D1101140

Everyone Has Their Reasons

a novel

Joseph Matthews

Also by Joseph Matthews

Shades of Resistance

The Lawyer Who Blew Up His Desk

Afflicted Powers
(with Iain Boal, T.J. Clark, Michael Watts)

Everyone Has Their Reasons
Joseph Matthews
Copyright © 2015 by Joseph Matthews
This edition © 2015 PM Press
All rights reserved. No part of this book may be transmitted by any means without permission in writing from the publisher.

ISBN: 978–1–62963–094–6

Library of Congress Control Number: 2015930875

Cover by John Yates/Stealworks
Interior design by briandesign

10 9 8 7 6 5 4 3 2 1

PM Press
PO Box 23912
Oakland, CA 94623
www.pmpress.org

Printed in the USA by the Employee Owners of Thomson-Shore in Dexter, Michigan.
www.thomsonshore.com

For Jesse

"The personal aspect of the problem was not what your enemies were doing but what your friends were doing."
—Hannah Arendt

"The terrible thing is that everyone has their reasons."
—Jean Renoir (Octave, in *The Rules of the Game*)

15 October 1940

Honorable Maître Herr Rosenhaus,

What was it I was thinking, when I shot Herr vom Rath? Or, what was in my mind? They are not entirely the same thing, are they, Maître? It was only a few hours ago that you were here, but I am not certain now which of them you asked me.

You might have suggested that I begin with something a bit less difficult, Maître. To describe my family's rooms in Hannover, for instance. On Burgstrasse. Where I was born. Altogether 27 years they were in Germany, my parents. Until that October. 1938. Which surely you know about.

Or to tell about my recent journey from Toulouse to Moulins, brought by the French police. And then to Berlin, in the company of the Gestapo. The very close company. To their building here. To this cell.

But I suppose you are right—where else should we begin? That moment. The revolver. The shots. So, how to describe it? I have heard people say "Time stood still." A truly stupid expression, Maître. Well, not actual people—in a film. Two films, I think. Many of them say the same things, films. Have you noticed that? Maybe that is why I remember. Anyway, I saw films often during my time in Paris. The two years there before I was in prison, I mean. Before the shooting. At least, as often as I could afford it, the cinema. In the afternoons, mostly, when it cost less. Not really so many films—more the same films over and over. You see, I learned that there were a few cinemas where I could stay for many hours during the daytime, no one bothered to check. And safe from the police. Especially nice in winter, these film houses. Somehow always warm there. Saint Martin was the best. And on hot summer days it was cooler. How do they manage that? The Mysteries of Paris. Have you heard that expression, Maître? Although now that I think of it, it was a mystery in most of the Paris rooms where I stayed. And there were quite a few of them. But an opposite

7

mystery there—when it was cold outside, these rooms were somehow colder. And on the awful August days, from most of the rooms I would head out into the melting streets—to cool off. But yes, at the cinema it was better. Cinema Saint Martin, on Rue du Faubourg Saint Martin. And two others near where I lived. Or, where I often stayed, I should say. Because to tell you I actually lived anywhere those two years in Paris would be untrue. Faubourg Saint Denis, the neighborhood is called, 10th arrondissement. Do you know Paris, Maître? Perhaps when you visit me again, we can talk of these things as well.

I am sorry, I have gone off the track of what I was saying. Or, writing. But that is one of the problems. The difference between saying and writing. As I found out. You see, when I was put in jail in Paris after the shooting, the juvenile part of the big prison at Fresnes, I was told to begin writing. A sort of journal, and biography, my life. Not just me—all the boys who are sent to Fresnes must do it. At least, the ones who can read and write. And so I did. It was very difficult at first. I was not used to writing. Except now and then a note to my family in Hannover. And the languages. At school in Hannover there had been writing, of course, in German. But at home, with my parents and brother and sister, we spoke Yiddish. And then in Paris, those first years, speaking Yiddish with Uncle Abraham and Aunt Chawa while picking up French in the street. And when I began to make friends, in Yiddish or French with them also. But not German. Hardly ever speaking German, those years in Paris. Well, except with a few. And then—nearly four years since I had left school—to write again in German, in my journal at Fresnes, because my French by then I could speak enough to get by for everyday things, but I had no experience of writing it. So, the people at Fresnes told me—the Social Counselors, or Moral Aides, something like that. I was never sure, in Paris, what these names meant. Many people who came to see me in the Paris jail, they worked for one state bureau or another, but mostly I did not understand which one exactly, or what their job was. I wonder if anyone really knew. Anyway, they told me, these people, "Write as you talk. Just let yourself talk, but on paper." So that is what I learned to do.

And it worked. I think. At least in some ways. Hundreds of pages, while I was at Fresnes. And so I do the same now, with what you ask of me. Talk to you, on paper. To prepare for trial here. As I did in France. There were lawyers for me there also, Maître. I once counted 12 that I had at one time or another. Or rather, who said they had me. I often argued with them. And them with each other. But I did finally realize that they might help me. Even understand me. Though not always both—I am not certain which was more difficult for them. Or which I wanted more. But I got used to talking to them. One or two of them, anyway. And it helped—my nerves, at least. Though I never did have my trial. France officials—so particular, so fussy, all their rules, and procedures. But then nothing actually happens. It drove me mad. And through all of this, 20 months, I remained in prison. As you know. The longest of any minor, without trial, in a French jail. Ever. Me. Did you know that, Maître? Another thing that made me famous.

So, if I did not express it clearly enough during your visit, let me say again how relieved I am to have you helping me here. And that I am most willing to talk to you. And write. Which you said will be useful. Also, Herr Rosenhaus, to address you as Maître, since that is what I became accustomed to with the lawyers in Paris, and so makes it easier for me now. Which you have kindly permitted. Even though Maître is a French word, and Germany and France are at war, so how do you feel about France? Or, were at war. I am not certain. Perhaps you can tell me. Because there was some kind of truce, I know. Though it was all very confused, in France, people not knowing what to do. And soon after, the French police brought me from Toulouse to Moulins, and handed me to the Gestapo. Very quickly. And not unhappily, it seemed. So, is anyone certain? And as you have told me, France will send people to my trial here, the France government, to tell their side. But what does that mean? Their side of what?

My apology, Maître—it seems I have lost my way again. The cinema. I was talking about films, seeing films, in Paris. And how I heard there that expression "Time stood still." To describe a moment of great danger. And fear. Also, in one film I think, about falling in love. Which I admit I know nothing about. Almost nothing.

Anyway, what total nonsense. It was not at all like that. Time standing still? That was before, my two Paris years before the shooting—no documents, no home, no work. No me.

But when I fired the shots? Just the opposite—time exploded. Out, but also in. Filling me. The whole room. My entire life. The past and future both. I was 17 years old. Of course, that you know.

So perhaps you are right, Maître. The place to begin—that moment. But the truth is, I must tell you, it was not the ending of Herr vom Rath's life that I felt in that moment. It was the complete unchangeable changing of my own. Yes, forever unchangeableness. My life. That is what I mean. What I felt.

The moments just before had been madness—vom Rath and I shouting at each other, then the shots, and the chaos afterward, people screaming and running in the halls, vom Rath staggering, falling, the gun in my hand, all the people, in and out of his tiny bureau, and soon the police. There are many different reports about exactly what happened when I arrived at the embassy that morning, how I managed my way in, and to vom Rath's bureau on the second floor, what people heard once I was inside. Versions. Confusions. Contradictions. But there is one thing everyone agrees—that after the shooting I sat calmly where I was. Did not move. Said nothing. It was because of what I felt, Maître. In that instant. Absoluteness. Is it a word? After nothing but worry and doubt and unknowing for so long, the sudden absoluteness of it all.

It is a bit later now. I have read these words again. And I am thinking that perhaps you were asking me for something else, Maître. Something more than just that instant.

But I have done the best I can. For now. For my first time writing anything since June, since the French jail people sent me out of Paris heading south, with the Wehrmacht and the Gestapo giving chase. Weeks on the move, across France, on the loose, the countryside, the roads, the villages. And the French—or rather, the humans. Ending up in Toulouse. And jail again. Then back here to Germany, to Berlin, these basement cells. The questions. So many questionings, examinations. For weeks now. I am tired, Maître. And through the walls, the floor—there are sounds. Human sounds. It is difficult to sleep. But yes, as you saw, I am well. No one is harming me, my body that is. You asked me to write this fact, and so I do. I am very tired. My stomach, as always, it troubles me. But otherwise, my body at least is mostly well.

So perhaps tomorrow, or the next day, when I write again, I will be able to tell more of what it is that you want to hear. Or, that you want me to say. About what was in my mind when I shot Third Secretary Ernst vom Rath. And just before then, on my way to the embassy that day. And the days before. The months. My mind. The why of it all.

Please realize, Maître, explaining myself is not easy. I have said this to many people before, at the court in Paris, the lawyers, the magistrates there. The doctors. And here, the questioners, in this building. And others. I have told them, all of them, that I am not certain who I was that day. What exactly I was doing. A sort of trance, you see. A delirium—a word I heard one of the doctors use. Killing someone? Was that truly in my mind on the way to the embassy? Or what else? In my mind's eye, what else?

But I will try, Maître. Because I want so much to get it right. And because you have said that my trial here will be coming soon. Where finally, you tell me, I will be able to speak. Nearly two years in that Paris jail, yet never a trial, never a place to be heard. And now the two months I have been in here. But soon that will change. Which is what we want. Is it not, Maître?

Most gratefully yours,
Herschel F. Grynszpan

Honorable Maître Herr Rosenhaus,

The "who" of it. That also you said was important. But as I think about it now, that could mean very different things. The people I saw in Paris? That is a long story, Maître—it will take some time in the telling. Or the people in Paris who saw me? Truly saw me? There were many fewer of those.

Perhaps five days ago or six, when you were here, I thought I knew what you meant by "who," and so I did not ask you. But for the three days after that I was unable to write, or even think about writing. And following those days my mind has been so fogged.

At a hospital, those three days. No, not what you might suppose, Maître—I have not come to any harm in here. A hospital where they examined my mind. Mostly. For the trial, they said. But more than that they would not tell me.

For the trial, yet during the first two days there they asked me nothing about what happened in Paris. Instead, all these questions about my childhood. And my parents. After a while I said, Now it is your turn—you tell me about my parents. Where are they? Are they all right? And my brother and sister? But they would say nothing. So I refused to speak any more to them of my family.

And you, Maître? You said, when you were here, that you will try to find out for me. Have you learned anything? My family, they also are part of the "who." What about them, Maître? What do you know?

Still, they had so many other questions, at the hospital. What I think about. Especially at night. Things I dream. Ridiculous—but not a surprise to me, Maître. At least, not most of it. I knew this kind of thing from my first months in the Paris jail, and the doctors there. Aliénistes, they are called in France. An odd word, I thought. Even more so when I looked it up. My lawyers gave me a dictionary, you see, French and German, in the Paris jail. To help with my French. And my writing, in German, my spelling. Not for anyone else in Fresnes.

Only me. There was special money for this. Most of it from the USA. The Journalists Defense Fund, it was called. Thousands of USA dollars they collected, to help me in French court. And famous people. Sinclair Lewis—world famous. Scott Fitzgerald—world famous. Even Edward G. Robinson, Maître—Little Caesar himself. For me. Just me.

So, aliéniste. From a word that means "other," my dictionary said. A doctor who decides if someone is other. Me, in Paris? This they needed doctors for?

But my lawyers there, they explained to me that the Paris court had asked these doctors to look into my mind. When I shot Herr vom Rath, was I sane? Or was I, instead, a kind of Christian? Yes, that is a word they use for it, the French—very strange. Though I did not actually hear the doctors there use it when they were examining me—in fact, they said almost nothing to me about what they were doing, or what they thought of me. But in Paris, before the shooting, that was a word I had heard the French use to describe someone whose mind is not right—a chréten, as they say it, or chrétien. I am sorry, but without my dictionary I do not know how they spell it. Or why they would say such a thing in a country with so many priests. Anyway, these French doctors, it seems that was what they were trying to decide—given what had happened to me, and what I had done, had I become some sort of Christian. Maître, could I make up such things?

And here again in Berlin, the doctors examining my mind. To decide who I am. Also my body. I am small, as you know. One meter 57. Though they said 56. And 45 kilos. Delicate, one of them called me— most of the time they spoke about me as if I was not there. Delicate, that also I had heard in Paris. Though not from doctors. And with more affection. Or appreciation, at least. Anyway, the doctors here, it seems they believe certain things of the body can tell them something about me. My skull, they measured. My eyes, my mouth. My nose. One of them said that I looked like a Slav. This sort of thing also I had heard in Paris. My "look"—Was I Arabian? Albanian? A Turk? I mean before I was in jail I heard these things. From Frenchmen. And others.

They even made a mask of my face, at the hospital here. In France, they make masks of the dead.

Three days and nights I was at the hospital. I told the doctors about my stomach, the troubles I always have with it, and at first they were interested. When did I have these troubles? What brought them on? I asked them for some medicine, but they said that was not why I was there.

They also asked the most uncomfortable things, Maître. About girls. What happened when I was with them. And what I wanted to happen. Dreamed.

And Maître, I must tell you this—about boys also. Are they permitted to ask me such things? I refused to answer. What is it they want?

A guard has just brought me more paper and pencils. As you promised. A stack of paper. And some envelopes, with your printed name and the address of your bureau. Perhaps you should know, they do not seem happy about it. And this makes me quite nervous. Which gives me problems in my stomach. You said that I will be well looked after. But Maître, I am the one who shot vom Rath. And then, all across Germany—Kristallnacht. The smashings and burnings. The beatings and jailings. And killings. Their fury from what I had done. And now I am here, Maître. In Germany. Back in Germany. The cells of the Gestapo. Grynszpan. Herschel Grynszpan. A name people cannot have forgotten.

Nor should they.

Yours sincerely,
H.F. Grynszpan

28 October 1940

Maître Herr Rosenhaus,

Since your visit this morning, I have been thinking about why my first writings to you have not been all that you had hoped. Many reasons have occurred to me. Some of which, I think, are best kept to myself. Let me just say, Maître, that I am someone who knows things. Only certain things, yes, to be sure. But some of them are knowings that others do not have. Or do not want. And are happier for it.

No, that is not exactly correct. I cannot seem to find it, Maître, the right way to say it. Perhaps it will come to me. Or perhaps it is one of the things I do not know.

But about your disappointment in what I have written—some things cannot be helped. When I am writing, I do not always go precisely in the direction I have intended. Or someone else has intended. Still, you left no doubt that I must make a greater effort. And so I will. My trial will be soon, you tell me. Finally. That is news that has certainly focused my attention.

Also that the press, the world press, will be there. I must admit this surprises me. Of course, yes, I am someone of importance. No, that is not what I mean to say. Not me, but what I have done—an event of importance. As was Kristallnacht, which followed from it. To my great sorrow.

Immediately afterward, the press was very interested in me. Did you know that? Though most of them not at all kindly. At least not in France. The big Paris newspapers. The Left and Right papers, both. The Yiddish ones also, who rushed to unown me—not that they knew anything about me. But abroad, Maître, in some places, Britain and the USA at least, they were different, the newspapers, journals. A few of them, anyway. I saw them, reports from these places, my lawyers in Paris gave some to me. Understanding what I had done. Well, not actually understanding. But trying. And the radio abroad also, I was told. People posted them to me, the journal clippings, and radio transcripts.

Along with letters. Hundreds of letters I got, Maître. From all over the world. And photos. From girls. Quite some photos, let me tell you.

But now? Two years later? All the press coming to Berlin, to a trial here, invited by the Reich? I must say, Maître, this is something of a surprise.

Anyway, since you have now told me of this I can see how important it is that we become clear. We—I mean you and me, Maître. I hope you do not mind me speaking in this way, but it is how I sometimes think now, these past weeks since you have begun to help me, and so it comes out that way on paper. I do not wish to offend.

Yes, how important to be clear about what I will say at the trial. And so, how important it is that we work out my thoughts ahead of time, as you have said. But can you imagine, Maître, how many thoughts I have had? Seven hundred days, since that morning I walked into the embassy. And nights. More than twice that many since I first set foot in Paris. And so many people wanting to know. Or telling me what I know. And what I do not. Police. Lawyers. Uncles. Aliénistes. Magistrates. Some of them trying to put a pin through me. Others trying to make sure that no pins would stick. Getting things clear, Maître—it is not something I have had much success with these past few years.

The days just before. A place for me to begin, you suggest. Perhaps you are right. 7 November 1938, the shooting. Odd, those words—the shooting. As if it happened by itself. I do not mean to separate myself from what I have done, Maître. But those are the words that come out of me now as I write.

So, those first days of November. Two years ago. Newspapers, I remember. Every newspaper I could get my hands on. And there were many, in French and Yiddish both. All the reports I could find. About the thousands in Germany, Maître, those with Polish passports, pulled from their beds, shipped to the Poland border. My parents. My brother and sister. Locked trains. And dumped there, on the border. Those were days for me of terrible waiting, for some word from my family. The newspapers were all I knew. Reports of the chaos there—but the reports themselves a chaos, impossible to know what was truly happening. Then the postal card from Poland, from my sister, at some barracks there, on the border, describing their terror, their misery. Pleading for help. Days for me of despairing, Maître. And yes, raging.

But why just those few November days? What about October? Poland's new law, for example—Polish citizens living abroad. Though now that I write "citizens," I doubt that was the word the Poles used. More likely they were careful to not use it. Anyway, this law, in October, that people living outside Poland would not have their passports renewed. Meaning who, Maître? Meaning my parents, who had fled Poland and the Poles so many years before. And everyone else who had done the same. A law to make sure they never returned. Twenty-seven years in Hannover, my parents. But never allowed to become citizens of the Reich. As perhaps you know. So, still with their Poland passports. But under this new Polish law they would become stateless. Also, my brother and sister, born in Germany. And me. Our whole lives in Germany. But Poland passports, all of us. And soon, none at all.

Then there was Munich, of course, also that October—the way that cursed month began, the Munich entente. Huge crowds on the Paris boulevards cheering Daladier, the French premier, on his return. Cheers he wasted no time turning into law. A new decree—the immediate arrest and deporting or jailing of anyone without residence papers, no appeals, no exceptions, no new papers issued. Also by that October my Uncle Abraham and Aunt Chawa had moved to a smaller workshop apartment in Paris—things were not going well for them. Not for anyone. Still they offered me a pallet in the kitchen of this little place, whenever I might need it. Except that I could no longer risk spending nights with them, as I had done so many times since first coming to Paris two years before. All my petitions for some kind, any kind, of papers—French, German, Polish, visa, residence, even an identity card, just an identity—by that August had all been rejected. And an expulsion order issued, with my name on it. I had become what the police called a "personnage clandestine"—meaning not just subject to arrest, but an actual target. Even at night. You see, there is a law in France, a very old law, that police may not enter a home at night just to arrest someone, except in the most serious emergency. A law taken very seriously there. At least by the French. Part of their liberté—it is a word you hear quite a lot in France, Maître. And with this old law, nights on a pallet at my uncle and aunt's had always seemed mostly safe, at least if I got out by dawn. But with another of the new decrees, this law no longer protected me, people like me. No law did. And if I was found with my aunt and uncle, they also would be arrested. As anyway they were, after the shooting. Adding still more sorrow.

So. How did I get here? What I am trying to say, Maître, is that to understand the days leading up to the shooting, the early days of November, you must first pay attention to October.

It is late in the night now, Maître. I am unable to sleep. I woke a while ago, in a kind of panic. From a dream. I was in Paris, in a cinema, and somehow trapped there, in a seat. And on the screen, right in front of my face, so close, these horrible masks, like the mask they made of me at the hospital, only enormous, with screeching mouths, and the sound so loud, but I cannot move, and my eyes are somehow forced to stay open. Then all around me, on the walls, the ceiling, other films running alongside the first, more masks, more screaming, my head being turned this way and that way to face it all, never stopping, four films running, eight, and more and more, and then I am not in the cinema but out in the streets, the Paris streets, but the masks are still everywhere next to me, screaming, screaming at me, and I run and run but screaming masks are in every window, every doorway.

I woke up trembling. But then saw that around me, in the cell, all was calm. The pages I had been writing, and the pencil, lying just where I had left them on the floor. The cell was quiet. The corridor quiet. And I was so relieved to be here.

Two years now I have been in jail. One jail or another. The thing is, in here I am myself. At least, compared with my days in Paris, on the streets there, those days of liberty—there is that word again. In jail, Maître, I know who I am.

They are not something new, these waking nights. My stomach is often a problem. More so here, because for some reason they force me to eat when I do not want to. I had to stop writing this evening when they gave me supper. Well, not exactly force me to eat. But the guards do not leave me until I do. And they are not happy about this task. Nor am I. Have you ever had someone just sit and watch you, Maître? While you try to do something? Some everyday, simple thing? It can make you crazy. Me, at least, it makes me crazy. Tonight, I forced down the food as quickly as I could, to get them out of the cell. Schnitzel. Twice a week they give me meat. Which also seems to make the guards unhappy. And tell me something, Maître—How can the diet of a great nation have schnitzel at its center? Yes, once or twice before I ate it, growing up in Hannover. But it was not something at my family table. Or the people we knew. We had our own foods. In part because of who we are, yes, the ancient diet rules, but it seems to me now that it was also just because of the food itself, the kind of food that most people ate—Christian people, I mean. Though I do not mean you, personally, Maître, perhaps what you eat in your home is different. But let me ask you—What German dish would anyone think back on once a meal is done? Except for having to digest it, that is.

Well, the schnitzel here. After gagging it down I could not manage to write again, and had to lie flat on my back. Until the dream woke me. The nightmare. It is curious, but in Paris before the shooting, in my dreams I was always in Hannover. Since I have been in jail, my nightmares all put me in Paris.

Now, since I cannot sleep, I am trying again to write. The light is always on in the corridor, shining in through the hole in the door. Plenty of light. Actually, for years now, nights have not been so different from days. Even before I was in jail.

October 1938. I said that you must know October before you can know November. But what of September? It was beautiful in Paris that month, late summer, warm, the trees still so full of deep green—I spent a lot of time then in the parks, in the west of the city, the posh arrondissements, which I realized was the best place then for someone like me to be safe. At least, if I made sure not to look out of place. Which my new Paris coat helped so much. The Parc de Monceau, or along Avenue Foch, even the Cimetière de Passy—so quiet. Always quiet in those districts, of course, but even more so then, nearly empty that September. Because in the weeks before Munich, so many people who live in those parts of Paris left the city. Quietly. For their country houses. Feared the start of war, you see, bombs falling on Paris. A month of terrible worry. For everyone. Many hoping so hard that something would happen, that someone would finally do something. But most hoping that nothing would happen. At least not in France. It was a strange time for me—long, peaceful hours alone in the parks or the little fenced-in squares. The quiet. A kind of liberty. Not so different from in here. Does that sound odd?

Mind you, it was not all quiet, Maître. I will tell you of a different kind of day that September. Late in the month it was. The start of our High Holy Days, and I had gone to a synagogue. A large synagogue, and the finest, they say, in all of Paris. A place for the old families, the real French. I was certainly not one of the invited, but I managed to get in. I had on my new topcoat, you see, and looked very fine, I must say. A most handsome coat. Beautiful fawn color. The latest Paris cut. Elegant—tailoring is something I know. You can see a picture of the coat, Maître. I was wearing it the morning at the embassy. All the newspaper photos, after my arrest, they show me wearing the coat. And in a pocket, the postal card I wrote to my family. Asking their forgiveness for what I was about to do. "My Dear Parents, I could not do otherwise." And so on. Surely you know of this card? It also was in all the newspapers. I suppose we will need to talk about it sometime.

I was young, and small. But with my stylish topcoat, and my hair brushed back, my high forehead, I could look older, if I tried. More sophisticated. By then, after two years in Paris, and the things I had seen, I knew how. Depending on the occasion. Look older, I mean. And so I did, on that day, going to the synagogue. Very proper, in my handsome coat. To seem like I belonged there, you see. I also mentioned a name, to help me get in—in French, trying hard to hide my accent. A family name I had come to know. I was hoping to see someone there. Someone I had met. Who did belong there. But never mind, that is something else.

What matters, Maître, for what I am trying to explain, is what I found inside. It was all certainly new to me—an organ, a choir, things I had never before imagined could be in a synagogue. Even in Paris. And the rabbis—there were two of them, with robes like the pastors I had seen at the churches in Hannover. You would have felt comfortable there, Maître. Well, I should not say that, I suppose. But familiar. And the prayers, except for the holiest few, were in French. All of this was a surprise to me. But not a shock—after my time in Paris, so many corners of Paris, I was not easily shocked. That is, until I heard what they had to say after the prayers that day, one of the rabbis, followed by some elder man, a French flag in his lapel. Not just shocked but angry. My French by then was good enough at least to get their meaning. Keep quiet, they preached. Say nothing. Only the most perfect behavior must be shown toward other Parisians. Above all, the rabbi told the congregation, sitting there in their furs and fine suits, be French.

Be French?

Other things he said were simpler for me to understand. Say nothing about Germany, he warned, nothing about Poland, Czechoslovakia. Not a word about war. Or peace. And keep plenty of distance from the "allogènes"—the "outsiders." Meaning me, Maître. As if the distance was not already enough.

Then it was the elder's turn to warn about the allogènes. Oh, they might recite the same prayers as we do, he said, shaking his finger. But do not be fooled. Because they are and always will be—and how he spoke these words, Maître, as if with bad fish in his mouth—"de l'Est." "Of the East."

I did not understand much of the rest of what he said because my head was now storming. Except at the end, I could make out his final warning to the congregation, not to remain in front of the synagogue following the service—they should not gather with each other in public, he told them, not set themselves apart from other Frenchmen. And so, outside, the crowd hurried away. West. To their peaceful streets. I had hoped to speak to my friend—well, this person

I knew. But they all left so quickly, in their big automobiles and taxis. I went in the other direction. Toward the neighborhoods where I had spent most of my Paris time. The not so peaceful neighborhoods. To the east.

It just occurs to me, Maître. That perhaps this was another of the Paris code words—"east." One that I never recognized before now. Of course, in one way, when French people spoke this word I understood very well, they meant Poland, Russia, all the uncivilized places. Unlike France. Or Germany. But now that I think back on it, perhaps they were also speaking about Paris itself—Belleville, the Marais, Bastille. The east of the city. Where we allogènes were. East—the word seems a bit more complicated now. One thing I slowly came to realize, in Paris, was that when finally I understood something, actually I did not.

So that particular day in September I went back to the east of the city, still burning inside about these warnings at the synagogue, for the congregation to stay away from outsiders. Well, we outsiders still met among ourselves—in the crowded east it could not be helped. I went to a café, the Tout Va Bien, a place where we were allowed to sit for a while even if we did not spend any money. And there I found Sam, a good friend. In fact I was staying in his room at the time, a place where the police would not look for me. Anyway, he is not religious, Sam, and so he was not at synagogue on the holy day. But many people in the neighborhood were in the local shuls, or at least were off the streets, and we saw no one else we knew at the café.

The two of us started walking. If we were heading someplace I cannot now remember where, but probably just walking. Neither of us had money to spend. Sam was earning some but used it all to buy medicine for his mother. And I had just spent almost all I had to buy my new coat, my topcoat. We could not afford cafés and such too often. Sometimes the cinema. Once in a while a street fair. But mostly, we just walked. And on this day, after a while we reached the Pletzl, the old quarter, in the Marais. The Aurore Sportclub was there, on Rue Vieille du Temple, a kind of social club, where we sometimes met friends. When we got there Sam saw someone he knew outside the Aurore and stopped to talk to him. I did not know this other boy, and while they talked I went over to a tabac—a small bar and shop—to get some tobacco papers or matches or something. As I did, I noticed an auto, a new Citroën, I remember—a Traction Avant, with the drive power from the front wheels, Maître—a beautiful machine. I had worked in the factory, have I told you? Well, not directly in the factory. And not for long. But I had learned all about them, Citroëns. Anyway, this new auto was going by, slowing down, and these faces, these bony pale faces, all ears and hair cream, staring out the windows at Sam and the boy on the pavement in front of the club.

When I came out of the tabac a minute later, I noticed the Citroën now coming back in the other direction. Suddenly it swerved and jumped over the curb. The doors flew open, but for a moment nothing happened—the people inside were fumbling around—and then four men got out, young men, but grown. Huge, actually. At least they seemed so to me. In the auto they had just put on these large floppy berets, country hats you almost never saw in Paris. Certainly not on young people. They stomped past me and across the road toward Sam and the other boy and began shouting at them, "Dogs, you want us to die for you!" "Germany is your problem, not ours!" And more things like that, but I could not understand all of it, the French was too fast and they were on the other side of the road from me, and then they started pushing Sam and the other boy, screaming at them, and all of a sudden hitting them, then Sam's friend fell, and they kicked him, and swung at Sam, who hit back, until some people nearby started shouting, and the four young men backed away, passing by me again, got into their auto and drove off. Sam holding his head, blood on his face. The other boy on the ground, not moving.

I was only a few feet away. They went right by me. Did not touch me. I was wearing the coat, you see. They did not realize I was with Sam. The fine Paris coat.

I had heard about attacks like this, Maître. They had been happening all summer. But it was the first I had actually seen. It was not the last. The next day, the very next day, I was near Place de la République when I saw Bertrand, someone I knew a little bit, sitting outside at a café table with another young guy. Bertrand had heard about what had happened in front of the Aurore the day before and asked me about it. We talked for a couple of minutes when all of a sudden some men from another table starting speaking to us, then shouting. "Boches!" they called us. "Sales Boches!"—"Dirty Krauts," it means, Maître. Bertrand cursed back in Paris slang, he is French, Bertrand, his parents from the East but many years in France and he was born there, Bertrand, in Paris. Then two of these men got up and came to our table and told us to get out, they did not want any Germans there, and when we did not move right away they knocked over Bertrand's drink, then pushed us out of our chairs. I swung at one of them, Maître, and Bertrand also, but Bertrand's friend pulled him away and so I backed up with them. A few of the other people at the café were sneering at us, and growling. Some of them joined the two men shouting at us "Boches!" "Sales boches!" as we moved away down the street.

Dirty Krauts. You see, Maître, in telling Bertrand about the attack from the day before, I had used Yiddish along with French. And these people thought it was German.

So. One day a beating for wanting war against Germany. The next day, for being German. September, Maître. That was September. That month also you need to know.

Yours most sincerely,
Herschel Grynszpan

Maître Herr Rosenhaus,

It is now some time in the morning. I know because the guards just gave me bread, which they do each morning. I slept for a bit before that, though I have no way of knowing what time I stopped writing last night. Or how long after that I fell asleep. I feel not at all well. My stomach is in confusion again. My back and neck also, they ache from the position I was in for so long while writing, sitting on the stone, the floor. But I woke this morning thinking about that September two years ago, Maître, and I want to keep it in my mind, the thread of it. So I will push on with the writing. Though most of me just wants to lie down again.

There was a bit of hope during the summer before that September. They cleaned the river. Pulled out the bodies. Which made the city seem less grim. And somehow—I do not know how else to describe it, Maître—less congested. Also there was to be Evian, the conference there, about us refugees, a hope that something would be done.

A wasteful emotion, hope.

The year had begun badly. In January I had gone to the German consulate. For a visa—I had a Polish passport, as I told you—to go home to Hannover. Yes, back to Germany. In 1938. Does that tell you something, Maître? About my life in Paris? I suppose it will come as no surprise to you that the Reich did not allow me to return.

Paris became even more crowded that winter and spring. In the east of the city anyway. More people who had fled. From pogroms in Romania. And then Anschluss, that March, the Austrians' turn. This time, though, the congregations of the upper type Paris families stood up. After all, these were civilized refugees, the Viennese—almost like Parisians. So, they gathered in their drawing rooms and in their country houses, these old time Paris families, to decide how to support their business associates and ski holiday friends from Vienna. And support them they did. Sort of. By going to their synagogues and offering prayers. Though only in Hebrew—so the France journals could not quote them.

And the rest of Paris? Yes, a few spoke of asylum for some of the Austrians. But not many. And not for others. Not for anyone from the east. Not for me.

Anyway, none of them needed worry, the French. Because the République, the France state, had its decrees. A flood of them that spring and summer. Decree—No new entries into France. Decree—No extending of residence permits. Decree—No more work permits. Decree—Anyone with wrong or expired documents to be jailed, then thrown out from the country. And if caught again, three years in prison—and then thrown out.

Plus the numerus clausus. Strange how a person learns things, Maître—Latin on top of French. Numerus clausus for all the trades, even if you had a proper work permit. I knew a boy, Izaly, he had some work now and then, in a balalaika orchestra. Just enough to keep him and his family alive. Fifteen years old and the only one in his family who had work. A wonderful musician, Izaly. But with a Russia passport. Then came a numerus clausus that spring—no more than 10 percent of not-French people in any music group. So, they turned him out. For being Russian. In a Russian orchestra. And then his family had nothing. Months later he finally found other work, this boy. In a clandestin, the Parisians call it—a hidden bordel. Above a hairdressing shop. Rue Saint Denis. A specialty bordel, Maître. He was not playing music there.

Fiches—permits. Even just to be a zammler, a scavenger, France law said you must have a fiche. In France, you need a fiche to sneeze. But that spring there were no more fiches given out. By decree. And if you were caught selling something, anything, without a fiche? And a refugee? Straight to jail, then deporting. Even if you had a residence card. Because the right to reside was not the same as the right to stay alive. And if you tried to stay alive by working, you lost your right to reside.

Whatever the question, the answer was No.

And by another new decree the employers also could now be

heavily fined—depending on how French they were, of course—if they hired a worker who did not have the right papers. So, suddenly the pieceworkers, in the worksheds and ateliers all over Paris, were being turned out of their jobs. Also thousands of new deporting orders. And more arrests, every day. Many people went into hiding. And worse. The boy Sam that I knew? He had a friend, Eli. Sam showed him to me that spring—floating in the river. His body stuck between two barges. Somehow his cap still gripped in his hand. After a winter on the streets, sometimes starving, sometimes freezing, he had found work, Eli, in a leather-making place, tanning hides, over by La Villette, the slaughterhouses there. Two weeks later there was another decree—I cannot remember which one now—and the leather workshop put him out. The next day, he jumped into the Seine.

Not the only one, Maître. Some of them just floated away, and we never saw them again. But many, like Eli, got caught on branches growing from the banks, or on boat lines, and washed back and forth, half sinking, surfacing, up and down, over and over. Whenever I passed by the river, I tried not to look down.

There were so many new rules and restrictions that spring, I cannot tell you all of them. Or remember exactly one from another. Even at the time, none of us could. But one decree, that spring, I recall very well. Not in France. Here in Germany. In Paris I received a letter from my sister Berthe. Every year, in spring, she and I together had always planted herbs, in little pots, on the windowsills of our old apartment building in Hannover. But this year, Berthe wrote me, there would be none. The Reich had issued a decree—only Aryans were allowed to farm, to grow food. She was afraid, she wrote me, that the parsley would send her to jail.

But the summer. I was going to tell you about the summer. The hopeful summer. They cleaned the Seine. Tourists would be coming. And King George, the England king. July he would visit, and they worked hard to prepare the city. He was to ride down the river, with a flotilla of boats. It was to be at the other end of Paris, the west, where the great Exposition Universelle, the world's fair, had been the year before. But they cleaned the river through the whole city, east past

Gare d'Austerlitz, all the way to Bercy. There was so much cleaning that even a few people I knew got work—some French workers would find foreigners and pay them, a tiny piece of their own wages, to do the foulest of the cleaning jobs. Fraternité or egalité, I am not certain which that was. But it was work. And people in Paris east were desperate for it. I knew a man doing this cleaning, he pulled his brother out of the river. The body, I mean. There were many rumors of how many bodies in all were found. I will not bother you with the different numbers, Maître.

Still, somehow, a lot of us got caught up in the excitement of the England king's visit. It is difficult now for me to remember why. I suppose it was part of an idea that in some way England and France would come together about the Reich, and about us refugees. Of course, in the autumn, in some way, they did—Munich. But in June and July there was still hope. And somehow the king's visit must have seemed a part of that. I know I planned to be there along the river, to watch it all, when he sailed by that July.

In people's heads, I think—at least in mine—the king's visit was connected with Evian, the conference that was held around the same time, called together by President Roosevelt. Did you know that I had correspondence with him, the president? But that was later. From jail. Well, not exactly correspondence, but a letter I sent to him. Which the committee for me in America, the Defense Fund, they wrote me that they would make sure the president received it. Did I tell you about this committee, Maître? Famous people? Yes, I did, Little Caesar, I remember. So, this letter, it asked the president for visas to the USA, for my family. I asked nothing for myself. My trial in Paris had to proceed, I knew. I was responsible. And it would allow me to speak to the world about what was truly going on. The trial. Which, as you know, never happened.

Evian. And President Roosevelt. To help us refugees. Was there much notice of this conference in Germany, Maître? I can tell you there was in Paris. At least in the east. Many nations sent their topmost ministers to Evian, where they talked long and hard. About people like me. For a whole week it went on, every day the newspapers guessing what was happening behind the doors of the grand old spa hotel where they were meeting. I remember wondering whether they were all sitting in the baths together, dozens of naked old men, talking about us as they soaked. Anyway, in the end, these great ministers produced a long statement of their intendings to help. The newspapers printed big headlines, which all seemed to use the word "commitment." And a photograph of all the politicians standing together, relieved. Finished.

We carefully read through this statement, my aunt and uncle and I, the other people I knew, everyone. Full of promises—to keep talking. We read it over and over again, in different languages, throughout Paris east, everyone arguing about the words, what this might mean, or that, for two or three days, looking for the flame inside the smoke. Until finally, one by one, we all stopped.

It was the photos that made me angriest. Their satisfied faces. And that word—commitment. "Do not piss on my back and then tell me it is raining." A Yiddish expression, Maître. Those days, we could all smell the piss. Excuse my language.

Oh, yes, and King George. He did come to Paris, a few days later. And rode down the Seine. I did not bother to watch.

The same day as the king's visit, the France ministries rejected my application for a residence permit. They even refused me an identity card. Which meant I was no one.

A month later, in early August, they issued an expelling order. It gave me four days to get out of France.

Yours most truly,
Herschel Feibel Grynszpan

7 November 1940

Maître Herr Rosenhaus,

Today. Two years ago, today. That morning at the embassy.

For a week now I have been so anxious that I have been unable to write to you.

I suspect that this has been a disappointment to you. But please know that I understand my responsibility. So, to make atonement for my failing, I have fasted.

Yours,
Herschel Feibel Grynszpan

10 November 1940

Maître,

Last night was a crouching beast—the anniversary of Kristallnacht, when people in the Reich learned that vom Rath had died. That my shots had killed him. And took revenge.

I thought I saw something in the guard's face yesterday when he brought my evening food. I had been waiting in fear, so perhaps I only imagined this. But not the rest of the night. That I did not imagine.

Just after they collected my plate—I have begun to eat again, Maître, I meant to tell you this, I know how my not eating troubles you—the noises began. From somewhere above. I could not tell where they came from, these sounds, whether inside the building or out. There was shouting, though I could not make out the words. And singing. Loud singing. Rough, like you would hear from a beer hall. And stomping, boots. It went on and on, then would quiet, but return again, as if the shouters and singers were circling in the nearby streets. Perhaps around this building. Or in it.

Finally, it stopped. I tried to sleep. But something in the tone of the shouting and the singing, in the guard's face, and knowing what day it was, made sleep impossible. After some time—I could not say how long, but a slow stretch of time, a sort of twilight where I have been so often these past years—I began to hear other noises. Glass. Breaking glass. Not crashing loud, smaller. And quiet laughter. Sounds, I know, that could not have come from outside. I have been taken in and out of this cellar many times now, Maître, and I know there is no opening down here directly to the street. No way that such small sounds could have come from outside, through the walls of stone.

Then, after another while, I smelled it. Faint, but I knew right away it was not tobacco. It is a terror, in jail, the smell of fire. In Paris, in the prison at Fresnes, the stories that were told, of jailhouse fires, of men abandoned, trapped, burned alive.

I must say that I did not actually see any fire last night. But smoke, somewhere close. I know it was meant for me. Breaking glass and burning—Kristallnacht, you see. But this time, Maître, just for me.

And all night long, off and on, scraping at my cell door. Sometimes a key in the lock, then out again. But never a word. Or a face. Just a scrape, or a tap on metal.

The guards here, Maître, they never speak my name. But they know who I am.

HG

Maître Rosenhaus,

Yesterday they brought me back from the hospital. The normal hospital, not the special one where I was taken before. I am feeling much better now. The medicine the doctor gave me helped quiet my stomach. And seems to have calmed my nerves as well. Of course, how difficult is it to be calm when you are asleep most of the time? Which is also what the medicine did. For three days, I think. Or four. So, I am not exactly sure of the date today. I asked a guard this morning what day it was but he did not answer. They almost never say a word to me, the guards, even when they are here inside the cell. When next you visit, I can ask you for the correct date. It is somehow very important to me in here. "Heaven gives us routines to take the place of happiness." Were you also taught this in school, Maître? Goethe. A schoolmaster in the lower form used to say it to us. It was also a favorite of the instructor in my final school year, when I was 14. Except instead of "Heaven gives us routines" he would say "God gives us discipline."

For days before they took me to the hospital I was unable to write anything, I felt so ill. I would like to ask you, Maître, is it possible for you to detain more of the medicine they gave me, to keep here in the cell? As they were getting ready to send me back here from the hospital I asked if I could have some of it to bring with me. But the Gestapo officer there said "Stop" before the doctor could answer. The doctor looked surprised, I thought, but he said nothing. The Gestapo man asked the doctor the name of the medicine, then left the room; the doctor also stepped outside and a policeman came in to watch me. When the Gestapo man returned a few minutes later, he spoke to the doctor in the doorway to the room, but I could not hear what he said. The doctor listened and nodded, looking through the open door at me. Then he came inside and told me that I did not need the medicine any longer. I started to speak, but he turned and left.

I am glad to have been taken to the hospital, Maître. But there are several things about my days there that I do not understand. And that continue to trouble me. I was not allowed to speak with anyone, not even the doctors, except to answer a few questions—a Gestapo guard was always in the room, day and night. I was not permitted to tell the doctors about who I am, or where I had come from. Not even much about my long stomach troubles, just to describe the problem from the past few days, nothing more. And they used this name for me—Schneider. Otto Schneider. Why should they not want the hospital people to know who I am? Or the guards? Yes, I am the one who shot vom Rath, and vom Rath became a great Reich hero, I know, a state funeral with the Führer himself, and all kinds of memorials and such. But the truth is, he was not such a hero before he was shot. I can tell you that. I mean, as far as I know. Just an embassy third secretary. With a postage stamp office. And perfect hair.

There was Kristallnacht, it is true, that terrible revenge after vom Rath died. And me who had shot him. But I am in protected custody. Gestapo custody. So, why the secrecy, Maître? The false name? People should know that I am here.

I have slept again. I was awakened by the evening food being brought. The guard did not stay with me this time. I ate a few bites. After a while he returned and took the plate away, without worrying me about how little I ate. This is an improvement.

I thought you would want to know these things, Maître. And that I am better, since I was feeling so poorly the last time you saw me. It was only after your last visit that they paid any attention to my being sick. For days before, the guards had ignored me. Then, the day after your visit, special Gestapo men came and took me to the hospital. And now the guards here are less difficult about me eating. At least for tonight. Whatever you told them, Maître, whatever you did, I thank you. The guards do not seem respectful to you when you are here, yet something about you helps me. That is why I thought perhaps you might be able to get me some more of that medicine.

I suppose I should tell you that I did hear a bit of what the Gestapo man said at the hospital, when they refused me the medicine to take away. "Murder" I heard him say to the doctor. Also the word "self." At the time I did not connect the two, because "murder" has so often been spoken around me, about me. But as I was waking a little while ago, I heard the Gestapo man's voice again, in my head. And this time the two words were part of one. True, the medicine is very strong. But suicide? Did they really think I would kill myself? After all this time?

Yes, I admit, there were times it crossed my mind, suicide. Often, in fact. Throughout much of that last year in Paris. With corpses carried out of neighborhood buildings every week in Paris East, and bodies in the Seine, how could it not? I even spoke of it with a few people I knew. But I did not do it. And yes, it was on my mind that morning I went to the embassy. Shooting myself there—an image I had. But only one image, you see. Among many. As I told you from the beginning, Maître, there were many things in my mind that day. But I could hold none of them steady. Shooting myself, at the embassy? In the end, I did not do it. Perhaps because always disturbing that image, Maître, paling and cracking it, were all the suicides that had gone before. That no one had paid any notice. Every day, more bodies. And no one did a thing. Except clean the river.

So I did not do it. That is my point, Maître. I did not kill myself. And now, at last, when I will have a chance to speak, to stand in front of what I have done and to speak, what sense would it make now?

Yours truly. Very truly.
Herschel Grynszpan

24 November 1940

Maître Rosenhaus,

Let me begin by again giving thanks for your visit yesterday. Even without bringing any of the medicine.

I had wondered, when I wrote to you about my recent time in the hospital, whether you might already know of it. And perhaps had decided not to concern yourself. I am relieved that you came to see me, about my health. Though it seems odd to me, Maître—I mean, that you should have heard of these things only from me.

I am sorry that you think me too thin. Now that I am feeling better, I will be able to eat, which I will do. As I have promised you.

Also, let me say how much I appreciate that you have made inquiries about my family. Since your visit, I have been thinking about your news that despite special efforts the Reich did not find them anywhere in Radomsk, where they had been last year. Did you know that my parents came originally from near Radomsk? Before moving to Hannover. Of course, it was Russia then, before the Great War, not Poland. Radomsk, I mean. And anyway, what does "originally" mean? Or matter?

Well, I have been thinking about what you have asked me, about where else we have family in Poland, where my parents might have gone to stay. Thinking hard about this. And I must report that I do not know. Or anyplace else where my parents might be. Also, I can imagine that searching for them further would require more special efforts. By whoever would be assigned the task. Which is not a burden I want to impose. Also, Maître, just thinking about this makes me feel slightly ill. And might begin again the whole problem of eating. And becoming so thin. Looking unwell. Especially without the medicine.

So, to avoid such things, perhaps it is best that I withdraw my request for news about my parents. Yes, I am certain that would be best.

Appreciatingly,
Herschel

4 or 5 January 1941
Sachsenhausen

Herr Rosenhaus,

Where are you, Maître? Are you asking the same about me?

I am somewhere away from the city. Another prison. Of a sort. An enormous place. And so many people—prisoners and guards, both. Spread out over several hectares, it seems, all flat and sandy. But surrounded by trees, which block it from whatever is beyond. Nothing like any of the jails I have been in before—which are now quite a few. I do not know what word to use for it. Except its given name—Sachsenhausen. I have been here four weeks. Or so. Yesterday they finally gave me paper and a pencil. Though not your addressed envelopes.

It is not very far from Berlin, this place—we traveled only a short time to get here, less than an hour I think, though in what direction I could not tell. The Gestapo took me out of their jail building suddenly. With no warning, I mean. From them. Or from you, Maître. Do you even know where I am? Next to the question of why they moved me, this is the thing I wonder most.

Late in the night they took me. Told me nothing of what was happening or where I was going. First to another part of Berlin, in an auto. To a building in the city that seemed to belong to the army, everyone in uniform. SS. Outside on the street there was no one, but inside the building was swarming with soldiers, even so late at night. The Gestapo brought me in, along with a file of papers, and stood me in a corner in a large entry hall, people going back and forth, while they spoke with an SS man. Then the Gestapo left and I was taken upstairs by four SS men—Why so many? I wondered—to a small room, a bare room where they left me, without speaking. At first I expected another examination, another questioning, though it was the middle of the night. But they asked me nothing. Two years of questions, endless questions, and now no one wants to hear me. Except you of course, Maître.

Finally they brought me downstairs and put me in another auto. Four of them, again. And brought me here. Again there was no talking.

I do not know much about this place, Maître. I saw very little as they brought me in and then moved me around through several buildings. But I am now allowed outside from time to time, where I can see a bit more. And from the small windows on the upper floor where I am kept I can sometimes get a glimpse of different parts of this place. There is a main camp, as I have heard the guards call it, built in a sort of triangle, huge with many low wooden buildings. Which is where the other prisoners stay. Thousands of them. There could not be a cell for each of them in those huts, not even two or three to a cell—there are just too many people. So I suppose they live in larger rooms, together. A dormitory, like in those boarding schools I have seen pictures of. Or the yeshiva school where I was for a short time. This must be a relief for them, to be all together.

Around the buildings there are fences, with many guards patrolling, most of them SS it seems. And dogs. Then another high fence outside these. And around it all a wall. Also something odd—in between the first two rows of fences there is a rainbow. On the ground, I mean. Rows of colors, with the surfaces looking different. Five or six of these rows, these rings, each a meter or so wide, going around the entire camp I think, though I can only see certain parts from where I am. Bright colors. When it is not covered by snow. Everything else here is grey.

Each morning all the prisoners in the main camp come out to the front of the huts. Lines and lines of them, standing there in their striped uniforms. I am usually in my cell and cannot see, but I hear them. Even though they do not speak. After a few minutes they are marched out of the camp toward the trees. And in the evening they march back, again in their lines. It is dark when they leave and dark when they return but there are lights on the towers and I sometimes get a quick look out a corridor window, on the second floor, if I am out of my cell. They must be working somewhere all day because when they come back at night they can barely move. Thousands of them yet almost no sound. Only the dogs. And some shouting from the guards.

Shots also, Maître. From time to time a shot. But the prisoners themselves, the thousands of prisoners, not a sound. Except shuffling feet. And crunching when there is snow and ice. Once in a while a small cry when someone is struck. But otherwise nothing. Just their feet.

Some do not leave the camp. When the others go in the early morning, these few remain outside the barracks. Just standing there. In the freezing cold. Maybe 30 or 40 of them. I think some of these may be the same men I sometimes catch sight of later in the day. On the rainbow. Walking around and around. Like an athletics track. All day they walk. Rain, snow. Each with a large letter chalked on his shirt. Some carry sacks on their back. Sometimes they fall. Perhaps it is a punishment. Why a rainbow?

There is also another area of the camp, with brick buildings, where the guards live. But I cannot see it well.

For me there is this separate place. A building apart from the rest of the camp. With its own high fences, razor wire on top and several other structures in between. Also a trench, an enormous trench, where slops are dumped. And other things, it seems. At night. The smell is horrible. As bad as in Paris. Did I tell you? About the quartier, the old neighborhood, where sometimes I stayed? The cesspools there? Yes, in the great city. No sewers in the old quartier, you see, but cesspools. Late at night the cleaners would come. And when they opened them? The smell? I cannot tell you.

Here it is the trench. Also a building next to it, a brick building, unlike all the other ones of wood in the central camp. With a large chimney. It smokes from time to time, every day, and when it does, the smell is different.

But the building I am in—a blockhouse. Brick, with windows, actual glass windows. A new building. Two stories. They are still finishing it. As if specially for me. Although that cannot be so, not completely, because there are also a few other prisoners in here. And three more buildings of brick being built nearby, very much like this one, it seems. There are also special guard towers for each of these brick buildings, very close, with a machine gun and a powerful light. Sometimes I can see the guards in the tower next to this building, out the corridor window. And hear them. Especially at night. The squeaking light as it moves. The guards coughing—it is terribly cold in here so I imagine it is worse on the towers. Their talking to each other. Their mumbling. Sometimes one of them sings.

35181. My number. I was told to memorize it. But I do not have to wear it, as I see on the prisoners' shirts in the main camp. Or their uniform with the stripes, I am not made to wear that either. None of us in here, in this separate building—we wear our own clothes. And they do not shave my head, as they do to all the prisoners outside. But my name, Maître. When they first brought me here they called me Otto Schneider. The same as at the hospital in Berlin. I told you, do you remember? Since the very first day here no one has said my real name. Not that they ever bother with names.

Since this past week I have been given work. Of the other prisoners in this building—there are eight—I am the only one allowed to spend much time out of my cell. The others are permitted out to wash and to exercise but only one at a time—every few days one or another of them is put out in a small space behind the building, to walk around for a few minutes. But always alone. I am also permitted this outside walking. And for me, every day. Fresh air. Well, not exactly fresh—it is next to the chimney building, and the trench. At least there is an earth wall that blocks the trench from view. Once in a while, in this outdoor space, I can see a bit of sun. When there is some. And not too much smoke.

Each day I move around, taking the others their food, to their cells. But in this building only, to the eight other prisoners here. I am not permitted near the main camp. So this is my work, Maître, to deliver the food. Later to collect the plates.

And now at last I am able to write to you. But without having your official envelope I wonder whether you will receive this. And when I will see you. I will have to wait. Which I certainly know how to do. Though not well. Never well.

Yours sincerely,
Herschel Grynszpan

7 January 1941
Sachsenhausen

Maître,

I am not often speechless. But it seems that yesterday I was, during your visit. I am sure I must have said something, but I do not recall what.

Christmas, of course. And the New Year. It was thickheaded of me not to realize, Maître. And thoughtless not to ask yesterday how this holiday of yours was, when you told me that you had been away. But that was from being embarrassed at my own foolishness, Maître. And from not knowing whether such a question would be proper. On paper it is easier for me to ask. And for you to answer. Or not.

I do remember telling you yesterday that I have already written to you from here, just a few days ago. Perhaps you have received that by now. Or soon. I will certainly feel better when I know that my writing has reached you. Perhaps if you provide me again with your official printed envelopes, the people here, the SS, will more likely appreciate how important this is.

But the trial, Maître. This decision you have told me, that the trial is to be delayed. I cannot make sense of it. And, as you could see yesterday, has upset me greatly. I am sorry that I raised my voice. I have never done that before. With you, I mean. And certainly I did not intend to cause you any discomforting, the guard coming into the cell at my shouting. My sincerest regret.

So yes, with this trial postponing I can see why it was not necessary for you to visit me for a while. Or be in contact. Also why I am no longer in Berlin. But the reason for the delaying—and yes, I understand, you made clear that these things are beyond your control. Still, this does not help me understand, Maître. Because what do the French have to do with it? Whether some French official will come to the trial or not, to speak about France and Germany? What difference could it make? This trial is about me. Or rather, what I did. And why. But the

41

official French know nothing of this. Nothing of me. They never did. So, what is the point? To postpone the trial because of them? Because of trouble getting the proper French people to Berlin? Proper, how? What people? What could anyone from there possibly say? I want to understand, Maître. But I do not.

You said yesterday that the delaying is actually a good thing for me. Gives me more time to prepare. To work with you on my writings. To expand, you called it. Well, I am sorry, Maître, but the idea of expanding while sitting in this cell I am having some difficulty imagining.

I need to get my thoughts in control. And my temper. So, for now I think it best not to continue.

Yours sincerely,
Herschel

I also forgot yesterday to wish you a very prosperous New Year, Maître. And your family. If I may be permitted to say so.

Maître Herr Rosenhaus,

Valenciennes. Where France began for me. On the border with Belgium. August 1936.

I had left Hannover in July. Not for Paris but for Brussels. To my Uncle Wolf, one of my father's brothers. But there was no room for me, not to stay for long, theirs was a tiny place, their family already crowded in. Also they had so little money, and I had none to help keep me. I had a proper exit visa from the Reich, to go to Belgium. And a proper Belgium visa also, though only temporary, to visit my family there. But just 10 marks in my pocket—all that the Reich laws permitted me to take out of the country. I did not want to risk being turned back as I left Germany, before I had even begun my journey, perhaps even arrested, so I brought only the 10 Reichsmarks allowed. Much later, my father arranged to send a little money for me to Paris. I do not know exactly how, since it was forbidden. But there were ways. When I arrived in Brussels, though, I had nothing, and it soon became clear that it was impossible for me to stay with them, my relatives there, who had so little for themselves, and anyway barely knew me.

We decided that I should keep moving. To Paris. My Uncle Abraham and Aunt Chawa there, they had earlier written to my parents that if I got to France, they would try to help me. Abraham, a tailor. Another of my father's brothers. They managed to make a living in Paris with their tailor work, Abraham and Chawa, though not much. They had no children to support—or give them worry—so it would be easier for them to help me. Also, they already knew me a little, had got on well with me when they had visited us in Hannover. And in Paris I had other family also. Though more distant. Very distant, as it proved. But that is a different story. I will try to stay on this one, for now.

Please excuse me, Maître. For having begun so directly. It is just that

43

I have been thinking so much of things to write, they started coming out in a rush. But that is certainly not polite. Because first I meant to say again, thank you for your visit this morning. And for the shirt and trousers. Soon I will take off the others I have worn for so long, to wash them, as you suggested. But for now if I wear all of them at once, the ones you brought and the old ones, on top of each other, I do better against the cold.

Thank you also for your strong reminder that we must continue to prepare, even though we do not know when the new trial date will be. Meaning that I should I begin to write again. Your insistence on it. So.

The deciding to leave Belgium for France. Because of my uncle and aunt in Paris, yes, but also the Popular Front. Just two months before, in June '36. We were not political, our family. And myself I understood little of all that. But the Popular Front, everyone had heard of it. Believed it was different, and so now France itself different. We imagined. Different from Belgium. And definitely from Poland, where also we had family I might have gone to, and a Polish passport which yes might have made some things easier there. But Poland? With the pogroms that had begun again there? The place that had yellow ghetto benches in their schools? In Paris, people asked me, French people I mean, when I was in jail—"You had so much difficulty here in France, why did you never try Poland? After all," they would say, "you are a Pole, your family, Poles."

It made me want to tear my hair. Poles? Us? Maître, who did they think drove my parents out of Poland in the first place? Well, and the Ukraines.

So, France it was. With the Popular Front. And Blum. Léon Blum, president of France. These were things it seemed would make a difference. Seemed at the time.

I had no visa for France—we had tried in Hannover, but from the French it was impossible. For someone like me. Blum or not. Still, once it was decided that there was no place for me in Brussels, my Uncle Wolf began asking quiet questions of some people there, then one day we went to Quevrain, a small Belgium town on the France border.

I think that is the spelling. Please excuse me if not. I try to be very careful with my words, Maître, I assure you. But in Fresnes, the prison in Paris, I had a dictionary—I think I told you—which I used with great satisfaction. Here I have none. Is that something you would consider?

And so Quevrain, in Belgium, on the France border. There was a tram line there. A short line of a few kilometers that crossed into France, to the city of Valenciennes. People went over the border all the time on this trolley—it was normal, many Belgiums worked in Valenciennes. The France guards checked papers at the border, my Uncle Wolf was told, but not very much—mostly they only looked closely at people who had valises or boxes. The Belgiums who crossed every day to work they usually did not bother. So several times we rode the tram, Uncle Wolf and I, getting off at the border and watching through the tram windows how things went onboard with the guards. Then a few days later, after we had made our preparations, we returned early in the morning when the tram was crowded with people heading to their jobs. I got on. Alone. If there was trouble, we did not want to risk Uncle Wolf being arrested also, on my account.

Many of the tram riders worked in the Valenciennes factories or rail yards, men with rough clothes and that flat cap they all wear. My valise with the few things I had brought from Hannover, I left it all behind at Uncle Wolf's. I carried only one of the little net sacks the people used there, with a small bit of food in it, one lunchtime's worth wrapped in a Belgium newspaper that you could see through the net. And I was wearing bleus, with one of those caps. Bleus de travail—France worker clothes. Do you know these, Maître? A bright blue color and a very strong, heavy cloth. Many of the France workers wear them. I mean, the ones who do laboring jobs. All exactly the same, les bleus—with this special color that stands out so much and marks the people who wear them. They seem almost proud of it.

Since many of the men who traveled daily on the tram wore the bleus, my Uncle Wolf bought a set for me—trousers, shirt, jacket. Secondhand, so they would not stand out from the others. It was difficult to find them small enough, but he is a tailor and was able to cut them down for me. Anyway, it was good they were too large—they could fit over a set of my own clothes, so I would have at least something to wear when I got to Paris. And which also made me look a bit bigger. More like a worker. So I boarded the tram wearing two sets of clothes, one on top of the other—just as I am now, Maître, with the second shirt and trousers you have given me. Except that day in 1936 was in August and miserable hot. I was sweating terribly. Even in the early morning. Though not only from the heat.

Yes I was terrified, Maître. I do not mind saying so. I think more than any time since—which includes quite a lot of terror, I can tell you. I had almost no French, you see, nothing I could say if I was stopped. Or even if someone just spoke to me. I had studied the language for some weeks before I left Hannover. But I had found out already in Brussels how little of it I had really learned. Not to mention my accent, my German accent. Later in Paris my French became better, and I also worked up quite some skills for such things. Situations, I mean. But not yet. Not then. I had never before been outside of Germany. I was 15 years old.

The trolley stopped at the border and the France police got on. They moved through rather quickly, just looking around, then spoke to two people near the rear door, looked into their satchels, checked their papers. I was standing at the far back, as close as I could to a group of young men, most of them also wearing bleus—though I realized, adding to my fear, that none of them were wearing a jacket in such heat, as I was. They were chatting, these young men, laughing, ignoring the police. I was frightened that they might catch my eye, the police, so I looked down at the floor, at people's backs, out the window. Soon the police left through the rear door. Just two minutes or three, the whole thing. Though some minutes, I can tell you, are much longer than others. They never bothered the back of the car. And none of the other passengers said a thing to me. We began to move again, and in a few minutes we arrived in Valenciennes. The trolley had crossed over. And so had I.

Boulevard Richard Lenoir. Paris. Near Place de la Bastille. My uncle and aunt, Abraham and Chawa, their rooms there, two small rooms.

Not just where they lived but also their tailoring workshop, the front room. Maison Albert—House of Albert—it said on a small plaque outside the door. In Paris, Maison Abraham would not have had the same tone. And that is what their few French clients, the real French, called my uncle—Monsieur Albert, they would say. Also the French people he bought materials or took store orders from, which was much of his business. But not his two workers—his machiniste and his finisher. To them he was Abraham. Other clients also called him Abraham, the ones who were not French. Or not quite. But who spoke French. At first, this was all very confusing—who was who.

They slept in the kitchen, my aunt and uncle. Behind a folding screen. The front room had the two machines, and the cutting table, and another small table for hand work. Also a corner with a curtain, where clients could be fitted. In the early days, that is where they put a small pallet mattress for me, which we folded up each morning and hid in the kitchen. Much of the work they did went to shops and large department stores, but they paid poorly, the shops and stores, so the private clients were important, and the fitting space needed to be clear and spotless.

They had very little, my uncle and aunt, but right away they began to help. It is true, we fought often during the next two years, Uncle Abraham and me. Some bitter fights. About many things. But they opened their arms to me. Took risks. Whatever else, Maître, he was a mensch, my uncle Abraham. Mensch in Yiddish, I mean—in German, of course, that would not make sense. I am sorry if this is also confusing.

19 January 1941

What to do with me? From the beginning, the very first day in Paris, this was the question. Abraham and Chawa's question. And the police. Not asked in the same way, of course. Or interested in the same answers. And my own question, to myself. Every day. With everything that has happened since, I suppose in the end it was not a question I ever managed to answer. Or anyone else.

The first thing was to try to get some kind of papers. Something that gave me permission to stay in France. It was the police who gave out such documents, though who actually made the decisions, there were so many bureaus and ministries and such, we never understood. But the police—everything seemed to begin and end with them.

I remember well the flowers, the smell so sweet you could feel it on your skin. And the colors, all the amazing colors. Coming up with Uncle Abraham from the dark of the Métro—the trains that run under the city—into the bright sun of that Paris September morning, and directly into a wild sea of flowers. It was like that children's toy, the tube you hold up to the light and twist, looking into it at the changing colors and shapes, do you know it, Maître? But instead of looking into a tube of colors, I was actually inside it—a flower market, on the square right outside the Métro stop. I told my uncle how wondrous I thought it was. Tears, he said. The flowers were watered by tears. I did not understand. Until later. It was the main prefecture of police where we were headed, an enormous set of buildings with a vast courtyard where people stood and waited. Its walls just behind this flower market. La Vallée des Pleurs, people called the courtyard. The Valley of Tears.

On that first visit in September '36—I had to make several in the next two years—there were not nearly as many people as later. Perhaps 100 or so were in the courtyard that morning, split up in front of different entrances to the building. Waiting. Plus twice that many inside. And the agents de police, in their dark uniforms. With those capes they wear. As if they were theater actors. I once saw a performance of Nosferatu, Maître. In Hannover. Our school class, we went together to see it, my last year there. At a small municipal theater. And the vampire, the dracula, he first appeared on stage with his head hidden behind a large dark cape. At the very end of the scene, just before he attacked a small child, he suddenly swirled the cape in the air and with a loud hissing sound revealed his horrible face. There were cries and gasps from all of us boys—we were truly startled, maybe even a little frightened, then embarrassed that we had been so. On the way back from the theater to school, none of my classmates would speak to me. That kind of thing was happening to me more and more in my final years there, but this was the first time every single boy refused me. The nosferatu, you see—they had given him a huge hooked nose, with horns on his head. Between the horns was a little round skull cap. And he spoke with a thick accent. An eastern accent.

Whenever I saw the police cape during my two years in Paris, I could not help a shiver of feelings from that day of the nosferatu. The fright and shame I had felt in the theater. And the hurt I felt afterward. Plus the danger that the police themselves were to me, in Paris. The constant danger. Altogether, the cape always made me jump.

I once mentioned it to my uncle. I asked him why the police wore a cape instead of a jacket with sleeves, which would not get so much in their way. Because with capes, he said, there is no need for tailors. I could not tell whether he meant it.

20 January 1941

It took us an hour in a queue just to get to the prefecture's first information bureau. Where they turned us away. We did not have the correct photograph—not an official one, they said. So they would not yet let us begin. We had to go find this particular machine, a photomaton it was called, near the prefecture. It was a little booth that you entered, and it took your photograph. I had never seen one before. Though I do not mean to say that the Reich does not have them also—of course they must.

At this photo machine there was another queue. And it cost 10 francs, I remember because my uncle was so angry that they charged so much. Later, I saw these same machines in other places—at street fairs, and at the World's Fair that opened the next summer, there were many of them there. Just for fun, at these other places. And cost much less—1 or 2 francs, the exact same machines. But when you really needed the photo, at the official place near the prefecture, it cost 10. La Vallée des Pleurs.

We finally got the photo and returned to the prefecture courtyard, then waited again in the queue. After another hour we reached the

49

long high counter in the information bureau. My uncle explained to one of the officers who sat in a row behind a wire screen that we wanted to apply for a permis de séjour—a permit for me to stay in France—as a refugee, with him as my supporting sponsor and guardian. They spoke in French, of course, my uncle and the policeman, which at the time I did not understand. My uncle had told me that he would not speak any Yiddish to me while we were around the police, and that when he spoke to me in French I should just nod and look like I knew what he was saying—the police expected that everyone spoke French, my uncle told me, and if they thought I did not, it certainly would not help things.

The officer asked to see my passport and papers. And my uncle's papers, as well. The policeman picked them up one at a time and almost immediately put each of them down. He did not so much examine what they said, it seemed, as check to see if they would crumble in his hands, or if some insect would jump out. He asked my uncle a few questions and began to write things on a form. When he finished he put all the documents together, got a slip of paper and wrote something on it, then placed this on top of the other papers. It appeared that he was just about to hand everything to my uncle when the officer sitting next to him leaned over and said something. The man who had our papers nodded, puffed out a couple of words at my uncle, closed and latched the opening in the screen, got up from his chair, and walked away. The other policemen behind this long counter, maybe six of them, who were also speaking with people through openings in the partition, did the same. All at once. Turning their backs, they began to chatter with each other and went out a rear door. Not looking back.

Déjeuner, Maître—lunch. It had struck noon, you see. They all got up and went to have their lunch. Exactly at noon. Not a minute later.

My uncle told me we had to stay where we were. If we left, we would have to begin again at the end of the queue. Anyway, we could not risk leaving my passport and Reich exit visa there, and also my uncle's papers, sitting just on the other side of the screen. And the form we needed, filled out, signed and ready, lying on top of them.

So we sat on the floor, as did most of the others waiting in the queue behind us. Uncle Abraham brought out from his pocket two bulkes—bread rolls—and some slices of smoked meat, wrapped in paper. He had been in Paris for many years. He knew.

It was half past two when the police returned from their lunch and we were given back our documents with a slip of paper instructing us to go to a certain staircase, up to a certain floor, to a certain numbered bureau. It took us some time to find it, getting lost in the corridors crowded with people who were standing and waiting, or wandering around lost like us. With each floor we climbed it got hotter, the air thicker. We finally found the proper bureau and entered a waiting room with grey-green walls and rickety benches. Nothing on the walls except patches of stain from smoke and damp. The benches were full of people. Waiting. In the center of the room was a single small, scarred wooden table. It was bare, nothing on it. Though many people had to stand while they waited, some of them holding stacks of papers, no one used the table. They seemed to avoid even touching it.

We were on the fourth or fifth floor. There were no windows in the waiting room. It was terribly hot and damp in there, with a powerful sour smell. Like sitting inside a dog's mouth. And quiet—people sometimes spoke to each other, but only in whispers.

Across from the entry was a glass door. Through it was another large room, with a long table. On the far side of the table six or seven police officers sat side by side, the table crowded with papers and folders. On the near side, their backs to the glass door, people were standing, presenting their documents.

Every few minutes a person or two or three would come out from behind the glass door, through the waiting room, and out to the corridor. Some looked lost, a few near tears, but mostly their faces were blank. Moments after someone left the glass door room, a French woman would come out through the same door and call a name, then one person or couple or family would rise from a bench and follow her back in. Once in a while a young woman clerk or a police officer carrying papers would come from the outside corridor into the waiting room and go behind the glass door. The time between the called names was only a few minutes, and with the movement into and out of the glass door room, and people settling into vacated places on the benches, and new people entering, there was almost constant motion. But the room remained quiet. Just finding enough air to breathe took effort, concentration.

After what seemed a very long time my name was called. We went through the glass door and to the near end of the long table. My uncle spoke to the first officer, who looked at the form the policeman downstairs had filled out, then we shuffled to the next officer in the row, who looked at my passport, visa and photograph. Then we moved along the row to another policeman who examined my uncle's papers and spoke to him a bit longer, then to the next one along, who said something to me and gestured me forward, then grabbed my hand and twisted it, pressing it onto an inkpad to make fingerprints. Finally we moved to the last man in the row. Abraham seemed startled by something this last policeman said, but he managed to answer and the man stamped the form and handed it back. I tried to pretend that I was listening hard to the conversations but of course it was in French, I understood none of it, and my attention kept slipping up to a row of photographs on the wall behind the officers. Each photo was the face of a policeman, in his uniform cap. The frames were wrapped in black ribbon. Underneath each frame was a small printed sign, with a name, a date, and the words "Mort pour la patrie." At the time, I did not know the words. But I could tell what they meant.

We were finished with the glass door room in no more than 15 minutes. Without speaking, my uncle led me quickly down to the courtyard where we went through a different doorway, into another bureau, with several small windows, behind each one a clerk. We got in the queue and waited. My uncle said nothing. In a while we reached a window where my uncle presented our papers, then handed over some money—almost all he had in his billfold—and was given some sort of receipt. He then took me a little roughly by the elbow and led me out of the office, across the courtyard, still without speaking, and away from the building.

Only when we had gone several blocks did he slow down, then

finally stop to sit on a bench. We were right in front of the great cathedral Notre Dame. Do you know it, Maître? My uncle did not seem to notice.

He then told me what had happened. And what had not.

Because I had no entry visa for France, the police had said I had to pay a fine. Meaning, Uncle Abraham had to. 100 francs. Not a small sum, Maître—an entire day's earnings for my uncle. On a good day. On top of the 10 francs for the photograph. But that money was not for a residence permit. No, all that did was give me time to apply for such a permit. Which had to be done somewhere else. And until I had this other permit, the police told my uncle, I had no actual right to stay in France. Paying the fine just meant they would not arrest me then and there and throw me out of the country. He was also required to sign a promise, my uncle, to support me while I was in France, which was what he had told them from the beginning he was willing to do. If he did not give me that support, the document said, he would be committing a crime. He also had to promise to teach me a trade—though the same document said that if I practiced that trade, or if I worked at all, both of us would be breaking the law.

I was completely confused, so as we walked back to Maison Albert my uncle tried again to explain. By paying the fine, he said, for a short time it was not illegal for me to be in France. But it gave me no right to stay in France. My uncle and aunt's rooms, for example—I was permitted to be there, but not to live there. Or anywhere else.

Distinctions. The word my uncle used. I tried to sort it out as we crossed the river, walking back toward Bastille, toward the rooms where I could be, but not live. I tried to sort out distinctions the entire time I was in Paris. Most of them I never managed.

Yours sincerely,
Herschel

P.S. The rainbow, Maître. On the ground. Circling the camp. I told you about it, do you remember? Did you notice it when you were here? Though with all the snow, perhaps not. I said it reminded me of an athletics track. And so it is, I have learned. Of a sort. For boots. A testing track. Prisoners are made to put on special boots, then march around the rainbow. Each stripe is a different surface—stone, dirt, pebbles, mud, sand. Around and around, many kilometers they march, each man on one color path. For the Wehrmacht. Different types of boots the army might use—they need to be tested. Carrying heavy sacks on their backs, the prisoners, like the equipment packs the Wehrmacht would carry. Even heavier, I was told—it seems the prisoners weigh much less than Reich soldiers, so they add weight to the sacks to make the pressure on the boots the same. To test how they wear, the boots. On different surfaces. In all conditions. How long they last. Extreme conditions. And what they do to a person's feet.

Which puts me in mind, Maître, that if you could send me a pair of socks I would be most grateful.

Herr Rosenhaus,

"Confine my remarks." A curious notion, Maître. Though perhaps not so much, given my present circumstances.

So yes, as you can see, I received the packet of your official address envelopes. And the pencils. Along with your instructions that I confine my remarks. But forgive me, Maître, who was it not long ago who said that the time I now had before my trial would allow my writing to expand? And in Berlin, who asked me to write about my well-being? That in Reich custody, I was well? At the time, I gave that request quite some thought. Though I may not have told you of my hesitation—I think about things considerably more than I write about them. Which I am sure you can understand. In my position. But I decided, back then, to agree with what you asked.

And once begun, describing my well-being, surely now I should continue. Which must also mean speaking about where I am. And what is happening around me. Because that is all part of what is happening to me, yes? Up to a point.

Also, Maître, certainly these are things you yourself must want to know. I assume.

Respectfully, your client,
Herschel Grynszpan

19 February 1941
Sachsenhausen

Maître Herr Rosenhaus,

Your note was given to me earlier today. Which is a relief. I was becoming very concerned, after hearing nothing these past three weeks. About whether my writings were reaching you. And yours to me, here in the bunker. Which is what this building is called, this special prisoner unit—the bunker. Perhaps you know that.

I have been worrying that there might be a problem, Maître. Because I know that sending things here to the bunker, things from outside, is not itself unusual. I move around the building for my work, bringing the meals and collecting the bowls, and I have seen many things in the cells—books, newspapers, foodstuffs, blankets. Things sent in to the other special prisoners here in the bunker. One man, he has four sets of clothes. Handsome clothes—high quality tailoring. Another has a cane chair. There are now 10 of us here in the bunker. I know little about the others—I am not allowed to spend much time in anyone's cell when I do my job, and we are not supposed to talk with each other. But I pick up things now and again. All of us are German speaking. A few with the accent of Austria, I think. Most with very fine manners and ways of talking. But perhaps this is all I should write about such matters. Confining my remarks.

So, not hearing from you left me wondering whether your writings take some kind of special journey before they get here to the bunker. After all, Sachsenhausen is not far from Berlin, I know, so it is not a matter of distance. There was no date on your latest note, so I cannot tell exactly when you wrote it. Or is it my writings that take some longer route before they get to you? Though you have never said anything to me about such things. Not that you should have to, of course.

What you now ask of me also adds to my confusion. That before I continue about France I should explain about Germany. How I left. Who helped me. You have never mentioned this before. Why this should matter I do not understand since I am writing to prepare for my trial, about what happened in Paris. Although I suppose it is true, that everything in Paris was always connected to everything else.

The short answer is that no one helped me. Except my parents, of course. But short answers may not be very useful, I can understand. Even about a short life. For our purposes. Perhaps this is something we should discuss again when you visit. Our purposes, I mean.

My sister Berthe, she was a singer. On the stage, even. Though only in small places. And only from time to time. But such a voice, Maître. From deep inside her. Like a cello. May you be fortunate enough to hear her someday.

But then suddenly it was gone. Not her voice, I mean, but any chances to use it. A new law, that only Aryans may perform in theaters, halls, anywhere in public. Spring of 1934. Just before my birthday. My 13th.

I am telling you this, Maître, about my sister, from two years before I actually left Germany, because I believe that was the real beginning for us, for my family. Of leaving, I mean. Of me leaving. The idea of it.

She did not earn her wages singing, Berthe. She was the secretary in the bureau of a small company, so this new law did not take away her pay. Still, something changed that day. The air. Its mixture. How it felt to breathe.

The news about the new law came to us on the evening radio. I remember it well, sitting around the table, my parents, my sister and brother and me. We all listened to the radio together each evening. We had only just got one a few months before—radios had recently become much cheaper for people, something the Reich had arranged, do you remember? My father had taught himself to repair broken ones, he had now managed to fix one of the older ones for our own, and it was still quite special to all of us. On this particular evening an announcement came on telling of this new law, the public performing law, and it was as if all the oxygen rushed out of the room. With something else beginning to seep in its place. Through the walls, the ceiling.

Even from the radio itself. Invisible. That we would now inhale, every day, and that would silently begin to rot our lungs, our insides, more and more, from then on.

A cello—I think that is right. How someone once described it. My sister's voice. It has been a long time.

During the months following that evening my parents began to talk quietly about arranging for me to leave. On my own. Leave Germany. They did not yet speak to me about it directly, but I could tell they were talking about me. I think they must have wanted me to know but without having actually to face it yet. It was a shock to realize what they were discussing, but we all felt what was happening around us, even if we avoided speaking to each other about exactly what it might mean for us. Like my older brother Marcus. Becoming a plumber. As my father had once been. He had some work then, Marcus, in 1934. For not much pay. And only the lowest of jobs. He was waiting to be accepted into the guild, you see, as an official apprentice. Still waiting. He had passed his examinations, had all his certificates in order. More than a year he had been waiting. By then, we knew it would never happen.

And for me, in school, things were getting all the time worse. At the beginning of each new term I had always been placed in the front row, because I am small. That was how they did it in the municipal school, the small boys up in front. But in the fifth form, all of a sudden they moved me to the last row. And from then on hardly ever called on me, the instructors. Or even spoke to me. And the boys also. Each year, each month, it got more difficult. Not including me in the games and joking and walking after school and such. Ignoring me. Then later, true awfulness—name-calling, fights. Which I did not shy away from, Maître. Judas Maccabeus, the boys sometimes called me, because I was always ready to fight, like the Maccabees. Later, they shortened it just to Judas—when they said anything at all to me—and laughed at their joke.

For my parents also, everything was becoming so difficult. I mean, even more than it always had been. They had come to Hannover from Radomsk, before the Great War. I think I told you this. Or you already knew? Anyway, at first, in Hannover, my father looked for work as a plumber, as he had been trained in Radomsk. But he could get very little, and only doing back labor, as he called it—without using his hands, he meant. His skills. Or being paid for them. So he soon gave up and instead began to work as a tailor. At this he did a bit better. People in Hannover—Germans, I mean—were more willing to offer him this kind of work. To use him as a tailor, you see, they did not need to allow him into their homes.

I was not born yet when these things were happening, but later my father spoke about them. Especially once he realized that Marcus would not be allowed into the guild, the plumbers guild. At the time, I thought my father was telling us these stories to remind us, especially Marcus, that there had always been such problems, and that in the end something else would work out. But thinking back on it now, perhaps that is not what my father had in his mind.

After some years in Hannover he decided to take a chance, my father, and opened a small shop, near where we lived. I was about 10 years old. He was still tailoring—most of it piecework, for the big clothing stores—much like Abraham and Chawa did in Paris, only with even less success. It was long and hard, the work, and poorly paid. He could only do so much, and it was never enough. We only managed because of the little extra money Berthe and Marcus earned. So, my father opened a tiny shop where he not only did his tailoring work but also sold some clothes—a few things he made, and some secondhand clothes that he would repair—and other old things that he picked up here and there, small furniture, tools, kitchen things, that he would clean up and fix. Make usable again.

A zammler, my father, I suppose you would say. Not you, Maître, I do not mean actually you would say. Because the word is a bit different in Yiddish than in German—zammler. Not just pronouncing it, the z sound instead of s. Is it spelled with an s in German? But also what it means. Someone who scrounges things, to make a living—that part of it is the same as in German, yes? But in Yiddish there is more. There is a kind of respect. At least some. Depending on who is speaking, of course. Though people who give it no respect would not be saying it in Yiddish anyway. A zammler. It requires a special talent—to know the value of something when others cannot see it. An intelligence. A useful kind. And not a common one. Though I must admit I did not feel that way at the time, Maître. In truth, I was a bit embarrassed by my father's shop. I was younger then, of course. But something else, also. I was more—what? Hannoverian? Is it a word? Anyway, later, when I was in Paris, I began to see things differently. Appreciated what it took to live by your wits. Seeing so many who could not manage it.

Also, in his shop he examined for shatnez, my father. People would bring him secondhand clothes, or fabric that they wanted to use. I can still see him squinting through his jeweler's glass or tasting a bit of cloth. Tasting, yes. And burning. To test the fabric. Do you know? I suppose not. I should explain. Shatnez, it means wool and linen threads mixed together. Which is forbidden by Torah, the ancient law. But people cannot tell these things for themselves. They need an expert eye. Or mouth—wool and linen taste different, you see. And burn different.

It was the most orthodox, the strictly observant, who brought their cloth to my father, for him to examine it for shatnez. Only the very orthodox worried about such things. Which was certainly not most people. At least, not in Hannover. Or Paris. There is the orthodox, and then the strict orthodox. And the not at all. There are also many people, like my father, who do not follow all the laws of observance but who know them completely. What people do may tell you more than what they say, yes. But it might not always tell you what they know. Or what matters to them.

To get something examined for shatnez, many people would go to a rabbi. But it did not have to be, and with a rabbi you must pay your respects, have a conversation, listen to what he has to say. And give some money for the shul, the synagogue. My father made it simpler for people. He was observant enough, and knew enough, the right things to say, and not say. So, the orthodox were comfortable with him.

This talk about wool and linen, Maître, it makes me think to ask again—Could you bring a pair of socks for me when next you visit? Or if that does not seem proper, to send me? My only pair is worn through with holes. If I try to wash them, they will surely fall apart. And as you have seen, it is terribly cold here in the bunker.

So, my father's shop. By 1935 it was doing poorly. More poorly than before. Not enough customers. Because by that time all the Germans were staying away. The Christians, I mean.

Then, it was losing the technical school. You see, I was always good with my hands—tinkering, fixing. I had watched my father closely in the shop, the way he took abandoned things, broken things, and made them work again. I learned from him. I had aptitude. My father said so. Even my teachers used this word about me. Aptitude. At least in the early years. Not later.

My parents and I for a few years we had a plan—or at least an idea—that I would go to the local technical college. Become an engineer. Some kind of engineer, we did not know exactly, but I would find out more at the college, where you were taught the trade. It was our idea, that is, until the decree—only Germans would now be allowed into technical colleges. At first, we did not realize that this was a problem for me. I was born in Germany. Had lived my whole life here. Spoke German. Thought German—although, I suppose some would not agree with that. By now, perhaps me among them. Though how would I decide? Anyway, it does not matter. Did not matter, none of that. Because my passport was Polish. And Poles—even if they were not truly Poles—were not Germans. No matter how German they were.

Early in 1935, this was. My final year of school, when I was to get my graduation certificate. Which, until this decree, would have allowed me to go on to the technical college. Instead, I left school. Two months before my diploma. Because, Maître, by then, what was the point?

20 February

Helping me leave Germany. About groups, you asked. Well, yes there were, that helped some people go out of the country. But I doubt there is anything I can say about them that you do not already know. Or at least, that the court would know. Because these were groups the Reich had approved. Yes, at the time, early in 1935, getting permission from the Reich to leave Germany was not so difficult—letting people leave meant almost none of them would come back. But having somewhere for me to go? That would allow me in? The Reich, Maître, was only the first of my problems.

So. When I left school it was with the idea also to leave Germany, but going to Belgium or France, to relatives there, at first did not seem sensible. I would be a burden to them—they had little themselves, these relations, and anyway barely knew me. I would be lost there, I remember my mother saying. Which I suppose is what happened. Given where I am now.

No, early on the idea was Palestine. Not because we knew anything about it, our family. Or knew anyone there. Before then none of us had even thought of the place. But if I managed to get there, my parents learned, at least I would not be on my own. You see, to be allowed into Palestine you had belong to an organization. Some group or another—unless you were rich. And you remained part of that group once you were there. The group made sure of it. Since my parents' great fear was that I would wind up alone, a group that could look after me seemed to them the best thing. So, Palestine.

First, we tried Ziraiy. I am just writing the sound of it, Maître—I do not know how it is spelled in German. I only ever saw it written in Hebrew. Young Spirit, it means—something like that. My family knew almost nothing about them. They had a small bureau not far from where we lived, and we would see them, boys from Ziraiy, also girls but mostly we saw the boys and young men, who were often on the streets in our neighborhood, always in groups of six or eight, with these sort of uniforms they wore, very smart looking, all exactly the same, with military style caps and shirts, brown shirts. They were always handing out leaflets, which talked about all the activities they had for young people—different sports, and summer camps in the forest, and marching groups you could join. Marching—they loved it. You often saw them in the streets strutting in soldier steps, around and around, not going anywhere, just showing off it seemed. And I must admit, Maître, it was something that caught your eye, all the identical outfits moving by, with this straight, upright posture, and boots, pounding the pavement all together, in perfect time. Plus the singing. To match their steps. Different things they sang, some in Hebrew that I did not understand. But one of the songs, in German, many times I heard it, and a particular line that stayed in my head. "With blood and sweat a race will arise, proud, giving, and cruel." I am not sure which of the words made the biggest impression on me. But all of them together, I remember it gave me shivers.

Anyway, these leaflets also said that they were looking for young people who wanted to go to Palestine. To make a life. And fight the Arabians. And the British. Though I do not remember that part, about the British, actually being in the leaflets. In fact, I think not. Only when you spoke to them.

They had some Palestine entry visas to give, the Ziraiy people. And permission from the Reich. So, I went to see them, with my father.

It was over quickly.

First they asked what we knew of Palestine. About the struggle there. That was their word—struggle. In German. When we first got to their bureau we spoke to them in Yiddish, but they replied only in German, these two large men, with shaved heads and starched outfits, sitting across the table from us in a tiny room that seemed barely able to hold them.

So, did we know of the struggle with the Arabians? And the British? Had we heard of the Irgun, the secret-but-not-secret fighters there? In Palestine new men were being created, they said. Men to make the desert bloom. And who could fight, would fight, to keep it.

It seemed odd, but at the beginning they asked nothing about me or our family. Our situation. It was difficult, this conversation, or interview, whatever it was, because my father and I knew so little about what was happening. In Palestine, I mean. So, he fumbled around a bit, my father, and began to speak to them about his fears, for our family, for all of us. For my future in Germany. My no-future. After a few moments, though, one of the men put up his hand for my father to stop. They were not authorized, the man said, to speak about such things.

The man then asked whether I had any skills. "He has just turned 14 years old," my father said, a bit of bother slipping into his voice. "How many skills could he have?" The two men just stared at him, so after a moment he told them that I knew some tailoring. "Are you a tailor?" they asked my father. When he said yes, they were silent, and their shoulders—it was so remarkable to me, I can still see it, exactly together, the two enormous men, their shoulders moved from leaning forward, toward us, to slightly back. Just a few centimeters, but it struck me, and for some moments I did not hear what my father was saying. He had begun speaking again, quickly now, something about how I also knew how to fix things, that I was very handy, from what I had learned in the shop, his shop. One of the men asked about the shop, where it was, what kind of shop, and when my father said it was now closed, their faces remained the same but again their bodies, their shoulders, moved slightly away. They asked nothing about what I had learned there.

I could tell that it was going badly. Then I had an idea. And spoke up. About Judas Maccabeus. My nickname. I told them about how I got the name, because I was always ready to fight if I had reason to. They looked at me sort of curious, then asked me to stand up. And take off my jacket. I am very small, Maître, as you know. I was even smaller then. They could barely see any more of me standing up than when I was sitting. And very thin. I had been ill. My stomach. A problem I often have. As you already know. Then—and this I will never forgive, Maître—they asked my father to stand up. He also is very small. They looked at us both, standing there, then glanced at each other, these two large men, and said thank you. And that was it. The interview was over.

They said they would contact us when a visa became available. We never heard from them again.

21 February

From people in the neighborhood my parents heard that the Commission had quite a few visas for Palestine. That was what they called themselves, this organization—just, the Commission. As if they were the one and only. It was run by a group in Palestine with some other name, my father learned, and they had a big bureau near Hannover's city center. You had to make an appointment many days ahead, it was all very formal. So, on our day we got dressed up, my father and I—he had made me a new jacket—and we went to their bureau. But before we got to speak to anyone there we had to fill out a form that asked which category of Pioneer I intended to be. That was also the way they talked, when we finally got to speak with them— Pioneers and such. To stock the new land. But only the best human material, they said. Human material, Maître.

Sitting in their waiting room we looked over this form, my father and I. The first category was the single word Capitalist. This was about the Haavara, we learned later, the transfer agreement. Between the Reich and the Zionists and the British, with Palestine visas going to people who could bring 1,000 English pounds with them—about 15,000 Reichsmarks. Altogether, my father, Marcus and Berthe earned maybe 600 or 700 marks in a whole year. We did not write anything in that column.

Next was a category about professional skills—doctor, engineer, electrician. I forget the other ones. My father wrote down something for me about repairman. He did not write much.

There was also a column about farming—Had the applicant ever worked on a farm? I had grown up in Hannover, Maître. I had never even seen a farm. But there was also something on the form about being willing to train for farming. We read it together, my father and I, then he looked at me and I nodded. He made a mark next to that spot.

Another category was Zionism activities. We had nothing to put there, so we moved on to the last column, which was political associations. My father had asked around and heard that the group in Palestine, the group in charge, was made up of socialists and the like, who wanted to build some kind of workers nation there. Since he had stopped being a plumber many years before, he had spent no time around workers groups—they had no interest in tailors. Or zammlers. But as a young man in Radomsk, for a while he had gone to meetings of the Bund, the laborers group in Poland. He was never actually a member of the Bund, he told me later. But he thought this was at least something he could put in that column, so he did.

We handed over the form and waited awhile, then were shown into a huge room with rows of desks, big file cabinets, lots of papers everywhere, men and women, mostly young, some of them talking across tabletops with people—well, like my father and me, I suppose. We were taken to a table where we sat across from a man and woman, only a bit older than my sister Berthe I would say, in their 20s. The man was small, though taller than me and my father, with a strong energy in his body, a sort of muscle energy—I do not know how else to say it. And the woman—like no one I had ever been near before. She had this wide smiling face, with skin very pale but colored by the sun. And freckles—on her face and neck, her bare arms. Her short hair was wavy but loose, not that curly fashion style that does not move. It was light brownish, her hair, but when you looked closer it was actually chestnut. And her eyes—both grey and green at the same time. I never knew that eyes could be grey. Or that grey could be so beautiful.

I am sorry if saying such things does not seem proper, Maître. When what I have to write about is so important. And here, in this place, to think such thoughts. But sometimes I cannot help it, the thoughts that come. Where my mind takes me, in the oddest moments. Time and again this happens to me, Maître. As it did during the moment I am describing, when all my force should have been concentrating on how these people might help me leave the Reich. Yet for some while there, across that table, my attention was only on her green-grey eyes and reddish hair. And her freckles. My life has turned a thousand somersaults since that day, but I can see this woman still so clearly. Because of Geneviève, I suppose. Who looked so much like her—at least, in my memory of them both. Their eyes and hair the same. Their skin.

Anyway, the young man and woman at the Commission, they were friendly and full of enthusiasm. Happy to be talking with us about Zion, chattering away about the new land. Such excitement. And confidence. If these two were going to be there, I also wanted to go. Completely different from what I had felt from the people at Ziraiy.

The young woman told us about the several kibbutzim the Commission was starting, about new fruit groves in the empty land. All the while, the man was looking over my application, his face growing darker. The woman continued to speak about the spirit of the new pioneers, their communalist principles, or some word like that—not Communist, Maître, I am sure of that, in case you would ask, but some other word like it—and my father spoke up, saying yes, since his days as a young man in Radomsk these ideas had been a part of him, and of course he had taught them well to his children. The woman started to answer brightly, but the man put his hand on her arm, and she stopped.

"It is written here that you were a Bundist," the man said to my father, looking up from the application form. My father did not know what to do. Whatever he had prepared himself to say about the Bund had now been frozen by the look on the man's face. He stumbled out some words, my father, about having been a Bundist in Radomsk, yes, but long ago, and he had not kept up with them in Hannover, since the Bund was in Poland but not in Germany—and other things he said, I do not remember what, though by some of them he seemed to contradict himself. What I do remember is the young woman—she had put away her smile. It was the first time I had a broken heart.

We did not know why, but it was now clear to us that this mention of the Bund had been a big mistake. Only later did we learn that the Bund had officially oppositioned against the whole idea of Zion in Palestine. My father understood enough from the man's reaction, though, to realize he had better change the subject and he asked, as cheerfully as he could pretend, about the farm training. I was a very fast learner, my father said, and willing also. He looked to me, and I said, yes, yes, I would certainly like to learn.

By now I felt I had to say something on my own, something to make them pay attention to me, because until then everything seemed to be about my father. And he was not doing well. But I did not speak about myself, or ask questions about what might happen for me, such as was there a space for me in the training—because I knew by now that in these bureaus there were never any direct answers. So instead

I asked them, the two young people, if they would tell me about their own training. To describe it for me, what it had been like. How much I would like to hear about it, I told them. It was to let them talk about themselves, you see. A tactic—we had studied von Clausewitz in my final year at school. Did you also, Maître? Of course, von Clausewitz also taught that tactics is not the same as strategy.

And so. The woman spoke a bit about their training, how it was for farming, yes, but also about the communalisms, or whatever that word was. And that it usually took a year. "Longer for some," the man put in. "We are creating Pioneers," the woman added, but without a gram of her earlier friendliness. Pioneers—it must have been the 50th time since we had been there, Maître, that I heard that cursed word.

They spoke for a few more minutes, but now as if they were just reciting from a text. They told us that the training was at small farms the Commission had in different places across Germany. All of them approved by the Reich. I do not remember any details from this lecture they were now giving us. Except when the man said, somewhere in the middle of it all, that the Commission did not accept Hitler Zionists. Pardon the expression, Maître—theirs, not mine. But one that certainly caught my attention. And sent my mind spinning. A few minutes later I found out what he meant.

At the end of their little talk the man said that for someone as young and small as I was, he thought the training would take at least two years, not one. If I was accepted at all. And there was no guarantee that the training, if I was able to complete it, would mean a visa. Things, he said, would remain to be seen.

By this time I just wanted to get up and leave. My father had shrunk down in his chair—become smaller, somehow, since we had been there. But he was stronger than I realized, and spoke up again.

"All right," I remember him saying. "All right, I understand."

I did not know what he understood. Maybe everything.

"So, Palestine is a complicated matter," my father said. "I can see that. But what about somewhere else for my son to go? Somewhere less difficult?"

The two young Commission people looked at him as if they could not quite make sense of what he was asking, as if he was suddenly speaking a broken language.

"But we are Pioneers of Zion," the woman finally said. "Why would we help someone go anywhere else?"

22 February

My parents would not give up. My mother knew some neighbor women whose children were in Mizrahi Youth. For the orthodox, this was. They had some social gatherings, the Mizrahi group, but mostly they taught Hebrew to children, and helped them study the religious texts. She learned, my mother, that the Mizrahi also had a few settlements in Palestine. And some visas. But they were different from the other groups we had tried. The Mizrahi were not interested in whether you knew anything about farming, or what other skills you had. Or your family's politics. No, what the Mizrahi wanted was young people who were very religious. That was how they saw their duty, the Mizrahi—to put enough orthodox in Palestine to make sure that the new land would be a strongly religious place.

Strictly orthodox, the Mizrahi were. And we were not, our family, as I told you. But becoming more religious was something I could do. Much easier than becoming stronger. Or taller.

So, we made a new plan. I started going to a small local synagogue, an orthodox synagogue, to show my devotion. I also began attending a religion class that the synagogue offered for young people. And a class in Hebrew language. Also, on Friday afternoons, before the Sabbath began at sunset, I would walk to the baker with my mother's stew, in a clay pot, where it would cook untouched in a special slow oven until I picked it up on my way home from synagogue the following evening, for the meal that marked the end of Sabbath. You see, an orthodox family is not permitted to do any work on the Sabbath itself, not even cooking. We could have managed to do this meal the same way at home, of course, as most people did, but this was a way to show how observant we were. Or, I was. For anyone who might be paying attention.

Also, my father made an arrangement for me. He knew a man with a small shop, a German man, something like the shop my father himself used to have—a place where old things were repaired and sold. My father had done this man some favors, so the man offered me a job, helping in the shop, cleaning up, fixing a few small things. But after only a couple of weeks, he fired me—because I refused to work on Saturday, our Sabbath, when his shop was open. Quietly we let people know in the neighborhood, and especially in Mizrahi, what had happened, which added to this idea of me as a boy whose religious feelings were strong, even more so than my parents—who after all had arranged the job at a place that was open on the Sabbath.

Even though the truth was that the man did not really need any help in the shop. The actual favor to my father was not giving me a job but pretending to give me a job, then pretending to fire me.

It seemed to make an impression—my firm religious beliefs costing me a job, particularly when work was nearly impossible to find. Plus the other religious things I was doing. Because soon after, Mizrahi took an interest in me. Not to give me a visa, though, as we had hoped. But to sponsor me for yeshiva.

Which reminds me now, Maître, of another part of the story, this long story of my short life. About how this little trick with the job came back to curse me later, in Paris. When I was in jail there, after the shooting, the magistrate asked some social counselor people, or whatever they were called, to prepare a report on me—what I was like, what kind of person. My character, they called it. And one of the things they ended up writing about me, in their report, was that I "appeared to be somewhat irresponsible" and was "perhaps lazy." Why? First, because I had left school without my diploma—it seems that my reasons for that were of no interest to them. Also, because they could find no record of any work that I had done during the two years I had been in Paris. Can you imagine? No record? When I had no work permit? Where people like me were never given work that anyone would write down and make official? Where if I was caught working, I could be thrown in jail, then out of the country? And they also looked into my life in Hannover. And learned that I had quit the one job there I had ever

70

had—I was 15 years old when I left, how many should I have had?—the pretend job, at the shop. So, "somewhat irresponsible," they decided, "perhaps lazy."

Well, I was talking about earlier, in Hannover, where the Mizrahi had now seen that I was a good boy. An observant boy. Which for them was the same thing. They had an arrangement with the central orthodox council of Hannover, to sponsor boys, and pay the fees, for religious study. They asked if I would be willing to study, and my parents said, yes, of course, since they thought this was a first step to Mizrahi sending me to Palestine. So, the council made the necessary applications, and Mizrahi agreed to sponsor me to attend yeshiva.

Yeshiva, Maître—I should explain. It is a place where boys are trained in religious studies, the ancient laws and texts—as early as four or five years old a boy can start, instead of attending municipal school. Some of them to become rabbis, or religious teachers. But many just to be in a school that is a separated place, and to gain the knowledge, or the diploma anyway, to be thought of someday as learned men in their communities. And part of this studying is to learn Hebrew, because of the texts. So, here in one place were the two exact trainings I needed for Mizrahi to sponsor me to Palestine—religion and Hebrew. What could be bad? Except that it was in Frankfurt, the yeshiva, not Hannover. In a few days I was on a train crossing the country. May 1935.

It was not easy at first, yeshiva. It was my first time away from home. And the routine there was very hard, very strict, with many hours of study, and several sessions every day of ceremonial prayings and readings and the like. Also, the boys, most of the ones my age were so far ahead of me, after years of study there. And so serious. So much in their tunnel, their hidden-away yeshiva cave. Not that I was unserious, Maître. I do not want to give you the wrong impression. I wanted badly to learn. At least, enough to get to Palestine. But these other boys, who knew so much—from the texts, and from endless discussing and debating—and at the same time knew so little.

Mostly it went all right for me, I did well enough. And there were two other boys like me, I discovered, who were also hoping to leave the Reich—although we only whispered this among ourselves.

You see, almost none of the other boys approved of such a plan, and did not want to hear anything about it. Nor about what was happening all around them, at home, with their families, in the Reich. For them there was no world except yeshiva. One night I remember well, Maître, soon after I arrived there, I sat up the entire night listening to a group of them argue, hour after hour, about whether old birdseed was chomitz—food grains that are not kosher for Passover and so must be removed from the house before that holiday starts. Full of learning, these boys. Full of argument. And nothing to say. Birdseed, Maître. Sometimes I wanted to scream.

But yes, I worked hard at yeshiva, and after six months their report on my progress was very good. I was proud of myself, I do not mind telling you. Then we all went home for a winter rest. By the time I reached Hannover in late November, things had become much darker.

The yeshiva hardly ever allowed us boys out into the city—part of keeping us separate—so we had not seen much of what was going on that summer and fall. My parents had written letters to me, but they had been careful in what they said. When I got home that winter, though, it was clear that things were very different. In September, the first of the new laws had come from Nuremberg, taking away citizenship. This we had heard about at yeshiva, and many of the boys had been quite upset. But it had not registered much with me, because my family and I were not citizens of the Reich anyway—we all had Poland passports. Just before I reached home, though, the next set of laws had come, with more restrictions and prohibitions and such, and we all could see it, the ball rolling faster and faster downhill. With us at the bottom. Waiting.

My father had by now moved his work from the attic of our building to a little single room, a shopfront, further down the street. At first I thought this meant that he had more work. Actually it was just the opposite. He was no longer getting any work from the clothing shops, so he depended completely on individual customers. But almost the only ones who could still afford to have new clothing made, rather than just repairs, were his goyishe customers. And since the summer, they had no longer been willing to enter our building, to be fitted.

Excuse me, Maître—Christian, I should say. The customers.

Also, a family we knew had their apartment taken away, and my father moving out his machine and work table gave them enough space to live in the attic. So, my father rented a tiny room down the street as his workshop. But the work was not keeping up with the added cost, small as it was, and for the first time in my life it was very quiet at our family table each night.

I went back to yeshiva just after the new year, 1936. Soon after, in February I think, Marcus was barred from any work as a plumber—another new law. And not long after that, Berthe lost her job. She was not barred, like Marcus, but the small company she worked for had shut. They had been gardeners to the city of Hannover, for the municipal parks. There are many public parks there. Do you know my city, Maître? I do not remember whether I have ever asked you. Forgive me. Anyway, this little business that Bertha worked for had lost its city contract. The official reason was that they provided the wrong kind of fertilizer—apparently, there was now Aryan manure and non-Aryan manure. Anyway, it would not have mattered. A few months later there was another new law, and all the company's workers would have been forbidden even to enter the parks.

Finally, my father gave up his workroom, to save the rent, though it was only a few marks. He now used our kitchen for what little work he had.

I learned all of this in March. On my birthday. I turned 15. Until then, my family had kept all these things from me. Their letters were shorter and shorter, with less news, less talk of what they were doing, and I had suspected that things had become worse. But I did not know how much so. Until my birthday. I was allowed to receive a telephone call. All the boys at yeshiva, on their birthday, or a parent's birthday, were allowed a call. And on the telephone, my father, it all came spilling out—the end of Marcus's and Bertha's jobs, giving up his workroom, the whole suffocatingness. My father told me then, on the telephone, that we should wait no longer. That we should now try again for a visa, to find a way out of the Reich for me as soon as possible. He said he would again contact the Mizrahi.

The waiting was terrible. I became ill, my stomach, and could barely eat. And this, plus not knowing if I would continue at yeshiva, made it difficult to concentrate, and I started doing poorly on my work. Which only added to my worry.

Soon my father heard from Mizrahi that if I returned to Hannover I could be interviewed again about a visa. He wrote to me with this news, and to the yeshiva to allow me to leave. A few weeks after my birthday, I packed my things and headed home.

It took some time to get another appointment. But when we went, we were prepared. My father brought a letter for Mizrahi from the rabbi of the local orthodox synagogue, where I had been attending before I left for yeshiva, praising me for my observance and my serious purpose. I told the Mizrahi people about my religious training at yeshiva, and how much I had learned of Hebrew. They seemed pleased with all this, but the talking went on for a long time, and I became nervous. I was sweating, dizzy. My stomach was beginning to pain. The people from Mizrahi could see that I was not well. They stopped and asked if I needed anything. I explained that recently I had been ill at yeshiva but that I was getting better. They said I did look very thin, but I told them no, that was not from the illness, I had always been small and thin, this was nothing serious, I was almost well. They brought me some tea, and offered to have me come back another day. They were very kind. But I did not want to let anything get in the way, so I told them that I wanted to continue.

They began to talk about what came next—a word I thought very hopeful. It would be training. I do not remember where, exactly. Perhaps they never said. They told us that it took some time, this training, about six months, to prepare for the very physical life on a kibbutz. I did not listen very well to what they were saying, the details I mean, because of feeling so poorly, but also having grabbed on to that single word—next. Slowly, though, I started to realize what they were actually saying. Since I was so small, and not up to full strength, they thought it would be best for me—they still spoke very kindly—if I waited some time before I was sent for such hard training. About a year. If I came back in a year, they would see how I was doing—if I was stronger, sturdier. And then they would be only too happy to consider again. If I was ready. Keep studying, they encouraged. That could only be a good thing, they said. No matter what.

23 February

I have been writing for several days straight, now. And it occurs to me that I should stop and send all this to you. Or else you may not know that I received your note.

So, Maître, that was the spring of 1936. Mizrahi. Come back in one year, they said, and then perhaps we will see. But it was not a year my parents believed I had. Especially not with that "perhaps" at the end of it. You wanted to know about groups, organizations? Well, we had now run out of them. Palestine would have to get along without me.

After that, things moved very quickly. Much to our surprise. The details will not be very interesting to you, I think. To the court, I mean. Because there was no one who helped us. So, I will tell you briefly. First my father and I went to the France consulate for a visa, to go to my relatives in Paris. But the officials there were not interested in me going to France. Very much not interested.

Then we went to the Belgiums. We prepared for this visit, after our experience with the French. I brought a reentry permit from the Hannover police, which they had given without any trouble—at the time, as long as you took no money with you, which they checked carefully at the border, the Reich was happy to see people like me leave, since most would not return. And we also brought to the Belgiums a letter from my Uncle Wolf in Brussels inviting me to come stay with them, but saying clearly that it could only be for a short time, while I recovered from my illness. They would take me to the beautiful Belgium seacoast, the letter said, where the healthy air would do me good, and to Spa, where the water was said to be a miracle.

The people at the Belgium consulate could easily see that I truly was in need of recovery. And they agreed—seemed quite proud, in fact—when they read in the letter about how good for my health it would be in their country. In just a week, they sent a note that I should return to the consulate. And gave me a visa. Simple as that. A visitor's visa, only one month, for the purpose of restoring my health. But a visa nonetheless. In my hand. I was amazed. Except for going to yeshiva, it was the first time anyone had said yes to me, about anything, in a very long time.

I had to leave almost immediately. Since it was supposed to be for my recovery, I could not delay. So, within a week I was gone. By train. Hannover to Brussels. July 1936. And the rest, about my journey to Paris, you know.

Yours sincerely,
Herschel

No, Maître, that is not true—about you knowing the rest. Of course you could not. And some things I cannot tell you because I do not know either. Most especially, what it was like for my parents to see me go. To make me go. I have one final picture of them in my mind. Because since two years ago, when the Reich sent them out of Germany, I have been unable to imagine them anywhere, my parents. Wherever they are. So, I continue to see them always on the platform, as my train pulled away. In the two years since they left the Poland border camp, I have not known anywhere even to send them a letter. It is now more than four years since they have seen me. Except in the newspapers.

Do you have children, Maître? You have never said. Pardon me for asking.

Maître,

The main thing was to find work. Any work. That, and food, was what pressed my mind the most every day, almost from my first hours in Paris. Well, and the police.

My Uncle Wolf, in Brussels, he had given me a bit of money when I crossed over to France, but he could not afford much, and it was soon gone. Uncle Abraham and Aunt Chawa, during those first few months in Paris, they would give me small amounts from time to time—it embarrassed me, they were already doing so much for me, and they had no extra for themselves, but every week one of them or the other would quietly press a few francs in my hand. The two rooms they lived in were also their workshop and fitting room—Maison Albert—with their two workers, and their customers, so I had to be out all day, during their long work hours, from early morning until well into the evening when I could return and Chawa would give me something to eat. I was so careful with the little money they gave me, but still—on the streets in Paris, hour after hour, day after day, eventually a person needs to spend a few sous. I remember that food was so often on my mind. More often than in my stomach.

My father wrote that he would get some money to me, whatever he could. But it was against the laws of the Reich for him to send money out of the country, and after a few months he still had not managed it, and anyway how much could it have been? I did not want to keep taking from Abraham and Chawa, so I badly needed work. Which in 1936 Paris was not easy to find. Especially for a boy of 15. Who was small. And foreign. And spoke so little French. And had no papers. Or priest.

After a while, we went to Bernard. Another uncle. Bernard Blücher. A real Parisian. Or almost. I was never sure who was and who was not—it seemed to depend on who you asked. He had been in Paris since before the Great War, Bernard. Legally. An actual citizen—a citoyen. Blue-shay he pronounced his name. And had lost the umlaut, soon after he arrived in Paris. You should hear his French, Maître. Beautiful.

Citoyen. I suppose you have never had occasion to consider this, Maître, but it occurred to me, while I was in Paris, how much citoyen and Citroën sound alike. When the French say them. At least to my ear. Citroën the automobile. And when I thought more about it, it made perfect sense. Because what is more French than a Citroën? But this is off my track, Maître. Pardon—as I learned to say so often in Paris.

It was sometime in October when Uncle Abraham took me to see Bernard. Several weeks after our first visit to the police, that I described to you, the Valley of Tears? By the time we went to Bernard, Abraham had already taken me to some committee for refugees and applied there for a foreigner identity card for me, as the police had instructed him to do. But all that committee could do was forward the request to an official bureau, some French ministry, and then we had to wait. How long, they could not tell us. In the meantime, nothing.

He is not exactly an uncle, Bernard. A cousin. Of Tante Chawa. So, we are related by marriage. Sort of related. Anyway, he was family—in those days, any relation was family. At least, so we hoped. For weeks Chawa had been telling Abraham that he should take me to see Bernard, who might have work for me in one of his several businesses. Also, she said, Bernard was a piston, as the French call it—a piston that moves the machine. Someone who knows how things work, and can get things done.

It pained Uncle Abraham, the idea of going to Bernard. I could see it on his face whenever Chawa mentioned the name. She would bring up the idea of going to see Bernard, and Abraham would immediately switch to speaking French with her, which otherwise they never did, except when a French client was in Maison Albert. When I finally saw the two men together, Abraham was uncomfortable in a way that was difficult to watch. As if he was allergic to Bernard. How to explain it? My friend Henri used to say that the world is divided in two, and even if you cannot describe either side, you have to know

78

which one is yours. Well, they had some things in common, but in the end I suppose Abraham knew that he and Bernard were on different sides.

Bernard's workers called him "le patron"—"the boss"—in that French way of saying it, with a kind of nod of the head, even though none of them was French, these workers for Bernard. Sidney and Berenice, the machiniste and seamstress who worked for Abraham and Chawa at Maison Albert, they also used this French word patron, which they would mix in with their Yiddish. But for them, it was part of a little joke, because patron, in French, it also means pattern—you know, the thing they use for the design of the clothes. So, Sidney and Berenice once in a while would say to each other—and of course in the crowded little space where they all worked, that meant also for Abraham's and Chawa's ears—that something or other all depended on le patron, and the two of them would laugh. Abraham did not seem to like it, this joke, but in the end he would have to smile. They understood each other.

It was very different with Bernard. He was patron of Au Courant Dame, a ladies dress shop. French ladies. Very chic. In Passage Diderot. Do you know of these places, Maître, these passages, in Paris? Curious places. A number of them in the center of the city. Very narrow, pressed-together little streets, connecting one boulevard to another. But not at all like a normal Paris alleyway, where people actually live. They are streets, yes, but above the rooftops they are covered by a glass and iron awning that connects the buildings on each side. Which makes these places both outside and inside at the same time. And so tight together, one side to the other, with no room for autos or carts or even to ride a bicycle. With no place to sit. Not even to stand, at least not for very long. Passages is certainly the right name for them—you are not meant to stay there, just to pass through. Unless you stop to buy something. Because that is what they are all about—shops jammed together from one end of the passage to the other, like piano keys. And only chic things, at least in Passage Diderot—no everyday shops there, not a greengrocer or a cobbler or a baker. Nothing people actually need.

Also, all the lovely things you saw in Passage Diderot, in the shops there, gave no idea of what you could not see. Because up inside the buildings, out of sight above, are workrooms—dark and crowded and smoky, with so many people pressed in up there and the work going on and all the machines, and the foul smell because the windows are always shut tight to keep the noise away from the shops below. Bernard had such an atelier right above Au Courant Dame, where his façonniers worked—the people who measured and cut and sewed for him. Crammed into four rooms, eight or ten workers to a room, and all the piles of material, and boxes of threads, and the racks of dresses and coats and cloaks in different stages of finish, and the machines rumbling and clacketing without stop. Turning out all this fashion. Not only for Au Courant Dame but also for the large stores, the famous ones, Galeries Lafayette and the like. They barely ever lifted their heads from the tables, these façonniers—for them, the passage below did not exist.

So, Abraham and Bernard. Both making clothes. They could have helped each other—Maison Albert could have made pieces for Au Courant Dame. Or for Bernard's other clients, the big stores. But Bernard would only use his own workers, stuffed into the rooms above his shop on the passage, and in three other large attics, over near Gare de l'Est, the train station where people arrived from the east. New immigrants. Refugees. Including tailors and seamers and finishers. Who would work for Bernard for less than Abraham and Chawa would. And make no complaints. At least, not usually.

Bernard never actually talked to me about any of this. He always spoke French, did I tell you? Even to Abraham. Although he could speak a little Yiddish, from his childhood—and he would do with me, when I first arrived. As long as no one else could hear, that is. And later on also, when he wanted to make absolutely certain I understood something. Anyway, one time I got up the nerve, not directly to ask him but to bring up the subject, from the side, about why he never passed on work to Uncle Abraham. I cannot remember exactly what I said, but I certainly remember his reaction. He looked at me as if he could not believe I could think such a foolish thing, as if the answer was so obvious. The clothes from Maison Albert, he finally said, are not French enough. That was all, and he turned away. I was so startled by this that I blurted out to his back, "But how can this be, since Maison Albert also has clients who are French?"

When Bernard turned around again, his face was dark. "You do not know what you do not know," he said. Not kindly. And in French. I did not understand. His anger, I mean. Which was partly because I did not yet understand something else—how much Bernard disliked being asked a direct question. Part of what made him a real Parisian. Of a certain type, anyway. They have a way about them, this type—not just few words, but almost refusing to speak at all. Certainly not to answer questions. At least, from people who were not of the same type. They often stare at you in their silence, as if to let you know that they are holding something back, some special knowledge, that they have no intending to share with you. But what I finally understood, Maître, after a long time in Paris, is that the silence is actually just their way of never saying anything they might be held accounted for, and so, most important, of never being caught out as wrong. I do not mean untruthful, Maître—that was expected. But incorrect. About anything. And found out to be.

So. Bernard. After several months in Paris and still no money arrived from my father, there seemed no other way. With his wide business, doing things all over the city, Tante Chawa was sure Bernard could give me some work. Or find some for me, so many people he knew. And later, I must tell you, he did. A bit. Which wound up leading to something else. But that is another matter.

At first he was not helpful at all, Bernard. I knew some things about tailoring, from watching and listening to my father, but I had no skills to actually do the work. Still, Bernard had so much business in so many places that Abraham and Chawa thought certainly he could find something for me to do. The first thing Bernard said, though, was that I would need to speak French well enough in order to manage with his contacts—that was a word Bernard liked to use, contacts. And after speaking French with me for a few moments that first visit, he dismissed the idea, saying I was definitely not ready.

Uncle Abraham was not happy about this—by that time I had picked up some simple French, on top of what I had studied in Hannover, and after all how difficult could it be, doing errands, delivering or collecting things, to say in French the few words that might be needed? No, it was not the language, Maître. It was me. Bernard did not want to attach my face, and my accent, to his name. Did not want to be thought of, by these contacts of his, as a business of immigrants. Even though behind his atelier doors that is exactly what it was. At least, this was what Uncle Abraham believed, and in his anger later said to me, about why Bernard turned me away.

Also, I remember Bernard making a fuss about the law, that first visit. He said he was obliged—as a citoyen—to honor the rules. Since I had no permit, not even a residence card, I would be breaking the law if I worked for him, and I could be arrested. Then where would we be? he said. Which meant, I suppose, where would he be? If they connected me to him. Though he seemed not to have such nervousness about the people working in his big ateliers, most of them without work papers. But as Uncle Abraham explained to me later, in fact Bernard had few legal worries about those workers, because they were not actually employed by Bernard. At least, not officially. Instead, they were paid by what the French call an entrepreneur—a man in the middle. Though with Bernard's money. For Bernard's work. In Bernard's workshops. And anyway, Abraham said, what did Bernard really risk? He was French. At least in Abraham's eyes.

So, Bernard put off the idea of giving me any work, that first time we went to see him. He told Abraham that we should go to a place Bernard knew, an organization, he would give us an introduction, some place he claimed could get me a receipt, as they called it, a temporary permit to stay in France, so that at least for a while I would not be completely illegal. Abraham told him that he had already applied for a receipt for me, at the central refugee place. No, no, Bernard said, waving a hand, the place he was sending us could arrange this much more quickly than "those people." After that, he said, this organization might perhaps help me get a permis de séjour—a residence card. And after that, Bernard continued, if someday I managed to get that card, perhaps I could try for a work permit. And then, if I managed to get that permit as well, he might be able to find some work for me. Perhaps.

2 March

If you want to know the real piston, Maître, it was Sam. Sam le Gamb. That was what people called him. Gamb for gambade—jumping around, a French word, like a goat, he could never sit still, Sam, always springing here and there, you could never tell which way he would move next. Henri though, my friend Henri, he said it was Gamb for gambit. It is the same word in German, I think, gambit. Because of all Sam's schemes. That was how Henri saw him. He and Sam often had different ideas about things.

We are about the same age, Sam and I—though I can hear him now, jumping in to correct me, telling you that actually he is a year older. And the same size. Maybe that is one of the reasons he took a liking to me—we saw with the same eyes. Not only because of our height. It was also true in other ways. Though not all the time. Because no matter what, Sam would see an opportunity. A chance to take. Always. You have asked me several times about who it was in Paris that helped me. Well, the list is short, but after Uncle Abraham and Aunt Chawa, Sam was near the top. Not exactly my teacher—I would not want to give him an even bigger head by saying that. But around him, with him, I learned.

The same height, but we look not at all alike. Sam has a square head, with lots of wavy hair. And he is much lighter color, his hair, his skin, his eyes. Also, if he jumps around like a goat, Maître, it is a mountain goat, with muscles like wire. And very athletic. Sometimes, in the summer, if he had no paying schemes going on, he would go over to Montparnasse, to La Coupole and Le Dome, the big cafés there, with their artist types, and the visiting English, and Germans yes, and he would do acrobatics on the sidewalk, in front of the tables. It was always good for some coins, he told me. And sometimes a paid hour or two. Giving company to a tourist.

He is a Litvak, Sam. Or, was a Litvak, until he became a Parisian.

Anyway, whichever he was, or is, I always called him Ostie—Easterner. It was a joke between us, because when we first met he called me a Bayern—I spoke German, you see. Or Yekke, he would call me—which is Yiddish for jacket—because the Easterners, the ones in Paris I mean, they said that people from Germany tried to be so proper that they always wore jackets, even to bed. It was the same kind of thing also in the other direction—to the old israélite Parisians, and to the real Bayerns, I mean the ones who had come from Germany many years before, to them anyone whose family came from east of the Oder was a Polak, no matter where they were actually from. They had an expression, these old-time German-French—"No Bayern marries a Polak unless he is krum, lum, or stum." I am spelling out the Yiddish words by sound, Maître, but it is almost the same as in German—crooked, lame, or mute.

The orthodox also had their us-and-them. To the strictly observant, anyone not religious like them was the goyim. Sam or Henri, for example. Or me. Though I would not agree. About me not being religious, I mean. On the outside—what I did, how I lived there in Paris—yes it was true. But only if the outside was all you took notice of.

About this naming of people, I remember waiting in the pantry of Bernard's huge apartment in the 16th arrondissement, in the west part of the city. Six of us were there to be servers at a party—this was later on—and one of them asked who these people were that we would be serving. He had heard someone say that they were israélite. Was it true? And another server answered with a little smile, "Well, that depends. If they make more than 100,000 francs a year they are israélite. But less than 100,000, just juif. If they make more than 500,000," he said, "they are français d'origine sémitique. And more than a million?—they are French."

I hope this is not confusing to you, Maître. But this kind of thing meant something there. At times it meant a lot.

Anyway, Sam. His family had come to France from Lithuania when Sam was seven years old or so. His father was a miner, had come to work in the France coal fields, in the north. Along with many others, mostly Poles and Czechs, Sam told me. After the Great War, there had not been enough Frenchmen who would dig in their own mines, dredge rivers, and such like work. So at the time, France gave out visas, actual official permits to live and work, to laborers from the east. And after some months, if it went all right, many brought over their families, as Sam's father did.

But it did not last. In a few years, when more French came of age, and then the Great Depression, the mines began to turn the foreigners out. Sam's father was an outsider not only to the French but also to the Pole and Czech miners, so he was the first to be let go. Then he faced a decision—back to Lithuania and the certainty of endless misery, or down to Paris and take a chance finding work there.

As it turned out, it was not much of a choice. They came to Paris, Sam and his family, but his father had no skills outside of the mines and found no work in the city. I do not know much about his father, or exactly how it all happened—Sam mentioned him only once, when he told me how his family had come to Paris. But after a few months the father went back to the mines, this time some other place, some different kind of mines, over in Alsace, while Sam and his mother stayed in Paris, in the little room in Belleville where they still lived when Sam and I met. After a while he came back again to Paris, the father, looking for work, then again went away. Sometime later, they got news that he was dead. Sam never told me what it was, and I did not ask—I imagined he had been killed in a mine accident, or had become ill there and could not afford a doctor, which was a common thing. But later, when I was in Fresnes, the Paris jail, this boy who knew Sam was brought in to serve a sentence, and I asked about Sam, how he was, because Sam sent me a card once in a while when I was in the jail but could not visit me because he had problems of his own with the police. This boy in the jail with me, he lived near Sam and knew him a long time. He told me that around Belleville, where he and Sam lived, it was said that Sam's father had killed himself.

I remember when this boy told me, we were playing dominoes in the jail's day room, and he was talking about Sam, and told me about Sam's father, so casual, not even stopping his play in the game. It gave me a shiver. But I was not surprised. These things happened.

Sam and his mother Rina, they spoke Lithuanian, Russian, and Polish—like so many of the other Litvaks I met in Paris. They had needed them all, in order to survive no matter which army happened to run over their district that year, or month, or day. But not German, Sam, he had no German, so we spoke Yiddish with each other. Sam's French was perfect, at least to my ears, he had learned it so well, Paris slang and all. And not just the language, Maître—there never was a faster learner about anything, our Sam. Even though he had not gone to school very much. In Lithuania, he told me, they had lived in a shtetl, and from time to time he had gone to a school in the nearby town—when the rules allowed, which depended on who was occupying the area at the moment. I forget the name of it, the town, but Sam's mother, the few times I heard her or Sam mention it, she would right away curl her lip and say "May it burn to the ground." As if that was part of the town's name.

In France also, Sam had little schooling. Not worth getting beaten up for, he said, when they were in the mining town to the north. And when they got to Paris, when he was 10 or 11, he had no time for school—he needed to work. Which he did, with his mother. He also had a sister. Rachel. A year younger than Sam. She was in Paris when I met Sam, but not in contact with her mother and brother. The year before, age 15, she had gone off on her own. Well, sort of on her own. That also happened often.

Rina, Sam's mother, was a colporteuse—a kind of peddler—with a small cart, moving around from street to street, market to market. They actually had a proper permis de séjour, Sam and Rina, from when Sam's father was brought into the country to work in the mines. Which meant they were legally in France. But only the father had been given a permis de travail, so Rina and Sam were not allowed to work. Not officially. And officially, they did not—though even to peddle on the street you were supposed to have a permit.

One of the places Rina would set up her cart was the Bastille market. An outdoor food market, at the end of Boulevard Richard Lenoir, just outside the building where Abraham and Chawa were living when I first arrived. Twice a week, this market, and a wonderful thing it was. With all the different fruits and vegetables brought in from the countryside, and not just sitting in boxes or piles but arranged into rows and shapes, these amazing pyramids of color, sometimes with the shades of light and dark shifting from one part to the other, or a three-dimension checkerboard with different color peppers or potatoes, have you ever seen such a thing, Maître? And the cheeses, so many kinds and shapes all lined up so beautifully, and fish, cart after cart of fish, and the ones in shells, in perfectly shaped mounds, on beds of ice. Oh and most of all, at least for me, the charcuterie, Maître, the dried sausages and smoked meats, and the pâtés that reminded me of the liver ground up with egg and onions that my mother used to make—those were torture to me because I could not afford to spend my little money on such things, though anyway later I learned that most of it was pork, so it was just as well. Then, of course, there was the wine, that anyone could afford if you bought it straight from the barrels, and I would bring empty bottles from Maison Albert and fill them up for Abraham and Chawa and their workers Sidney and Berenice, who all would have a glass or two with their midday meal, just like real Frenchmen. And also coal that I would bring back for the brazier as the autumn became more chill in the old stone building, coal sold by the wine men, or wine from the coal men, whichever way it was, anyway coal and wine from the same people, that was the way it was—Bougnats they were called, these people, from the Auvergne, who brought their coal and wine together on the same barges down the rivers to Paris, all so strange and wondrous to me.

The Auvergne, in the middle of the country—I was there, Maître. Later. Did you know? Much later. Passing through.

So, Sam's mother Rina, and her colporteuse cart. I first saw her at this outdoor Bastille market. There were many others like her at the edges of the market, I mean people with carts selling cheap clothes and jewelry, household tools, and little things for the kitchen, all kinds of leftover things that had not sold in shops, or had some small thing wrong with them, or were secondhand, just about anything, depending on what the peddler had been able to come up with, somewhere, during the days and nights before. Valises, Rina used. Old pasteboard valises that she would carry her wares in, then just flip open the tops when she set up the cart. They were also useful to protect her goods from the weather, and from sneaking hands, as she moved around the city. And easy to close up if she had to move suddenly. Because she had to be careful, Rina. The police, of course, but also not to be noticed selling something at a market that a Frenchman was also selling nearby. Or to set up in a spot that a Frenchman usually had. They would chase her away, and she knew enough not to do more than say a few nasty words before moving on, because if she stayed, the Frenchmen could get rough, or might wind up calling the police. Which could mean more trouble than just going hungry for the day. Even though it was considered a low thing, to call the flics, the cops, because the market people did not get along with the police, you see, and so always settled things among themselves. But it was not quite such a low thing to do if it was about a foreigner, so Rina could not take the chance of standing her ground.

And that is where I met him, Sam. At the Bastille market, which I never missed—it was something to do, and so much to see and hear, those first few months in Paris. Not actually met him there, but first saw him, noticed him, the way he hopped around, talking to everyone, hawking whatever his mother had on the cart—his French was much better than hers—and jabbering and joking with the shoppers and the other sellers, managing to get a free piece of bruised fruit or a petit rond of cheese that had become too squashed to sell. He talked to everyone. Even the marketeers who hated foreigners—and there were plenty of those. He did not care, Sam, if they snarled at him, it did not stop him, or even seem to bother him. He was definitely not shy, our Sam. Afraid, from time to time—he must have been. We all were. But Sam, you could never tell.

6 March

I had already seen Sam quite a few times before I actually met him. Which was after the Bastille market one night. He would always manage to get a few bites of food during the market, one of the stands or another would give him a little something, and once in a while a seller would trade a bit of food for some frock or trinket on Rina's cart. But the real stomach-fillers, the heftier hunks of food you could snatch up, that was after the market ended. A lot of food falls to the ground during the market but is perfectly fine to eat, and other food is left behind because it did not sell but is too much bother for the sellers to take away with them. Incredible, Maître, how much is there, left behind. And in those days of hunger for so many, the race to gather up this food was fierce. And got worse, real battles, by '37 and '38, when more and more people crowded into the city. Winning was a matter of knowing where to look. And moving quickly. And not being afraid. All of which seemed easy for Sam. Sam le Gamb.

Easy for him, but important. You see, Maître, for me it was just about getting a bit extra—something during the long day when often I did not eat. And a chance to eat things I did not see at Abraham and Chawa's table, and I could afford to buy so little on my own. Also, it made me feel better, to get my own food, instead of taking so often from my aunt and uncle. But for all that, it was never about me going completely hungry—even if I did not eat all the day, there would always be something for me if I returned at night to Maison Albert. For Sam, though, it was far more serious. He had no family in Paris except Rina. And she had no one but him. Well, and his sister, who had disappeared. So, when Rina did not do well from her cart—and sometimes she would go days without selling a thing—it meant that Sam had to get food for both of them some other way. And twice a week that meant the Bastille market. He had many other ways, also—other street markets on different days, the trash outside certain bakeries at closing time, some restaurant back doors he knew. Plus other schemes, for cash, to pay for their room in Belleville—most of which I need not talk about. And others that I never knew. But the market, the Bastille market, he had learned it so well, he knew he could always get things when the market was over. He never missed it.

First of all, you had to get to the good things before others did. There was always a crowd of glaneurs—people who scrambled for leftover food. And just like the market sellers, some of these people staked out certain places as their own. The hungrier they were, the more trouble they would make if you poked around their territory. Or the greedier. Because not all of them were eating the food—for some it was a business, taking the food away and selling it to old war pensioners and other especially poor people who could not collect food for themselves. The glaneurs who were real French, some of them were especially rough. They felt entitled to the food—before us foreigners, I mean. Even if they were just going to sell it. "Terroir français!"— "French soil!"—they would shout at you. I took them very seriously, Maître—I thought they were saying "French terror!" and did not know what they might do. Not all of them were like that. But enough.

There were also the sweepers. You had to get to the food before they broomed it into piles along with the other trash, then into their bins. They were hired by the market, these sweepers, or by the arrondissement or whatever it was, to clean up after the market, to get the street ready for the evening's traffic. And to keep down the smell, from rotting food. And rats. Although there were so many cats around, these tough and wiry cats, with no homes, and very smart at findings ways to stay alive—kind of like Sam. Anyway, with these cats coming for the leftovers, the rats were less of a problem, at least for the first few hours after the market closed down. And that is how it happened. How I met Sam. The cats.

In those beginning few months in Paris I was not usually out beyond the evening hours—I did not know my way around, and had not yet learned the places to be at night that were safe from police, or from rough types who could make trouble for a foreigner alone, especially a small one like me. But that November Abraham and Chawa were moving out of their rooms on Boulevard Richard Lenoir, and things became even more complicated. Between packing up for the move and still trying to keep their clients happy so they would stay with Maison Albert when it relocated, their work hours went almost round the clock and I was even more in the way than before, so I tried to stay out as much and as late as possible.

On this one evening I had picked up something to eat at the

Bastille market. After it closed, I mean. Probably just a pear or apple, or a few carrots, because those were most often the easiest to find that autumn without having to fight over them. I suppose after that I just walked around for a while without any particular place to go, as usual, and sometime after dark I headed over to a spot I had found nearby, a beautiful square in the Marais, a neighborhood that was mostly poor and run down, old buildings with workshops and small factories and such, but right in the middle of it this large and fancy and perfectly tended square, totally enclosed by very fine stone and red brick buildings with sloping slate roofs, completely different from the rough plaster buildings of the district, and with passages only at two corners to enter the square, which kept it mostly hidden away—I had walked nearby many times before I even realized it was there. The center park area of the square had four carved fountains and was planted with large trees and perfect grass and a ring of smaller trees all around the edges, just inside the metal fence that surrounded it. There were benches to sit on, and if it was cold or raining there were covered archways in front of the buildings all the way around. After dark they locked the gates to the center park but I found it easy to boost myself over. So, I would often take the food I picked up at the market and go there to sit for a while in the evening, to pass the time, the entire park to myself, before going back to Maison Albert.

That one evening turned out different. Because I was trying even more than usual to keep out of Abraham and Chawa's way, I stayed longer at the square, even stretched out on a bench, since in the evening after they closed the park the whole square was nearly empty and quiet. It was not too cold an evening and the enclosed square of buildings kept out the wind, so I was quite comfortable there, after eating my food, and lying on the bench with the soothing sound of the fountains I fell asleep. When I opened my eyes again, I was facing one of the handsome brick buildings and saw someone, a woman in a black dress, watching me from between thick curtains at a tall second-floor double window. I was groggy, but it did not take me long to realize that she might have made a call to the police—people had their own telephones in houses like that. I had learned a few things about Paris by then, and knew that lying down, even on a bench, was just not done in certain places, like this well kept square, and certainly not after the gates had been closed. So, even though I was warm and comfortable, I recognized that I needed to move, and slowly I got up. As I made my way to the fence I looked up again at the woman in the window, who until then had been standing perfectly still. I saw her hand, down at her side, move up in front of her waist and make a small flick of the wrist, in the direction I was heading.

Oh, that set me off something terrible, Maître. I was already unhappy about having to move, and when I saw that little sweep of her hand I felt a sharp pain in my gut—not like the other pains I so often have, but as if someone had just punched me, which was also a feeling I knew well, from my last year at school in Hannover. I hopped over the fence to make my way out of the square but stopped and turned back toward the building. When the woman saw me stop and turn she quickly moved away from the window, pulling the draperies shut. I do not know what I would have done, Maître—probably nothing, really, because what could I?—but just then on the opposite side of the square I got a glimpse of two capes, police capes, coming in my direction. I ducked under the arcade, then hurried along the wall toward the passage at the east corner, trying to get out of the square as quickly as I could but without making too much sound. When I turned the corner, I began to run. I headed east, back toward Bastille, but not really thinking about where I was going, just running, hoping not to hear any shouts, or that awful whistle the police carry, and finally after six or eight streets I ducked into a pissotière and listened. There was nothing, and after a few minutes I came out and continued walking east, though looking over my shoulder for quite a while.

It was the first time I had been really frightened in Paris, Maître. And the first time really angry—that woman's hand, I will never forget it.

Never? What does that mean?

Eventually I calmed down, and wandered over to the Bassin de l'Arsenal—a small waterway off the Seine where barges unload, and a few pleasure boats tie up, just behind Bastille, and where I had often spent time in the longer, warmer days and evenings earlier in the autumn, watching the bargemen and their boats, and the débardeurs, the ones who do the unloading. There were also the rich people there, on their private boats, going to or coming back from a day's cruise, or an outing someplace where they had their meal on a riverbank—they had a small part of the bassin just for themselves, these private boats, away from the barges. I remember being amazed, sometimes when I went there in the mornings, to see these people pack in so many things for the few hours they would spend out of the city—not just bread and cheese as you might expect, but hampers full of food, whole meals, with proper silverware and china plates and bowls and serving dishes, and linen serviettes. Even chairs and tables, Maître. And the wine, of course. With labels on the bottles. And proper goblets.

As always when I went to the bassin, especially after dark, I made sure to keep moving. It was a place, I already knew, where I could not stay in one spot for very long. The police came around from time to time to keep an eye on things, because of all the merchandise on the barges and the docks, I suppose, and also for the pleasure boat part of the bassin—special protection for the particular people whose boats they were. So, I never made myself too comfortable there, and on this night my nerves were already rough from my brush with the police earlier at the square in the Marais. It was something important that I kept learning more and more over the next two years—where it was possible to sit down in Paris, and for how long.

After a while I headed back toward Bastille. At the north end of the bassin there is a tunnel where the water goes underground, right below the Métro station and Place de la Bastille, then travels underneath Boulevard Richard Lenoir until it comes out again, a kilometer or so further up, into the Canal Saint Martin, in the lower part of Belleville. As I passed by the tunnel entrance I noticed something moving, a cat, sniffing along the ground at the edge of the embankment, then heading down the slope, along a walkway and into the tunnel. These scrawny cats were all over the place after the market, and usually it would not have caught my attention. But there was something strange about how this one was sniffing the ground the whole time as it went, and then I noticed another cat, also sniffing the ground the same way, coming along the pavement about 50 meters further back toward Bastille, stopping every once in a while, then sniffing some more and looking cautiously around. I stopped to watch, and over the next 20 or 30 minutes there were three more cats, one by one, that slowly made their way from Bastille to the embankment and then down and into the tunnel. None of them came out again.

I had been by that spot quite often and had seen cats nose around the other side of the bassin, if the barges were unloading food of some kind. But I had never seen any around the tunnel, and certainly not this strange kind of tracking they seemed to be doing. I had nowhere particular to go, so I decided to climb down the embankment and have a look. It was very dark down there, the walkway to the tunnel narrow and slippery, and I had no idea what was inside. I was getting nervous, but as I got closer to the tunnel I felt that I had to keep going, even if I did not know where I was headed.

Perhaps that makes no sense to you, Maître. If not, I am sorry. So be it.

I reached the edge of the tunnel and looked inside but could not see a thing, it was pitch black. As I peered in I heard a snarling cat screech—just one awful short howl, then nothing. A few moments later there was a kind of muffled mewling, this time from what sounded like more than one cat. I took a step inside to get a closer look, and from somewhere deep in the tunnel a sharp voice spoke at me in a way that clearly was not happy I was there. It was in French and I did not understand, except the tone, which was plain enough and made me stop. I could only make out a shadow—I suppose he could see me better, with the light from the Métro windows right above me, and the bassin and the far bank of the Seine behind. He snapped at me again in French, and again I could not reply because I still did not know what he was saying, but something must have come out of my mouth, maybe in German or in Yiddish, because he suddenly switched to Yiddish and said, "Get out of here. Unless you want the same." Or something like that. I could see his outline a little better now, could tell that he was small, and heard in his voice that he was young. And

94

since he spoke Yiddish, I knew that he was not French—not all the way French, I mean—so I was a bit less afraid and spoke back, in Yiddish, something like "Who do you think you are?" Trying to sound like I knew who I was, and what I was doing there. I remember clearly what he said next, because I had never heard the expression before. "Well, Bayern," he kind of spat the word, "at least I am not one of you." I did not know yet that, from an easterner, the word Bayern meant a person whose family was from anywhere in Germany—he must have recognized my accent—so after a moment I said, "No, you are wrong. I am not Bayern. I am from Hannover."

It was quiet, then he burst out laughing. The sound echoed through the tunnel. I did not understand why the laughter but I knew I did not like it. So, I started to move toward him—I think I told you, Maître, that I have something of a temper.

"Stay where you are," he said, not laughing any more. "These are mine."

His voice was quieter now but serious—so serious that I realized whatever was going on in there meant much more to him than my curiosity did to me.

"All right, little pisher," I said, "you can have your tunnel." Me calling someone little, how often did I get a chance to do that? "May you all be happy together," I said as I backed away, "you and the cats and the fish"—it smelled strongly of fish down there—"and the rest of your little family."

"Pisher?" he sputtered as I left the tunnel and climbed back up to the road. "I will see you again, Bayern," he shouted after me.

But I did not leave. There was something about the boy's voice, and his seriousness. Not to mention the strange proceedings of cats. So, I found a bench against a low wall on the other side of the road, above the embankment, and sat down to see whether he might come out soon, and maybe I would learn more of what was going on. I kept watch for a quarter of an hour or so, during which two more cats made their way down and into the tunnel. And did not come out. But after a while there were no more cats, and no movement from the tunnel, it was getting cold, and I thought it was probably late enough to go back to Abraham and Chawa's, so I got up to leave. I had only gone a few paces, though, when I heard a noise, a sort of grunt, then a yell, behind me. I moved over to the edge of the embankment and looked down and could see three people below, struggling. One of them—much smaller than the other two—was holding onto a large sack that the others were trying to pull away from him as they fought. Under the bassin lights, the small one holding the sack seemed somehow familiar to me. And without thinking, I rushed down the bank.

I can hear you asking why, Maître. Why not mind my own business and walk away? I mean, the little one had just called me names, and laughed at me. And anyway, someone else's troubles was certainly not what I needed to add to my own. Perhaps it had something to do with having to run from the police a little while earlier. Or that woman's hand, the woman in the window, that flick of her hand. Perhaps you could ask the doctors who examined me in Berlin, when I was held by the Gestapo. Or the aliénistes back in Paris. Perhaps they can tell you. Because as I have said before, Maître, I do not always know the why of things. Which never used to bother me, not knowing. But now is unfortunate, I suppose. Since that is a question you seem often to ask me.

So. The three of them were struggling over this sack, down by the tunnel, the two bigger ones had knocked the small one to his knees, and here I come jumping in. I mean exactly that—jumping. I had some speed coming down the hill and as I reached them I launched myself, and my fist, toward the man who was closest to me.

Not just speed, Maître. Momentum. Coming down the slope. They are different. I know. I was going to be an engineer.

I landed a flying punch on the side of the man's head and he howled, let go of the sack, and toppled over. It was pure Schmeling, Maître. Worthy of the great Schmeling, that punch. A lightweight version, of course. The other two stopped fighting, in surprise, and maybe amazement when they got a look at me. I also stopped. It was all of a sudden quiet. We three just stood there, stupidly, with the other man on the ground, and then the small one seemed to wake up and shouted Run! and the next thing I was scrambling with him up the embankment, then into the streets behind Bastille and through the Rue de Lappe with its crowds of drinkers and dancers.

Looking back now, Maître, maybe it was the feeling I got when I leaped at that man. And hit him so hard. A feeling I wanted so badly. And so completely opposite to all the shrinking, scurrying away feelings I had earlier that night. And almost every day and night since I had been in Paris. Maybe that is the why.

We ran into the back streets and alleyways of the Faubourg Saint Antoine. It was dark in those alleys, but the boy seemed to know where he was going, and I just followed the burlap sack bouncing on his back, which was about all I could see, the sack, with his feet looking like they stuck out of the bottom. Finally he stopped at a corner and took a quick look behind. We were alone. We listened for a moment. Nothing. We stood there, staring at each other, for the first time seeing each other's face up close, and me finally recognizing him as the boy I had seen so often at the Bastille market. Sam.

Then I heard them. Faintly. Cats. In the sack. Barely moving. Tiny meows. And a grin spread over Sam's scratched and dirty face.

8 March

So, Maître, that is what Sam was doing in the tunnel. Trapping cats. He had six or seven of them in the sack. Wild cats that lived in the alleys and roofs of Paris east. No one would miss them, but still Sam did not want to be seen grabbing them off the street. Which was why he used the tunnel. Not only for the official trouble it could bring him but also because of the competition—like the two men who had jumped him, he told me. Others who wanted the cats. And would wait to take them from Sam, after he had done all the work.

As we walked up toward Belleville, he explained how he went about it. After the Bastille market, he would pick up fish heads and other seafood scraps that had been dropped or thrown aside. Then, when it got late and few people were around, he would use the fish parts to make a trail, smearing the ground, from behind Place de la Bastille down to the tunnel, with more fish bits inside so the smell would be strong enough that the cats, who were smart and wary, would be tempted to enter. When a cat came into the tunnel, Sam would grab it—he did not always succeed, he admitted, but because he was experienced now, most of them he managed to hold onto. Still, the scratches on his face told me that, experience or not, this was no easy job. When he got a grip on a cat, he would dunk its face in a pot of wine he had there, and hold it until the cat stopped struggling, but not long enough to kill it—it was important, he told me, to keep the cats alive. With this also, he said he did not always succeed, but mostly by now he had developed the skill. The near-drowning, plus the alcohol the cat would accidentally drink, would help keep the animal quiet after he put it in the sack. "This is science," Sam told me. I had appreciation for that.

After he had stunned a cat, he would wrap it up tightly in old rags. Like some people do with babies, do you know? To keep the cats from fighting with each other in the sack, or moving around much at all, and from making much noise. Sam had learned all this from an old clochard—a tramp, I suppose we would say. Although in French it does not seem to be as harsh a word. And it was curious, Maître, but I only heard people use the word clochard about a Frenchman. For a foreigner who was hungry and without a home—well, there were many other words the French used. Anyway, after fighting in the Great War this particular clochard had lived for years under the bridges of the Seine and had taught Sam to help him with the cats after the old man had become too slow to do it himself. Sam stopped his story for a moment and looked at me with a very serious face. "I carry on tradition," he said. "That is very important to France."

By now we were in Belleville, and Sam led me up the hill through winding narrow streets. I had no idea where we were—I had never been that far east before, and a thick yellow fog made it feel like we were suspended in air. The buildings looked older, shabbier than around Bastille, and it seemed colder and darker up there—there were few street lamps, and only faint light through some grimy windows. The yellow damp held a smell of boiled cabbage. And urine. Also the sulfur that people used to drive away bugs, so many bugs in the walls.

Sam stopped in front of a low building that looked like some kind of small factory, or had once been, with a porte cochère—a wide opening for carts and small trucks to enter the courtyard, very common there. He knocked on a heavy door that must have been salvaged from somewhere else and propped up to fill most of the entry space. As we waited, I looked around. Maybe it was the fog, Maître, but the taller buildings so close across the narrow street seemed to be tilting forward, as if at any minute they might topple over and bury us.

A man came to the door and looked at us through a crack. He did not open immediately but spoke to Sam in a mumbled voice and a language I did not understand—Russian or Polish, I do not know. The man was asking about me, I could tell by the way Sam kept turning, but after a short exchange the man let us in.

Wooden boxes and other junkish things—I could not see very well—were piled against the courtyard walls, and in one corner an open stone staircase led to the roof. We started toward a room with a pale light coming through a window, but after just a few steps I staggered at an awful gagging smell. Of waste. Also some kind of acid. And though I cannot say this for certain, Maître, of blood. Sam noticed my painful face and said this would only take a minute. The man opened the door to the room but I decided to wait there in the yard—despite the cold and damp, going inside this place, whatever it was, just did not feel like a good idea. So, Sam and the man went in and closed the door. From somewhere above, maybe the roof, I could hear muffled sounds. Whimpering cats.

The room's single window was coated with coal soot, the light only a small smoky oil lamp, and I could just manage to see inside. Sam and the man were talking and looking into Sam's sack. I do not know why I remember this, Maître—I could not tell you anything else about the room, or what the man looked like—but directly behind them were two rickety shelves, barely hanging onto a wall. They were completely bare, the shelves, except for three things. On the top shelf, a wooden shoe-clog with a bunch of garlic or onions sticking out of the top, and another clog holding a chunk of brown bread. On the shelf below, a glass of water, and in it a set of false teeth.

Sam was soon back in the courtyard. His burlap sack was now empty. When we were again outside in the street he said he wanted to buy me a drink. We went to a little bar nearby, a dark rough place with sawdust on the floor, and over a glass of strong wine—at least to me it was strong, I had never drunk alcohol, Maître—we introduced ourselves a bit more, and he told me more about the cats. The man we had just seen bought cats from Sam and others. There were several places like that in Belleville, run by people who had learned their trades in the slaughterhouses or tanneries of la Villette, which was just on the other side of the hill, or in one of the many fur ateliers spread around the east parts of the city. The man would clean up the cats and feed them throwaway fish guts and the like for a few weeks to fatten them up—which is why you had to catch them alive—then kill them and sell the meat to certain butchers, or directly to people in the neighborhood, much cheaper than any other meat. No one was tricking anyone, Sam told me. When they sold it they did not pretend it was something else—they just called it meat. Everyone knew. In that part of the city, at least.

There was also another part to sell, which together with the meat made the whole operation worthwhile, barely. It was the coat, which would be cleaned up and made into small fur items. Usually mittens. Which the brocanteurs and colporteurs, like Sam's mother Rina, would sell in winter. You would even see them for sale in the pharmacies, at least in the poor neighborhoods. No one bothered to ask what fur it was.

By the time Sam finished his tale of the cats it had become quite late and I thought I should return to Maison Albert in the hope that Abraham and Chawa had not yet gone to bed. I had already spent several nights getting not much sleep on outdoor benches when I had wandered a bit too far in an evening and, by the time I got back to the Bastille district, it was too late to disturb my aunt and uncle. That night with Sam it had turned quite cold, and rain seemed on the way, so I told him that I needed to head for Bastille. As he walked with me—it would have taken me forever to find my way on my own, especially with what the wine had done to me, which maybe Sam could tell—he offered to share with me the money he had got for his sackful of cats. I had saved the whole lot from the two men at the tunnel, Sam reminded me, and maybe a bad beating for him also. So, giving me a part of it, he said, was the righteous thing to do.

From our talk, and the cats, and the look of him, it was clear to me that things were more difficult for Sam than for me, who had Abraham and Chawa. So I said no thank you, I had enough money just then—though that was anything but true.

All right, he said. But you will still get a share.

A month or so later, when the real winter cold had set in, he presented me with a pair of ear muffs. Tabby color.

Yours,
Herschel

Maître,

I did not see Sam again for some weeks after that night with the cats. I was busy helping Abraham and Chawa with their move. There were only the two rooms to pack up, but they were stuffed full, and we had to carry it all three floors down the narrow twisting stairs, then into the small hired wagon, and the horse just barely managing to pull the load over to Rue Martel, then all of it out of the wagon, up four staircases and into the rooms they had taken over there. Three times we had to make the journey. And it was raining, so we had to cover everything in oilcloths, and tie it all down, which took so much longer, and do it carefully—because it was not just their personal things, Abraham and Chawa, but also the tools and work tables and machines and fabrics and fitting dummies and such of Maison Albert—to keep it all dry. Also, the wagon could not hold very much. And the old dray horse, well, he moved so slowly we called him Statue. It took all day and into the night.

When we finally had dragged the last load up to the rooms on Rue Martel, we spent more long hours through the night and the next day putting it all in order—the machines and tools and materials, especially, and the fabrics for the orders they had—so that Maison Albert would lose as little work time as possible. At the end of that second day, when at last we finished in the evening, I went up to the top floor of the building, to a little attic room Chawa had found empty and put down a paillasse for me, a straw mattress, and I fell immediately asleep. It was still dark when I woke. Except that actually, it was not still dark but dark again. What I mean is, I had slept all through the next day. I remember being terribly foggy when I opened my eyes in this odd little empty room with the eaves just above my head, and no light, and I became quite afraid as I tried to find the proper staircase, and the correct floor, in the dark corridors, and then the door to their rooms, in this huge old building I did not yet know. And when I finally found Abraham and Chawa I became even more upset when they explained that it was not Tuesday evening, or Wednesday evening, or whatever day it was when I had fallen asleep, but the next day, the next evening. That I had lost a day. In those early months in Paris I tried to hold on tightly to the few things I knew for certain. So, waking in a strange place, with day and night turned upside down, it was all very disturbing of me. And in all the many nights I spent in one or another of those tiny attic rooms—off and on over the next two years—I never once woke without a jolt of fear that was part Where am I? and part Who am I? and which had begun with that very first confusion.

It was in another part of the city, Rue Martel, though not a great distance from where they had been in the Bastille—now in the 10th arrondissement, the old rooms not far to the east, in the 11th. But it seemed quite different. Which in fact was their idea, Abraham and Chawa. About the move. To have a bit more space, yes, but also to be closer to the center of things. And in a neighborhood less rough than Bastille with all its dark little bars and rowdy bals musettes—dance halls—that crowded around the Rue de Lappe, just behind where the old rooms had been. Abraham and Chawa hoped to receive more clients at the new Maison Albert, instead of doing mostly just piece-work for the big stores, which did not pay as well. French clients especially, they were aiming for—the small boutiques, and the personal customers, who would need to come for fittings. There were several other fitting-tailors in this neighborhood, so more clients would be comfortable going to Maison Albert now that it was in this same district. At least, so they imagined, my aunt and uncle. And were willing to pay more for these rooms, even though they barely got by as it was.

Faubourg Saint Denis, it was called, the district—some years earlier, quite a few years, it had been very much chic, though certainly not anymore. And the building itself, Maître, an enormous impressing old place it was—two connected buildings, around two courtyards, six floors, plus the street level. You could tell that it had once been home to people of some money, in those earlier years. The entrance was an archway, two stories high, a porte cochère with beautiful carved oak doors, and more oak above, with glass that was also the street windows of the concierge's loge. The concierge—the great Madame Corbin. May she know that I think often of her kindnesses. Which was not my experience with other concierges, I can tell you.

So, the building. The apartments on the first two floors were very large, with tall windows over the street. And ironwork balconies, all pedigree detail, along the front of the second floor. They seemed once upon a time to have been quite grand, these apartments—I would get a peek inside sometimes when I was on a stairway and a door was left open, and could see how big the rooms were, and hallways leading deep inside, with some kind of sculpture decorations high along the apartment walls, and even their own toilets, Maître. Though I was never actually inside one of these apartments. We did not know anyone who lived on those floors. And even if we had been introduced to any of them, they were not the type to invite in neighbors. Certainly not people from an upper floor. The district was by then very different from the high tone it had once been, Maître, and the building itself down many steps of the ladder, but this was still the way of things there, among certain people.

The upper-floor apartments and their rooms were much smaller. Still, Abraham and Chawa's place on the fourth floor had three rooms, instead of just the two they had before in Bastille. And with its own electricity connection, though with the cost Abraham and Chawa did not use electrics much. Also, it had its own running water—quite an improvement from their old place, where there was only a water tap way down in the courtyard, next to the privy. All the smaller apartments on the fourth and fifth floors had water, and nearby privies under the staircases in each corner of the building.

Something else showed that the building had once upon a time been quite different. On the top floor, the sixth, were chambres de bonne—tiny single rooms under the eaves, where the living-in maids used to sleep in older days when they had worked for the families on the first two floors. By the time Abraham and Chawa moved to the building, these little rooms were rented separately, most often just to one person or a couple, but sometimes to a family, despite the tiny space. Madame Corbin, the concierge, as long as there was not too much noise, she did not mind how many. Or who. Often one or another of these maids rooms was empty, though, and if Abraham and Chawa got word of it, I might spend a few nights there until a new paying tenant moved in. Madame Corbin said nothing. And sometimes, when one of these rooms had no paid lodger for a longer time, I would even move in my clothes and the few other things I had. Which got me more out of Abraham and Chawa's way—and avoided the more difficult arrangements I got myself into at other times, when the chambres de bonne were all occupied. Over the next two years I spent many nights in one or another of those attic rooms. Even after Abraham and Chawa had left the building. They were a place, these tiny rooms, where no one would come looking for me. Two meters square of floor that was my own. Well, sort of my own. The only one I ever had in Paris. Until I was in jail.

14 March

This new district, Faubourg Saint Denis, was where I met Henri. Who became my friend. And taught me about Paris. And other things. As Sam did. But so different from Sam. They almost never saw anything the same way, those two. They got to know each other a little bit, from me. But like milk and meat, Maître—I tried not to put them at the same table, so to say. Still, a few times the three of us wound up together. Which did not always go smoothly.

Henri is two years older than me, and tall, with a long thin face and narrow nose—all bony angles, Henri, his head and shoulders and elbows. And very soft light hair, like the silk on top of maize. Also the way he dresses, so different from Sam. Almost always in laborer's bleus, Henri, at least the jacket or the trousers, whether he is working or not, and a rough white shirt with long sleeves rolled up to his elbows. Never short sleeves like the Paris students, no matter how hot the weather. And with whatever he wears, winter or summer, day or night, inside or outside, always his cap—that flat cap with a small front brim that most Paris laborers wear, and is so much a part of Henri's head that I cannot remember what he looks like without it.

Altogether—partly the way he looks, but also how he speaks, and carries himself—the biggest difference from Sam is that Henri is French. That is the best I can describe it, Maître. He was born right there in Faubourg Saint Denis, and his Paris worker's slang is a fast and tumbling wonderful thing to hear. But his parents had come from some eastern part of the Pale that had been Polish, then Russian, then back again—so even though he was born in France, right in the center of Paris, to many people there Henri is not French. Though to himself he is. A Parisian, if not exactly a Frenchman.

He speaks a little Yiddish, Henri. From his parents. But not very well, and with a strange pronouncing to my ear, so we spoke a back-and-forth mix with each other, him with his bumbly Yiddish, and over time more and more Paris French from me. He would often laugh at the way I chewed up the sounds, though he was always careful not to discourage me. After a while, he began telling me that my French was becoming very good. I knew it was not true. And he knew that I knew. But still he said it. And I liked that he did.

Henri and his parents had papers, all the proper papers to live and work in France. Though their passports were not French. They were in a workers' group, the parents and Henri both, always part of meetings and strikes and such, so in '39 when the first rafle happened—the roundup of the particular foreigners that the French police most wanted to get rid of—Henri's parents were among the first to be taken. They had been released after a few weeks, though, because they had a son who was born in France. But early in 1940 the rafles began again, and again they were on the first list to be grabbed. This time they were put in Roland Garros stadium. The tennis place. Do you know it, Maître? Hundreds of them held there, kept underneath the stands so nothing could be seen from the outside. Except for the razor wire. Prisoned under there for weeks, in the dark, with no air, no chance even to move around, though I learned that the stadium itself is huge, with plenty of space. I was in jail then, in Fresnes, but one of my Paris lawyers told me all about it—he was trying to help some of the people there also, and knew the details. They were kept all the time underground, he told me, because of the clay. Some officials had asked the police to make sure to protect the clay. The courts, Maître. For the tennis. Made of clay.

After Roland Garros they were sent to one of the camps, Henri's parents. French camps, I mean. In the south, most of these places, but others all over the country. Did you know that the French have such camps of their own, Maître? Something like this place where I am now, I suppose. I do not know who had the idea first.

Henri escaped the rafle. I know because in jail I got a letter from him telling me that his parents had been taken away. I had not seen him for many months, but he wrote to me several times while I was in Fresnes—learning about where I was from the newspapers, of course. I enjoyed the funny puzzle of reading his letters, which were in French but with a few Yiddish words also, though he had no idea how to write it. I could not learn much about what was happening with him or his parents from this particular letter following the rafle, because Henri was careful not to say anything in it about himself, and there was blacking out by the censors of the lines about Roland Garros. I suppose they did not want people to be put off the next tennis matches. It is one of many odd things about my long time in jail, Maître, but I was able to keep up with things, through my lawyers, much better it seems than most people on the outside. Anyway, from that letter I learned that he had not been taken. At least, not in that rafle. But there were many more rafles to come. And after that, no more letters from Henri.

How we met, Henri and I. Handing out leaflets, on the street. Him, I mean. Typical—he was always stirring the pot for something or another. That time it was David Frankfurter. Do you know the name, Maître? I suppose you might. Especially given your profession. Which maybe we can discuss one day. Other than helping me, what is your other work? Perhaps knowing more would help me better understand what it is we are trying to do together, you and I. Only if it is proper, of course. To discuss it.

So. David Frankfurter. The boy from Croatia who was studying in Switzerland. And who shot Gustloff, the Nazi Party man there, earlier that year, 1936. I suspect you might remember, Maître, because of all the news and publicity about it, the special state funeral train bringing Gustloff back to Germany, and all the honors, after his death, for this Gustloff, being made a bright star of the nation, even the Reichsführer himself at the memorial. Yes, exactly the same as for vom Rath, the man I shot—the special train, and the Führer at the state funeral for a nobody who was suddenly a Reich hero. People pointed this out to me, when I was in jail in Paris, that everything for vom Rath was exactly the same as it had been for Gustloff two years earlier. Maître de Moro-Giafferi, especially, showed me how much these things were the same. Not Frankfurter and me the same, or vom Rath and Gustloff, but what the Reich made of them both. Except for Kristallnacht, of course, when vom Rath died. Which made everything different.

De Moro-Giafferi, in Paris, chief of all my lawyers. Which I suppose you know. The great Corsican bulldog—he looked like one also. And that was another thing the same—just like for me, de Moro-Giafferi had been one of Frankfurter's lawyers, two years before. Did you know that, Maître? Perhaps not, because in the end the Swiss would not allow him to plead in court there—he was French, you see, and in Switzerland it was being French that was wrong. De Moro-Giafferi, who I first saw that day when I met Henri.

15 March

I am sorry, Maître. Things went a bit zig-zag yesterday, in what I was writing. Starting in Henri's direction, then heading off toward Frankfurter and de Moro-Giafferi. Let me try to find again where I was going.

He was on the street, Henri, the first time I met him. In front of the Saint Lazare women's prison, just a few blocks from Abraham and Chawa's rooms on Rue Martel, quite soon after they moved there. It was perfect for Henri and his leaflets, that prison. Which is now a hospital. Or hospital and prison both. I am not certain how much it is one or the other. It is a huge place, with several large buildings over three or four blocks. A hospital originally, I was told, but became a prison long ago, for women, especially women who were prostitutes with diseases, and some who had lost their minds. Anyway, they were tearing down some of the old prison buildings then, in 1936, and putting up new ones to make it officially a hospital again, a public hospital for women. Mostly the same women. So, at the end of '36, December sometime, on the day I met Henri, this Saint Lazare place was still a prison, with people coming to visit the women there, but also a hospital, with patients coming and going, many of them rough-looking women, and also an enormous constructing site, with all the tearing down and building up, and many workers on the project. So, altogether a perfect place for Henri, with so much foot traffic and mostly people who might be interested in what Henri and his leaflets had to say. Which this time was about a big meeting that evening for David Frankfurter and, I suppose I should tell you, against the Reich.

I do not know what interested Henri to spend time with me that day, to tell me all about the leaflet, and later to bring me with him to the meeting. That was one of the things about Henri—he never explained himself. A thing was just right or wrong to him, it was obvious, there was no need to say why. He was full of believing, Henri. And depending on how he saw you, believed that you also believed.

I noticed him that day as I was walking around the neighborhood, getting to know this new district where Abraham and Chawa had moved. Henri was handing out these single sheet printed papers, calling to people going by, talking fast to the ones who took an interest, grinning, growling, singing, yes even singing. He knew how to make people pay attention, and even get them to smile. He noticed me staring—I had been standing across the road from him for a long time, watching him—but he did not seem to mind, and said nothing to me, until finally he took a break and crossed the road toward a small spot of sun near me, and as he passed me he smiled and said, "Come on," then went and sat down on a ledge, without looking back, as if he was certain that I would follow. For a moment I thought to walk the other way—that was my first reacting always in Paris when someone noticed me, which I tried to make sure was not often. But instead I found myself going over to sit next to him. He began to speak to me in his speedy Paris French, but when I struggled to answer he slowed down, and when he had sorted out my accent he tried out some Yiddish, his strange and awkward Yiddish, mixing it in with French. After a minute or two he pulled out of the deep pocket in his bleus some bread and cheese wrapped in newspaper and offered me some, which he proceeded to cut with a very serious-looking snap knife.

He asked me a little bit about who I was and where I came from and such but did not seem that interested in my answers, and anyway I was careful not to say very much. Within no more than two or three minutes he scrambled to his feet, pulled some coins out of his pocket, handed them to me and asked me if I would go around the corner to a café he named, on the street behind, and buy from them a demi, a small bottle, of vin ordinaire—inexpensive wine of the house. Not to the closer wine shop on the corner, he said, they are petit bourgeois thieves. These were not words I knew, petit bourgeois, but I remember them from that day because I heard them from him often in the two years to come. And by the end of those two Paris years, being frowned on nearly every day by one tradesman or another for some invisible mistake, eventually I knew what he meant. As I stood there blinking at him, he put a leaflet in my hand, said "And read this," then took the rest of the leaflets and crossed over again to the front of the hospital prison, beginning his cries and songs even before he had reached the other side of the road.

Despite some nerves about facing the café people, I felt happy to do what he asked—as I later saw, he usually had that effect on people. When I brought back the wine, though, he said, "But where are the glasses? What, are we barbarians?" and explained that I should return to the café, tell them that the wine was for Henri Vladin, and ask for two glasses. "And here," he said, "take the bottle with you. It needs to be open, right?"

I had a sudden uncomfort in my gut about returning to the café asking for the bottle to be opened and for the glasses, worried about my poor French—with a German accent—and maybe being ignored, or even told to leave, for breaking some rule or other I did not even know about. Instead of which, as soon as the woman at the bar managed to understand my pronouncing of Henri's name, she smiled and took the bottle, pulled the cork, then brought out two small thick glasses and handed it all to me. Just like that.

I returned to Henri and waited while he finished speaking with someone about the leaflet, then he led me back over to the sunny spot across the street. He poured us each a glass and said, "Well, what do you think?" I had seen and heard so many things in the short time since I had begun watching him that I did not know what he meant. The wine? The café? His performance on the street? "Frankfurter," he said, pointing to the leaflet, which he supposed I had now read. "Fighting back against the fascist Boches something-or-others"—I am certain it was quite nasty, what Henri said about the Reich, though I did not actually know the French words he used. And even if I knew them, and could remember them now, perhaps it would be best not to repeat them here. Although you have told me several times that I must write what actually happened. So, if I repeat something that offends, Maître, that does not mean that I myself mean to offend. And anyway, you have also read I am sure about the things they say I shouted at vom Rath, when I fired the shots. Also very nasty. Which I do not doubt is true even though I cannot remember. Some embassy people claimed I shouted "Sale Boche!"—Dirty Kraut!—just before the shots. Which is strange, because why would I, from Hannover, shout French words at a German official? So, like many things about me, Maître, what you first hear may not be exactly right. Although it is possible that I did use those French words. Because during the two years before in Paris I had heard "sale Boche" again and again when a German name was pronounced. Or a name that someone thought was German. Including my own. Anyway, whatever it was I said at the embassy about vom Rath and the Reich, or what Henri said that day two years earlier, please know that of course it would not include you. I mean, if it was up to me.

So, while we sat there with the wine—Henri drinking it and me pretending to—he spoke to me about Frankfurter, and his trial and sentence, and the protest meeting that would take place that evening. I had not understood most of what was on the leaflet—my French was still quite small then, as I have said, and reading it even less. But I had already heard about Frankfurter from a newspaper, the Pariser Haint, a paper in Yiddish, published in Paris, that my Uncle Abraham read. So, I knew that Frankfurter had shot and killed Gustloff, and that just that week the Swiss had sent him to prison for 20 years. This newspaper seemed to be of two different minds about Frankfurter, and in the same way my aunt and uncle were unsure how they felt—partly understanding for him, and sad for him going to prison, and maybe even proud that he had done something that could not be ignored. Though without coming right out and saying any of these things, not Abraham and Chawa or the newspaper. They kept their distance from it, my aunt and uncle, because anyway, they would say, what did it really have to do with them? But also a kind of anger at Frankfurter, from them and the newspaper both, that even if it had nothing to do with them it could only bring them trouble. So, to see from Henri's leaflet that some people were standing up for Frankfurter, even gathering to make a protest, was quite a surprise to me. And an impression.

Henri said that he would soon be finished handing out the leaflets and that I could go along with him then to the meeting, the rally. I was very pleased to be included, and so struck with this boy, his way of being, his confidence. His Frenchness. And how friendly he was to me, though we had just met, and the two of us so different. His invitation to the rally meant that I would be included in something French, for the first time since I had arrived in Paris. If I had learned of the rally some other way, on my own, I am certain I would not have gone—I tried to make certain, at least in those early days, to stay away from anything that might bring me more trouble than I already had. And anyway, this was to be a meeting of French people speaking French, neither of which I understood very well. Also, I was afraid of moving too far from the streets that I knew in Bastille, and the ones I was now just learning in the 10th arrondissement, but this meeting was far over in the 5th, across the river. I had only been a few times on the left side of the river, as they call it, and only along with my uncle to help with carrying things for his work. I did not know my way around over there, and when I had been on that side it did not seem that there were many people there I would be able to talk with. Later on I got to know the other side of the river, or parts of it, but on this first day with Henri, all of Paris was still quite new to me. Each day I stepped onto the streets I felt quite odd. Month after month. The fact is, Maître, I was in Paris four years in all—counting my jail time—and there never was a day I did not feel strange.

18 March

The meeting Henri took me to, the rally for Frankfurter, was in a big hall. By the time we got there it was already crowded with people inside and out. Lots of worker type people—French, I mean, or so it seemed to me. Some still wearing their work clothes. There was a small entry fee, but Henri immediately announced "Chômeurs" to the ticket seller and paid for us both. The sign next to the entry showed half-price for chômeurs—unemployed. Though not simply someone who is not working, a chômeur, but someone who is ready and able and wanting to work but has no job. At least, that was how Henri explained it to me. He pronounced the word as if it was a title.

Inside the hall it was packed and smoky and loud, some people sitting in rows of chairs up near a stage, but most huddled together in groups that were clearly separated from the other groups, backs turned to everyone else in the hall, talking seriously among themselves. Except for one group against a wall near the door—actually not a group, just a portion of people—who seemed a little different, not wearing French worker clothes, or the caps, or other French type things. More like the people I had seen working in Bernard's atelier, the cutters and sewers. Also their bodies somehow different—not their size or shape but how they held themselves, more hunched over, chins low to their necks. And quiet. Each of these people seemed to be alone.

I stayed close to Henri as he moved around the hall. We paused for a few moments while Henri spoke to someone in a group that was talking among themselves in a mix of French and Italian—at least, I think it was Italian, maybe Spanish—then past others until Henri finally reached a group where he was greeted by several people. Do you know that French greeting, Maître? I mean, between people who know each other—people of a certain type, anyway? Those sort-of kisses once to each side that are not truly kisses at all because the lips never touch anything except air and only the cheeks might make some little brush of contact? All the while they are so careful to keep their bodies apart? Very odd, the whole thing, I never understood it. What is the point of going so close but making certain not to touch? Anyway, with Henri and these people he greeted in the hall it was different, there were actual hugs and kisses—what I had seen before, I mean between real French people, only at the Bastille market. Henri's parents were part of this large group in the hall, and he introduced me to them, for some reason calling me H, which in French is pronounced "ahsch." And which is what he always called me, from then on. I never asked him why—I suppose because I wanted him to continue. It was something just my own. And sort of French.

Henri's parents were friendly enough to me, but after we were introduced they said nothing more, just accepted that I was there, without paying me any attention. The hall kept filling up, and soon a number of men in suits and neckties came onto the stage and began to speak. I do not know who they were, except for Maître de Moro-Giafferi, who became one of my lawyers two years later, although I did not know who he was that night at the meeting. And I did not understand most of what they said, because it was all in speechmaker's French, which was more difficult for me than when I was talking directly with someone. But I did notice that while some things were said about David Frankfurter, most of it was about the Reich itself. In angry forceful voices. Not afraid.

After the speeches there was a lot of activity in the hall, with people moving again into what seemed were the same groups as before the speakers had begun.

Yes, I can hear you asking me already, Maître, Who were these people, these groups? I do not know exactly which ones were there, but Henri said that several groups were worker foreign sections, as he called them, including the group he was with, each one from a different country's background. I did not understand why "foreign," because they all seemed very French to me. But later on I learned that these were people who lived and worked in Paris with all the proper papers but who originally had come from different places and so to protect themselves as workers had formed their own special groups. Even though by then many had been in France for years and spoke the language perfectly, and some of the young ones even born in France, like Henri. Yet no matter how long they had been in the country, if their parents were not born there, they were considered foreign by the French workers—the other French, I mean, the real French, as they think of themselves—who made up the big trade unions, the syndicats as they are called, that these groups, these sections, were connected to but were officially separate from because they were foreigners. Though not a foreign as I was, since they had papers. Perhaps you can see why, at first, all this was quite difficult for me to sort out.

Henri and I stood to the side as he tried to explain about these foreigner section-things, which was made even more difficult because of the French-Yiddish jumble we spoke together. But somewhere in the middle of his explanation he mentioned that these foreign sections sometimes had work for young people.

Work. I might not have understood most of what he had been telling me, but he now had all my attention.

The groups from these French-but-foreign sections were now spreading themselves around the hall to talk with the people who had been watching from the edges. Pairs from the sections plucked a person here and there and brought them back to their main group to do the talking. Henri's parents were speaking to a tall, broad man with a stone-cut face. I could tell the man was having trouble, because he only spoke once in a while, short sentences in a very grunty stop-and-start French that sounded as bad as my own, but Henri's parents rattled on without slowing down. As they kept talking the man said less and less, until Henri's parents seemed to lose interest in him, and finally turned away, as if they had been giving the man an examination and now knew that he had failed.

With Henri and me it was different. He did his best that I understand what he said to me, although I must say he seemed not to take quite as much care understanding what I said to him. He told me that in the new year—it was then December—there would be some work opening up, and that maybe through one or another of the foreign sections there would be something for me. He said it in such a way, though—at least, as far as I could tell such things in our choppy languages—that I sensed another shoe had not yet hit the floor. I mean, that getting this work might not be so simple. Still, I was so excited about any prospect of work, and about this new friend—this French friend—being so kind and helpful to me, that I immediately buried the worry. When I think of it now, of how little I understood then about trying to get real work, it makes me laugh. If I could.

20 March

After the rally, I left the hall with Henri and some others from his group, some of the younger ones. He did not actually invite me to go with him, Henri, but he made it seem a normal thing for me to do. It was very cold and wet in the streets but the group was in a big mood. Big, yes. What do I mean? Still angry and serious from the rally, but at the same time in high spirits, as if being together had been a celebrating as well as a meeting. They walked together in the rain, the young men and women, in several bunches of five or six. Henri's parents were in a different group, older, and did not look back to see what the younger ones were doing. A few men still wearing their work clothes headed off on their own but called to some others, seeming to make rendezvous for later, as much as I could tell from their Paris slang. We moved up the narrow night streets of a hill behind the meeting hall, into a neighborhood that I later learned was the Montagne Sainte Geneviève, different small groups turning down this small street or that, while others headed another way, calling salutes to each other as they parted. On the hilltop was a church and a large library, and the great Pantheon monument building, but the side streets and alleyways were dotted with little bars and cafés and music halls. Henri and our group stopped outside a place with little red lights flashing on-and-off all around the doorway, and the name above in fancy lighted cursive the way they liked to do in Paris, long curved blue electric light tubes shaped into letters. I remember getting into an argument with Henri about it another time, these neons as they call them there. He mentioned that he knew someone who worked at a place that made these lights, and started talking about how amazing it was what they could do, these French workers, and how these lights were a great French invention, and on and on, until I got so fed up and told him "No, you are wrong, it was German, these are nothing but Geissler lamps, we studied it in school, it was a German invention, by Geissler, long before the French." It is true, Maître. Perhaps you know. Or you could look it up in a book. Which is what I told Henri. "A German book," he said, "or a French book?"

So, this place on the hill with the flicking lights in front, a little dance hall—a bal musette, they call it, which is some kind of musical instrument, a musette, though I do not know if I ever saw one. The group Henri and I were with stopped in front and stood there for a moment, deciding something. I tried to get a look inside but the big front windows had been painted and it was impossible to see. Two men next to me headed into the place, so I followed, thinking we were all going in, but Henri grabbed my sleeve, laughing, and said, No, no, and some others laughed also, and then Henri and the rest moved on, with me following.

Why do I remember such a small moment, Maître? Because I had done the wrong thing. And hated it. Especially when I did not know why it was wrong, and so might do it again. It was only the first of several bad steps that kept piling up on me that night, and which by the end had darkened my spirits and chilled the hopefulness that Henri's mention of work had given me just a few hours before.

The strange thing is, I did go into that very same bal musette, the one with the painted windows and flicking red lights. Many months later. But that is something else. Something very different.

Henri and the group moved on through the streets as if the wet and cold were nothing. Of course, they all had their caps, the men, and the young women, there were three of them in our group, also had hats, these loose round things that covered their heads but somehow did not fuss their hair, two of them each keeping a perfect single curl on their forehead, like a question mark, it was the fashion. How did they manage it? But I had no hat—I had gone out in the clear afternoon and had been with Henri ever since. So now my head was becoming soaked and cold. And worse, I must have looked foolish.

It is odd, Maître, the thing about hats there in Paris. The worker type people all had those flat caps, as I have told you. The men, that is. Every one of them. But the other French wore different sorts. Bernard and some upper types I later saw, at least the older ones, wore stiff homburgs, the kind I remember seeing in the central district of Hannover. But many other French wore these softer fedora things, sometimes pushed back on their heads and the brim folded down in front, or tilted a bit to the side, the way James Cagney wore it. Did you see him in Public Enemy, Maître? Do a lot of people in Paris want to be James Cagney? But then there was Uncle Abraham, and many others in the Marais and Belleville and the other foreigner neighborhoods, who also wear a kind of fedora, but stiffer and always black. Who did they want to be? Me, I never knew what to do. Back in Hannover I had worn the cap that all students had, but I certainly would not in Paris. I mean, those were for schoolboys. And they were German, those caps, so I never even saw one in Paris. But none of the French hats seemed right for me. So most of the time I went around without anything on my head. Even in the rain. Almost as if I had not yet earned a hat, any hat. As it seems to me now. I cannot explain it.

Just a few streets further along the group reached another bal musette. Fortunately, this time we all went inside. And unfortunately.

It was like nothing I had ever seen before. The room gave the feeling of being tiny and large at the same time. In fact it was not a big place, not much more than most neighborhood cafés, with a bar and very small tables, and a red leather bench running around the walls, and a little empty space in the middle for dancing. In one corner was a raised stand with a low wooden railing around it, and on the stand three men with their instruments—accordion, guitar, two drums. Enormous old mirrors covered the walls, which made the room seem bigger than it was, but also more packed, with the jammed-together people multiplied in the glass. And making it feel even more crowded were paper decorations hanging everywhere from the low ceiling, four long ones criss-crossing the room from the corners and meeting in the center at a dangling ball of glass, tiny pieces of glass, that slowly spun around, with colored lights shining on it and bouncing off the mirrors making the whole place glitter as if we were caught in the middle of a spinning red and blue Milky Way.

Everything in there was strange to me. The music was very loud and fast. I had heard music like it before, coming out of the doorways of the bals on the Rue de Lappe, behind the Bastille, those places that Abraham and Chawa had wanted to move Maison Albert away from. Inside this small space the sound was different, though, not just entering my ears but banging against my body. Also I must tell you, Maître, many French love it, you hear it everywhere, but what pleasure they find in the accordion is a complete mystery to me. Bavarians also love it, I think. Who also are a mystery.

The floor was crowded and the tables all taken, so our group made its way around the dancers to stand at the bar. I noticed one small table in a corner that seemed to be empty—no glasses on it waiting for dancers to return—and I moved toward it, gesturing to Henri, but he immediately shook his head and came over to shout in my ear that it might belong to regulars and we did not want any trouble, and that anyway drinks cost less at the bar. I looked around—no one seemed to be watching me, which was a relief, but I was reminded again how much I did not know.

The dancers were doing a fast short step that I later learned was called the java, but because of the small space they could not move around very much. And there was something quite shocking for me, Maître. Not only were the dancers pressed close together but some of the men had a hand directly on his dancing partner's behind.

When the music stopped, a man next to the band stand yelled out something to the crowd and the men who were dancing dug into their pockets and put coins into a bowl that a woman from behind the bar held out as she moved around the floor. People then went back to their tables and the bar, and I was surprised to see that most of the dancing couples split up, going back, I suppose, to the people they had come in with.

Henri and his friends ordered drinks, and as casually as I could I said to Henri "Vin ordinaire"—to avoid speaking to the bar keeper and perhaps making another mistake—which was the only drink name I knew. Since Henri had asked for it that afternoon I thought that was what all of them would drink now, with a bottle or two coming to be shared. When the drinks arrived, though, they were individual glasses, with different strange bright colored liquids. I got my small glass of red wine and held out some coins to Henri, but he waved them away with a generous smile.

Soon the drummer began some introduction tapping and immediately I heard strange noises, tsking or hissing sounds, and saw that they were coming from different men around the room, directed to other tables or toward the bar. After Henri's warning about avoiding trouble in this place, these sounds from the rough men now made me think that something ugly was about to happen but the men only got up and approached different women around the room, who joined them on the dance floor. The band soon began blasting another java tune, and away they all went, spinning tightly around the floor like pairs of wind-up dolls. Once I realized that the sounds were just some way of dancers pairing up, I relaxed a bit and began to watch again how close the men and women were pressed together, and so open about it all.

While the music was playing it was too loud to talk, so I did not have to return anything more than a nod or a smile to the young men and women of Henri's group. Then the music stopped again, and I quickly turned to my glass of wine and began sipping, staring straight ahead, sneaking looks at the room from the mirror behind the bar. I felt safe enough in my little space there, but in a few minutes when the drum announced the beginning of a new song, one of the young women in the group put her arm on mine and said, Come dance. Immediately I shied away, but Henri was looking at me and smiling, encouraging, and the others also, and I did not want to disappoint him, or again do the wrong thing, and suddenly I was on the dance floor with this woman who immediately put an arm over my shoulder.

We were about the same height—well, she was probably a bit

taller—and so I was looking directly into her face, just a breath away, her warm arm on my neck, her other hand taking mine, and my other hand on her lower back—being careful that it went no lower. She was smiling kindly but all I felt was fear. The band started the next dance song, another loud fast java, and we began to move, but of course I did not know the steps, what to do, and I stumbled and bumped into the dancers around me, and this kept moving me up against my partner's body—despite trying not to, Maître, I assure you—and that plus the music and the wine and the spinning lights altogether made me dizzy, and all I could do was stare as hard as I could at the single amazing perfect curl on her forehead and hope that I did not fall down.

The dance ended but the torture did not. Because now the man by the bandstand again made his announcement—"Pay up, pay up!" or something like that—and I realized that I was supposed to put some coins into the collection bowl. But I had no idea how much, and was afraid that I would look cheap by putting in too little or the fool by putting in too much. The woman I had been dancing with—I never did learn her name—must have noticed my uncomfort because as I tried to make out the different coins in my hand, she quickly picked out a few and put them into my other hand.

After this rescue, and my relief that she now led me back to the bar instead of expecting another dance, I felt a wave of gratefulness to her. I suppose I just smiled stupidly for a few moments, and then noticed my wine glass and had the idea to offer her a drink. I had already been spending some afternoons in the cinema, and although I could not yet understand much of the speaking in the films, I had seen this gesture several times, the offer of a drink, so I knew that it was something normal for a man to do. So much for films, Maître. Because the woman seemed quite surprised at my offer, and backed up slightly, looking me over as if I was a fish at the Bastille market, deciding whether it was fresh enough to buy. Then a small smile came to her face, and she said something that I did not understand but that I could tell was not a simple "Yes I would like a drink" or "No thank you." Henri now turned toward us and seeing what must have been the terrified look on my face said something quietly to the woman, who spoke back in his ear. Henri stared at me, then must have realized that I had no idea what was going on, and came around to the other side of me and told me what was what.

It turns out that in this bal musette, and in many other places like it, if you offer to buy someone a drink that means you are asking if the person will go away with you for that night, a kind of code. To have relations, Maître. And if the person accepts the drink, it means Yes. As soon as I heard this from Henri, my dizziness rushed back, worse than before. Then, although I tried not to, I peeked at the woman, saw that she was still smiling, and realized with a sudden sickness that she was actually thinking about accepting the drink. Now I felt like I might black out completely, and the only thing I could think of was to run. I spluttered something to Henri—"Sorry, I have to, sorry"— and rushed away through the crowd. As I reached the door, I heard laughter behind me. It could have been anyone, of course, laughing at anything. But despite their kindness to me all that evening, for the rest of that night, and for a long time afterward, I imagined that it had come from Henri's group, and that the laughter was at me.

I saw a lot of Henri over the next two years. But he never mentioned that night. And I never asked.

Yours sincerely,
H.

21 March 1941

Maître Herr Rosenhaus,

    I have just learned something about this place that is very difficult for me. That many people who were dragged off the streets on Kristallnacht are here. In this Sachsenhausen camp. Have been here ever since that night. The entire two years and a half.

    Not here in the bunker, Maître. Out there.

Herschel Feibel Grynszpan.

Maître,

I am thankful for your visit. It had been many weeks. Also, that you came when you did, on the eve before my birthday, was especially pleasing. Though you did not mention the occasion. For the awkwardness it would have caused, I am sure. Which is something I appreciate.

I have been eating again these past three days, as I told you I would. Only small amounts, but my health, which seemed to worry you, is improving. I am grateful for your concern.

To explain myself to the world is one thing, Maître. An important thing. More than important—necessary. But when I learned that prisoners have been here in Sachsenhausen since Kristallnacht, still here after all this time, explaining myself just did not seem enough. Which is why I fasted. But when I did not eat, I became too weak to write. And in the end, which is more important—Atonement? Or speaking to the world? Is that a spiritual question, Maître? As they might have said at yeshiva. And argued about for days. Or a political one? As everything is, my Paris friend Henri would say. Then again, I can hear Sam, Sam le Gamb, saying, Question? What question? There is only living. Or not.

As yet, Maître, I have little strength. But I will write again soon. I wanted you to know that I was eating again. In case you do not know already.

Sincerely,
Herschel

6 April 1941

Maître Rosenhaus,

When last you were here you asked if I kept up this connection with the foreign section—the foreign but French workers, or French but foreign—that Henri had introduced me to. Well, yes. And no.

When I ran off from the dance hall that night, I had made no plan with Henri to meet him again. In the weeks that followed I held on tightly to what he had said about his group having work to offer, but I did not know where Henri lived, or where else to find him. I kept a lookout for him in the neighborhood, especially by the Saint Lazare hospital where I had first seen him, and often put my head in the door of the café where he had sent me to fetch some wine. But I never spotted him. He had told me his family name, Vladin, but I heard it only once that first day and by the next morning I did not remember it correctly, let alone how to pronounce or spell it, so I did not have even that to use in looking for him.

I told Abraham and Chawa nothing about that night at the bal musette. After my first few months in Paris they had stopped trying to keep watch over where I spent time and what I did, because the answers I gave, honest as far as they went, were always the same—walking here and there, I would tell them, at the cheap matinee cinema, at the Sportclub Aurore. Getting to know my way around, I would often say, which were convenient words for all of us because it could truthfully include almost anything while actually saying nothing. And when in later times I did tell about things that I got involved in, with Sam for example, or Henri, and later with some others, it often caused an argument with Uncle Abraham. Yes, you may have heard, it was mentioned at Abraham and Chawa's trial, we argued often. Abraham was always worried that I might do something that would put me in contact with the police, and end up being jailed, then sent back to the Reich. Which, of course, in the end is what happened—here I am— though not in any way he was imagining. And worried also, perhaps, that he and Chawa would themselves somehow end up in jail—which is also what happened, to my everlasting sorrow. For harboring a fugitive. That was the official charge. Which is what I became after my expulsion order in August '38, a fugitive—a personnage clandestine, as the police there call it. Protecting me was Abraham and Chawa's legal right and duty, but France had made doing so a crime on that August day when it declared me illegal. To my enormous relief, from the efforts of Maître de Moro-Giafferi, Abraham and Chawa were released after not too long.

Yes, a legal right and duty—my parents had sent a document making Abraham my official guardian. But being a guardian and being able to guard are two different things. Abraham and Chawa already had all they could do, working from early morning into each night, just to pay their two workers and the rent, especially since their move to the larger rooms on Rue Martel, and food for the table— including always a bit extra for me if I showed up in the evening. There were many times in Paris when I was hungry, Maître, but never for more than a day or two—and knew it would not be longer than that, which was just as important—because of Abraham and Chawa. And when my stomach pains would become especially bad—because of something I found on my own to eat that was too old or too strong or too French, or because of too long with nothing at all in my gut except the acids of worry—they would spend what little extra they had to buy me medicine. Tante Chawa and Uncle Abraham, wherever they are now, may they live and be well. From my mouth to God's ear.

So, the foreign section. Paris is a huge crowded city, even just the eastern part, and by several weeks into the new year 1937 I had still not spotted Henri. Things in general seemed very dark. In fact, it actually was dark most of the time, the low skies trapping coal soot and sulfur, the winter sun barely appearing, the streets cold and wet. The winter days and nights were even harder for me to fill because there were so few places to be out of the weather that did not cost money. Sam introduced me to the Aurore Sport Club that winter, where we could spend some time inside, and once in a while I would go with him on one of his expeditions, collecting something or other from a far corner of the city, something he or his mother could sell. But the winter made Sam's street life more difficult, and like so many others in Belleville and Bastille, all over the east, he stayed more in the little room he shared with his mother, just trying to keep warm, so I did not see him as often.

By early February the local police bureau still had received no paperwork about my applicating for residence, as a refugee. It was the police who kept track of foreigners, and notified of any decisions, though some central bureaus, some ministries, had a part in deciding. Which of these was the most important no one seemed to know. Or what might make a difference. The whole process was a saw-puzzle, but without knowing whether you had all the pieces.

Since the police had not received anything from a ministry saying that I had filed the proper papers, they would not issue me even a receipt that showed at least that I was following the proper procedures, as Abraham and I had been instructed to do on that first visit to the prefecture. I tried not to bother Abraham about it too often—After all, what really could he do?—but I was desperate to have some kind of paper to show to the foreign section people whenever I had the luck to see Henri again. If I ever did. And if he was still willing to help, after I had run away that night at the bal. If he even remembered me. And if his foreign section really did have work. Yes, many ifs, but I was holding onto Henri's words as if they had been an iron promise that was only a matter of time. By February, though, it had been two months since that day, the only day, I had seen him, and the iron seemed turning to rust.

Late in the month I again asked Abraham what might be happening with my papers. He just shrugged, as he often did, in that way that says the workings of the world were beyond him. I lost my temper. As much about the shrug, I think, as the lack of any news. I hated it, that shrug—of clerks behind windows, of "never mind, my son" rabbis, of schlemiels. This time, at least, Abraham managed to keep his own temper—perhaps because he could see how near to crazed I was—and said he would once again return to the refugees bureau, where he had filled out the application, to ask if they knew anything. And this time, after sitting there for three hours, someone actually gave him news. A clerk reported from some list he consulted that yes, just as they had promised, they had forwarded the papers to the ministry—a week before. Four months after Abraham had completed them. As for why the delay, the clerk had no idea. Or so he told Abraham.

When a few weeks later I convinced Uncle Abraham to go again to the local police station, to our great surprise and relief they had received notice from some ministry that my application had in fact been filed. So they issued me a receipt. It was not much—it did not give me any right to live in France and certainly not to work. But it showed that for the moment anyway I was not completely unlawful.

Now I was again excited to look for Henri but did not know where to turn. So, I decided to tell Uncle Abraham about meeting Henri and about the chance that I could find work through one of the foreign sections.

A mistake.

"Bolsheviks!" Abraham shouted, furious—but at the same time fearful, it seemed.

"No," I said, "they are French."

That stopped him for a few moments, confused. "Well, yes, maybe so, some of them," he finally said, quieter though still fuming. "But they are all of them trouble."

It turned out he knew quite a lot about them, the foreign sections, from the year before. The bigger clothing ateliers had been under attack for months, according to Uncle Abraham, until just before I had arrived in late summer. Or I should say, according to my memory of what Abraham told me. Because I am not certain now that I have all these things the right way around. Anyway, it seems that the guilds, the craftsman guilds, were pushing for a 40-hour work week for the façonniers—the atelier workers—just like the big labor syndicats were doing at the same time for workers at the large factories. Even though almost all the façonniers were immigrants and so not members of the guilds. But some of the façonniers were in the foreign sections, and the sections and the guilds together had sent their members to fight against the big ateliers.

According to Abraham, what the guilds were really after was for the big ateliers to hire the guilds' French workers instead of lower-paid foreigners—who not only had no guild certificate, as the laws said they should, but in many ateliers had no work papers at all. Well, this move by the guilds threatened the whole set-up of the ateliers—not just clothing but also hats and leather and furs and furniture and jewelry and more—which offered one of the only chances in Paris for refugees and other new immigrants to work.

Despite never having been allowed into the guilds or syndicats, most of the façonniers took the guilds' advices—Abraham shook his head when he told me this, as if still disbelieving—and went on strike against the big ateliers. Many of the foreigner façonniers had once been in guilds or syndicats wherever they had come from, Abraham said, and hoped by following the guilds' lead to be so again in Paris. But there were also others, either with different backgrounds or simply too starving for work, who instead of striking became yellows, as the French call them, taking the spots of the workers who had gone on strike. Which led to many bloody fights in the streets of Paris east during this time—older immigrants against newer refugees, French foreign against more foreign, poor against poorer. It must have been an awful thing to be a part of. Or even to see.

Abraham himself had not had any direct trouble with the guilds or the foreign sections, he told me—Maison Albert was too small for the guilds to bother with. And anyway, Sidney and Berenice, the machiniste and the seamstress finisher, had worked for a long time with Abraham and Chawa, were almost family. They had their midday food together, the four of them, every day clearing a work table and sitting properly at a meal like French people, talking about their work and their lives and the world outside. And it was true, I had seen for myself—Maison Albert felt very different from Bernard's ateliers, the one above Au Courant Dame and the others near the Gare de l'Est, where the workers were crammed together and never permitted to lift their heads from their work. Still, what had happened at Bernard's ateliers had also shaken Abraham and Chawa.

Because Bernard had so many workers, all his places had been targeted by the clothing guilds, with help from the foreign sections. And all Bernard's workers had gone on strike, in the spring of '36. Not only that, but the ones in the workrooms above Au Courant Dame—the fancy boutique that carried Bernard's name—all had work papers and so were bolder, and had actually taken over the atelier and locked Bernard out. Then, to make it worse—much worse, in Abraham's telling—the workers had flown a huge red flag out the window, right over the entrance to Bernard's shop below.

With this takeover of his main atelier, and facing syndicat and foreign section support for his workers, eventually Bernard made a deal that gave them a bit better pay for shorter hours—though nothing near the 40-hour week and paid holidays that the syndicats had won from the big employers—and his façonniers went back to work.

When it was all over, some of Bernard's workers who had valid working papers applied for membership in the guild. But still they were not allowed in—still they were not French.

Then one at a time, slowly over many months so that it did not draw too much attention, Bernard began to fire the façonniers who had gone on strike. Eventually he replaced almost all of them. The foreign section complained about it to the guilds but the guilds did nothing, said nothing. Still, the whole thing had cost Bernard dearly. And had badly frightened Abraham. So upset was he when he described all this to me that I asked him nothing more about how I might find Henri.

Though we spoke no more about it, Abraham's story of the strikes carried on in my head. Before this, I had the clear idea that Maison Albert was completely unlike Bernard's workrooms. Yet here was Uncle Abraham so disturbed, months later, by what had happened at Au Courant Dame. Even so, I told myself, he and Bernard were obviously on different sides. But which sides, exactly? Later, I heard Henri call Uncle Abraham a petit commerçant while Bernard he said was a nouveau bourgeois—with a different tone of voice for each. This was supposed to make things clearer for me, Maître? The only explanation I could think of was that there must be yet another side, with neither Abraham or Bernard. Where Henri and the foreign sections were.

All right, I said to myself, so there are more than two sides. But if the guilds would not allow Bernard's façonnier workers to become members, and did nothing when Bernard later fired most of them, then the guilds must be on a different side from the façonniers. But the façonniers were certainly not on the same side as Bernard, the boss who had put them on the street. So, what sides were which? Do you follow me, Maître? And what of Sidney and Berenice, who did not strike at all? And who broke bread every day with Chawa and Abraham? What was their side?

With this sifting and sorting in my head, Maître, eventually I came around to myself. What was my side? Other than outside? I had no answer. I wonder now whether, at the time, it might have been any side that would have me.

Sincerely,
Herschel

10 April 1941

Maître,

Sportclub Aurore. On your list. For me to say more about. I suppose I have mentioned it, the Aurore. Or did it come to your attention some other way?

It is in the Pletzl—the old district that surprises you right in the center of Paris, a few small streets with kosher food shops and Yiddish window signs and booksellers with volumes in every language east to the Urals. My friend Sam introduced me to the Pletzl. And to the Aurore. Which is where I became a pongiste. Although actually it was later, in jail at Fresnes, that I reached my highest level. None of the boys at Fresnes could defeat me. Or even the guards. Some of them were quite friendly to me, the guards—you see, Maître, my crime was against the Reich, and that changed how they looked at me, at least some of them. But two of the guards in particular were not like that, and it used to make them so angry when I would defeat them in the game, which of course was not a very smart thing for me to do, but I could not help myself. And then they would call me names. "Monkey-boy" was their favorite—because I moved so quickly to defense their clumsy hits. And "Banania-boy," that was another—it sounds like it would be the French word for banana, Maître, which come to think of it is another monkey thing, but actually it was the name of a chocolate drink, with poster advertisements all over the city which showed a big grinning dark African face. Most of the names they called me, I noticed, had something brown about them.

So, the Aurore. It called itself a sport club, but it was really more just a gathering place for young people of the Pletzl, and Paris east. Mostly people like me, who came from somewhere else. Though there were also some who had been born right there in the Pletzl and who remained more part of that little district than of Paris the great city.

They did have some sport at the Aurore—the table tennis in the old cellar that used to be a wine cave, and outings to nearby parks to play raggy games of football.

Excuse me, Maître—pongiste. Instead of table tennis, in Paris they like to say pingpong, which sounds more Chinese to me than French, but anyway from that they call players pongistes. At least, very good players. Like me.

It was sometime in January or February '37 that Sam first brought me to the Aurore. They served hot food there every midday in winter, a soup or stew of some kind—"the cabbage patch" we sometimes called the place, because that was the main ingredient in every cooking pot there, and the rooms always had that smell. They would give a bowl to anyone who came in, whether or not you could pay the small 10 sous they charged. You had to arrive early, though, and get in a queue—they could make only so much on their two little spirit burners, and there were always a lot of young people there looking for something to eat. Sunday was the busiest, and they cooked extra then, since on that day all the French food shops were closed, which on other days were places where some young people in the east managed to scrabble a bit of back door throwaway food. In the east of Paris, Maître, Sunday was the hungriest day.

Also it was a place to get out of the cold and rain for a while, the Aurore, when there was nowhere else. Well, not completely nowhere else, because Sam had also brought me to these new low price department stores—the Monoprix and Prisunic and a few more. We often went to one or another of them. Huge places, they were dry and warm, and the people who worked there did not look at you crosseyed if your clothes were old and you did not right away ask them for a particular thing you meant to buy, the way small shops did, and also the fine large magazin stores, the Galeries Lafayette and such. There were always many people wandering through these low price places, which is what these stores wanted—all kinds of people coming in to look around. They even allowed people to pick up the clothing and other things the stores sold—they seemed to sell everything, all under one roof—and to handle it, look it over, even try things on right there by themselves, without any kind of fitter or helper or someone to make sure things were done Paris properly. So, it was quite a good show, to be there with people in good spirits, trying things, showing each other, jabbering about this and that, even if few people had enough money to buy very much. Also, there was something about these places that allowed people, strangers, to talk to each other, which was not something I had seen much of in Paris. Except at street markets. Or the bateaux-lavoirs, the floating washhouses on the river. Places where there was no point pretending, and so people did not bother. Perfect for our Sam, these stores. The French shop girls he met there were his favorites. They liked me also, the girls. At first even more than Sam—his clothes were more scruffy, and he could not always hide the scabies rashes he so often had. Yes, they seemed to like me, but when my poor French speaking came out, and my accent, they usually shied away. Though not always from Sam. We went together to these places, Sam and I, but we did not always leave together. He was a great talker, that boy.

Sam also had other reasons for visiting these stores. If he or Rina, his mother, had managed to latch onto some goods that she would be selling from her cart—slightly damaged and so dumped very cheaply, or that one of these very stores had not been able to sell, after maybe earlier not getting sold in one of the fancier stores, and so then sold off in lots for almost nothing, or that maybe had just fallen off the back of a lorry—Sam needed to see how much similar things sold for in these discount stores. So that Rina could set her own price lower but not too much lower. Also, Sam knew that at the end of the day, after these stores had closed, they put out their trash and sometimes there were sellable things to be found there. Sam le Gamb.

I am sorry, Maître—the Aurore club. I was talking about how you could almost always go there to get out of the weather, or just to spend some time. There were also newspapers and journals to read, in French and Yiddish both, and each with its different politics. Several of these papers delivered copies free to the club. And once in a while they would send someone to talk with the young people there. Also the boys and girls among themselves, whoever was at hand, there were always discussions in strong spirits about almost anything on their minds. Yes, boys and girls both—part of the sense of the place was that anyone could get together there without worrying about wagging fingers or tongues. It was also where people shared what they knew about troubles back home, wherever home was—mostly Poland, but also Russia, Lithuania, Ukraine—and also about what was happening there in Paris, the decrees, rules, arrests, places to find food, sometimes even work. There were speakers also, at the Aurore, usually in the evenings and Sundays—often about politics, but also about books, or advice about how to deal with documents and the police and such. Also what to do when you were ill, which was often a problem with hardly ever a solution that did not cost more money than people had. Sometimes there were debates, which usually ended in fierce arguments. And from time to time there was music and even dancing—though my allergy to the accordion drove me away on many of those evenings.

So, who were they, the people who ran the Aurore? The Gestapo asked me this several times when they were holding me in Berlin, before you began coming to see me, Maître. Were these people communists? they wanted to know. Or socialists? Or bundists or anarchists or cabalists or zionists? I cannot even remember all the ists they asked me about. What did the Aurore people say about France and Germany? Did they encourage people to go out and cause trouble about the Reich? Turn the French against the Reich? To throw France and Germany into war? Were they the ones, the Gestapo asked, who told me to avenge my family, my people? To draw the world's attention? To shoot vom Rath?

Why is it they were so convinced that someone told me what to do? And even if, that I would simply follow? That I did not see the world for myself? Or perhaps they were not convinced but just wanted me to say that it was true. And so asked me over and over—What groups, what parties, what people led me on? Not so different from what you sometimes ask, Maître. But of course not in the same way.

It was through the Aurore that I finally saw Henri again. Henri Vladin. Who had introduced me to his foreign section that night, after the rally for Frankfurter. You recall me telling you? Yes, of course—you have asked me to say more about it, the foreign section. On your list.

It was in the early spring of that year, 1937. Sometime in March. Mild weather had returned after a long cold winter and the Aurore sponsored an outing, a trip to the countryside. Well, they said it was the countryside, but it turned out to be not exactly. Instead it was to Bonneuil, a town on the Marne, a river not far from Paris. And it was not exactly the Aurore. The sponsor, I mean. It was arranged through the Aurore but actually paid for by one of the newspapers—I do not remember which one. They had several of these trips a year, the Aurore, to get young people out of the city for a day. Always backed by some journal or charity or society of this or that, because the Aurore had no money of its own to spend on such things. And whoever the official sponsor was, there would also be some other group behind that, and always some of their people along on the trip—usually talking politics. Or telling us to avoid politics. Everything always seemed to have something else behind it, in Paris. In those days. Maybe always. Well, I suppose that is why the Gestapo kept asking me.

So, Bonneuil. Or Bonnueil. I am not sure how to spell it. Anyway, on the Marne, a river that runs just east Paris, and connects with the Seine. Which is how we got there—by boat. We left from the Bassin de l'Arsenal. Just near the tunnel where I had first met Sam, when he was trapping cats. He came on this Aurore trip as well, Sam, and we had a small laugh together when we found out where we were departing from.

At first Sam was not interested. He told me he had no use for the countryside—too many French people out there, he said, and nowhere to be invisible. And he did not like being trapped by the world-savers, as he called them, the people who always went along on these outings and made you listen to their spiel. But after a while I convinced him to come. There would be a free picnic lunch, I told him. And I pointed out that from the boat there would be views of places on the city's edges that he did not know about but that might be good new territory for his scavenging. How did I know that? Or, rather, how did I think to say that? Since of course I did not actually know any such thing.

It was on a weekday, the outing, so the only young people who came were those who had no regular work. It had to be during the week, the Aurore people said, because Saturdays were too crowded— so many French workers and their families went out to the countryside on that day, huge numbers of them every Saturday, ever since the summer before when the syndicats had won the 40-hour week. Also, some of the young people who spent time at the Aurore were religious, so Saturday was not a day for them to travel. Sunday also was not so good because there was very little transport that day, and we would have a hard time getting out of and back into Paris. That did not stop the French working people, who went out Sundays on their bicycles, but almost none of us had bikes. I realized later, though, that the real reason for going on a weekday for this particular trip was that on a Sunday the factories at Bonneuil would be shut.

About 20 of us gathered at the dock, very early in the morning darkness. Part of the excitement of it all was that we were going on the river. Most of us had never been on a boat before. Including me. Though it turned out to be not much of a boat. Just a barge, one of the coal barges that come to Paris from the east of the country. They do not have as much to carry back with them out of Paris, these coal barges, so sometimes they are willing to take on passengers. Of course, not many people travel that way—it is very, very slow, and uncomfortable with no real place to sit, and we all wound up covered in coal shmutz. Also, to return to Paris we had to find a different way, since the full barges coming into the city had no room for passengers. So, the sponsors of our trip had made arrangements, and we returned to Paris that evening packed into the canvas-topped back of a small, half-filled farm truck—for days afterward I smelled like goat cheese on top of the barge coal. But I suppose space on the barge and the little truck cost them much less than the train or bus would have, for 20 people, and in the end being on the great rivers was quite special.

As Sam and I were waiting on the quay near the barge that morning, I heard someone call "Salut, Asch!"—"Hello there, H!" I had forgotten that this was the name he had given me—H. I had almost forgotten about him altogether. But the nickname and the sound of his voice right away brought back to me that evening at the Frankfurter rally and the bal musette and I turned to see Henri approaching with two other men.

He embraced me like we had known each other for years, then introduced me to his two companions, both young Frenchmen, it seemed, and asked how I was getting along, all in his speedy French. By then I was able to carry on simple conversations in French, so I said some empty things about being fine, how everything was fine. Then I noticed that Sam had moved back a few paces, watching. Quiet. How often was Sam ever both silent and still? I introduced him to Henri, and they exchanged a few words, each sizing up the other by the way he looked and spoke. They both had some kind of invisible microscope—all Parisians did, it seemed—to sort out these things.

It turned out that Henri's foreign section was connected to the newspaper that was sponsoring this outing, and that Henri and his two friends were to be our guides for the day. His foreign section liked to keep its hand in at the Aurore, Henri told me later, to get to know the young people who spent time there. Especially those who had convictions. I did not know what convictions he meant, and I did not ask—remembering how I had acted the last time he had seen me, fleeing out of the bal musette that night, I did not want to ruin this reunion by straightaway seeming foolish again.

There was a lot of activity getting everyone ready for the departure, with Henri busy being an organizer. And once we were on our way, we were packed quite closely together, with Henri on the other side of the barge from me, so I did not get a chance to speak with him. I did not mind, though, since it was a relief just to have found him again, and soon I was distracted by moving along the great river. Also, Sam seemed a bit put-off, I do not know why, and since I had convinced him to come along I decided to stay close to him, both of us looking out at the passing river banks. It did not take him long to brighten up and begin chattering away, giving me a running story about the places and buildings and people we were seeing, though I doubt he knew much about what he was saying—he admitted later that he had never been on that part of the river before. But that was an extra from spending time with Sam—right or wrong, true or made-up, listening to him rattle on about the streets and backways and shadows of Paris was always an education. Not to mention an entertainment. And I had very few things like that.

12 April

It was midmorning when we arrived at Bonneuil, too early to just settle on the river bank and have our lunch—they must have planned it that way—so Henri and his two friends led our Aurore group away from the docks and toward what they said would be something "very interesting." These were words Sam said to be wary of, since they could stretch a long way, in any direction.

We walked toward the town but stopped, before reaching it, outside a huge set of connected buildings, a factory, set on a open flat area next to one of the canals that led from the river. Hundreds of people were gathered in front of the factory gates, and dozens more inside the fences. They were workers from this factory, Henri told us, a Lancia automobile factory, and the ones outside the gates were on strike. Yes it is Italian, the Lancia, but they were making them specially for French people, at this factory in Bonneuil. Exactly like the original cars, but built by French workers. Also given special French names, the models made there, instead of the original Italian, even though they were the same cars. And beautiful machines they were, Maître—there were several rows of them parked at the side of the building—with gorgeous lines and shapes and bright colors.

It turned out that the workers outside the gates, the ones on strike, were French, and the ones inside the fence, still on the job but for the moment out of the building, were Italian, brought over from Italy to live and work in Bonneuil because of their knowledge of the Lancia's constructing. They had been members of the metalworker syndicat in Italy, Henri told us, and supported the Frenchmen's Bonneuil strike but were unsure about actually striking themselves because of their position as foreign workers in France. The French syndicat workers were now trying to get the Italians to join them outside the fence, even though these same local workers had never allowed the Italians, who were doing the same work side by side in the same factory, to join their syndicat—because they were not French.

It was difficult for us to sort out what was going on, with shouting and speechmaking by the French workers outside, and some of them yelling to the Italian workers inside the fences, and all of it in a worker French slang that I could not follow. So, Henri gave us a quick picture about who was who and what was what. He seemed to know the situation well, Henri, and it turned out that the two French friends that had come along on the trip with him were actually Italian—French-Italian, or Italian-French—who were part of a different foreign section from Henri's, a specially Italian section. There was a whole League of Nations of these foreign sections, Maître. The Italian section was one of the biggest—there were so many Italians living in Paris then, many who had first come to work on farms, plus many more from the big cities of Italy who had wanted or needed to get out of the Mussolini world. And thought they had.

Anyway, these two friends of Henri, they moved to the front of the crowd to call out in Italian to the workers behind the gates. This livened up the Italian workers, who called back in Italian to Henri's two friends, and even some things to the crowd, in their funny-accent French. By now Sam had become restless and said to me "Come on," nodding in the direction of the town. Henri heard Sam and said to me, "Wait a few minutes. It will be worth it." This made me curious, even though all this workers chaos seemed to have nothing to do with me, or for that matter with any of us from the Aurore. Also, I did not want to be a disappointment to Henri again, so I turned back to the crowd, ignoring Sam. Anyway, there was no point trying to explain myself to Sam. What would have made sense to him? What would have mattered?

The back and forth calling continued between the workers outside the gates and in, and with Henri's two French Italian friends. Soon an automobile arrived and several men got out, quickly greeted by some of the striking workers. One of the new men seemed to be the center of attention, and when Henri's two friends noticed him they called out in more excited Italian to the workers inside the fences, then went over to greet this new arrival. He was middle age and mostly bald, this man, wearing a waistcoat suit that I can tell you was very well-made, though not French, and with small round glasses—altogether looking more like a professor than a syndicat man. His name was Rossini or Rossetti, something like that. Henri told me the name but it did not stay in my head, Maître, I am sorry. Anyway, you could look it up, in the newspapers from the time, and from that summer—it turns out he was famous somewhat, especially after what happened a few months later. So, this Rossetti came over and spoke with some of the French strikers, who welcomed him, then he turned to face the Italian workers inside the gates. He did not give them any kind of speech or anything like that, but moved close and spoke to them through the fence, in Italian I suppose, talking not at them but with them, and listening to them. This went on for a while, and while it did the French strikers respectfully stopped their shouting and chanting.

Sam was now nudging me again, saying he was bored and was leaving. Henri heard him and with a kind of challenging smile to Sam, but not unfriendly, he nodded toward a group of people arriving behind us, who were carrying several long tables and boxes, and some of them huge armfuls of long loaves of bread. "Dejeuner," Henri said—lunch—just the one word, then turned away, allowing Sam some space to react but also giving the idea that he would not mind either way Sam decided. Sam watched the food arriving, and when I took a peek at him a minute later he had settled down, not paying attention to what was going on with the crowds but not wiggling to get away, either.

After a few more minutes of talking between Rossetti and the men behind the fence, first two and then four and then a dozen or so of these Italian workers headed for the gate and out into the crowd of French workers, who cheered them on. They were slapped on the back and embraced by some of the Frenchmen, though the Italians still seemed uncomfortable, unsure of where they stood. The French did not hold back, though, and began a celebration—singing and dancing around with each other, a few of them taking off their caps and tying handkerchiefs on their heads like the laundry women wear, allowing themselves to be twirled about as if they were women dance partners.

The food tables were now ready and Sam and I and the others from the Aurore got in a queue with the workers—I realized that this must be the picnic lunch that Henri had promised—and we soon reached huge piles of what turned out to be tinned sardines. We were given one tin each, a glass of wine poured directly from barrels rolled up next to the tables, and a hunk of bread torn from a mountain of those very long crumbly loaves that the French think so much of. At least it was proper hefty bread. Not those skinny little baguettes the Parisians love. Do you know those, Maître, the Paris baguettes? So narrow, with a hard crust. And when you open them up, pure white. And full of air. Sort of like Parisians.

So, our little group took our sardines and bread and went along with Henri back to the river, where he led us to a quiet grassy spot on the bank under some willow trees. "Now here it comes," Sam said to me, "the party line." But Henri just settled in to eat and did not try to lecture us about what we had seen. Still, it had been quite a show, and many of us wanted to know more, so as we ate and drank—Henri had brought a sack with several bottles of wine filled from the barrels— we talked for a good hour or so about the syndicats and the foreign sections and all the strikes and actions and factory occupations and such—the world turned right side up, Henri called it—that had been going on all around Paris the past two years. Finally, the whole group stretched out on the grass for a petit somme—an after-lunch nap—as if we had all suddenly become French. Except Sam. Because when I opened my eyes again, he was gone.

No, not Parisians, Maître. Being like the baguette. That is not what I should say. Certain types of Parisians is what I mean. I once complained to Henri something about "the French" and he said, "Oh? There are 40 million of them. Which one do you mean?" Or maybe he said "40 million of us." Depending on when he said it. So, I try to be more careful about such things. Still, Maître, some truths are true, and in some parts of Paris the bread is thicker and rounder than in other parts. And darker.

Anyway, in a while Henri roused us and we headed back up to the factory. The strikers were still outside the gates, though some of them were now stretched out on a nearby patch of grass. Rossetti was sitting in a circle of men under a tree, talking, and if there were any Italian workers who had not come out to join the strikers, they must have gone back inside the building because there was no one within the fences. It was quieter, people talking in small groups. And to my great surprise, there was Sam, standing with a few men near the food tables, talking and gesturing and shifting from leg to leg as if he was back at the Bastille market. Henri now led us past the factory toward Bonneuil itself, and Sam called to me to go ahead, that he would catch up with me shortly, which he did just as we reached the little town.

In Bonneuil there was not much to see—the church, an old church, always a church—and we passed through the town quickly on our way, it turned out, to another factory that Henri wanted us to see. There was nothing special happening there, and if Henri even mentioned it I do not remember what they made at the place. But he wanted to tell us about how the owner of this factory, who was also the town mayor, had tried to sack the syndicat's foreman the year before, but the syndicat, with the help of the confederation it was connected to— some initials or other, I do not recall which one—had not only forced the owner to back down but had rallied the local people to defeat the owner in the town's next mayor election—replacing him with the very same foreman he had fired. "This town is liberated," Henri said. "Paris next."

By now it was late afternoon and soon we had to meet up with the lorry that would take us back into Paris. We headed toward the river, passing the Lancia factory where Henri stopped to say a few words to Rossetti as the Italian was preparing to leave. While we were walking toward the Paris road, Henri told me a few more things about Rossetti, how he had fought against the fascists in the civil war in Spain, and how he had been a socialist but then become an anarchist—or maybe it was the other way around. He often worked outside proper structures, Henri made a point of saying with some disapproval, but still Rossetti much impressed him, and he said I would likely see more of the man. I never did. Two or three months later he was murdered. It was in all the newspapers, and when I asked Henri about it, about who had killed him, a great sadness came over his face—this was in the summer of '37, Maître, a new and terrible time for Henri and his foreign section, though only a short time after his high spirits on this trip to Bonneuil. "The Italy Fascists, I suppose," he said. And added after a moment, "Unless it was the France Stalinists. Whoever got there first."

Well, that is a different subject—what happened to Henri that summer. Allow me to finish what I was telling you about Bonneuil.

The grinding engine and banging wheels made it impossible to talk in the back of the little lorry as we bumped back into Paris. We arrived in the late evening, near the narrow streets and lanes of Les Halles, where hundreds of trucks and horse carts and wagons from the countryside were already gathering for the next morning's vast daily marketplace of food there. Henri took me aside and told me where I could find him, the address of his foreign section's meeting place, and advised me to come visit. "You have seen us in action," he told me proudly, "and there will be much more to come very soon. With work to go along with it. The Exposition," he said—he meant the huge world's fair they had been building for the past year along the Seine—"will be ours."

Then he noticed Sam, who was standing across the road, waiting for me to finish my conversation. "Your friend," Henri said, "he is clever and a half. But be careful—he has no discipline."

Discipline. The word made me think of my schoolmasters in Hannover. But Henri had already turned and was now speaking to some others in the group, so I did not have a chance to ask him what he meant. Of course he was right about Sam being clever, but as I moved over to join Sam for the walk back to our neighborhoods in the east, I wondered how Henri could have decided such things about this boy he had barely met. Sam and I began to walk, and I noticed a clacking sound coming from the deep pockets of his baggy jacket. After a while I stopped and asked him what the strange noise was. He smiled, proud, and pulled five or six sardine tins from each pocket. I suppose Henri had spotted Sam taking them at Bonneuil, and I wondered what Henri had thought about it—Was that Sam's clever part? Or the no discipline part?

The occasion to ask Henri what he meant about discipline never came up again. Because after what happened to the foreign sections, and to Henri, a couple of months later, it was not a word I heard him use again.

Yours sincerely,
H.

16 April 1941

Maître,

I cannot say for certain that my telling them about the trip to Bonneuil was the cause of it. I was careful not to mention Henri or his foreign section, but even my short description of the factory strike made Uncle Abraham and Tante Chawa nervous.

One night a week or so later Chawa and I were sitting at the table in the front room at Rue Martel when we heard a loud clattering up the stairs and along the corridor, then Abraham burst in, out of breath. He often went on work errands in the evening, so I had not bothered to ask Chawa where he was. But this entrance was a shock, because I had never known Abraham to rush anywhere—I think he believed it would make him appear less dignified, less Monsieur Albert. Now, without taking off his coat, he dropped into a chair and immediately began talking.

He had been to see Bernard—given how much he hated going to Bernard for anything, you can see why I guessed that my trip to Bonneuil might have been behind it. Abraham had asked if Bernard, the piston, could somehow help speed up the ministry's procession of my refugee papers, so that I might have some legal status in France.

Bernard had first scolded Abraham for not asking him to get involved in this matter of documents months earlier, when we had first gone to see him. But Abraham quickly left behind that uncomfortable part of the story in his excitement to get to his real news. Bernard had agreed to set up a meeting for me at the Consistoire, the organization of longtime, top line Paris families, the Rothschilds and their like—not simply israélites but real French. I am sorry, Maître, I do not know what it means, Consistoire. Neither did Abraham, when I asked him. All he knew was that other times, when the regular French used the word, it had something to do with the Catholic church. Why this Consistoire's people chose the word for their own organization you will have to ask one of them. Anyway, Abraham said that this Consistoire had several doors into the Quai d'Orsay—one of the important France state ministries—and many ways to help those they decide are worthy. Bernard himself was not actually a member of the Consistoire—he was three or four generations too new in France—but he had many contacts, he told Abraham, to people who were.

I am certain that having to listen to all this from Bernard must have pained Abraham, but in the telling of it to me he did not show any bother and raced on to say that this was not yet the best part. Bernard had told him something else, something extraordinary, that Bernard himself had just learned when he contacted the Consistoire. It seems that during the summer before, in '36, there had been some kind of proclamation or agreement—Bernard did not know exactly what—by the League of Nations, in Switzerland or wherever they are. And this agreement said that any refugee from Germany who had left the Reich and entered another country between 1933 and the summer of 1936, when this agreement thing was enacted, was given the right to stay in that new country. An actual legal right to live there, Maître, which in France would mean a permis de séjour—the golden paper that so many hoped for and so few received. Abraham sort of recalled hearing something about it back then, but at the time I had not even left Hannover, and I was anyway headed for Belgium not for Paris, so it had not stuck in his mind, especially with all the other decrees and proclamations about refugees that none of us could keep track of.

So, the Consistoire. An official France organization—meaning that whatever they did had the approval of the state. Normally, they only dealt with matters involving israélite France citizens, Bernard had told Abraham, but because of the difficult times they had decided to make an exception. They had begun a program of assisting to refugees from Germany. But only from Germany—since many of their important business associates were in the Reich. This last bit of information Abraham added in a way that made me think it had not come from Bernard. Anyway, one help the Consistoire was giving was to process people under the League of Nations agreement.

Our appointment at the Consistoire was a week later. This was late March, I think. They had their own entire building in the 9th arrondissement, which is on the right side of the river and west toward the Champs Elysées, which might help locate it for you, Maître—the kind of place it was, I mean. Bernard went with me. I do not know what was said between him and Abraham, but I could see that Abraham suffered when I left him behind at Rue Martel that morning. Once Bernard had made it clear that Abraham would not be going with me to the Consistoire, Abraham had asked Bernard to sit down with me sometime, to talk about what would go on there and how I should act. But Bernard had waved off the idea. "He is not the one who matters," he said. Meaning me.

Abraham and Chawa wanted somehow to participate, to help out, and so had tailored a suit for me. Chawa told me to use only the top of the two front buttons—that was the new style, she said—and to quickly unbutton it as I sat down, so no wrinkles would appear.

"Where did you get that suit?" was the first thing Bernard said when I met him outside the Consistoire building that morning. "Ah, I can imagine. Well, it cannot be helped now."

So, we went into the Consistoire building together, Bernard and I. In a large entry hall was a reception desk with a young woman who looked like what a tawny leopard would be if it turned human. She had a long neck and light flowing hair, long arms that a very stylish silky dress left uncovered almost up to her shoulders, with beautiful hands and perfectly manicured nails. Her arms were lying in front of her on the desk, comfortably crossed at the wrists like a cat, as if she would never have to ask them to move. After hearing Bernard's confidant announcement of who he was and that we were expected, she turned her head slightly—as if registering what he said but also wondering about it—then gestured, again with just a slight move of her head and a barely hearable "S'il vous plait," for us to take a seat against a side wall of the reception room. Only when we had been sitting for several moments did she very slowly reach for the telephone on the desk. She spoke a few quiet words, put back the receiver, and returned her arms to the same crossed position on the desk. She did not speak to us, or even glance our way. Was she one of them, I wondered, not a mere israélite but a française d'origine sémitique? Or only someone to give a first impression for them? Perhaps Bernard knew the difference. Not me.

We sat silently in the entry hall for a while. Bernard was not happy. He had not expected to be kept waiting. There was nothing else to see while we sat there for so long, so my eyes kept returning to the young woman, which is perhaps why I recall her so well. I imagined that, under the desk, her legs were the same smooth gold as her arms.

Finally a man came in through a rear door. He took us upstairs to a large, very fine bureau with dark polished wooden floors, which turned out to be only the reception room of the actual bureau, which was even larger and finer, with walls of books in floor-to-ceiling shelves of the same dark wood. Around from behind a grand desk came Monsieur—I am sorry, his name did not stay with me—who smiled in a formal way at Bernard, shook both our hands, and asked us to sit in the upholstered chairs in front of the desk. He was a thin, cold-looking man, with pale skin under dark brows. Somewhat younger than Bernard. And more refined. As we sat there, I was impressed by how his high forehead, and his long hair brushed straight back and smooth, helped make him look so distinguished.

Bernard seemed to relax now that we had passed through the assistant-types and reached someone of position. He gave me a small grin, Bernard—something I had ever seen before. I think it was a grin for himself.

Monsieur whatever-his-name now waited for Bernard to speak. This made Bernard uncomfortable again, as if the fact that Bernard must be the one to open the business at hand was a proof of where each of them stood. Still, Bernard spoke easily, with monsieur smiling and nodding and adding an "Oh, yes," and "Mm, a fine man," when Bernard mentioned three or four people they both knew, which was all Bernard spoke about at the beginning. It was probably the first time in all the months since I had come to Paris that I was able to follow fairly well two French people's conversation—though many of the particular words I did not know. They both spoke so handsomely, without any slang, clearly pronouncing each syllable. And slow—as if there was all the time in the world.

Eventually Bernard came around to the subject of "the little one," as he spoke of me, saying that I had come to Paris from Hannover the previous summer. Monsieur smiled and said, "Ah, Hannover," then turned to me and in excellent German said, "A most energetic city. I have visited often. A number of commercial relations there. And most wonderfully, the Schützenfest, where I was invited to shoot in '33 and '34. In the First Order competition. An Iron Cross in '34. Yes, some excellent memories I have from my time there. Especially among their fine marksmen."

I was happily surprised by monsieur speaking to me in German, but I could see that it upset Bernard. From Budapest originally, Bernard spoke no German, and being left out of the conversation disturbed him. Monsieur must have noticed, because he switched back to French and told Bernard that speaking German was something quite useful in the present world. "N'est-ce pas?"—"Isn't it so?"—he finished, the little phrase seeming to carry a kind of challenge. Bernard's jowly face sagged.

Bernard now let drop entirely the etiquette egg he and monsieur had been so carefully handing back and forth, and asked directly whether the Consistoire could help me get residence papers based on this League of Nations thing. Monsieur smiled just a bit before answering—enjoying for a moment, I think, that Bernard had been the one to show his cards first. Then monsieur went into what sounded like a speech he had delivered many times before, about how any assistance the Consistoire offers must "of course" be first and foremost for those who are French. He then turned to me and repeated the speech in German.

"One must never forget that we are the Consistoire de Paris," monsieur continued in French to Bernard, "and that Paris is in France."

After letting this sink in for a moment, he smiled that formal smile again and said, "Well, let us see now if we can assist the little one." He pressed a button and although I did not hear anything through the thick walls, it must have summoned the man who had shown us in, who now came into the office as monsieur rose from behind his desk to let us know, without saying so, that this interview was finished. We were to go with the assistant to have my request processed, monsieur said, and extended his hand to us. Bernard and I were both taken by surprise at how suddenly this was all over with, and it took us a moment to rise and follow the assistant out the door. It was only when I got up to leave that I noticed that there was not a single paper on monsieur's desk.

We were taken downstairs to a small office toward the rear of the building where we were turned over to a serious young man who sat behind a table partly covered by neat stacks of dossiers. He also spoke German well, and got straightaway to business. Bernard showed no reaction to the young man—I think his mind was still on monsieur upstairs—and as the interview went on, Bernard allowed it more and more to happen in German, without him.

Almost the first thing the young man said was just my family name, pronouncing it with a question mark in his voice. I did not know what he meant by this, and so I said simply "Yes, Grynszpan," and spelled it for him. He tilted his head slightly but did not respond, and wrote down something. Then he asked for the details of when and where I was born, the names of my family, where I had lived, and finally the date when I had entered France. I did not know what the right answer was to this last question, so told him that I was not certain of the exact date but that it was in the summer of the previous year. He said that was good, because the protection of the League would only apply if I was in France before the previous August. He then described what the League agreement actually offered, which was not what Bernard had believed and given me hope for—permanent residence in France—but only a special temporary refugee status. It would give me a legal right to be in France, but technically only while I was "en route" to somewhere else. Bernard and I looked at each other, both of us surprised, as the young man explained all this in alternating French and German. But Bernard and I both understood that even this would be better than the complete nothingness status I had up to then, that any document I could get was better than none, so we hid our disappointment—less difficult for Bernard than for me—and said nothing.

The young man then told us that my French entry visa would give the exact date I arrived in France and asked to see it. I had not expected that, and my heart dropped into my stomach, which had already been paining me for days before the appointment. I must have blanked for a moment, because the young man now asked again, slowly explaining in both German and French, repeating himself as if we had not understood in either language. Finally I had to tell him—that I did not have an entry visa for France. He said, "Well, that will make it something of a problem to show that you entered France within the time set out by the League agreement." But he did not make this sound like the end of the world. "Have you applied for any French documents," he asked, "which could show when you were in the country?" I told him of my trip with Uncle Abraham to the Vallée des Pleurs, but that was not until later in the year, sometime in October, and so did not establish me in France early enough. I also told him that of course Uncle Abraham and Tante Chawa would be able to say that I had arrived in July, but when the young man asked some questions and learned that they were not French citizens, he asked no more about them.

He now turned and asked Bernard if he was a citizen of France. Bernard rose in his chair and said, "Of course"—as if it should have been obvious. Well, the young man said, if Bernard could swear that I was in the country in July, then perhaps—together with other evidence—that would be sufficient. The problem was that, although we had not discussed it, Bernard probably knew from Abraham that I had not actually arrived until the end of August. To my surprise, though, Bernard simply said, "Other evidence? More than my sworn word? As a citoyen?"

"Well," the young man said slowly, "you may be a citizen. But— please excuse me if I am incorrect—I have the sense that you were not born in France."

Bernard was stone faced.

"That your family is not French," the young man continued. "So, if perhaps there are some documents or papers that might support what you would claim."

Now I could see the embarrassed anger rising in Bernard, and I feared that he would say something that would destroy any chance I might have. Although the man had been speaking French to Bernard just now, I had understood enough to know what kind of thing he was looking for, and realized that actually I had it.

"Yes, yes," I said in German, "my exit visa from the Reich. With a stamp on it that shows I left Germany in July—before the deadline."

"Excellent," the young man said—now we were speaking only in German. "Even if it does not show exactly when you entered France, it could show that you became a refugee that summer. Do you have it with you?"

I had brought my papers, the few there were, and from an envelope in my jacket I retrieved my passport with the Reich reentry visa inside, and slid it across the desk to him. He did not pick it up but just stared at it, then slowly raised his head and looked at Bernard and me, from one to the other and back again.

"But this passport is Polish," he said.

"Yes, the passport. But not me. I am from Germany. A refugee from Germany."

"Perhaps," the man replied, then addressed Bernard again, speaking French. "But not a German refugee. To receive the League's protection, the boy must be German."

Bernard could not manage a sound. A red stain spread under the skin around his perfect white collar.

"In fact," the young man was now saying, pushing the papers back toward me but continuing to speak to Bernard, "we cannot help him here at all. With the League agreement or otherwise. You see, the Consistoire has agreed to give refugee assistance, but strictly limited to Germans."

"Yes, German," I quickly put in. "As I am. From Hannover. Born there. My whole life there. As I have told you. German."

"No, I am afraid you have not understood," the young man said, shaking his head. "Whether you are German is not for you to say. It is for us. And others."

Sincerely,
H.

Maître, I argued with myself for several hours about whether to put this letter in your envelope as I finished it above, and give it to the

153

guards when I reported for my work. Or to wait, and write to you about something else that has been troubling me, which is what I have decided to do. My trial, Maître. I have now been almost five months in Sachsenhausen, and so far you have given me no word about when the trial will be. I believe that you also must be interested to know, since after all that is what we are preparing for, what we are working toward, together. And I can only suppose that the authorities also would want to hold the trial soon. I cannot imagine that the Reich would fail to bring about proper and orderly proceedings against the one who shot vom Rath, a state official, after all—especially after the many honors and salutes the Reich provided him, following his death. Yes, of course I can understand that there are likely to be many who are not keen to hear me speak out in the courtroom about my family's treatment, their shipment to the Poland border, their fate. Which would also bring up, I suppose, the question of the thousands sent with them. But that has not seemed to overly trouble the Reich before, since they have chosen from the beginning to invite the world press to the trial. Though I must admit, I have yet to understand why.

So, Maître, I feel that I must break my silence on these worries and ask that you do your best to learn when the trial will be scheduled. To speak with those who decide. I do not assume to advise you on your responsibilities, Maître. But I think you will agree that a trial soon would be the right thing. Not just for me. For all concerned.

26 April 1941

Maître Rosenhaus,

It was in the 16th arrondissement, Bernard's new apartment. A posh and quiet part of the city—in the west, near the Bois de Boulogne, the huge park and woods there. Though the place being new for Bernard meant nothing to me, since I had never before been to his home, this or any other. The few times I had gone with Uncle Abraham to see Bernard, it had always been at the atelier above Au Courant Dame—Bernard's fancy boutique in the central city—or at one of Bernard's big workrooms near the Gare de l'Est train station. But now I had been called to Bernard's home. I did not know why.

I stood outside the large impressing building, wondering where I should go. I was facing the front gate, part of a high black iron fence that stood between the pavement and a garden that was almost like a small private park. The building was set in the middle of this garden, about 15 or 20 meters back from the fence. I was not certain that this was where I should enter, because there was also a cinder path outside the fence along the side of the building, and a gate toward the back where I saw two young women wearing thin, poor coats—something I could easily see, Maître, even from a distance—scurrying along the path, through that gate, and into the building by a rear door. Also a coal deliveryman, with black smears on his work clothes and empty sacks, coming out the same door and heading to his wagon that waited further down the road.

The building itself was smaller but from the outside not so different in style from the one on Rue Martel where Abraham and Chawa now lived, with iron balconies on the first two floors and a narrow top fifth floor under a slate roof that slanted back from the main walls. It was the setting that made it feel so completely different—the neighborhood, the quiet street with no traffic or shops or even people walking by, the large trees along the pavement, the high fences and gardens in front of and around all the buildings, and quite some space between one building and the next. Also their condition, the houses, the whole street, with soot-free walls and gold-painted railings and gleaming brass fittings and polished hardwood doors.

This was about two weeks after our disappointment at the Consistoire. No, that is saying it too softly—Bernard had not even been able to look at me as we left the Consistoire bureau that day. And for him not just anger at their refusal to help but also a terrible embarrassment, it seemed, the failure of his famous contacts, right in front of my eyes. He had left me standing there in the rain that had begun while we were inside, with barely a grunt of goodbye as he put up his umbrella and rumbled away.

The experience at the Consistoire, plus Bernard's cold turning away from me, had gone straight to my gut. By the time I made it back to Rue Martel that day—I walked all the way, despite the rain, afraid to go down into the Métro or onto a bus I felt so ill—I was thoroughly soaked and had retched two or three times, badly staining my new suit.

For the next several days I kept to my pallet in a chambre de bonne in the attic at Rue Martel—fortunately, one of the little rooms had again become empty, and I had moved in my straw paillasse two days before—so ill that I did not even go down to see Abraham and Chawa. I scribbled them a short note a few hours after I returned, saying only that the interview had gone fine but that we would not know anything for a while, and that I would be out spending time with friends. I did not want to worry them with either the bad news from the Consistoire or my illness, so I simply slipped the paper under their door and crept back up to the room tucked below the eaves.

Several times over that day and night I had to stagger out and downstairs to the toilet on the floor below, then crawl back up and collapse onto to the pallet. My awful retching sounds, and the noises I made in my fevered sleep, must have been quite disturbing, because in the early hours of the next morning I heard a soft tapping and "Monsieur... Monsieur?" in a strange accent. I managed to get to the door and there was a dark-haired, dark-eyed young woman standing out in the hallway—she took a couple of steps back when I opened the door, perhaps at the sight of my vomit-stained and still rain-damp trousers and waistcoat, which I had not had the strength to remove.

"Are you all right?" she asked in French, with what I learned was a Spanish accent. Or Basque, as she made a point to me later. From the Basque country. Which is in Spain, but not Spanish. At least, as close as I came to understanding it. Mirari is her name. Mirari Iriguay.

"Do you need help?" She had a thin robe wrapped around her, as if she had just come from her own bed, and at a noise from the door of the neighboring room I turned to see two little heads sticking out into the hall, small children, a girl and a boy about six or seven years old. Most recently I had again been spending nights downstairs at Abraham and Chawa's, and before that in a different empty attic room on the other side of the building, so this was the first I had seen of them. Mirari and her children were living crammed into the tiny room next to the one where I was now staying. Or I should say that Mirari, the children, and piles of stiff leather were crammed into the room. Because that is what she and the children did most of the day and night—cut leather for the bottoms of shoes, for some atelier that paid her a few sous per sole. Her husband was fighting the war in Spain, she later told me, and when the Franco army was about to run over the town where they lived, she and the children fled in the night and made it to the French border, which was the closest place of safety. After a month in a small village there, paying to live in a barn, she was able to get a message to her husband. He put her in touch with some supporters in Paris, who helped her find this room and arranged for her to get the leather work. Other than that, she and the children were on their own. She had not heard from her husband for two months.

That first morning when she came to the door, I could manage to say only "I am sorry—my stomach," before retreating into the room and crumbling again onto my pallet. A while later there was a soft knock, and when I made some small noise but could not get up, Mirari eased open the door and came in. She had a bowl with her, and in it some sort of creamy milk food, warm, with rice mixed in. She told me it would be good for my stomach, helped me eat a few spoonfuls, put the bowl on the floor next to me, and left. I waited, and when the strange mixture did not come up again from my gut I tried a few more swallows, and eventually managed to eat all of it. I was feeling a bit better in the afternoon when she again knocked on the door, and as soon as she noticed the empty bowl and me sitting up, she nodded, as if she expected it. "My name is Mirari," she said with a small sad smile—which is the most I ever saw her manage. "It means 'miracle.'"

For the next two days Mirari made me this sweet milk and rice mixture on the little spirit stove in her room, until I was feeling well enough to move around again, and to visit Abraham and Chawa downstairs, and within another day to start going out. Mirari and I became friends. She said I reminded her so much of her little brother, who was also caught up in the Spanish war. She showed me his picture. The photo was not very clear, and it had been badly creased when she stuffed a few things into a sack in the rush to flee their town, but I could see how much he did look like me, in his size and color and long black hair, even the shape of his head. So, after my arrest when those French doctors measured my head and wrote about the race type I could have been, they should have added Spanish. Or Basque.

Sometimes I helped Mirari work on the leather, when she or the children were ill, or for some other reason she fell behind, and at times I would look after the children when she needed to go out without them. Euskadi ta Askatasuna—Land and Freedom—the children taught me, in the Basque language, and how to count in Basque and Spanish, always with laughter at my pronouncing. It was good to give them something to laugh about. In the following months I always tried to snap up extra food for them when I went to the Bastille market. And nights were still damp and bitter cold in the draughty top-floor rooms there, so I got Sam to bring me mittens for the children. Fur mittens.

27 April

My apologies, Maître. I had begun to speak about going to see Bernard at his new home, and somehow got onto a side road about Mirari and her children. Allow me to redo my steps.

That day I reported to Bernard's home—which is what it felt like, reporting to the school headmaster's room—I did not know why he had called on me. I wore the best clothes I had other than the new suit Abraham had made me for the Consistoire appointment, which Bernard had disapproved of, and anyway was soiled by my sickness of the previous week. But apparently even these best clothes of mine, and perhaps something else about me, sent a message to the concierge, who arrived at the building's large double entry doors after I decided to come in through the front gate. Because as soon as she saw me she scowled and demanded "Where are you going?" Though perhaps she met everyone in that same irritated way, since a visitor meant obliging her to come out of her little loge on the inner courtyard. Or maybe it was the opposite—she was bitter because so much of the time she was stuck in there.

I told her that I had come to see Monsieur Blucher—that is Bernard's family name, did I tell you? "What is your business with him?" she asked roughly—she was large and pale and scary, and when she spoke, her fleshy jaw and cheeks moved up and down and side to side all at the same time, like the rear end of a cart horse. I said, truthfully, that I did not know but that I was expected. She looked at me oddly, as if trying to decide on the answer to another question that she had not asked. Finally, she motioned me to the side of the building, saying "Service entrance," and stood with her arms crossed as if barring my way should I decide not to follow her instructions. I started out the door but then turned back to her and managed to croak out "I am a cousin."

She stared at me for a moment, then said, "Ah, that explains it." What did it explain? "Wait here," she said and went back into her loge. I could hear her speak on a telephone but could not make out the words. After a minute she stuck her head out and said, "Second floor, first door on the right," then disappeared back into her loge.

I made my way up a big winding staircase and found that the door to Bernard's flat, which took up the entire second floor of the building, was already open. Waiting for me there was a woman with narrow bony shoulders and a pinched, bird-like face, wearing a maid's uniform. This was Clarice, Bernard and Elsa's French femme de ménage—the housemaid who worked for them all day but did not sleep there.

Elsa. Have I ever mentioned her? Bernard's wife? Who was Aunt Chawa's actual cousin? Maybe not, since I had only met her once before, at Bernard's atelier, and who had barely spoken three words to me. She did not work at Au Courant Dame or Bernard's ateliers—or anywhere else as far as I know—and she and Bernard never visited with Abraham and Chawa, so I had never but that one time crossed her path. She was a small, pear-shaped woman with a lovely soft voice, who spoke French as well as Bernard did, or so it seemed to me. She had been in France almost as long as he had, marrying him in Budapest before the Great War and accompanying him back to Paris, where by then he had established himself. In all her years in Paris, though, she had never been able to lose entirely her Hungaria accent. Which might explain why she spoke so softly, and often hesitated when she needed to make a decision or give a direction. Though perhaps there was something else behind this hesitating, something that Clarice the housemaid understood and took boldness from. Clarice showed none of the respect and carefulness around Elsa that I later saw from other servers in fancy Paris households. True French households, I mean.

Clarice let me into the apartment, with Elsa standing almost imme-diately behind her—something Clarice's expression said she thought was less than entirely proper. Elsa did not seem to notice Clarice's unpleasure and greeted me quite warmly, to my surprise. She brought me into a salon, or salle de séjour, or some other type of parlor, I am not really certain what they called it, or why—there were several names for rooms like this, rooms that all seemed alike to me, and I could never make out which name went with which one or how it was decided.

In the minute or so it took to reach the parlor and get settled, I wondered what it was about the place—besides the obvious things, the large rooms and fine furnishings, the electric lights—that made it seem so different from Abraham and Chawa's apartment on Rue Martel. And I realized that part of it was the smell—perfume, floor wax, silver polish. Nothing like the sewing machine oil and kerosene at Maison Albert. Or the onions and mold, and sulfur against bugs, in the rooms where I had followed Sam on some of his ventures.

Elsa asked Clarice to fetch Monsieur, and perhaps thinking that I did not understand even such simple French, told me quietly in Yiddish—once Clarice had left the room—that Blucher would join us right away. Elsa did not say anything else while we waited, as if she felt that Bernard needed to be present for even the smallest of talk. It seemed so curious to me that she used Blucher, his family name— their family name, for after all she was Madame Blucher—when she spoke of him. And as it turned out still more curiously, even when she spoke to him directly—"Ah, Blucher, there you are," she said when he finally entered. At first I thought it was just a way for her to show their high respectability. And of paying some kind of honor to him, or at least to his position. Though at the same time that placed herself somewhat lower. But as I saw them together over the next months, I sensed something else—a kind of distance in the way she said the name, even a hurtfulness. Perhaps because Bernard encouraged such a difference in their positions, or at least had allowed it to exist over all their years together.

Bernard began speaking to me almost as soon as he came through the doorway, ignoring Elsa and leading me out of the room, down a hallway, and into the kitchen, which was connected to a large pantry and on the other side to a rear hallway and door, and where a cook—a round red-faced woman whose painted hair did not quite cover the gray—was busy taking out of an oven something that smelled wonderfully of butter. Bernard did not bother to introduce us, and there was nothing particular he showed me in the kitchen. I suppose it just seemed to him the right place for talking to me.

He had work for me, he said. I was jolted. Abraham had told me nothing about the reason Bernard had asked to see me—probably Bernard never told him. Since he had not before offered me any work in the eight or nine months I had been in Paris, I thought later that that this might have been his way of covering over his failure at the Consistoire. But at the time I was too surprised to think about the why of it.

In a few weeks he and Elsa would be having a dinner party, Bernard told me, the first in their new apartment. There would be a dozen or so guests—people of substance, he said, business associates, some of them important members of "the community," as he put it. The cook, with help from an assistant specially hired, would manage the food duties—he spoke about the cook as if she was not there in the same room—but he would need people to serve drinks and hors d'oeuvres to the guests, and then at the table during dinner. Bernard spoke French to me, slowly and clearly, pausing once in a while for me to indicate that I understood. I think he wanted to repeat some things in Yiddish, to be certain that I was following what he said, but he was not willing to with the cook there and with Clarice coming in and out, so after a few minutes he took me into another room, a small sitting room, where we were alone. I realized now that the perfume I had smelled was coming from him.

In Yiddish mixed with French, he explained that he was putting together a group of six or so of his atelier workers—ones who had picked up French well and could speak it without heavy accents—to be the servers at this party. He did not tell me why he was not hiring French people who were experienced in such work. At first I imagined it was simply because it would cost him less to use his own workers but later I doubted this was the reason. I did not understand about people with money, when they decide to spend it and when not. Particularly someone like Bernard, whose money had not been around very long. But when I served at the party itself it was clear that Bernard had spared no expense, and would not likely have worried about paying the price for French serving staff. Something else must have been going on with Bernard, because using foreigners brought some real risks—What if they did poorly? Made faux pas? Showed their foreign-ness? No, thinking back on it afterward, it seemed there was a different, greater risk that Bernard was trying to avoid, something that worried him far more if he did use French workers—the possibility of their disrespect to him in front of his guests. The kind that seemed to crouch behind the eyes of Clarice the maid, the French maid, every time she was in the same room as Bernard or Elsa.

He told me that he had been impressed by how I had handled myself at the Consistoire, and at my greatly improved French, and thought that I was now ready to take on work from him, beginning with this dinner party serving. I had never before heard a positive word from Bernard, let alone compliments. I was flattered. And so accepted them as true. Which they were, as far as they went. But I knew from Sam's teasing that actually I still spoke French with a heavy German accent, and as Bernard continued to talk, I sensed that something else was going on about why he was offering me the work.

We were family, Bernard was saying, and the bonds of family are a source of great satisfaction. He leaned back in his chair, as if he was now a patriarch blessing me with drops of wisdom. Family is a source of trust in hard times, he said. And of strength.

Well, something like that—I was not paying close attention to what seemed just blabber from him. Especially since this idea of family had not moved him before now to lift a hand for me in all the months I had already been in Paris. Also, his Hungaria Yiddish was odd to me, and quite simple and thin, worn away by lack of use over his years in Paris, so getting any real sense of him was anyway not so easy. But finally he got around to what this family and trust talk was truly about.

On the night of the dinner, he told me, he would have some special duties for me, which he would explain later. But he also wanted me to keep a "family eye" on things that night. These atelier workers of his would need to cooperate with Clarice and the cook and her assistant, and working with French people was not something these clothing façonniers were used to. They also were not used to this kind of high proper serving—although I soon learned from Bernard that we were all to have training sessions the following week. And they were not used to being around people "of a certain dignity," as Bernard put it—meaning his guests, his French guests. He and Elsa would be busy as hosts, he said, and they would not be able to keep an eye on what was going on in the kitchen and pantry. Or elsewhere in the apartment. He would count on me to let him know of any problems. And—he finally mentioned as if it was the last and least thing on his mind—there were many things of value in the house.

It is Sunday night, Maître, and although I want to go on writing, I feel somewhat weak, so I will stop now. Which will allow me to give this to the guards in the morning to post, or however it travels to you, since I know that I will not write tomorrow. You see, I have decided to fast on Mondays. Every Monday. Until my trial date is set. I have written to you about this, asking when the trial will be, but I have heard nothing from you in return.

In the Paris jail also I fasted every Monday. To atone for my actions. The taking of a life. And the horrors of Kristallnacht that followed. But also for my other unrighteous acts. Of which there were more than a few. So, from those months in the Paris jail I have experience of fasting, and know that it robs me of my concentration. I was unable to write in my diary at Fresnes on fasting days, and often the day after, when my stomach would trouble me. And so I feel quite certain that I will not be able to write to you tomorrow. I am confident that you will understand.

Yours, H.

Maître Rosenhaus,

I am most appreciating of your visit yesterday, after not hearing anything from you these past weeks. Though as you saw from my condition, my own silence during these weeks was not due to illness. Or my fasting—as you seemed to have worried.

No, Maître, it was a decision, not writing. My life is reduced to one idea—the opportunity to speak. And these past months I have come to believe, as you have urged me, that my writings are the best way for me to prepare. Which means that setting aside my pencil was not easy. But as I tried to explain when you were here yesterday, over the past weeks I became determined not to continue until I knew that my trial would be set in due course.

So, an inditement, you tell me—pardon me if that is not the spelling, but I forgot to ask you—the first formal part of the Reich's trial procedures. I learned a great deal about French proceedings during my long time in the Paris jail, but I know nothing of law things here. And yes, from your explaining I can see that it could take some time to gather the evidence of support—Is that what you called it?—needed to prepare this thing, this inditement. Especially since it all happened in Paris. Well, most of it. But the court being in Berlin.

And yes I can also understand when you say that part of the delay is how carefully things are done by the Reich. Which I appreciate. Have always appreciated. But still, Maître, it has been nine months since I was brought back to Germany. Of course, it was 20 months I was in the French jail and still they did not manage it, a trial. But surely, Maître, the Reich is more certain than the French about what it is doing. Officially, I mean. Well, at least this inditement is underway. Preparations for the trial. Progress. I am encouraged.

So. The work Bernard would have for me. At his dinner party. I was telling you, yes? But other things had begun to happen also. All of a sudden. It was the start of busy months for me. The first time there was a slight crack in the Paris walls. The only time.

I had several days between that first visit to Bernard's apartment and the evening when I was to report back there for my beginning to train as a server. Meanwhile, I went looking for my friend Henri who had been so positive, so promising, at the end of our trip to Bonneuil. The day after seeing Bernard I headed to the address Henri had given me for his foreign section, on a small street near the Gare de Lyon train station, not far south of Bastille. I found the place easily enough, a little storefront with three or four people busy inside. But no Henri. The people there said that I could most likely find him at their larger bureau, that Henri was now there most days, over near the Citroën factory at Javel, on the river, in the southwest corner of the city.

I had no idea how to get all the way over there—I had gone in that direction only a couple of times before, with my friend Sam leading the way, and only as far as the Montparnasse cafés where Sam some-times did a bit of pavement performing, trying to catch a tourist's eye. Walking now all the way to this other bureau was not something I was willing for—it was across the whole width of the city, and an unhappy rain had already soaked me on my much shorter walk to this closer foreign section bureau in the east. I had just bought, secondhand, one of those flat caps that Henri and his worker friends all wore, and this was my first time to use it. But somehow I could not manage to fit it on correctly, it kept shifting around, and in the end did not keep much rain off my head and neck. I could have got onto the Métro, the under-ground tram, but I was still not used to it, and anyway the bus cost less. So I crossed the river to the nearby Gare d'Austerlitz, knowing that many buses depart from outside the train stations. It was so calm and orderly that day, the station. Nothing like the chaos and misery I would see there three years later—my last ever view of Paris.

Outside the station I found a bus that went to the Tour Eiffel, which I had never seen up close but now realized from a map at the bus stop was not far from where I was heading. I watched as best I could out the steamy bus window as we traveled through the rain past the edge of the French student area, down the long crowded bustle of

Boulevard Montparnasse, and finally out onto a road that runs beside the Champ de Mars—a huge rectangle of fields and gardens that starts at the Tour Eiffel and stretches a kilometer or so in from the river. At the time, though, none of the gardens were left there, no green of any kind. Instead, it looked like a small city inside of Paris but somehow completely separate from it, and which was recovering from a war or giant earthquake that had magically stayed only and exactly within its boundaries. There were enormous piles of stone and brick and lumber and dirt, and machinery and half-built buildings of every size and shape all over the huge space, only a few of them finished—including two towering cement-block monuments just on the other side of the river, each with giant statues on top, facing off like guard dogs on chains, straining to get at each other. They were separated, these two massive buildings, by an open space that led up to a huge, wide Roman sort of palace on a hill overlooking the construction and river below. There was scaffolding everywhere—red flags hanging from some of it—and thousands of people, most of them doing constructing but some just marching around outside particular building sites where there seemed to be no work going on. All of this in the endless dreary rain, which more than anything else left me with an impression of the place as a sea of mud, everywhere mud. This was to be a main section of the Exposition Universelle, Maître—the World's Fair—scheduled to open in just a few weeks but seeming, as I passed by it on the bus, more likely by then to have sunk into the Seine.

The bus stopped next to the famous tower and I got off and started walking south along the river, forced to go a few streets inland from the river itself, though, because also along the banks there was constructing going on for the Expo, as well as on the other side of the river and even on an island in the middle. The rain had now stopped, so I slowed my steps to get a better look at this district of the city where I had never been before. At one point I saw down a side road a building that looked, from a few blocks away, like a slightly smaller version of the train station where I had started the bus ride, five or six stories high with a massive glass and iron roof. Except I could not see any train tracks, and while a few people were going in and out, there was no hurrying crowd as at a station, and no one carrying baggage. I decided to take a closer look, and when I reached the entrance I saw advertising signs that showed bicycle races inside the place, on a large oval track—a vélodrome, they called the place—with enormous tiers of spectator seating all around, a kind of stadium but all indoors. There was also an advertisement showing ice skating in the open center of the oval, although those dates had passed, and another for roller skating. I took a peek inside, and saw people on the other side of the entryway, hiring skates at a cloakroom counter.

Roller skates. I had a pair in Hannover, Maître, and used them often during summers. Secondhand, the skates, but good as new after my father had repaired them and cleaned them up. Did I tell you that he was a fixer of things, my father? I wrote to you some about my family, and my time at school. But it has been quite a while now, and I cannot remember what I said. Probably nothing about roller skates.

I walked for another few minutes until I found the foreign section bureau. It was bigger—two large connecting rooms—and much busier than the one on the east side of the city, with groups of men in worker clothes, and a few groups of women, scattered around the place talking with each other and looking at paperwork and newspapers. I spotted Henri as soon as I reached the doorway. He was in an agitating conversation—his hands darting around in front of him in a way that did not seem very French to me—with three other men, but he saw me almost immediately and waved me in as he went on with his jabbering. I stood just to their side for a few minutes while they continued their argument but they were speaking so fast and with so much slang that I had no idea what they were talking about. Finally they seemed to agree on something, the little group broke up, and Henri took me over to a quieter corner of the room.

Before either of us said anything, I pulled from my pocket the receipt the police had given me, showing that I was properly registered in the country now, and handed it to him. I could not help grinning. He looked at it for a moment and nodded, but said only "Good," and handed it back to me. What did "good" mean? I stopped grinning. He was glad to see me, he said, and told me I had come at the right moment. Action—that was his single word of explaining this moment, pronounced in a way that let you hear all the letters both separately and together and the saying of it almost lifting him off the ground. He gestured with his head for me to look around the room at all the busy people, then told me a bit of what was going on. This bureau had been set up there several years before, Henri said, because of the big Citroën factory down the road and the huge Renault works just across the river in Boulogne-Billancourt, and other factories also nearby. All the big industrial guilds and syndicats also had bureaus near there. Most of the foreign sections were now connected with the CGT—the biggest laborer confederation of them all—and over the last two years or so, especially since the beginning of constructing on the Expo Universelle, things had been moving heavy and fast. There was organizing and strikes and other action at the giant auto factories, not to mention battles there between different syndicats, and also lots of new work at the Expo, with many work-stoppages and strikes and such there also. In fact, Henri said, he and several of his comrades—I remember being impressed by the word, the way he used it so ordinary—were about to head up to the Expo to look in on one of the building sites, to see whether there was any extra work today for people from his foreign section. Did I want to go along?

Eight or ten of us walked in the direction I had just come, including one boy a few years older than me who I had seen around the Sportclub Aurore, a Russian Polish boy who was often part of politics arguments at the Aurore and who had been along on the trip to Bonneuil. I also thought I recognized one of the men from the group at the bal musette, the night of the Frankfurter rally, and worried that he might remember me from that time of my embarrassment, but he did not seem to. Or did not care. Despite the break from the rain, the few men who were not already wearing their flat caps immediately put them on when we stepped outside. I had earlier stuffed my own unfitting cap into my back trousers pocket, under my jacket. I left it there.

After a couple of blocks a lorry rumbled up. The driver called out to us and stopped so we could climb into the open back where we rode, standing alongside piled sacks of cement, the rest of the way up to the Expo. I remember trying to avoid the pools of rain-mixed cement powder that was spilled all over the lorry's bed, then saw that the others did not bother.

Up close, the Expo site looked even more of a mess than when I had passed it on the bus. We got off the lorry and picked our way through the mud, past crowds of dirt-caked workers and machines, around piles of materials and the skeletons of buildings. In the half-built jumble it seemed impossible to know one place, one building site from another—there must have been 100 of them. But as Henri and his friends moved steadily forward, he would sometimes point out a particular shell and tell me what it was to become—the Alsace Pavilion, the Hall of Rail Travel, that sort of thing—and the particular syndicats that were working on it, though the names meant nothing to me.

We finally reached the far side of the Champ de Mars, then moved beyond it to another area along the Seine where Expo buildings were also going up. We stopped at a site that backed onto the river, a building that seemed almost finished and that had more workers, with more activity, than any of the others we had passed. Red flags flew from the building's scaffolding, and most of the workers had red kerchiefs around their necks. Henri explained that this was the Hall of Work, dedicated to the laborers of France themselves, and that although it had been approved and funded only recently, it was further along than most other sites, and would be ready—unlike most of the buildings—for the Expo opening the following month. That, he said, hunching himself up to his full height, was because only CGT members were allowed to work on this building.

Henri's group gathered around a couple of men who they seemed to know, while Henri moved over to shake hands with someone else, introducing me as H and calling me a "copain"—a pal—which I remember gave me a small shake of pleasure. At least, until I realized that everyone else there he called "comrade."

Henri discussed with this man how the constructing was going and whether the site could use more workers that day from Henri's foreign section. This man then went over to the group we had arrived with and set them—including the boy from the Aurore—to work on a pile of building materials. I watched them for a moment, then realized that Henri was already headed elsewhere and had stopped to wait for me.

We walked around to the side of the building, where Henri spoke with another of the workers. Just then there was a commotion behind us, 20 meters or so out away from the building, with two or three red-kerchief workers arguing, yelling, cursing at several other workers, who were giving it back just as strong. The groups were standing on two different temporary wooden walkways they each were constructing to give safe passage across the mud, one out from the Hall of Work and the other coming from another building site across the way, both aimed toward a more permanent cement pathway. The two temporary walkways were headed to cross paths in the middle of the open space, and apparently neither group intended to give way. Now several other men joined in from the other site, and were quickly matched by men from the Hall of Work. Suddenly several of the men were fighting, and others from each side rushed in, swinging and kicking. It was wild and ugly and frightening, the men breaking through the makeshift wooden handrails of each other's walkway, crashing onto the boards and wrestling in the mud. More men rushed from the Hall of Work into the fight, which now took up much of the space between the two building sites.

I do not remember how or where I got it from, Maître, but when I felt Henri pulling me back toward the Hall of Work I realized that I had a large piece of wood in my hand and had been wading out in the mud toward the fight. Henri took me back to the edge of the pavilion, and from that safer distance we watched for a minute as the fight carried on, other men pouring in from neighboring sites. After a few minutes the battle slowed and eventually stopped, with the fighters retreating to their own sides. Henri looked down at the wood I was still gripping tightly, and I threw it aside. He said nothing, but a quick smile sneaked across his face.

Henri now led me away from the trouble and out of the Expo. We found a small bar a few blocks away, after Henri had passed up several other places—too fancy he said of two cafés, looking in at well dressed customers, too "catholique" he said of another bar, somehow able to recognize that the men in work clothes who filled that particular place were not of his liking. At a corner table at the place where we finally settled, Henri gave me a sort of word map of the Expo, and of what had just happened there. It seemed to me a long story, though I suppose it was actually a very short version.

19 May

All the arguments of Paris were jammed together there. The way Henri explained it, the Expo sounded like a giant laboratory where the scientists were all competing against each other but had to use the same test tubes. When the Expo construction had been planned several years before, Henri said, the business people of Paris had all been strongly behind it. The government—and other countries also, for each one's own pavilion—would spend incredible amounts of money, the companies in charge of constructing the different Expo sites would be hugely paid, and many of the other businesses of Paris would make millions from the people who came to visit during the half year the Expo was to be open. The workers, on the other hand, were not all of the same mind about it. Not all of the same mind about much of anything, Henri said. There were dozens of different guilds and syndicats in Paris, not just depending on the jobs they did—metal workers, constructing workers, electric workers and so forth—but also larger worker groups, confederations they were called, that the individual syndicats were part of. And each confederation was connected with a political group—left parties, right parties, more left, more right. They were so big, some of these confederations, they were political movements all by themselves.

I hope I am making sense to you about all this, Maître—I cannot recall the details of what Henri told me that day, or of other bits and pieces I heard over the following few months, and to be honest I did not understand it very well even at the time. Please excuse me for speaking about things I do not know well, but they are part of what happened to Henri during that spring and summer of 1937. And so, in the end, to me.

At the start of constructing the Expo there were several worker groups who were quite happy with things. These were the syndicats catholiques, Henri called them, though he never explained to me exactly why—I mean, all the real French are catholique, as far as I could tell, so? Anyway, these syndicats catholiques seemed to get along very well with the employers and so were happy to have all the Expo work with no questions to ask. But many of the other syndicats, the ones connected to the left parties, were not so keen. They were in the middle of long struggles with the employers, and though of course they were tempted by all the work that building the Expo could offer, they did not want to give up their bigger fight. Also, many of them were furious that in the middle of the terrible Great Depression the government was spending so much on what Henri called a giant circus. So, the confederation that Henri's foreign section was connected to became a part of a larger one, the CGT, along with other left confederations and syndicats whose initials I cannot give you because I could never keep them straight. And for the past year, Henri said, they had taken their fight against the employers onto the Expo grounds, where they led many slow-downs and strikes and occupations. Also combat with the syndicats catholiques. That brawl Henri and I had just come from, in the mud outside the Hall of Work? About nothing. And everything. Left workers and catholiques, going at each other, once again.

Yes, and also Communists, Maître. Part of Henri's confederation. How many times when I was in the Paris jail, and then at the Gestapo—though thinking back on it, not nearly as often from them as from the French—was I asked, "And what about the Communists?" As if, in the end, the answer to that question must be the answer to everything. Well yes, the CGT now had official Communists in it, Henri told me, but also socialists and anarchists and syndical-anarchos and councilists and I do not know what else. So? They were even in the France Chamber of Deputies, the Communists. I mean, they were not some secret society, Maître. It is not as if they were Masons.

Was Henri a Communist? I am sure you would ask me that next,

Maître, if you were here. But I do not know. He never said. And I never asked. Never thought to ask. But the foreign sections, yes, it was the Communist confederation they were connected to. For a time. After what happened later that summer, though, if Henri had himself been a Communist, he certainly was not any longer. Except, perhaps, somewhere deep in his broken heart.

Let me go back, Maître, to how Henri explained things to me. I mean about the Expo and its strikes and all its other chaos. In 1936 the Popular Front had become the government in France—well, of course that you know. And after some big strikes by the confederations, to let everyone know they did not intend to wait around for the politicians to do something for them, the workers won a big agreement from the employers—the 40-hour week, paid holidays, and other such things they had long been fighting for and which had included many dis-ruptings during the first years building the Expo. But then it became the Popular Front that was responsible for finishing the Expo, and since they had helped pressure the employers into the big agreement with the confederations, they wanted the left syndicats to cooperate, to make the constructing go smoothly. And to add meat to the pot, they promised the syndicats that when the Expo was finished, the government would also spend money on new public works—a big hospital, sewers for the old parts of the city, and other such things. These projects would not only give more work for the syndicats but also bring some good to parts of Paris that would get nothing out of the Expo—except higher prices and more batons for the police.

So, the left syndicats had begun to work hard at the Expo sites. Then the shoe moved to the other foot—it was now the syndicats catholiques who were not so happy. They did not want to make the Popular Front—the Socialists and Communists they hated, and also Léon Blum—look good by finishing the Expo on time, so now they began to cause troubles there. And then it got even more complicated. Early in 1937, a few months before I first showed up at Henri's foreign section place, word had leaked out that the government was backing out of the big public works projects they had promised for after the Expo. So now the left syndicats were striking again, off and on, at the same time as the syndicats catholiques, off and on, with the two sides of workers still fighting each other, and the Expo became one giant muddy brawling pit, with nothing getting finished. Except for the German pavilion. And the Soviet. Because their governments had separately poured extra money into the construction and so had them completed early—these were the two huge cement blocks directly facing each other across the plaza on the right bank of the river. Also the Hall of Work, where Henri and I had just been, was nearly finished—because the CGT had demanded to build it without help or interference from any syndicats not in its confederation, and they wanted to show Paris and the employers what they could do when they decided to. But for the rest of the Expo? It had been scheduled to open May 1, in just a few weeks, and already the government had postponed it. So, in the push to get it all finished, there was now a lot of extra work, most of it for people connected to the CGT, like Henri's foreign section was. Though which buildings would actually be done in time, and which ones not, was anybody's guess, Henri said. And did not look the least bit concerned when he said it.

I was so captured by how Henri told me this long tale—not so much what he said, Maître, or his knowledge of it all, but his feeling, the way his voice became so full of gravel—plus the glass of wine I had drunk, and the warmth of the little bar on my wet head and feet, that I did not realize he had finished. Or if not finished, at least decided that was as much as I could take in one go. He was standing up, and said he was going back to his bureau to hear the reports from the Expo that day. Was I going that direction? At that moment I would have said yes if he had told me he was jumping into the Seine.

But I had another reason to stay close to him. Despite his mention of work on the first day I met him, and again at Bonneuil, and his telling of how the Expo now offered a rush of extra jobs, he still had not said anything about work for me. Even after I had shown him my paper, my official French receipt. After all, that Polish boy from the Aurore, or Russian, whichever he was, he had been put to work. So, as Henri set out again toward his foreign section bureau, I tried to keep up conversation about what I had seen that day, though without asking directly about anything for me. You see, Maître, Henri is French. And one thing I had learned—from Bernard, from shopkeepers, from concierges, from the fonctionnaires behind every public desk or window—was that asking a direct question marked you in some way, with something they wanted no part of. And was never met with a straight answer. Though for me to have included Henri in this type of Frenchman shows how poorly I understood him at the time. Or Paris.

We had not gone far when it started to rain again, harder than it had in the morning, so despite my uncomfort about it I pulled out the flat workman's cap I had stashed in my back pocket. If Henri thought anything of this he did not say, and just being able to put the cap on without getting a strange look seemed to me a step in the right direction. We were now almost running to get out of the rain, with conversation impossible, and I feared that once we got to the foreign section bureau Henri would immediately dive into the commotion of his comrades and I would lose any chance to bring up the subject of work for me. The rain became so heavy at one point that we ducked under a corner awning, but after a few moments a concierge leaned out of a window in the courtyard behind us and croaked at us to move along. As she and Henri exchanged insults, down the side street I noticed the big bicycle racing building, the vélodrome, and without actually thinking about it I said to Henri "Over there, I know a place, come on." He gave me a strange look but after a moment followed me down the block—I think he was so surprised I had stuck my head out of my shell that he wanted to see where it would lead. If he had seen into my mind at that moment, he would have realized that I had no idea.

We raced through the rain to the vélodrome and into the huge entryway. Spotting the cloakroom where they rented the roller skates, I said to Henri "Over here," as if I was an old hand at the place. I went up to the counter and without looking at Henri asked for two pairs of skates. "Chômeurs"—unemployed—I announced, remembering the reduced-price tickets Henri had bought for us at the Frankfurter rally.

"The skates will not know the difference," said the girl behind the counter in a flat voice. "So," she tilted her head toward the ticket price sign, "two francs, one hour." I peeked at Henri, who could not help laughing a little. But it was a friend's laugh, and I grinned back. Before he could make a move to pay, as he had done at the café, I paid for us both. Four francs was no small thing for me, Maître—I barely had enough in my pocket. But sometimes you just have to do something. Also it was worth it just to take off my wet jacket for an hour. And the cap. Henri kept his cap on. Of course.

He was full of smiles and laughter, Henri, the entire time he stumbled and skidded around the skating rink, with me circling around him, trying to help him stay upright and to keep him from getting run into when he fell. I was surprised that Henri had not objected to us skating, that he was willing to leave behind the foreign section and the Expo and everything else serious during our hour on the boards. When we finished and were getting ready to head out into the rain again, he told me what a great idea the skating had been, and thanked me for it. Blood rushed to my face. "After all," he said, "if there is no dancing after the revolution, then leave me out."

"Revolution?" I asked, surprised. And more than a little disturbed.

"Yes, well," his voice trailed off and a hand twirled in the air. Then he told me a name, whose words those were, about revolution and dancing. I was embarrassed never to have heard of the person. But like many things, I kept that to myself.

The rain had let up as we headed back to the foreign section bureau. At the door Henri stopped and told me that he had things to do inside, and that he would be busy for the next few days at one of the auto factories, where some kind of action was happening. But that I should return and look for him there soon after. "I do not know what we might find for you," he said, looking away from me slightly and toward the people inside, "with you being German, you see." He paused, and when I said nothing he went on. "But I am sure there are things to do for someone who can skate that well." And he grinned. "Even before the revolution." He put his hands on my shoulders as a sort of embrace, looked at me for a moment, then disappeared behind the black and red painted windows.

It must have taken me two hours to walk back to Rue Martel. I had a little change left in my pocket, enough that I could have taken the bus back to the Gare d'Austerlitz. I always made a point, though, never to spend my very last sou—I never knew when Abraham and Chawa would again give me a few francs, and I refused to ask them. But that was not the only reason I decided to walk. "With you being German," Henri had said. I could not face sitting on a crowded bus. I did not want to be near anyone.

22 May

A day or two later I reported to Bernard's apartment for my first training as a server for his dinner party. Not wanting to again face the nasty concierge, this time I went directly to the service entrance at the side of the building. It was in the evening, this training, because the others who were also to be servers—two women and two men—all worked during the day in Bernard's ateliers. The two women and one of the men were young, in their 20s, all of them quite handsome, I noticed, in that thin bony way that the French upper types seem to like. The other man was older, silver-haired, with delicate hands and a refined manner, who spoke excellent French with a slight Russian type accent. Bernard had chosen him, I learned, because for a time the man had been Maître d' in an expensive restaurant in Kiev, where the customers had liked to be spoken to in French and were served in the proper French way. I met them all in the kitchen, where Clarice the maid insisted that we remain while waiting for Bernard and Elsa.

Clarice looked unhappy about having to be around this group of foreigners and seemed even more pained when we spoke Yiddish among ourselves, though when any of the others spoke to Clarice or the cook, I noticed, they all spoke much better French than I did. At least, I think it was contact with these atelier workers that was making Clarice unhappy—it was difficult to tell, because during my earlier visit on my own, as Bernard and Elsa's relative, she had also looked pinched and crabby the entire time. After a while Clarice left us alone with the cook, who banged around with pots and pans for no purpose I could see except to let us know her feelings without having to speak to us. She also took out her unpleasure on a young kitchen maid who was doing the washing up and who was almost in tears by the time she finished and fled out the rear door.

Eventually Clarice returned and brought us all into the dining room where she remained hovering when Bernard and Elsa came in. Bernard explained that we would have very specific duties the night of the dinner—the two women servers would circulate with hors d'oeuvres while the other young man and I served aperitif drinks, the older man supervising. At dinner itself only the men would serve at the table, with the two women and Clarice bringing food tureens and platters from the kitchen to the dining room but then remaining at the sideboards. In this kind of French home, it seemed, only men are considered proper to serve at the table. No one said why. The older man—his name is Mordechai but Bernard said we must address him as Monsieur Maurice—would actually serve the food at table, while the other young man and I would hold the serving plates, pour wine, and perform smaller duties. We two younger males were also supposed to clear away the plates and such after each course, but just to hand them off—and we were instructed never to fully turn our backs on the table—to the women servers who were waiting in the corners of the room and would carry them to the kitchen. Strange, yes, but those were the rules of serving, Maître. And only some of them.

It was Elsa who instructed us about these dos and do-nots, including very particular lessons about which liquids went into which glasses. This was so important to her that she repeated it several times, at each of our training evenings—Clarice the maid looked disgusted at our ignorance—and I believe Elsa would have called us back for a special examination on the subject if Mordechai-Maurice had not finally told her in a calming tone that he would make certain there were no errors on the night of the dinner.

Elsa also gave us the few French phrases that were meant to cover all exchanges with guests. And no matter what, Bernard put in—even among ourselves, even in the kitchen—we were never to speak anything but French.

The cook gave us specific orders about where we were permitted to stand in the kitchen, and how we were to receive the food dishes from her, and where to put the finished dishes when we brought them back in, and even how we were to move in and out of the kitchen door. Once she understood how well Mordechai knew this serving business, she seemed glad to have him as an ally, and even warmed up to him a bit. It probably did not hurt that he was handsome and distinguished looking, with a cultured way of speaking and moving, and clothes that were well-tailored though worn and a bit loose fitting, as if he had once had a different body. The cook's face was always red so I cannot be sure, but I think I even saw her blush once when Mordechai—or Maurice, as she thought of him—spoke privately with her about some matter of kitchen practice.

At the end of that first session, Bernard sent Clarice and the cook home for the night, then Mordechai took very careful tailor's measurements of us all. One of Bernard's ateliers—maybe even these same men and women—would be making fine uniforms for us to wear the night of the dinner party.

Which calls to mind, Maître. Would it be possible to send me a shirt and trousers? I am still able to wear the ones you brought me a while ago, but the others, the ones I was wearing when I arrived back in the Reich, are in tatters. Other prisoners here in the bunker have family outside who send them things. But you are the only person I have. I mean, the only person who knows me, and where I am. At least until my trial.

Yours sincerely,
Herschel

Maître,

I waited almost a week before I returned to Henri's foreign section bureau. Until I thought certain he would be there, returned from the actions at the automobile factory where he had told me he would be busy for a few days. I was also waiting until I had gathered the nerves to face him again—"Being German."

The morning I headed again to the foreign section my stomach felt like it was hosting the workers' mud brawl that Henri and I had seen at the Expo. Henri was there at the bureau when I arrived, and from his smile he seemed pleased to see me. Before either of us said anything, I brought out my passport and held it in front of him. "Here," I said. "See? Poland. From Germany, yes, but Polish."

I had known for a while that the people in Henri's foreign section were connected to Poland—some from years ago, the leaders in particular, and many others more recent arrivals. Henri's parents had originally come from somewhere over there, I knew. But they had just seemed French to me, as did the foreign section people working at the front desks of the two bureaus, who spoke with each other in easy Paris slang. True, when I had gone with the group to the Expo work site I heard Polish as well as French, including from Henri. And I suppose its Poland connection was why this particular foreign section sent people around to the Sportclub Aurore, where many of the young people who spent time there had come from Poland. But until the moment when Henri had said that me being German was a problem for getting work from his group, I had paid little mind to the fact that the foreign sections all were divided up this way, not only kept officially outside the parties and confederations but also separate from each other—Henri's section for the Poles, another for Russians, one for Lithuanians, the Spanish, the Italians, and so on.

Henri looked at the passport in my hand but did not take it. "No, no," he said, "for us, papers are not important."

It was the first time since I had come to France that anyone had said that.

"It is different," he continued. "You see, we are a foreign section because of who we are not—not all the way French. According to some. Not French enough. But we are this particular foreign section because of who we are. What we share. Places and experiences. Politics. Language. Have you ever been to Poland?"

I shook my head.

"Speak Polish?"

I lowered my eyes, shook my head.

"Russian?"

No, again.

"Look, H," he said quietly, "there is a separate Yiddish foreign section, but they have no part with the big factory syndicats, the metal and electric trades and such, or in the building trades that are constructing the Expo. They stay over in the east, with the leather and hat and jewelry makers—the atelier work. I could put you in touch with them, if you had one of those skills."

I had no such skills, Maître. I stared blank at Henri.

"And there is the German section," he continued. "But it does not always get on well with the Paris comrades. And has even less favor these days—being German—and so has no work to offer. Which is why I encouraged you to come to us instead. Besides, they probably would ask you for papers, the German section. They are like that." He looked down again at the passport, my Poland passport. "And you have the wrong ones."

"As for working at the Expo," he continued, "Well, think about it. With a constructing crew who have building skills and broad backs? Speaking fast French and Polish? Imagine it, H, does this sound like a spot for you? Or your German accent?"

By now my chin was on my chest.

"So, what will we do with you? I have been wondering about it for some while, without having any good ideas. It is not simple, in these times. Nothing is simple. But a few days ago something came up. What are you doing just now? Could you maybe come along with me for a bit?"

Since I had just journeyed across the city to see him, he could not really have thought that I had something else to do, yet he was always careful to give consideration. To ask, not tell. A kind of respect. Even for me. For anyone. Henri.

We walked together south from the bureau, Henri telling me about the actions the previous week at the auto factory, though the more he talked the more excited he got and the faster he spoke, all in French now, and so the less of it I understood, especially with all the particular words about syndicats and workers and factories and bosses, which I knew nothing about. After 20 minutes or so we passed the Port de Versailles and reached an area of broad open spaces scattered with large buildings that did not look like apartment houses but neither did they look quite like factories. It turned out they were exhibition halls. This was the Foire de Paris—the Paris Fair—which was built for another kind of large expo that was held every year, for showing off farm foods and animals and fabrics and ceramics and what all else is produced from everywhere around the country. A national market of France. Henri headed for the largest building of them all, the Hall of Wines.

At one side of the hall were loading docks swarming with workmen and jammed with lorries and horse wagons. After a few minutes of sorting through the crowd, Henri found a man he knew who led us to a door and called to someone inside. A tall, broad shoulder middle age woman soon appeared, with dark hair lying flat against each side of her head, making a square frame for her large glowing cheekbones. She wore a wrap-around work smock on top of a cheap print dress with the sleeves rolled up to the elbows of her muscled arms. When she saw Henri she hesitated, her face taking on a very cross expression, but after a moment she grinned and grabbed him and gave him a big hug that almost completely disappeared him. Then she held him out at arm's length and said, again looking cross, "Where have you been? Why have you been hiding from me? And why are you still so thin? You only have another year!"

"Two years," Henri laughed, then introduced me to the woman, Rose, saying to her, "Here, now you can work on him instead."

"What makes you think I could not take both of you?" she said.

This was part of a long joke between them, Henri told me later, that when Henri turned 20 years old Rose was going to take him into her bed, and that before then he should put on a few kilos of weight—so he would have enough strength for her. She almost immediately began the same story with me, and over the next few months Rose hinted many times what she was going to do with me, and with me and Henri together—please excuse me, Maître—once I came of age. And put on some weight. "At least enough to hold onto," she would say.

Rose brought us inside the building. I was amazed at how enormous the place was, and how much activity. It was a single gigantic open hall—maybe two or three full-size football pitches, Maître, truly—with metal girders every 10 meters or so holding up a crisscross of white painted iron beams supporting the roof, which must have been 30 or 40 meters above. Dozens of men and women workers were moving around, calling to and shouting at each other as they carried and shifted and constructed and arranged things in different parts of the hall. Against one entire long wall were stacks and stacks of thin pallet mattresses, hundreds of them, the numbers growing as workers brought in new piles from the loading docks. Along the other side wall were teetering towers of bedcovers and hills of small pillows, also rising with fresh deliveries from the wagons and lorries outside. Most of the center part of the enormous hall was empty, with teams of men and women scrubbing the cement floor, others moving long wooden planks from piles at the rear of the hall and laying them in even rows on those parts of the floor that had been cleaned, while others placed signs on the girders—A1, B16, T33, and so on.

"Five thousand will be able to stay in this hall alone," Rose said, both impressed and proud, "and another ten thousand in six other Foire buildings." She was marching with great strides deep into the hall as she spoke to us. At the same time she was calling out to and being called by people working around the hall, her voice booming off the cement walls, friendly insults heading in both directions. I was not able to understand most of the words flying back and forth, but the spirit of it all seemed clear. Henri's big grin also told me that

I understood correctly the warmth of this human wave that Rose created as she charged across the floor.

We headed out a door on the far end and crossed an open space to another building, similar to the Hall of Wines but maybe only a fourth the size. Rose greeted a couple of people outside a door but bustled straight through it without slowing down. We stopped just inside, hit by a thunder of hammering and sawing and banging as people worked on and moved around huge slabs of wood and metal bars being made into long tables and laid out across the floor, and by other noisy doings in a different part of the hall separated from the main floor by a long, low counter but which I could see was an enormous kitchen area with stoves and tables and shelves and sinks, and masses of huge cooking pots and plates, and stacks and stacks of food tins.

After a moment of letting Henri and me take in all of this, Rose turned to face me and said, "Alors, qu'est-ce que tu peux faire?" Before I could think about what she was asking me—"So, what can you do?"—I was struck that she addressed me using "tu," the familiar form of "you" that most French reserve only for close friends and family. I had noticed that the people in Henri's foreign section all used tu with everyone else in the group, as Henri did with me. But I also knew that adults used tu when they spoke to children. I was not sure which way Rose meant it now, and somehow in the moment that was more important to me than what she was asking.

Henri jumped in right away. "H? He can do anything. Smart as a stray dog."

"Oh, I am sure of that," Rose said, "or else you would not have brought him to me. And said such good things about him the other day." My cheeks burned, and I avoided looking at either of them. "Though knowing you, cheri," she continued to Henri, "half of it I will wait to see for myself. Anyway, he could not weigh more than 40 kilos"—which was not true, Maître, I was close to 45—"so most of it better be brains." She turned to me. "All right, then, I will ask a different way. What skills do you have?"

Neither of us, Henri or me, was prepared. We looked at each other, then Henri blurted out, "Well, he certainly can skate." Rose looked at him strangely. "Roller skate," Henri added, embarrassed by a remark that made no sense and that he did not know why he had made. By now I was getting uncomfortable and found myself saying, "I know how to serve. Food, I mean. I have training. Top-level training," even believing it as I said it, suddenly convinced that the sessions at Bernard's, with another to come that very evening, actually gave me a skill—and that learning the difference between a flute de champagne and an apéritif glass might possibly be of any use in the huge open rathskeller they were building here.

"Good, good," Rose said, my simple claim apparently enough for her. Henri looked at me, surprised, but said nothing. "We will get you a place in here, then," Rose told me, "when things are a little further along. Before then, we will find something for you to do in the main hall. Come see me in a few days," she said as she headed off toward a group of people who were arguing near another door. "In the meantime," she called to me over her shoulder, "red meat! I want to see more flesh on your bones!"

As we walked back to his foreign section bureau, Henri told me that Rose was a syndicat steward, or some title like that, for women workers at the giant Citroën factory nearby at Javel. She was also a longtime organizer in the big left labor confederation that had recently joined with the CGT. The one with the Communists in it, yes. Anyway, these huge halls at the Foire de Paris were being turned into low-cost dormitories for visitors to the Expo, Henri explained, mostly for young people. And the CGT's syndicats were in charge of setting them up. So, when Rose was not at the Citroën plant, she had her hands on a lot of work to give people there at the Foire. Most of it went to actual syndicat members, but there was so much to go around in these last hectic weeks of getting the Expo ready that Rose was able to spill over some of it to several of the foreign sections. And unlike most other official confederation people, Henri told me, Rose was not interested in people's papers.

I asked Henri when he thought I should come back to see Rose. He thought for a moment, then said the following Sunday. Saturday was May Day—no one would be working. And though Sunday was usually a day off for all workers, the confederation was making an exception now to finish those Expo jobs they had won exclusively for their workers. This was also a jab at the syndicats catholiques, Henri told me, who would not allow Sunday work for any reason.

"Oh, but wait—Sunday will be the day after the big May Day parties," Henri now remembered. "And the morning after, who knows where Rose will wind up. No, better wait until Monday."

We had reached the foreign section bureau. "By the way, what about Saturday?" Henri added. "May Day. Where will you be?"

I suppose he expected me to have plans already, on this biggest holiday for workers, but in truth I had no idea. Henri read this on my face, I think, and invited me to join him and his parents, if I was free—as always, offering room for me to say No. They would be marching with their foreign section in an afternoon parade, from Place de la République to Père Lachaise cemetery and the Communards' Wall there—I nodded, trying to look as if I knew what that was—then joining the other foreign sections in a giant outdoor feast that night in the Parc de Belleville. All this was not far from Faubourg Saint Denis, Henri reminded me, the neighborhood where I was staying at Rue Martel. He told me I could meet them before the parade at the east bureau of the foreign section, the one where I had first gone to find him, near Gare de Lyon. "Action," he said, using his favorite word. "There will be plenty of action."

29 May

Just a few hours later was my third and final training session at Bernard's. Elsa was still all worrisome about which of all the different glass goblets were for apéritifs and which for red wine and which for white and which for water and which for dessert wine and which for digestifs and on and on. Do you realize how many they use, Maître, these kind of French? For each person? Glassware—that would be a business to do in Paris. I mean, for someone who was allowed to do business.

That evening we got our server uniforms—for the men a smooth black jacket and trousers, white waistcoat, white shirt, collar, and tie. And gloves, Maître. White gloves. I suppose if the diners saw a server's actual hands, they might unhappily imagine where those hands had been. Anyway, the uniforms fit all of us well—the tailoring had been top form. Then Bernard instructed us to report to two shops—one for the women, one for the men—where we would be given new shoes to wear at the dinner. We were expected at the shops the next day, during the closing time for lunch. I was not sure whether that was so the other four servers, who were also Bernard's laborers, would not miss any work time in his atelier, or so we would not appear at these shops when actual customers were there. At least we got to keep the shoes. Which turned out to look quite nice. Though they must have been the cheapest the shops had to offer—mine had completely fallen apart by the next winter. Even with the new heavy soles I cut for them from my leather supply. Well, that is another matter, Maître, the leather.

It was not until Bernard's instructions that we only had one day, the next day, to get the shoes that I thought about when exactly the dinner was. Saturday. The same day that I was invited by Henri to join him and his parents, and the foreign section, at the parade and then the festival. May Day.

Well, Maître. How many actual French people knew that I existed? And cared? One—Henri. Not to mention that his foreign section might open onto the confederations and the syndicats and the whole Paris world of laboring jobs. But work from the foreign section was still just a "Come see me later" said over Rose's shoulder. Rose, who did not even know me. While the serving work at Bernard's dinner was actually here, now. Definite. Besides, Bernard had his hands on so many things, Tante Chawa always said. And now that Bernard had finally offered me work, and if I did a good job for him at the dinner, other things could follow, he had said so—maybe there was some truth after all to Bernard's talk about family. So now, if suddenly I did not turn up? That would be the end for me with Bernard. Before it had even begun. And Abraham? After he had swallowed the bitter herbs and taken me to see Bernard? How would I face him?

I walked all the way back to Rue Martel from Bernard's flat, an hour of chewing hard on these thoughts. And as I lay on my pallet that night, the different images—of the dinner at Bernard's, of the Hall of Wine, of Rose in the food building, of May Day with Henri—kept rolling and crashing in my head, over and over, like tumbling down a flight of stairs.

By early morning I knew that I would be at Bernard and Elsa's dinner, the only certain work I had. I could only hope that so many people would be at the May Day events that Henri would be too busy, too much alive with the day, to notice that I was not there. It was painful to imagine that he would notice, and be put off me. But another thought was worse, and I was unable that night to stop myself from returning to it, over and again, tongue to a sore tooth—that Henri might notice I was not there, and not care. Eventually that idea blotted out all the others. And nearly made me weep.

1 June

When I think back on it now, Maître, it seems remarkable how smoothly things went with us servers at Bernard and Elsa's dinner party. Mordechai-Maurice was a master, and the rest of us at least did nothing that seemed to embarrass.

At the end of the night, the four of us younger servers waited in the kitchen to be paid and dismissed, while Clarice the maid and Mordechai-Maurice moved back and forth to one of the salons, continuing to serve the guests as they carried on smoking and drinking. By the time they all finally left and Mordechai-Maurice joined us in the kitchen, we had long since finished the baguettes and cheese the cook had given us as our supper. Bernard came in soon after. He looked exhausted, from nerves and perhaps too much wine, but also pleased. Or as close to pleased as I ever saw him. He told us that we had done well and that he and Madame were quite satisfied, then said nothing more, standing there red-eyed and content, as if this king's blessing was all that we could have been waiting for. The other servers looked at each other, shoes scuffling, their hands awkward, and I realized that maybe I was the only one willing to speak up.

"Excuse me, uncle," I said, and he winced at the word. "Our wages?"

Bernard blinked and I realized that, at the moment, the matter of our pay was simply nowhere on his mind. Instead of admitting it, though, or even just making up an excuse, he immediately recovered himself and put on an expression that tried to pity my foolishness. "You are very thoughtful, my boy. But all that is arranged." The other servers glanced at each other, said nothing. Bernard moved the lower part of his face into what he must have thought resembled a kindly smile, then told the others that he would see them at the atelier on Monday, reminding them to bring with them the server uniforms we were all still wearing. He also said goodnight to the cook, which was the signal she had been waiting for to finally begin closing up the kitchen. Mordechai and the other servers gathered their things and headed out the rear door. I also made ready to go, but Bernard said to me, "No, wait. I want to have a word."

We went into the small parlor where Bernard had taken me once before. "You did very well," Bernard told me, "especially with the von Hensbrucks"—or some name like that, with the "von" in front. You see, Maître, there was a German couple at the dinner. An important business connection of Bernard's from Berlin, a big garment business there of some sort. Herr von Hensbruck spoke a bit of French, but Frau von Hensbruck none at all. And as maybe I already told you, neither Bernard or Elsa spoke German. So, before the guests arrived, Bernard had given me special instructions. He would point out the von Hensbrucks, and I was to approach them with an offer of apéritifs, at first speaking French to them, to establish myself in their eyes as a Frenchman. But as soon as there was a moment when they were alone, or only with Bernard, I was quietly to speak German to them, to let them know that they could make themselves understood with me, if needed. Which would also show them that Bernard had "thought of everything," as he put it. "Your best German," Bernard had instructed me. "And whatever you do," he had poked his finger in my chest, "no pronouncing that sounds like Yiddish."

It turned out, Maître, that this was the real reason he had included me in this serving crew. For a German voice. That he could count on.

And he was right. About the von Hensbrucks, I mean. I could see immediately that a very stiff Frau von Hensbruck relaxed a bit when I spoke to her in German. And at one point, just before dinner was served, she was even quite grateful—her eyes said so, at least—when I was able to tell her where the powder room was. Bernard now said that because I had done so well, he would be thinking of more things for me to do, and soon would be in touch. Then he reached for his billfold, fingered some notes and handed one to me. Fifty francs—to me, a huge sum, Maître. I suspect that the other servers did not receive anything close to the same.

Bernard now took me by the arm and steered me back to the kitchen, nearly shoving me out the back door, but I broke away to get the clothes that I had come in. As I did, the cook excused herself for bothering Bernard—Madame had already retired for the night, she explained—and asked him what she should do with a large pile of shellfish—some kind of shrimp I think it was, I am not familiar—which had been left unused at the dinner but which, the cook said, must be eaten soon. I suppose she was hoping he would tell her to take it home with her, but instead he looked at me and said, "The boy, give it to the boy," then turned around and disappeared into the apartment.

Shrimp. Thank you, Bernard. You see, Maître, shellfish is traif—forbidden by the ancient food rules. Though apparently not for him. And while I did not always follow all those rules myself during my time in Paris, I had never in my life eaten these strange-looking shell-covered things, with their dead eyes staring up at you, and so even if I had wanted to, I would not have known what to do with them.

The cook was not happy about this. She quickly wrapped the shrimp in a soiled length of butcher paper and shoved it at me, without a word. Since I was not going to eat them, I am sure I would have offered them back to her, once Bernard had left the kitchen. But the way she had treated me, treated all of us—except Mordechai-Maurice—since we had first begun coming to the apartment, and the way now she almost threw this at me—well. So, I took it, the package. And as I stepped into the quiet night of the 16th arrondissement to begin my long walk east, I wondered how many hungry cats Sam might snag with a kilo of shrimp. And only the very best shrimp, I am sure.

Yours sincerely,
Herschel

Something is bothering me, Maître. Of what I said. About that night when I was thinking of Henri, of how he might react when I did not turn up on May Day. That I nearly wept. I do not want to give the impression that weeping was something I did. In fact, just the opposite. From the time I left my parents at the train station in Hannover, when yes I cried I admit, until this very moment now, I cannot remember a single time when I was unable to stop myself if I got to the edge of weeping. It cost too much, crying. I could not afford it. Just so you know.

2 June 1941

Maître,

The Monday morning after Bernard and Elsa's dinner, I went back to the Halle aux Vins—the giant exhibition building they were turning into a dormitory for Expo visitors. Though only certain visitors, as it turned out. The original plan was to offer inexpensive sleeping pallets there to anyone visiting Paris for the Expo, especially workers and young people from the provinces who could travel on the reduced-fare trains they would run during the summer months. A pallet, two meals of a sort, and entrance to the Expo, all for 22 francs. Over three or four days in Paris, that—plus the cost of travel and whatever else you spent on your special visit to the great city—would take quite a bite out of a worker's wages or a small farmer's bit of extra cash. Even so, the dormitory was a very good bargain, since a cheap hotel bed by itself—without meals and the six-franc daily Expo ticket—could cost that much or more.

I cannot remember the politics that Henri later explained to me—how some big characters in the government owed something to the city's hotel owners—but behind ministry doors the hotel people complained about the low price dormitories, and suddenly the rules changed about who could stay there. Now it was only for young people, and mostly groups that made special arrangements—such as countryside schools and churches, or Boy Scouts or Girl Guides. Also for the people who would perform at the Expo, or who were playing some part at the region exhibits. You see, Maître, everywhere you went at the Expo they had these halls and pavilions for all the regions around France, each one showing off the traditions of doing things in that province or département or whatever it was. And not only pavilion exhibits but actual—well, pretend-actual—village streets and farm buildings and such, human-size doll houses right there in the middle of the Expo grounds, with people in all these strange costumes that locals wore in those parts. Supposedly. Though I must say, Maître, that when I was in the countryside, I never saw any such things. And I crossed almost all of France, from north to south, three years later. As you know. Or know some of.

Anyway, there were hundreds of groups whose job at the Expo was to perform local dances or music, and thousands more people to show off the different regions. Though many of these people did not actually do anything—they were there just to dress up in old-time local clothes and walk around the pavilions and the made-up villages. "Authentiques," the Expo people called them. But some of these dance and music groups were from right there in Paris, hired to wear special countryside clothes as they performed supposed local songs and steps, pretending they came from that pavilion's region. And others—many of them chômeurs and chômeuses who needed any work they could get—were hired simply to stroll around in costume and pretend to speak in the accent of the place, so that the region's exhibition would not have to pay for their own people to travel and stay in Paris. Some of the pavilions spent even less—they just put local costumes onto figures made of straw and wax.

Most of these countryside pavilions and toy villages were in a special part of the Expo called the Regions Center, just next to the Tour Eiffel. Each pavilion or make-believe village showed off the things that were produced specially in that region—lace or silks or ceramics or cheeses, or whatever they grew there, and of course wines, as well as the local music and dance and clothing. But there was also a separate, larger made-up village that was just called Old France— whatever that meant. And another site they called the Rural Center, where they built a pretend farm with a house and a barn and even a silo. Over the entrance was a sign that said, "The land does not lie."

There was something very strange about all this cheering for the countryside, Maître. I mean, the Expo's official name was Technology and Modern Life—or something like that. And the biggest French pavilions, as well as the advertisement posters you saw everywhere in the city, were all about the latest French inventions and technicals— the new aeroplanes at the Palais de l'Air, the automobile pavilion with futureworld models that looked like they could drive themselves, and the photo-cine pavilion, with the television machine that everyone was so crazy to see. All of it meant to show off France as the most advanced, the most modern. But at the same time, and right next door to all this, they built all these old-fashioned farm and country village things. Almost as if they had become nervous that with all the fancy modern pavilions of so many other places—the Soviets, the Americans, and of course the Reich—visitors to the Expo would realize that other places were actually just as modern as France. Or more. So, they had a sort of panic, you might say, and decided also to fill the Expo with all these old countryside things. Especially the kinds of things that were nowhere else because they were only French. La France profonde—deep France—they call it. Yes all right, they seemed to be saying, so someone else might send an aeroplane to the moon, but only France soil can grow a Frenchman.

On the way to the Foire dormitory that morning I stayed well away from Henri's foreign section bureau, afraid that he might spot me and I would have to give him some false excuse about why I had not turned up on May Day—serving rich people at Bernard's fancy dinner party was not something I wanted to admit. I was also worried that he might stop by the Halle aux Vins during the day to ask where I had been, but fortunately he did not appear. Though part of me hoped he would.

Rose was there at the hall when I arrived. And remembered me. Put me right to work—shaking out bed covers, dusting them with sulfur powder, folding and stacking them against a wall. And the pallets also, cleaning them, putting them in piles, later setting them out in rows. For the next three weeks I did this over and over, as well as other cleaning and sorting jobs. Those days are now a blur of sameness, but not the little envelope of francs I received at the end of each day's work. I remember the excitement flowing up and down my arms and legs as I stood in the queue waiting to be paid the first day, waiting with workers who were either actual French or officially part of a foreign section. I was proud to be with them, even though mostly they ignored me while I was working, which was fine with me. They were not especially unfriendly to me, at least not most of them, and it was enough for me just to be one of the crowd. A French crowd. And to be earning a day's pay that was coming from a Frenchman for work that had been given to me by a Frenchman—or Frenchwoman, it being Rose. Still, as I waited in the pay queue the first few days I was also frightened, Maître, that before I reached the front someone would shout "Alors!"—"Hey!"—and grab my shoulder, pull me out of the queue, and say "You! Who are you? Where are your papers?"

But it did not happen, and as the weeks went on and I worked first in the big dormitory, then in the kitchen hall, I began to feel less worried, less of a cheat waiting to be found out. Less foreign. My weeks at the Foire dormitories were the best I ever spent in Paris.

After 10 days or so of me working there, the dormitories began to take in their first overnight sleepers, even though the Expo itself would not officially begin for another week. These were people who would be part of the big opening ceremonies at the regional pavilions—dance troupes and gymnastics teams and bands and choirs, plus the people who would appear in the pavilions to show how they made cider or wood saws or ceramic dishes with paintings on top, or whatever other local things, and who needed to set up their equipment or displays or to rehearse on the sites. Part of this early wave was four men whose job was to show off a new machine that automatically packaged hay into huge cakes, all tied up with rope, like a birthday gift. They set up this huge rolling petrol-powered mechanical thing in the field outside of the main dormitory, running it through great heaps of hay that had been dumped there. But then came an argument about where at the Expo they would show the machine. The plan had been to use it at the farm in the Rural Center. But then someone realized that this farm would also have old fashioned haystacks—these tall cone things, with a bushy top that looks like someone's hair blown by the wind, that the French claim are different from haystacks anywhere else. And are very proud of. Yes, haystacks.

Bride of Frankenstein. That is how the top of the haystack looked— like her hair, the bride, but after a storm. Did you see it, Maître, the film? It showed in the Paris cinemas when I was there. I am sure you know Frankenstein, everyone does, but in this Bride film they make a woman for him. I saw it three times one winter afternoon in Paris and twice more the next day. That was the winter after the Expo, when things had gone very bad again for me and I was spending many afternoons in the cheapest cinemas. I often watched the same film five or seven or ten times even, over two or three days, keeping myself warm in the film house and away from trouble on the streets—the police, and the gangs that had begun to roam around attacking foreigners. Most of the time I only half watched these films, dozing in my seat quite a lot since some of the rooms where I was bedding down those winter nights were so cold and damp that I slept very poorly. And my troublesome stomach again in those worrying days. But not this film, sleeping through it, I mean. Because I so much loved watching Elsa Lankaster, who was Frankenstein's bride, and also played the writer of the Frankenstein story, but looked completely different then from when she was the bride with that hair that stuck straight back and up, making her look so beautifully strange and also somehow dignified. Elsa, her name—maybe she is German, Maître. Do you think?

Well, the hay packing machine. At the last minute some people at the Expo thought that if they showed this machine at the Rural Center it would take away all the attention—the machine was not only very modern but also very loud—from the peaceful old time scene they were making up there, of a couple and their children and grandchildren who all worked this perfectly clean little farm together, and who were the true French who needed nothing from the world beyond their land. And especially because part of this scene was the old fashioned haystacks that were carefully arranged in the pretend field next to the pretend silo on the pretend farm.

In the end, instead of showing the hay packing machine itself, they decided to make a moving picture of it. And in the field outside the dormitory they began filming this hay packer, with plans to screen it in one of the pavilions that showed off modern machinery, or maybe it was in the cinema-television hall. Not only pictures of it spitting out the hay packs but also the detail insides of the machine at work, which would also let them brag about some special new camera lens the French had made that could film things clearly from very close up.

So, working at the Foire meant that I got to see a film being made. They had to rig up all these special lights and cameras to show the working insides of the machine. It took them three days to get it right. For five minutes of film. Of a hay machine. I snuck outside to watch them once in a while. I must say, it was not very interesting. They needed Elsa Lankaster.

Anyway, things became hectic as these first groups of overnight sleepers began to arrive at the Halle aux Vins, because they had not yet finished setting up all the beds and fixing up the washing and dressing areas and such, and now they had to get the giant kitchen producing so many more meals, and most of all to sort out the organizing—who was supposed to go where and when, workers and overnight visitors both. So there was a rush to get everything ready. But at the same time there was some kind of syndicat trouble at the nearby Renault factory—or Citroën, I cannot remember—and the car factory workers who were doing extra work at the dormitories dropped everything and headed over there. Rose and her other confederation comrades now started bringing in all kinds of other helpers to the dormitories. There were new people from foreign sections, chômeurs from other syndicats—though not the catholique ones—and even some workers' children on the weekend. Which gave me an idea.

I had not seen Sam for the past two weeks, not since the morning after Bernard's dinner when I gave him the shrimp. That was a Sunday, at a street market by République where I knew Sam usually showed up. But after that I was busy every day working at the Foire. And though for the first time since I had arrived in Paris I had a bit of extra money in my pocket, in the evenings I was too tired from the day's work, plus travel back and forth across the city, to go to the Aurore Sportclub or to the Tout Va Bien, a café on Boulevard Saint Denis that was a meeting place for Sam and me. Now I went looking for Sam, and when two nights in a row I could not find him at any of the regular spots, I went up to Belleville, to the little room he shared with his mother Rina. Normally I did not go there—it was a shabby little room, and I knew Sam did not like having visitors there, especially with his mother often in her bed from being ill or exhausted. I knocked quietly and Sam opened, then stepped out onto the landing for us to speak. I could hear Rina behind the door, coughing from deep in her chest. Sam looked poorly—pale and tired and without any sign of the grin that normally crouched, ready to spring into action, at the corners of his mouth. He told me that Rina had been very ill for weeks now, and that he had been spending most of his time taking care of her. He did not have to say what else that meant—that neither Rina with her cart or Sam with his scavenging and schemes had been able to earn much if any money during that time. And probably had even less than usual to eat. Which made me gladder still to bring him my news.

3 June

"Quelle pâtisserie!" Sam said when I brought him into the Foire dormitory early the next morning. At first I did not understand why he would say that, since we had not yet gone to the kitchen building, which I was holding back as a surprise for him. Pâtisserie, Maître—pastry shop. But then I realized where Sam was looking, over at a far corner of the hall where dozens of girls from visiting folk dance and song troupes were moving back and forth between their pallets and a closed-off washing area. When he had met me at the bus stop early that morning, the possibility of work had already much improved Sam's mood from the night before. But now, seeing the girls, a light suddenly switched on behind his eyes and he bounced from one foot to the other, a racer at the starting line.

After a few minutes I spotted Rose, and when there was a small opening—as she marched across the hall from one work group to another—I hurried Sam over to her and said simply that he was a friend who knew how to work. She paused and looked him up and down with that scary scowl that I was finally learning not to believe. Sam said something to her in fast Paris slang and after another moment she gave a big sudden laugh and said, "Right, go to it." Then she charged away. I took Sam over to a foreman who knew me a little by now, and began to explain that Rose had given her okay, but he just straight away said to Sam, "Name?" wrote it down, and sent us off on our first job of the day among the pallets and bedcovers. From then on, every time Rose and Sam crossed paths, Sam would say something quick to her in slang, and she would laugh and wave him away.

Sam was a great worker—small, but very strong, an athlete, I think I told you—and with his street Paris ways of doing things, in just a few hours some of the others on the work crews had become friendly with him. At least appearing so. Anyway more than I had managed in my two weeks there. Sam's concentration on the work that first morning was helped by the fact that all the girls soon left the dormitory, along with everyone else who had stayed the night, headed for a breakfast in the kitchen building and then to the Expo itself to practice whatever it was they would be doing there once it officially opened.

At noon I was able to show Sam the next good news—our workers meal in the kitchen hall. The people who stayed overnight in the dormitories were given bread and jam and coffee in the morning and an evening meal for those who returned in time for it. But the Foire kitchen also stayed busy at midday, feeding a hearty warm meal to Expo performers who took a break from the fairgrounds, as well as to us dormitory workers. That first day with Sam, we dropped what we were doing exactly at noon, just like all the French workers, and joined the queue at the door to the kitchen building. When we got inside and Sam got a whiff of the cooked food waiting for us at the serving counter, then saw even more food piled up back there for meals to come, his face showed a surprise and pleasure far more serious than when he had spotted the girls earlier that morning. As we moved forward in the queue, I could see him looking around carefully at what was going on, at the people serving, at others preparing and cooking, at the stacks of bread loaves and tinned food, the mounds of vegetables, and the cool box doors opening and closing in front of large hunks of meat, some of which had joined potatoes and leeks in the steaming pots of our midday stew. It was not long after that first meal that Sam began asking around about who got to work in the kitchen.

That afternoon the day turned warm and with the physical job we were doing, and all the sulfur powder in the air, it was very sweaty even in the huge drafty hall. By the middle of the afternoon most of the workers had stripped down to their undervests, and I joined them. But not Sam. Not only did he still wear his thick overshirt but he kept the long sleeves down and buttoned. I did not say anything while we were working but as we walked together to the bus at the end of the day and he happened to mention the heat, I took the chance to ask him why he had kept his top shirt on. He stopped and looked around—to see if anyone from the job was nearby, I soon realized—then rolled up one of his sleeves. The scabies, Maître. Up and down his arm. On his chest and back also, he told me. It was a problem for many people in Belleville, the scabies. A plague. All over the east of the city. But so common that I did not think the workers at the dormitories would be at all bothered by it. Until Sam finished explaining. If they saw the scabies, he said, he might never get to work in the kitchen. Then he showed me something else. Handfuls of sulfur that he had snatched from the big boxes of it at the dormitory—we scattered it on all the bed covers and pallets—and had dumped into the oversized pockets of his big loose jacket, the same useful pockets that had held so many sardine tins on the way back from Bonneuil. Mix the sulfur with a little oil, Sam told me, and it does a job on the little bastards—pardon my language, Maître, but that was what he always called the scabies. Every day of the next week it got warmer but Sam always wore his jacket to the job, and kept his shirtsleeves down while he worked.

The official opening for the Expo came closer. The setting-up work was now finished at the dormitories, and the pallets began to fill with performers and craft makers and the other people whose Expo job was—one way or another—to be an authentique from one of the provinces. Now there was much more work in the kitchen hall where the growing dormitory crowds had to be fed, and one morning when Sam and I appeared for work, Rose sent me to the kitchens— I suppose because of the serving experience I had invented for her that first day when Henri brought me there. I could see that Sam was disappointed not getting a chance himself to spend time around the food, but when I met him at lunch that day, he said he was not so bothered by it because actually he was lucky still to have any work at all. Now that things were all set up at the dormitories, they needed fewer workers, and Sam thought that his joking around with Rose might have saved his job. Anyway, he said, smiling back toward the dormitory, there were treats to be had in both halls.

6 June

Sam definitely had energy. After a few days, as we were heading home together in the evening, he began babbling about the girls from the Jeunesse Ouvrière Catholique—Catholic Worker Girls, sort of like our Girl Guides, I think—who had been pouring into the Foire dormitory the past couple of days. Sam went on and on about these sturdy girls and how terrific they looked in their uniforms—skirts, white blouses, and berets. Something about it made him go strange in the eyes. He told me that he had to watch out for the girls' chaperones, and that Rose did not like them, these girls, and gave Sam a dirty look whenever she saw him buzzing around them—they were a catholique group, you see, which meant that even though they were from worker families, the confederation people like Rose had no use for them.

I never learned whether Sam actually got to know any of those girls. Closely, I mean. I had moved over to working in the kitchen hall and so did not get to see him in action, so to say. Besides, Sam liked to keep details to himself. Never let people know exactly what he was up to. And especially not what he was thinking. This was something Sam practiced very strongly. It made being his friend difficult sometimes. But after a while in Paris I learned to value this myself. Of course keeping things from the police and other officials, that was obvious, and even from people who were supposedly meant to help me. Also, most things were best not told to Abraham and Chawa. And certainly not Bernard. There were also some things I definitely did not tell Henri. Or Geneviève—well, almost everything I kept from her. Then, when I was in jail, after the shooting, I always thought carefully before I spoke, and held certain things back from the magistrate and the counselors and the aliénistes. Even from my lawyers. Though with you, Maître, I believe I can speak my mind. Mostly.

So, for the next week or so I worked in the kitchen hall and Sam in the dormitories. At the end of every day we would head back together to our neighborhoods in the east, me to Faubourg Saint Denis, him to Belleville. Although later there were times Sam did not appear for our trip back across the city—perhaps those evenings he had managed a rendezvous with one of the Jeunesse girls. I did not ask. Anyway, that first week when we arrived back in the east we would separate, with Sam anxious to return to his mother Rina who had been so ill, to see how she had managed the long day without him. But after 10 days or so things had improved—with his pay he had been able to buy medicine for Rina, and some decent food, and she was starting to feel a bit stronger, he told me. So, one evening he said that we should celebrate our good fortune, that there was a dance at the Eldorado hall, a place on Boulevard de Strasbourg where we sometimes went. I said immediately yes, excellent—I was so pleased that things were going well for him, with the work, and Rina getting better. And that I had been the one to bring it to him.

But then I remembered that it was a Friday. And every Friday I made certain to show up in the evening at Abraham and Chawa's, to join them for a Sabbath supper. It was not that I was so observant of all the rituals, Maître. Or them, either—often they would open Maison Albert on a Saturday for a delivery, or for a French client's fitting. With Chawa and Abraham, it was not about what you were supposed to do but what it was important to do. Important in your own mind. And for them, one of these things was to pay at least some attention to the Sabbath. Not to follow all the rules, but just to make a point of it. So, every Friday evening they closed the workshop a bit early, said a single short prayer while lighting the Sabbath candles, then had a quiet supper where we talked—about what had happened during the week, about what was happening around us in Paris east, and of course what was happening in the Reich, with my family, with everyone. Especially if I had received a letter from my parents that week, or from my sister Bertha, who was so good about writing to me. These Friday nights were very much the same as they had been with my own parents, when I was growing up in Hannover—the candles and their one short blessing, and a family supper. It marked something. And this reminder of home was part of why Friday night at Abraham and Chawa's felt important to me.

I had once brought Sam to Friday supper there, and I saw that he was uncomfortable, having to sit still through the candle lighting and prayer, and making nice conversation with Abraham and Chawa during the meal. Now, as we returned from work at the Foire and I told him that no, I would not join him at the dancehall after all, because of Sabbath dinner, I could see that he was impatient with me. Irritated, even.

"You know," he said, "if you recite a prayer every day, when you die you will be a very holy man—but you will still be dead."

There were many people in Paris east who followed strictly the ancient rules and rituals. But there were also many like Sam, who went their own way. Henri also was without feelings for such things. But Henri was different from Sam—Henri had his politics, something else to hold onto. Sam had nothing. Though not from confusion or uncertainty. No, Sam believed fiercely in his nothing. Held it close. Does that make sense, Maître?

Let me tell you another way, about Sam and believing. Once, soon after I had met him, we were scrounging together after the Bastille market and had come up with a beautiful round cheese, an enormous thing, perfectly whole and untouched, that had somehow been left under an overturned wooden box. We were just congratulating ourselves when a big Frenchmen, rough and cursing and looking very hungry, came up behind us, pushed Sam away, and grabbed the cheese out of my hands. He looked wild, the man, ready to do whatever it took to keep the cheese. I was about to jump at him, but Sam's experience of Paris told him that this was not a fight worth fighting, even though there were two of us, and he held me back. If this man had been a market regular, Sam told me afterward, it would have been different—even if Sam took a beating from the man, he would have fought, to keep up his reputation there among the other scavengers, or else the next time someone else would try to take away his pickings. But he had never seen this wild man before, so Sam had backed away, pulling me with him. Never fight with a crazy, he said, because they do not understand when they have lost.

Just after the Frenchman left with our cheese, I happened to look down into a pile of throwaways. And there, under some trash, was a crate that turned out to hold half a dozen melons. They were bruised and soft, but still good enough to eat, so Sam and I grabbed the crate and carried it away. As we sat down on a bench, Sam's jaw was still grinding about the man who had taken the cheese. I thought in the end we had done pretty well for ourselves, and I wanted to relax Sam a bit, help him enjoy what we had, so I repeated to him a Yiddish expression I used to hear from my mother. "See," I said holding up a juicy chunk of melon, "God never hits with both hands."

Sam looked at me hard for a long moment. "No?" he finally said. "Wait awhile."

Yours,
Herschel

Maître,

Things went along the same for a few weeks, me working in the kitchen hall at the Foire de Paris, Sam in the dormitories, the two of us able to spend some evenings together with a few francs in our pockets—though Sam had to use most of his pay to buy medicine for his mother, and for their room rent. You should have seen him at the daily midday meal they gave to us workers, Maître—he ate enough for three, in sneaky extra bowlfuls and leftover ends of bread. The more he could pack in then, you see, the less he had to worry about eating in the morning or evening.

It was a good routine we had then, Sam and I. Simple. It did not stay that way for very long.

The first complicator was just two weeks after the Expo opened—I needed to be away from the Foire, and it took some arranging. The Expo and the dormitories were open all seven days, with the Foire kitchen hall going from early in the morning straight through until late evening, so it needed two different crews every day. And the dormitories went around the clock, which meant three crews—the first to clean up after the sleepers left for the Expo and to prepare for and settle new arrivals, then another crew to manage people who showed up in the evening, and a third crew to stay overnight as cleaners and watchmen. So to fill all these shifts for seven days—and without asking anyone to work more than the 40-hour week they had just fought so hard to get—Rose and the other foremen had to schedule and juggle a lot of people.

The problem that had arrived for me was the Poland consulate. And later, the German. Plus Uncle Abraham. It started with my passport, my Poland passport, which was soon to go past its expiring date. In Paris east those days, there were stories of how the Poland consulate was making it difficult to renew passports for people unless they could show they had actually lived in Poland, or at least that their families did—an early taste of the much stricter law that was to come the following year. There was talk about this at the Sportclub Aurore—many young people who went to the Aurore were from Polish families—where one evening it caught my ear. Not that I had any idea to go to Poland, Maître. But my passport and the Reich reentry visa were the only official documents I had. When I told Uncle Abraham what I had heard, and that my passport would soon run out of date, he became very nervous. Without a passport, Abraham said, whatever chance I had of getting regular papers to stay in France—or to go anywhere else, if I had to, and was able to—would become even more difficult.

Earlier that year I heard a Polish boy at the Aurore tell about how he had been punched up one night by some French mecs when they found him asking for work at Les Halles, the huge old central city market. You see, Maître, there are very strict rules at Les Halles—not written down rules, but even stronger—about who is allowed to work and where, with almost all of it for French only. They also took everything this Polish boy had in his pockets, including his passport. But I had seen this same boy again just a few days before, telling how he got a replacement passport from the Poland consulate, and that the new passport turned out to be dated for longer than his original one. When I told Uncle Abraham about this, he agreed that it was worth a chance, so we made a plan to go to the consulate, not to ask for a renewing of my passport but to report it stolen.

The Poland consulate was only open a few hours a day for passports and visas—two hours in the morning, and again two hours in the afternoon. Abraham expected that we would have to wait in a long queue, as we had whenever we had gone to see about papers at the police or the refugee bureau, and perhaps we would need to spend more than a single day there. Abraham had to go with me, you see—I was a minor and he was my legal guardian. Also, he could show his own good French papers to the consulate, and explain the receipt I had been given by the Paris police. Most of all, he could put on his Frenchness—Monsieur Albert, with his business card—which might pass in the eyes of a Poland official. Abraham wanted to make certain that once we went there we could finish what we started, even if we had to return the next day, and the next, which meant that I might miss several days in a row from work at the dormitories.

So, this is why I began telling you about how I needed to arrange for time away from the Foire. The work assignments in the kitchen hall were made by a foreman who had no soft spot for me, or for any foreigners. So, I was not sure how he would react when I said I needed to be gone for some days. He told me he did not care what I did or why, but that if I wanted the work when I came back I would have to organize someone to take my place while I was gone, who could handle the work but would be willing to give up the shifts when I returned. Well, I did not have to think too far about that. Sam was very happy to get into the kitchen hall and came in during his off-time from the dormitories to watch and learn what I did there. Then he changed his own work schedule so that he would be able to take over my spot, doing double shifts, when the days came for me to be away.

At the Poland consulate there was a separate desk for lost or stolen passports, with a much shorter queue than for other passport and visa business, and we got to see someone by late the first afternoon. Uncle Abraham immediately began speaking his best French with the consulate person there. This not only made a good impression but—and this had been the plan—kept the consulate man from speaking to me in Polish, which I had not a word of. The man also seemed to approve of Abraham's French papers and Maison Albert business card, and nodded at my receipt from the Paris police. Then he made noises that sounded both believing and understanding when Abraham told him a made-up story of this young and not very wise nephew—he patted me on the head like a small child—having his passport pocket-picked while traveling on the Métro. The consulate man said that he could not issue a replacement right then, because confirming information would have to be telegraphed from Poland, but that we should check back with them in two weeks. Which we did. And, thanks be, a new passport was waiting for me. Which was valid for a year. A year that my old passport did not have.

The evening after we picked up the passport, we sat over cups of tea in Maison Albert. Abraham proudly told Chawa the tale of the consulate again—in more detail than the first time, now that he knew he had been so successful—while she looked at the passport itself. After a minute or two Chawa looked up. Her face had changed. Something was wrong. Abraham stopped talking.

"The visa," Chawa said. "It does not have the reentry visa."

My Reich reentry visa, Maître. For travel to Belgium and return to Germany. It was in my old passport. But not in the new one. Which had not occurred to me, because I had no intending of going back to Belgium, and as difficult as things had been in Paris, I had no thoughts of returning to Germany. Not yet, anyway. But Abraham understood immediately what Chawa meant. One of the things the French police were very keen on when they looked at a foreigner's papers was whether there was someplace other than France where the foreigner could go. If you had a visa for somewhere else—or at least a reentry permit for the place you had come from—they were more likely to let you stay in France, at least temporarily. But if you had no place else to go? Then they wanted you out right away. There you are, Maître—life.

9 June

Uncle Abraham wanted me to go with him the next day to the German consulate, to try to extend my reentry visa. But I had only arranged with Sam to fill in my work at the kitchen for one day, and I was nervous about keeping my place at the Foire. Abraham and I argued, as we often did. But staying connected—with Rose and the confederation, with Henri and the foreign section, with the dormitories and kitchen hall—had become too important to me. For the people as much as the work. So, the next day I returned to the Foire. The Expo itself was in full action by now and the dormitories were getting crowded, though not as much as they would later in the summer, when students would pour in from the provinces. Sam had even managed to arrange extra work shifts for himself, which made him a little less disappointed to leave the kitchen hall when I returned to take back my spot there.

I was speaking with Sam in the main dormitory, telling him about the passport and my problem with the Reich visa, when Henri walked in. I had not seen him in several weeks, and it had mostly slipped out of my thoughts that he was the one who had made all this work possible for me, and so also for Sam. I suppose I had not even mentioned Henri's part in it to Sam, because as Henri came toward us, a sour "What does that guy want?" expression came over Sam's face. Henri greeted us, though without any sign of his usual high spirits. I thought maybe seeing Sam there was the reason. But that idea soon disappeared because, after asking how I was getting along, he turned to Sam and asked if he was also working there, and when Sam nodded, Henri said, "Good, good. I am glad." And from his serious eyes and quiet voice, it was clear that he meant it.

But that was all Henri said. He gave me a small smile that took some effort, put his hand on my shoulder for a moment, then said, "So long," using one of the many expressions the French have that all seem to say the same simple thing when parting from someone but which have different meanings depending on when they actually expect to see you again, and which it took me a long time to sort out—until I was in jail, in fact, the Paris jail I mean, when I spent a lot of time wondering when this person or that might next visit me. I did not pay attention to such things that day when Henri left us in the dormitory, but thinking back on it now he probably said something like "A la prochaine"—Until the next time—rather than "A bientôt"—See you soon. He walked away from us to the other side of the hall where he met up with Rose. I did not see any of the joking that usually began every meeting between them. The two of them moved off to a corner and spoke together quietly. Alone.

Yours,
Herschel

Maître,

So, Geneviève. I suppose I must have mentioned her to you, since she has found her way onto your list. And yes, I ignored it the first time you wrote asking me about her. But not trying to hide some evil secret, Maître—I just did not see how speaking about her would be of any purpose. For the court. Or for me. But now you have asked again about her, and all right it gives me no concern. Certainly not for her. I did not yet finish telling you of my time at the Expo dormitories, but the two were connected, the Expo and Geneviève, at least when I first came to know her.

Genève, they call her. Perhaps because that was where her parents had been sending her to school, to boarding school, the Switzerland city, since she was small. Or not. Probably not. Pardon, Maître, but this habit has got hold of me, this looking for reasons behind the reasons for things. Maybe because so much of what happened while I was in Paris I only later understood. Or never did. But there I am again—the habit.

Her family name is Lazare. Like the famous saint. That they love so much in Paris, it seems—the Gare Saint Lazare train station, the giant hospital Saint Lazare. I first met her at a party, her parents' home. Or rather, I saw her at the party, because I was not one of the guests and we certainly were not introduced. This party was a few weeks after the Expo opened, a month or so after the dinner at Bernard and Elsa's. One evening when I got back to Rue Martel from work at the Foire dormitory there was a note from Tante Chawa under the door of the top-floor maid's room where I was sleeping at the time, asking me to come downstairs to Maison Albert. Chawa had a message from Bernard for me to go see him, something about more work, though Chawa did not know what—Bernard never told Abraham or Chawa more than he absolutely had to. I was working almost every day at the Foire and had no energy for anything more, and certainly no taste to see Bernard. But Abraham reminded me that the Expo, and so my work there, would only last through the summer. And from this message it seemed that Bernard had changed his mind about work for me. Who knew? So, later that evening I dragged myself down to a café to telephone him. He seemed surprised and annoyed that I called—which I did not understand until we made an appointment and he insisted that I come not to his home but to his main atelier above Au Courant Dame. I realized then that he had expected me to reply to his message by contacting him at the atelier rather than—crossing some line I had not seen—telephoning him at home.

On a day off from the Foire the following week, I went to see him. It turned out not to be Bernard himself who had work for me but someone he knew, which gave him even more of a pinch-mouth than usual. Me working for someone else, you see, Bernard would have no control, or even know what I was doing, though I would be carrying his name, as someone he referred, and his relation. His uncomfort was also partly because of the people who had asked about me. Top, top crust, Bernard said in a tone like a warning. They were a very old and wealthy French family, the Lazares, friends with government ministers, and important to Bernard's business—they owned textile factories, a major part of a bank, and interests in several big Paris department stores. They were also important in the community, Bernard made a point of saying. He was proud to tell me that the Lazares had attended the party where I had been a server, which had led them to contact Bernard about me. But I later learned that this was another reason Bernard was even more thorny than usual that day—the work I was being called for was again to serve at a party, but Bernard and Elsa had not been invited to it.

When Monsieur and Madame Lazare were at Bernard and Elsa's dinner, Monsieur Lazare had noticed me speaking German with that couple, the von—whatever their name was—and later contacted Bernard about me. When Monsieur Lazare learned from Bernard that I was Bernard's relative, or sort of, that apparently made me reliable enough, but it was being German that would make me useful to him. I began to ask Bernard about my papers, about what I should say to these people about the récépissé—the receipt from the police—being my only official paper, but he waved me off, saying that for people like the Lazares such things would not be a concern.

The Lazare home, Maître—well, the one of their homes that is in Paris—how possible to describe it? It made Bernard and Elsa's fancy flat seem like Abraham and Chawa's two old rooms in Bastille. It was in La Muette, a section of the 16th arrondissement with enormous houses, each one with its own private green and wooded grounds that made it all feel like part of the Bois de Boulogne, the great forest park that stretched out just behind. High stone walls surrounded the Lazare property, the house itself made of stone the color of salmon poché—I am sorry, I do not have the German word for it—that was one of the many dishes served at their party that I had never seen before. The main house was two stories high and wide enough to have eight or ten long double windows across the ground floor, and four double windows on the sides, so how many rooms, enormous rooms, would that be? I was only once—much later—in the main house, and then only in one room. But I remember during the party, which was held in the rear gardens, looking up and counting 11 or 12 chimneys, not including the service annex, a separate large building of its own, with the kitchens and pantries and sculleries and laundry rooms, as well as the rooms where the household servers lived, and where I first reported for instructions a few days after my meeting with Bernard. Once again my friend Sam happily took over my shift in the Foire kitchen that day—he always needed the money from an extra shift, and he was eager for the chance in the kitchen hall to fill his pockets with whatever leftover or unattended food he could manage to liberate, as he called it.

There were five or six people bustling about the kitchens and pantries in the Lazare annex building when I appeared at the door there, and it took a few minutes for someone to decide to pay me attention. Finally, one of the maids said she would fetch Monsieur Philippe. After 15 or so more minutes waiting, in walked a tall, dignified-looking man in a beautifully tailored formal dress suit with a striped waistcoat. He was very proper but quite polite as he took me into a small parlor room, still in the service building. As he began to explain the upcoming event and what my duties would be, I slowly realized that this was not the master of the house but the chief butler or manservant or whatever they called him—anyway, the head of the household servers.

Monsieur Philippe explained that there was to be an afternoon garden party with about 50 people, and several of them would be visitors from Germany. Although I would carry around a bottle of sparkling water on a serving tray, my real job was simply to be available for these German guests, to hover around the edges of the party and keep them in sight so I could make myself useful if they needed something and wanted to express it in German. If the request was anything that I could not simply and immediately fulfill myself, I was to inform him, Monsieur Philippe, directly. It was unlikely that I would actually be called on to do much of anything—I was more of an insurance, he told me, for the special comfort of these particular guests. He gave me the card of a shop that would arrange for the uniform I was to wear, then told me when to report for the event—Saturday midday, in a fortnight. And that was it. No training sessions, unlike with the terribly anxious Bernard and Elsa. No mention of papers. No further instructions. Whatever arose, Monsieur Philippe told me as he sent me out the rear door, I was just to let him know and he would take care of it.

In the meantime, I continued working at the Foire kitchen hall. But soon I needed to be away from work again. Uncle Abraham had kept at me about trying to extend my German reentry visa, so I arranged for Sam to take over my kitchen shift for two days, in case it took that long, while I went to the Reich consulate. Not the embassy, where I went much later—the shooting. No, this was the consulate, a different place, where they processed passports and visas, over near the Luxembourg Gardens. There were quite a few French people waiting there for visas to visit Germany but there was a separate queue for residents of the Reich. I can report that the bureau was very well organized.

I showed my Reich reentry visa for Belgium, which was in my old passport, and explained that once I had arrived in Brussels I had also decided to visit my family in Paris, that they had then invited me to stay with them for a while—Uncle Abraham was there to confirm this—and so I was asking that my visa be extended. The man who processed the papers said my name, or a version of my name, and looked coldly at my Poland passport. Otherwise he barely raised his head and said little, writing down the information and telling us that I would be notified by post to Uncle Abraham's address once the consulate had received an answer from Berlin. When that would be, the man responded to Abraham's question without looking up, he could not say.

14 June

The week before the party at the Lazare house, my scheduled day off from work at the Foire was to be a Friday. Which I had been waiting for. Bourgeois Friday, the workers at the Expo called it. You see, the Popular Front government had insisted that the Expo offer half-price admission one day a week, so that chômeurs and other people without much money might afford to visit the nation's great exhibition. But in return the Expo officials were allowed to set aside one day a week to be double-price—for those who prefer not to be jostled by crowds, or to mix with the types who make up the crowds. That day was Friday. Bourgeois Friday.

You see, Maître, I wanted to bring three people with me to the Expo, to give them an outing, but the cost for four of us, plus at least some food and drink while we were there, would have been quite an expense even if we went on half-price day. I now had regular work at the Foire, but the pay was not exactly hefty, and I was trying to save as much as I could, knowing that the work would not continue once the Expo finished. I considered asking Rose if she could help get the four of us into the Expo, but she was so busy, and had so many people constantly asking her for things, that I did not feel right about it. Then I thought of Henri. He did not work at the Expo himself, but he and his foreign section had many connections to the place. I had not even seen Henri in two weeks or so, not since the short strange exchange with me and Sam at the dormitory, when Henri had come to speak privately with Rose. And I had not spent any real time with him since before I failed to show up at May Day, which was now many weeks before. So, it occurred to me that wanting help getting into the Expo was also a good excuse to go see him. Though with Henri, I really needed no excuse at all.

I found him in the foreign section bureau early in the evening, after my day's work at the Foire kitchen hall. It was 21 June. The bureau was crowded, but there was very little of the movement or noise—the sense of action—that I had always found there before. People were huddled in groups, talking quietly. Henri barely looked up when he noticed me, then after a few moments slowly made his way over to where I was standing by the door. He took me by the arm and led me outside. On the pavement in front of the bureau he smiled and asked how I was doing, but the smile was tired and the question only half called for an answer. I told him that I was working steadily at the Foire kitchen, and said how grateful I was to him for introducing me there. He nodded but said nothing. It was uncomfortable. Henri had always before been the one to grab the moment and take us in some direction or other—except for that time I brought him to the roller skating—but now he seemed a blank.

I decided that I should at least tell him the reason, the practical reason, for my visit, so I explained that I had three friends who I thought badly needed some relief from their every day and night in a little room making soles for shoes, and that the Expo might be a great distraction for them but they could not afford it. Was there any way he could help me help them? He asked did I know about the half-price day, and I told him yes, but two of the friends are small children and the enormous crowds on those days might mean the little ones would see nothing. Also, I told him, they do not speak much French, the children, or even their mother, and trying to understand what was going on with all the noise and people on that most crowded of days would be difficult for them. "That is why I am thinking of Bourgeois Friday," I said. "But that would be double the expense—if we had to pay the entry fee, that is."

Henri's expression changed only slightly, but he seemed to like what I was hinting at, of sneaking them in, and the extra naughtiness of doing it on a Friday.

"Well," he said slowly, "they guard the entrances specially close on Fridays, which makes it extra difficult. And we certainly have no friends among the Expo security goons." He paused to think for a moment, and without meaning anything by it I rattled on a bit about Mirari and her children, how they were hiding out in Paris without any papers while her husband was still in Spain.

"Spain?" Henri suddenly perked up.

I told him the little I knew, that the Franco army had driven Mirari and her children out of her hometown in Basque country and that her husband had remained behind, fighting against the Fascists. Henri listened carefully, then drifted away for a few moments. "The husband," he asked, snapping out of it, "which group?"

"Group?" I had no idea.

He stared at me with big eyes, trying to see inside my head, to find whatever else might be in there about these people from Spain.

"Is it important, which group?" I finally said, trying to hide my disappointment at disappointing him with how little I knew. "For getting into the Expo, I mean?"

Henri continued to stare, then slowly closed his eyes and lowered his head, shaking it. "Stupid," he muttered, "so stupid," then looked up. "Me, I mean. Forgive me. Yes, H, we will get them in, your friends." He shook his head again. "That, at least, I think we can still manage to do."

21 June. Why do I know, Maître? Because the next day was history. The newspapers all said so. The day the Communists left the government. It was complicated, all the reasons, I never sorted it all out. But without the Communists, the Popular Front was finished. And with it, the confederation's weight with the government, and its hold over much of the work at the Expo, was also finished. All of it, finished. Which Henri, when I saw him that day, surely already knew.

Yours,
Herschel

Maître,

I am sorry not to have written for some days but it was impossible. Because of the fever. I am not ill myself, Maître, but I have learned that a terrible storm of it has hit this place—the main camp, I mean. So, to keep it from getting to us special prisoners, they cleaned out our cells and everything else here in the bunker.

One at a time we were ordered to collect our clothes and bring them down to the shower room on the ground floor. There I had my head shaved and then was made to sit in a small metal tub where they poured bucket after bucket of scalding water on me, which smelled like it had some kind of chemical in it, against whatever it was they were trying to kill. It was screamingly painful, Maître. Though for moments, alongside the pain, there was another feeling—it was my first hot water since the public bathhouse in Paris, before the shooting. Soon it will be three years since I first went to jail.

My clothes were dumped into another tub of water that was boiling over a fire on the shower room cement floor. Then I was given a shirt and trousers, much worn and much too big, and sent into the small open space behind the bunker building. It was the first time in days I had been outside—none of us from the bunker had been allowed our usual outdoor air time. And still we are not. When I got outside, several other bunker prisoners were already there, also with shaved heads and raw red skin from the scalding, and wearing worn, bad-fitting shirts and trousers. We were made to wait there while the others from the bunker—there are now 12 of us altogether—went through the same treatment and joined us outside. We were not allowed to talk, though anyway we were all trying to keep our mouths closed and noses covered—because the chimney next door, in the main camp, was choking us with smoke and ash. For several days the chimney has been busier than ever, thick black smoke pouring out of it without stop.

While we were out there waiting, inside the bunker everything was being pulled from our cells. Once all 12 of us were outside, we saw some main camp prisoners brought into the bunker building, then later saw them shuffling away. They had dragged our pallet mattresses and bedcovers out in front and dumped them into a pile which the guards then set on fire, adding to the rain of ash. We were then sent past the smoldering pile back into the bunker, and were herded to the showers again where each of us was given a bucket of water scooped from the boiling tub. Burning our hands, we were made to carry the water up to our cells, which we found completely empty. We tossed the water onto the floor of our cells, and twice more were sent back down to the shower room, to repeat the process. Then we were given brooms to sweep the water, as best we could, all around the cell, then out, down the stairs and outside. At the end of all this, each of us was given a single bedcover, blanket and a replacement pallet, which for an hour or more I held standing on end, balanced on the tops of my feet, until the water slowly dried from the floor of the cell—thanks be that it is summer. Over the next several days we were allowed, one at a time, to retrieve our personal things from a dark storeroom where it had all been thrown together in a huge pile.

My clothes did not do very well in the boiling, Maître. I can still wear them, but I do not think they will last for long. I was allowed to keep the extra shirt and trousers they gave me after the scalding. They are both much too large, though the trousers are actually quite well made, with a label inside from a tailor in Hamburg. They will be my only clothes once the others fall apart, which will be soon, I am sure. So, if perhaps you could send me one other shirt and trousers, I would be most grateful. Also, in all the gathering and dragging and dumping of things, most of my paper and the addressed envelopes were ruined, and my second pencil broken. So, it would be a good thing for our work if you could renew my writing supplies.

At least my cell is clean.

Yes, I know, Maître—confine my remarks. But I thought you should know about this big illness, though they call it just "camp fever." And believed that you would not mind me reporting how they have tried to keep it away from us here in the bunker.

So. I do not remember what I have already said about her, Maître, but I know I was beginning to tell you about Geneviève. Seeing her, the first time, at her parents' party—though at the time I did not know she was their daughter—where I had this curious job of tending to the German guests.

There is not much for me to say about the party, except seeing Genève. I arrived at the Lazare property at midday, and in the service building one of the household staff gave me the uniform that had been delivered there for me, which I had been fitted for at a shop several evenings before. It was similar to the outfit I had worn at Bernard and Elsa's party—formal jacket, waistcoat, collared shirt with bow tie, white cotton gloves. But this time everything was slightly, well, more—more pleated the trousers, more styled the collar, more tailored the jacket. And all of it white this time, except the trousers. The household staff were also all in white—because the party was in summer, you see, outdoors, and in daytime. So many things I learned in Paris, Maître.

By the time I arrived, chairs and tables covered in linen had already been set up on the back terraces and in the huge rear garden. There was still plenty of activity, though, with the cooks finishing the hot dishes, and food platters being prepared, flowers arranged, and cutlery and bottle coolers and such set out. All the other servers seemed to know exactly what they were doing and no one asked me to help. Before the guests were due to begin arriving, Monsieur Philippe—the head of the staff, I think I told you—called all us servers, 15 or more, into a large rear room of the main house. After a few moments Monsieur Lazare, who only much later I learned was Genève's father, entered from deeper inside the house. I was immediately impressed. Everything about him. He was perhaps 50 years old, tall and trim and handsome, with a full head of straight, deep brown hair swept on the sides with silver. He said just a few words, in a very soft voice. So soft, in fact, that I noticed the absolute silence in the room, the lack of even the slightest movement by any of the staff, in order that he could be heard. I was fascinated by the way he could stand there so erect and so relaxed at the same time. He praised the staff for their hard work in preparing the garden and thanked them in advance for making the guests comfortable. There was no sense of bossness in any of this, no worry or threat, no effort to press us with concern. In fact, no effort at all.

As Monsieur Lazare was finishing his few words, Madame Lazare came in. She was small and small-boned, with fine features, light eyes, and a mass of chestnut hair piled into a form that would soon support a garden party hat. The room was very large, and Madame Lazare stood with her husband on the far side of it, maybe four or five meters of empty space between them and us. Like her husband, Madame spoke in a very relaxed and undemanding tone, simply reminding us of certain matters regarding the order of serving. She smiled slightly—whether actually at us, I could not tell—then disappeared with her husband back into the house.

Guests soon started arriving and I began my job of walking around the gardens with bottles of fizzy water—one each from France and Germany—balanced on a tray. At Bernard and Elsa's party, the von-whatever couple had been obvious as the only Germans among the French, and anyway Bernard had pointed them out to me. At the Lazares, though, I could not tell who was from where, and neither Monsieur Philippe or any of the servers bothered to tell me, if even they knew. Neither did the guests' looks give me any hints. The women were all wearing similar outfits—long white or pastel dresses with bare arms and matching color enormous flat hats that looked like serving platters, worn slightly atilt. The men were in fine suits, most of them with a type of snug, cross-the-chest tailoring that I had never seen before, in France or Germany. And none of the men wore a hat, whose style might have helped me spot the Germans. So, I just drifted around the edges of the garden, occasionally pouring water and overhearing bits of conversation, including some quiet laughter about the fall of the Popular Front, but not any German spoken, or French with a German accent. Then Geneviève appeared.

It was about an hour into the party when she came through the large open double doors at the rear of the house and out onto the first terrace. I did not take much notice of her right away, except that she was the only person I had seen who was near to my age, and that the outfit she wore was nothing like any of the other women. She had on a narrow blue jacket with faint white stripes and dark blue silk trousers, very stylish but certainly—and as I learned about her later, certainly intended to be—different from all the others. And instead of one of the platter hats, or any hat at all, her thick flow of light reddish brown hair fell loose to her shoulders.

I did not get a close look at her until later, when on my circuit around the gardens I came across her standing with two of the younger, but still middle age, men guests. One of the men gestured to me. As I poured the fizzy water for them, I heard the three of them talking in German. Though they spoke slowly and pronounced things carefully, I suppose for Geneviève's benefit, the two men sounded like native speakers. Genève's German, on the other hand, was awful, barely a beginner's and with no sense of the sounds, so bad that at certain mangled phrases the three of them could not help but laugh. I was about to move off again when one of the men gestured to a single small plate on the table next to them, empty except for a bit of oil, and asked the others whether they wanted any more of it. I say "it" because, although he named it in German, I had never heard the word before. Neither Genève or the other man had any interest. I noticed that this was the only food plate on the table—it was remarkable to me, Maître, how much beautiful food there was at this party and how little of it the people there ate. What is it about rich people, Maître? How is it they need to eat less than other people do?

Anyway, the man then spoke to me in French—I could hear his German accent, now—asking that I bring him some of that, ah. He paused, because he did not know the French word for it, and turned to Genève for help. She made a face as if to say "I cannot help you" because, as she said now in French, he had eaten whatever it was before she had joined them and so did not know what it had been. My brain did a quick race over all the foods I had seen on the serving platters, many of which I did not know the names of—in either lan-guage—but I remembered a particularly strange-looking pale veg-etable preserved in oil that was served along with a miniature fork and which I had heard one of the servers name when mentioning to another how delicious it was. One of those same little forks lay on the edge of the plate, and I decided—well, something in me decided, because I did not really think about it—to speak up.

"Artichoke?" I pronounced in French as well as I could recall it.

"Yes," the German man said in French, "that was it."

"Of course, then," I replied in German, "I will see if I can locate some and if so I will be happy to bring it."

All three of them now turned to me in surprise at my speaking fluent German, and for the first time I got a close look—we are the same height, so I was staring straight into them—at those eyes. Green with velvet grey, or velvet grey with green, depending on the day and the time and the light—and, as I found out later, her mood. Add to those eyes her light chestnut hair and a faint mask of freckles on pale skin, and she was either quite lovely or quite peculiar looking but any way you viewed her, a surprise.

"Who are you?" she asked me in French, not as a challenge but with interest. Or at least curiosity. The man who had asked about the food looked doubly surprised—first, that I had spoken to them in German, and now, it seemed to me, that Genève was bothering to ask something personal of a server.

"No one in particular," I answered—or however that came out in my foreigner's French.

Genève continued to stare at me for a moment, then said, with a small, still interested expression, "Well, artichoke it is." She looked at me a moment longer, then turned back to the two men. I went off in search of artichoke. By the time I returned with it the two men were still there, now chatting in French with a couple, but Genève had moved on to another part of the gardens.

I continued wandering around, once in a while filling a glass and on one occasion speaking German to a German guest, more as a bored volunteer than as a rescuer, but mostly trying to find another chance for an encounter with Genève. I did not find one, and after a while realized that she was no longer there, at least not out in the gardens. At the end of the day I returned my uniform, received a pay envelope from Monsieur Philippe, and went on my way back to Paris east without another word from any of the Lazares, parents or daughter.

Yours,
Herschel

Maître,

After the Lazare party, my next time off from work at the Foire kitchen hall was the following Friday, when I hoped to take Mirari and her children to the Expo. And somehow Henri managed to arrange it. We went to a certain entrance gate on the Quai d'Orsay, near the Hall of Work, asked for someone whose name Henri had given me, and found ourselves on a list—or at least, the man Henri had sent us to pretended that we were on a list—that allowed all four of us into the Expo for free. It was not easy for Mirari to give up a whole day's working on her leather, and I had to suggest it several times before she agreed. But now that she saw her children's faces—six-year old Suela and her smaller brother Abel—when the Expo was spread out in front of them, I could see her pleasure in it and knew I had done a good thing. Or thought so.

The Expo felt quite different this double-price Friday than it had two weeks before, when I had gone there on a Sunday to get my first look at it since the official opening. On that day it had been packed with people—Sunday is a day off from work in Paris. At least for the French. The jumble of pavilions and halls and stages, many still constructing, had been so confusing on that Sunday that instead of being able to choose where to go and what to see, the detours and long queues and surges by the enormous crowds had decided for me. I left after only an hour. But on this Bourgeois Friday there were so many fewer visitors that it seemed almost like a private showing for them, the Friday people who strolled around as if they owned the Expo. Which I suppose they did.

As soon as we were inside the grounds I took Suela and Abel by the hand—Mirari trailed behind, so tired, moving slowly, relieved I think for me take over the children for a while—and led them directly into a giant amusement park that the Expo had built on the Esplanade des Invalides, just next to where we had entered. Straight away the children were amazed by a rollercoaster that snaked through the area. The crowd was quite thin in this amusement park, there were few other children, and no queue for the roller ride. So, with Mirari waiting below I took the two children onto the ride, which made them wildly happy and terrified at the same time, little Abel screaming at the top of his lungs while Suela sat with a brave frozen smile.

When we got off the roller, the children spotted one of the tiny, toy-like open electric trams without rails, that could carry altogether maybe 15 or 20 people in its little bucket cars, zig-zagging through the grounds. The tram stopped nearby. I asked the driver where it was going and he just twirled his hand in the air as if to say "Around and around," so the four of us got in. There were only four other passengers. The tram rattled off, heading toward the central part of the Expo, the great Champ de Mars fields now covered with all sorts of pavilions and exhibition halls and places for food and drink, and which led down to the Tour Eiffel and the foreign pavilion area across the river. The tram stopped a few times to let one or two people on and off, but we did not budge—it was slowly making its way toward the great tower, and Mirari and the children were hypnotized by it. They had never seen it close up. In fact, they had never before been to the west part of Paris. We got off the tram at the base of the tower and I asked how we could get to the top. A guide pointed to a queue that stretched around the back, even on this less crowded Friday, and with the children as wiggly as they were, I immediately gave up the idea of waiting. Nearby was the photo-cinema pavilion, with the television machine that all Paris had been talking about, so I headed us over there, but it turned out this was the only other place that day that had a crowd at the entrance, so we gave it a miss also. To make the children feel better I bought a sugared crêpe for each of them, then we crossed the bridge to the right side of the river.

Immediately over the bridge we passed the enormous Germany pavilion, which was matched, directly across a plaza, by the almost as big Soviet building. I was curious to see what the Reich had brought to show at the Expo, but from the outside the building was not very welcoming—it looked like a single mammoth block of concrete—and it certainly did not interest the children. When I turned to see whether Mirari wanted a look inside, the twisted muscles of her face gave an answer without me having to ask.

We kept moving, and a few paces past the Reich pavilion Mirari stopped and said simply, "Espagne." The Spanish flag flew in front of a three-story building with rows of large photographs mounted on an outside wall. Mirari explained some of the photos for me, as best she could with the small French we struggled to share in our very different accents. The photos were of schools and hospitals and power stations, groups of people playing sport or camping, land watering systems, farmers learning new techniques from a government helper—things the Spanish republic, and especially its Popular Front, had accomplished before the civil war had begun. Mirari was pleased and proud at what was in the photos, but the pavilion was not finished and not yet open to visitors.

The children were now jabbering at their mother and she finally quieted them with a sharp word, looking around almost worriedly. I asked what the children had said, and Mirari told me, a bit embarrassed, that they wanted to go back to the amusement park area. Well, there was far too much at the Expo to see in any one day, and there was just as much near the amusement area as anywhere else, so I said to Mirari why not we go back there and visit a pavilion or two while mixing in amusement park things for the children. She nodded gratefully and I grabbed each child by a hand and swung them around in the air, crowing "Here we go!" People near us did not look pleased.

We found another tram and after a few minutes crisscrossing the Champ de Mars we made it back to the edge of the amusement grounds. The children wanted to go onto a parachute drop contraption, but we were told that they were too small. The Expo worker who turned us away told us that there were singing and dancing performances, and sometimes tumbling and juggling and such, on a stage across the way, so we headed over there, to a section of the amusement grounds called Old France—which was a collection of tiny pretend country village houses in local styles, built around a central square, and people walking around in fairytale costumes.

There was nothing happening when we got to the raised stage in the square. A sign said the next performance would be in three quarters of an hour. That was too long just to wait around with the children, but nearby was a remarkable building that all of us had been impressed by as we passed it on the way into the grounds. The front of this building—several stories high—looked like a giant ocean liner, or a great zeppelin, except it was made of glass and from the outside you could see in to a sculpture of enormous intercrossed metal rings hanging from the ceiling, and suspended in the middle of the rings an actual airplane, tilted to make it look like it was flying. This was the Palais de l'Air—the air travel pavilion. We walked around to the front and the children's eyes grew wide when they saw the hanging plane, so Mirari and I decided that after the Old France stage show we would return straightaway to this Palais de l'Air. Some frites potatoes and cool drinks that I bought for us—the children almost could not believe their good fortune—helped pass the time.

At the Old France village square some performers were gathering on stage, a troupe of young women and girls in some kind of local countryside costume—layers of skirts and aprons, with a white lace head cover that peaked in two points—and behind them three musicians. As the girls got into formation, someone stepped to the front and announced that this troupe performed authentic—that word they loved at the Expo—music and dance from the Allier region. I had never heard this name before, had no idea where it was—in the Auvergne, Maître, the center of the country, as I later learned—but at the time it did not matter. We just wanted to see the show.

It was clog dancing, wooden shoe clogs, and not at all clumsy as you might imagine but very fast and complicated and precise with the way they struck the floor in rhythms and weaved patterns in and out. I was surprised and impressed. The children loved it, not least because of the loud noise the clogs made on the stage.

It was during the second dance that I saw her. A few moments after the music began three young women stepped out of the troupe of 20 or so and moved to the front of the stage, where they performed special steps together as featured dancers. In the middle, in front of the other two, was Genève. It took me a few minutes to recognize her. We were at the back of the crowd, and I had little Abel on my shoulders for him to see better, so I could not move up to get a closer look. Right away she seemed familiar, but at the same time I began thinking it might be Genève I also doubted it. I had only seen her the one brief time at the party, and this odd costume made her look quite different. Not to mention the place and the company—What would a rich Paris girl be doing in the middle of countryside folk dancers? I finally became convinced that it really was Genève, though, and did not take my eyes off her, not wanting to miss the moment when she might notice me.

It did not happen. There was one more dance, with Genève again taking a solo turn—she really was quite skilled at this odd, complicated dancing—but then the troupe was finished. I had the urge to go behind the stage, to tell her that I had seen her, that I remembered her, and to let her see me, the real me, not the one in a server's uniform. But I had the children and Mirari, and we had planned to return to the Palais de l'Air, and the crowd stood between us and the stage, and there were all the dancers and the musicians and chaperones. Anyway, what would I say? "Hello, remember me, I once served you fizzy water at a party?"

The announcer returned and told the crowd that the same performers would be on again in the afternoon, so I had an unexpected boost of hope that I could come back and see Genève again then. Mirari and the children and I now headed to the air pavilion. As we left the stage area, I noticed in the crowd what I thought were the two German men from the Lazare party, the ones who had been talking to Genève.

The Palais de l'Air, Maître. An incredible place—the building alone, with its three-story high glass dome entry hall and the suspended airplane inside the ring sculpture, plus many other remarkable airplane displays all through it. In the entry hall the children were a little frightened but amazed by the huge airplane engine on a pedestal that roared to life every few minutes, its workings explained by a French military man. We moved on to the huge galleries further inside, which were filled with planes of all types, some of them large models on pedestals but others full-size and hanging from the ceiling. On the walls were pictures of old time planes as they developed over the years, as well as huge maps of the continents showing all the places that were now connected to each other by passenger airline companies.

In a large central gallery, French military men were explaining some of their special planes, the walls showing photos of parachuting soldiers. After a few minutes with the children walking around this gallery, I returned to Mirari who was waiting near the exit. Her head was down. Quietly, she was weeping. I asked her what the matter was. She glanced up at me, and for a moment her eyes flicked toward the ceiling, but she did not speak before looking down again. Now I looked up at what I had only glanced at before, the ceiling entirely covered by a startling realistic painting—or perhaps it was a super enlarged photograph, which was one of the Expo's favorite new gadgets, these huge clear photo prints—of squadrons of bomb-heavy military planes, flying low in perfect formations as if they were right above us. The children saw Mirari's tears and now clung to her, their joy and curiosity of a few moments before wiped away by their mother's unhappiness, and it was clear to me, without knowing what was going on, that we should leave this place.

Outside, Mirari still could barely speak through her tears, and managed to say only "I need to go home." So I walked with her and the now silent children to the bus, rode with them, still without speaking, back to Rue Martel. At the door to their garret room, Mirari sent her children inside, then thanked me, still with difficulty getting her words out. I could see that she wanted to explain, but it just seemed too difficult.

"Guarnika. My family. I am sorry," was all she managed, then went into her room and closed the door.

The town in Spain, Maître, the Basque part of Spain—Guarnika. That had been wiped away by bombs, just a few weeks before, and so many killed. It was very close to where Mirari was from, this town, a place where she had family. For many days it had been in all the newspapers, with photographs of the terrible destruction. Mirari had kept several of these pictures in her room, and since she had learned of the bombing she had spoken little, about anything, and had seemed even more sorrowful than before. Which was part of why I thought that getting her and the children out of their little room, to the Expo, would be a good thing.

The Palais de l'Air, Maître. The Guarnika bombs had been dropped from airplanes. Squadrons of airplanes flying low. Just like those on the palais ceiling.

Because of how long it took to return to Rue Martel, I knew I would not make it back to the Expo in time for the dance group's second performance. I went anyway. I hoped there would be a still later performance and went straight to the Old France village, after paying—Henri's contact was no longer at the gate—the Friday double rate entrance fee. I tried to find out if the group would be there again but I did not know its name, and could not even remember Allier, the region, so my asking two different guides there about clog dancers got me only the assurance that yes, such dancing was very popular in la France profonde, very special, only in France, and the countryside girls all beautiful, as a foreign visitor I should certainly see it, there would be plenty of such dancing at many of the regional pavilions, all over the Expo, be certain not to miss it, I would surely take home wonderful memories. I waited there for two hours, through two more performances. Heard some lovely lute music. And fiddlers from some-where in the south. But no Genève.

When I got back to Rue Martel that night, I thought I would knock on Mirari's door, to see if she was feeling any better, but I heard no sound inside and did not want to disturb them if they were asleep, so I decided to leave them be.

26 June

The next morning I was back at work in the Foire kitchen hall. Among the masses of people who moved through the breakfast queues I saw some of Genève's dance troupe, in their costumes. Stupidly, it just had not occurred to me that they would be staying at the dormitories, like so many other groups from the countryside. I waited for Genève to come in, trying to think of what I could say to remind her that I "knew" her, but without simply putting in her mind the image of me as a server at the party—just another one of the many people who regularly served her. Especially because, as I spoke to her, what would I be doing? Serving her breakfast.

After a while she had not appeared, at least not at my end of the hall, and the girls from her troupe were readying to head to the Expo. I was stuck behind the serving counter. Also, there were rules about Foire workers not bothering the dormitory guests. Anyway, how would I ask one of these dancers about Genève since I did not even know her name? I tried anyway. I slipped out and spoke to three girls from the troupe, asking could they tell me where to find a girl from their group who had long reddish hair and grey-green eyes and—but I did not know the French word for freckles. The girls may have been instructed not to talk to the men who worked at the Foire dormitories—though Sam did not seem to be having that problem—but perhaps it was just the directness, or clumsiness, of how I asked. Or my German accent. They barely looked at me before marching out the door.

I stayed around the kitchen hall after my shift was over late that afternoon, hoping Genève would show up with her group for the evening meal but I did not spot any of them. Eventually it occurred to me that they might be doing an evening performance, so I raced up to the Expo, paid another entrance fee, and hurried over to the Old France stage. Accordion music. From the Alsace. I cannot tell you how painful, Maître. Followed a half hour later by a church choir. Which was an improvement. But no Genève. Her troupe could have been performing somewhere else at the Expo—I could have tried the Auvergne pavilion in the Regional Center, but at the time I did not know that the Allier was in the Auvergne. Or by then they might have been back at the kitchen hall having their evening meal. Or out somewhere in Paris, country girls enjoying an evening in the big city. In which case, where would sophisticated Paris girl Genève be?

I decided to try one more thing. I knew Sam had been working the overnight shift at the dormitories that week. So I walked back down to the Foire and waited for him to show up, then asked if he would switch shifts with me—him to the kitchens tomorrow, me taking his dormitory shift that night. I could have just stayed around the dormitory that night without working, but I had missed several shifts recently, and had spent a lot of money on all my different entry fees to the Expo, plus what I had spent for food and drink on Mirari and the children, so I felt that I badly needed the pay. Sam was not too keen on the idea—one of the kitchen hall foremen had given him a hard time about the switching we had done before, these foreigners who could not just work the shifts they were assigned. Of course, Sam owed me his job here in the first place. But I did not want to again ask a favor, so instead I decided to sweeten the pot and offered to switch with him permanently, him to the kitchen, me back to the dormitory. He looked around while considering—there were hundreds of young females moving about, just in our immediate area. Also, the late night shifts he had now were very easy work, he had told me, mostly just guarding against thieves and troublemakers, and left him daytimes to work on his other schemes, and to tend to his mother who was ill again. But after a few moments the idea of all that food in the kitchen hall—not only the amounts he could wolf down while working but also what he could smuggle out for himself and his mother—won him over. So, he quickly explained what my simple overnight duties were at the dormitory, then headed out. And I immediately began surveying the enormous hall, hoping to get a glimpse of Allier clog dancers.

It was ridiculous. There were thousands of people spread out over the hall, and though I imagined I might be able to spot the whole troupe together, in their costumes, once they had changed into their regular clothes it was hopeless. Not to mention that there were six other Foire halls serving as dormitories, and the troupe could have been in any of those. In the morning I headed to the kitchen hall with the idea of seeing if the troupe came in, but of course there were thousands there also, and after being awake all night I could barely keep my eyes open, let alone pick out one country costume from all the others. I gave up and went back to Rue Martel to get some sleep.

I worked the rest of that week on the late night shift, hoping to spot the Allier clog dancers and so Genève, but I never did. By the end of that week I had given up the idea, and wanting a more normal schedule again—so I could have an evening meal once in a while with Uncle Abraham and Tante Chawa, go over to the Aurore now and again, take a stroll and get up to who knew what mischief with Sam, and maybe even have a chance to visit with Henri—I got Rose to switch me back to a daytime shift. The first thing I did when I got home for my first free evening in a week was to look in on Mirari and the children. The door to their room was ajar, the room empty—clothes, bedding, spirit stove, the valises they had stacked up to use as a table and workbench, all gone. The only thing left was a bare pallet, some newspaper clippings, and a stack of the leather that Mirari had used for making shoe soles.

As I waited and waited for sleep that night, I imagined them arrested and on their way to one of the camps in the south where so many thousands of Spaniards fleeing Franco were being prisoned by the French. After a while, though, I grabbed onto a straw of hope—of the many foreigners I had seen being arrested in Paris east, I had rarely seen any allowed to take all their possessions with them, as it seemed Mirari had. And I thought back to the last time I had seen her, to the only thing she had managed to say through her tears at the Palais de l'Air—"I need to go home."

Yours,
Herschel

Maître Rosenhaus,

Your note. The Communists. Who have not seemed to interest you much before. Though the France police, after the shooting, could not stop asking me about them. Did they have a hand, as you put it, in my Paris life, the Communists? Well, yes, of a sort. And I have no problem telling you so. Though perhaps not a hand that the Reich will find useful. Yes, Maître, we hear things in the bunker. For one, the guards have a radio. And there are other paths in here for news—despite the rules, words rarely sit still. So, Operation Barbarossa, the Reich's surprise attack on Russia last week. Allies suddenly become enemies. And now, also suddenly, you ask me about the Communists. Well.

It was early August, the dog days. I was fortunate that in the afternoons my work kept me in the giant high-roof dormitory, the Hall of Wines, which was much cooler than almost anywhere else in Paris. At least, anywhere else that I would be allowed. That month many French people—the ones who could afford to—streamed out of Paris and its grimy city heat. But the crowds continued to pour into the Expo, especially young people from the provinces who used some of their school or work holidays to come to the great city. So the dormitories were packed, and there was steady work there, even some double shifts for people who wanted it, like Sam and me. But when neither of us was working the second shift, Sam and I often spent the evening together—if he did not have a rendezvous with one of the girls from the dormitories, that is—walking by the river near the Expo, staying outdoors late to avoid our sweatbox rooms, and watching the passing show of nighttime crowds going into and out of the Expo grounds, light beams and fireworks brightening the west Paris sky, lit-up party boats floating down the Seine. Despite the heat, Sam still worked in his jacket with the oversized pockets, and we would make a supper from whatever he had managed to poach from the kitchen hall that day, though he always saved some to bring home to his mother Rina.

I also tried several times to visit with Henri after my work shift. It had been weeks since we had seen each other, except for a passing wave when he came to talk with Rose at the dormitories, as he did quite frequently now but without ever detouring to speak with me. The only place I knew to look for him was the foreign section bureau near the Foire. Each time I stopped by there, large meetings were going on, with ferocious serious faces and voices, much heated arguing. No one said anything to me when I appeared at the door, but I was certainly not encouraged to enter. Twice I saw Henri there, but each time he was in the middle of something and if he saw me he did not signal me to wait.

It was all beginning to fall apart.

Rose was away from the Foire for two days, and when she returned there was none of the joking and chattering, none of the bigness—that is the best way I can think to describe it, Maître—that had always been so much a part of her. In the killing August heat there was a chill in the dormitory air—certain workers now refused to speak to others, several got into shouting matches, others argued and cursed with the foremen. I tried to stay out of the way of all this, asked no questions. Sam saw the same sort of things in the kitchen hall, and because of his fluid Paris French he picked up some of what was going on. In the evening he told me that the problem—though he did not know details—was between the confederation, with its many Communist members, and the foreign sections. Between French workers and workers who were French but not quite French enough.

One morning Henri appeared in a doorway to the main dormitory, near where I was working. When he did not enter, I went over to speak with him. In a hoarse, almost choking voice he said that he could not visit with me just then, but we made an appointment to meet at the end of my shift that afternoon. Henri remained in the doorway as I went back to my work. Eventually he was spotted by several workers from his foreign section, who went over to speak with him. The conversation was short, and as they came back into the hall they called to others from the foreign section, who also went over to

Henri. Some of these workers returned with their heads and shoulders slumped, others with chins in the air and anger on their faces. After a while, when Henri was speaking in the doorway with the last of his foreign section members on that shift, I noticed Rose leaning against a wall—one of the rare times I had ever seen her standing still, and by herself. She was watching Henri. Eventually he saw her, and when the workers he was talking with came back into the hall, Henri and Rose stared at each other for a few moments. I could not see their expressions. Neither moved. Finally, Henri turned and walked away.

The foreign sections were out, Maître. Not just Henri's but all of them. The Party, the official parti communiste français, had decided to cut its ties with them, Henri told me that afternoon. And since the foreign sections now no longer had this connection, the whole confederation was happy to turn its back on them. Also, Henri told me, the Party, or maybe it was the confederation I cannot remember, had regularly given money to the foreign sections, and without it he did not know how his group—or any of the foreign sections—could keep together. We are no longer a section of anything, he said. And take "section" out of "foreign section," all you have left is "foreign."

I asked him why all this was happening. He sighed—he and his comrades must have been chewing on this, arguing over it, for weeks, months. And they had lost. Henri's face showed how tired he was. His answer came out in a rush, not bothering to make his French slow and simple for me, as he usually did, but I did not feel right stopping him to ask what one thing or another meant, so I had some difficulty understanding it—except for his enormous sadness.

"It is full." That was the line the Party had begun to use, Henri said, more and more often and more and more loudly over the past few months. "The boat is full."

Some French syndicats had been complaining for years, Henri told me, that the reason so many Frenchmen were out of work was that there were too many foreigners there. Never mind that the whole world had been in the Great Depression. Or that so many foreigners in France—almost all of those in the foreign sections—had been invited into the country to work exactly because there had not been enough

Frenchmen laborers after the Great War. In recent months, Henri said, this complaining about foreigners had become much stronger. And because of it, the syndicats catholiques and the fascist parties, which had been complaining the longest and loudest, were beginning to win supporters away from the confederation. So now the big left syndicats, with the Party in the lead, had decided to join the chorus singing "France for the French!"—somehow alongside the Internationale.

Almost everyone in the foreign sections, like Henri and his parents, had proper work papers. Which meant that officially, for work at least, they were French. But no longer French enough for the Party. Complaining about foreignness did not quite fit the larger Party line, though, so they added another reason for abandoning the foreign sections—"Lack of discipline." From the way Henri looked at me as he said this, I knew he remembered using the very same words, months before, to warn me away from Sam.

Henri said that things were going to be chaos for a while and that he did not know how soon he would have another chance to visit with me. I must have looked worried—I certainly felt it—because he put his hand on my shoulder and promised that we would not lose each other. If I did not find him after a while at the foreign section bureau, he said to look for him at a rooming house near Place de la République, where he and several friends were staying. I was about to give him the address of Maison Albert, as a place he could always leave a message for me, but I remembered how crazed Uncle Abraham had become at just the mention of the foreign section, and decided against it. So instead, I reminded Henri that for the next four months while the Expo continued, he could always find me working at the Foire dormitories. This seemed to make him uncomfortable, and he did not reply. Instead, he gave my shoulder a light squeeze, then turned and left.

2 July

A few days later a message from the German consulate arrived at Maison Albert, calling me back about the renewing of my visa, my Reich reentry visa. I arranged with Sam to take my following day's shift in the dormitory before his evening shift in the kitchen hall, and the next afternoon I put on a collar and necktie and the suit Uncle Abraham had made for me and went with Abraham to the consulate. As we rode the bus across the city I was taken over by different feelings, one after the other and back again—some of them connected to specific thoughts, others just shivers I could not identify. Abraham had made clear to me that a reentry visa was important for me in Paris—a chance, at least, to keep the French police from getting too agitated if I stumbled into their path. But the visa would also be a permission to return to the Reich. To my parents and Berthe and Marcus. Home. My work at the Foire would be over in a few months, and then what? Other than that one-time stretch of work, my struggles with Paris had not improved after a whole year there—except somewhat my understanding of the language, and of Paris French people, which only made it clearer that things for me were not likely to get any better. Plus this blow to Henri and his foreign section, my one bright spot that now seemed to have gone black.

The idea of giving up on Paris, my endless empty drift there, had already been slowly growing in me—though I said nothing about it to Abraham or Chawa. Now the downfall of the foreign sections, plus going to get this new visa that would allow me to return to Germany, brought it pushing to the surface. On the other hand, letters from my parents and my sister in the recent months had been darker and darker. It was the middle of 1937—I do not suppose I have to tell you, Maître, about the tightening then in the Reich. My parents wrote no details of it, but Berthe's letters told how my father's always small income had been shrinking even further—most of his regular customers could no longer afford the help of a tailor, even one as low on the pole as my father, and almost no work was coming from Germans.

Despite this, and for the first time since I had left home a year before, some money had just arrived from my parents. I do not know the details of how it traveled to me out of Germany, illegally yes I know, so please do not ask. It was not a great sum, a few hundred francs worth. But the note with it from my mother hurt badly. She said how sorry they were that it had taken so long to save this much,

239

and also that it was so little. It made me miserable, Maître, not just that things were going so badly for them but that they should be even poorer on my account, and worse that they should feel badly they could not do more for me. All because I had left the Reich.

The note had led to an argument with Abraham. I wanted him to send the money back to my parents. He said he had no way to get it back into Germany—sent by any normal channel, it would have been taken by the Reich, as I suppose you know. Abraham also reminded me that if I had no other money, he and Chawa would be even more responsible for me than they already were, and as I could see for myself, no more work was coming into Maison Albert than when I had arrived the year before—despite their move to Rue Martel which, Abraham pointed out, sometimes even gave me a room to myself, one of the chambres de bonne. I raged at him, Maître—to my great shame now—telling him that I did not need their help, I could find a room on my own, and did not need their money, or from my parents, because I had been saving from my work at the Foire, and I would work extra shifts and save even more during the coming months until the end of the Expo, four more months of saving, they would see!

With all this on my mind, by the time we reached the Reich consulate that day I was very jumpy. I just wanted to snatch the visa, go off by myself, and not see Abraham or Chawa again until I had sorted out what I was going to do. But at the consulate we had to wait. It was more crowded than the previous time we had come, and as I sat there stewing it all became unbearable—the waiting, my suit and collar, the square-headed clerks, even the German language, the sound of the language, and for some reason especially German spoken by the French who were there transacting their consulate business. With that accent of theirs.

Then I saw her. Or, rather, she saw me, because she was already staring at me when I noticed her. Geneviève. Standing at the consulate entrance desk with Monsieur Lazare—though I still did not realize that he was her father—and one of the two German men who had been with her when I had served them at the garden party. I was so surprised to see her there, and to find her looking at me. I must have had a ridiculous expression because a small laugh escaped her—though not unkindly, I thought. The three of them waited there less than a minute before someone came from an interior office and with extreme politeness escorted them behind closed doors. Genève took another glance at me as they went in, and again coming out just a few minutes later—Abraham and I were still waiting to be called. They were all relaxed smiles, Genève and Monsieur Lazare and the German man, as they glided through the entrance foyer and out the front doors. I could not see for certain that they got in it, but a limousine pulled up almost the moment they went out the door, then soon rolled away.

After scrambling after her without any luck those two days at the Expo and the Foire dormitories, she had almost completely dropped out of my mind. But now here she was again, adding another drum in my head, which made it difficult to give all my concentrating to the decision about what to do once I had the Reich reentry visa.

Uncle Abraham and I were finally sent to a rear room of the consulate where I gave my name to the clerk at a desk and offered my passport. The man did not take the passport, instead looking down at a paper on top of a large pile.

"Your request is denied," he said without any particular tone. Since Uncle Abraham did not understand German, I should have explained to him, but I was too stunned. I could not understand, and asked the clerk what he meant.

"Just so," he said and read from the paper in front of him. "You are a Pole who resided, at the Reich's pleasure, in Hannover. You asked to go abroad to Belgium to recover your health, so that you might return to the Reich and then permanently leave, to Palestine. You were given a certain time to do so. The time has long expired. You are no longer in Belgium recovering your health. And staying with relations in Paris is not migrating to Palestine. So. Denied."

Finally, he looked up at me. I tried to ask something more, I did not know what, but immediately he cut me off. "Berlin has spoken. Good day, junger Herr" he looked down again at the paper, then looked up to pronounce—mispronounce—my name, as if it caused him pain, "Gruenspahn."

I did not do a very good job of explaining things to Abraham as we stood on the pavement outside the consulate. Not that I needed to say much—he had understood the verdict. I could see that he was quite disturbed, but my own confusion was too great at that moment to worry about him, so I turned and walked away on my own. For a while I staggered around the nearby streets, eventually finding myself in the Luxemburg Gardens where I sat on a bench and tried to bring my thoughts together. It was quiet there, a wide green space in the middle of the crowded city. But there was something about it that before long made me uncomfortable—the huge handsome palace, the perfect groomed lawns and flower beds, the nannies and au pairs and their well-fed children, the students from the nearby university so sure of themselves with their turtle-back eyeglasses and pre-made cigarettes. So, I left the gardens and started wandering, without knowing where, until I found myself heading west and south, toward the Foire.

It was a long walk, and by the time I neared the Foire I realized that the afternoon work shift would just then be finishing, so I could speak with Sam before his evening shift in the kitchen hall, to tell him what had happened. There was a commotion going on when I arrived, several dozen workers gathered in groups outside the kitchen hall and the main dormitory, arguing among themselves, people breaking out of one group to curse or threaten another group. Off to the side, squatting alone against a wall, was Sam. His oversized jacket, the one he never took off, lay on the ground.

He barely looked up as I approached, so I squatted down next to him and waited for a moment, holding back my news about the visa.

"Easy in, easy out," he finally said, staring ahead at two men swinging fists and wrestling each other to the ground. I recognized the two men fighting, had worked with both of them for several weeks. While together at the Foire these two had learned that they came from nearby towns in Belorussia and had become friends.

"I am out," Sam continued, without looking at me. "All of us in the kitchen without work papers, out."

This yanked me away from thoughts of my visa. "Ducroix?" I asked, meaning the confederation foreman who always gave a hard time to me and Sam, and to the several other workers who were not members of either the confederation or a foreign section.

"Well," Sam said slowly, still staring ahead at the two men fighting in front of us, and the circle of arguing men and women around them, "in the end it was Ducroix. But it did not start with him."

This Ducroix never liked having foreigners working at the Foire but Rose seemed to carry more weight there than Ducroix did, and she had taken on people—like me and Sam—who Henri's foreign section sent over, even though she knew that many of her fellow confederation people did not approve. When a few days earlier the foreign sections had their connection to the confederation cut by the Communists, though, the section workers at the Foire began to fear for their jobs. And in the kitchen hall they had decided to take action. The foreign section workers there had met among themselves at noontime, and had agreed to identify for Ducroix which of the other kitchen workers were not in one of the foreign sections and did not have proper work papers. A surprise attack, Maître. Allies suddenly become enemies—Operation Barbarossa. So, Sam and several others had been told, just a few minutes before I arrived, that they were out. And the two Belorussian friends—one a foreign section member with work papers, one not—were beating each other into the mud.

Another fight broke out next to us, so Sam and I escaped through a door into the Hall of Wine dormitory. We found a bench along the wall and sat down.

I realized that not only was Sam out of a job but that if I had not switched places with him it would have been me kicked out of the kitchen hall. "I am sorry, Sam," I said, and decided to tell him then about my rejection at the consulate, thinking in some way that my own misfortune might make his hurt less.

I gave him a brief report on what had happened and he slowly turned to look at me. "So tell me," he said. "How many hands does God have?"

"Ah, this must be where I know you," came a French voice behind me.

Geneviève.

"May I?" she said, in German now, and without waiting for a reply sat down next to me. I took a quick glance at Sam, but his expression gave away nothing—Genève's entrance must have been almost as much of a shock to Sam as to me, but he had developed great skill in not revealing anything until he knew what would serve him best. So, here was this French girl, dressed in the expensive suit she had worn to the consulate earlier in the day, speaking not only her upper crust French but German as well, boldly approaching and joining these two foreigners, without being asked, and perhaps most surprising of all, seeming to know me. Not to mention her striking face. No wonder Sam did not know how to react. Neither did I.

"When I see you this morning on the consulate," she continued in her mangled German, then halted and leaned out to look more closely at Sam. "Pardon," she said to him in French, "if my German is too poor."

Sam pulled himself up and at the same time rolled down his sleeves, to cover his scabies. "German? Nothing to do with me."

"Well, then," Genève went back to addressing me in German, struggling but determined. "When I see you at the consulate I know that I know you but I did not knew how I know."

She was mixing up the tenses so badly, and her pronouncing was so awful, that I told her my French was good enough at least for simple conversation and that maybe we would do better to switch.

"Yes," she said in French, "that is exactly the problem. And I was hoping you might be willing to help."

Despite Sam's general interest in anyone young and female, the blow of losing his work at the Foire was too hard and fresh. He may also have felt an uncomfort—an odd man out—sitting in his soiled and sweaty work clothes with the two of us next to him in consulate-going dress. He got up and told me in Yiddish that he would see me soon, at the Aurore or the Tout Va Bien café, and we would talk then.

"What a curious accent, his German," Genève remarked about his Yiddish when Sam had left. "Where is he from?"

"Belleville," I said.

If my answer threw her off her mark, as I think some part of me intended, she did not show it. Though I now suspect—after getting to know her—that she might not have missed what I meant. She did not seem to miss many details. Only larger things.

Immediately she picked up where she had left off, telling me that when she had seen me that morning at the consulate she had recognized me but could not place me. And though she did not hear me speak, and there were many French people at the consulate, she somehow had the strong impression that I spoke German. She was traveling to Germany for a two-week visit at the end of the month, she told me, accompanying her father on a business trip, but she knew her German was terrible and since she realized that we had met somewhere before, or at least been among the same people, she had the idea that I might help her with her German—just by having conversations, she said quickly, no formal teaching, which her father had already arranged for her but which was boring her to tears and would only do her any good if she got to Berlin and someone asked her to conjugate a few simple verbs. So, she had waited in a café across the road from the consulate, hoping to catch me when I came out. When I did finally emerge, though, she saw that I was in a serious conversation with the gentleman—Uncle Abraham—and did not want to interrupt us, so she had remained at her table. Then she saw me leave him and she decided to hurry after me, but by the time she got to the street where I had turned, I had disappeared. So, she went for tea and cake in a favorite Alsace pâtisserie café, where they were willing to speak with her in German—"You probably know it," she said, "The Strasbourg, in the 5th?"—until she headed to the Foire to say hello to some friends from the Allier, girls in a singing chorus, who were to arrive that day to stay at the dormitory while performing at the Expo. And then she saw me sitting here and thought that maybe this was where she had seen me before, at the Foire, though she did not remember, did I have any idea?

Finally she paused, and after a moment I felt it must be my turn to say something but nothing came out.

"Oh by the way," she said, "my name is Geneviève."

I still said nothing.

"Like the saint," she continued, then added—almost modestly, though maybe something else—"but not too much like her. What shall I call you?"

"I am Hersch," I finally managed, shortening my name to make it sound more German.

"All right, so tell me, Hersch, am I correct that I have seen you? And that you are German? Or have I simply made all this up?"

Of course, I could have told her the truth about me having been at the garden party, but that would immediately reduce me to a server and would probably end her interest in me. Or, I could have agreed with her that maybe she had seen me here at the Foire. But then I would have had to make up a story about why I had been there, because if I had told her that I worked in the dormitories that would be barely a step up from carrying water bottles around the garden. All this calculating took place in the few moments it took for me to say Yes, she was right, we had seen each other before. Then I came up with a solution that was neither entirely true or false. It had been at the Expo, I told her, where I had watched her dancing one day, the clog dancing, she must have noticed me in the crowd, and for some reason my face had stuck with her.

Genève nodded as if this sounded possible, but before she could give it anymore thought—if she would have bothered—she spotted the girls she had come to see, the singers from the Allier, who were arriving on the other side of the hall.

"So, we could start tomorrow." There was so much confidence in her voice that I thought for a moment I had already agreed. "Lunch will be my pleasure," she added. I could not tell whether that was a polite way of offering me payment or just the normal way rich people did things. Anyway, the chance to spend time with her was more than enough for me to say yes even without the lunch invitation, though the thought of a restaurant meal, likely even a real French meal, certainly did not hurt.

Then I remembered that I had a work shift at the dormitory the next day, and so I could not meet her, at least until evening. But what if tomorrow she again came to see her friends in the dormitory and happened to see me there in my work clothes, mopping floors or cleaning the washrooms? Sam. Maybe I could get Sam to take my shift, he certainly needed the money now that he had been sent out of the kitchens. But I also needed the work—I had spent all that money buying things for Mirari's children at the Expo, and the entrance fees I had paid trying to find Genève, plus I had just missed a work shift so that I could go to the consulate. Also, I desperately wanted to save as much pay as I could so that my parents—and Abraham and Chawa—would not have to help me anymore. Also, I thought, what if I could not find Sam tonight to ask him? Or he showed up tomorrow and they turned him away here in the dormitory also? No, I had to work the next day. I would have to risk that she might come back to the dormitories and spot me there—I would keep a careful lookout all day.

All of this raced through my mind as I stalled for time by saying, "Yes, of course, if matters allow, I would be happy to help you. As much as I can, not being a trained language instructor, of course. But we will have to see what is possible"—or some drabble like that. Finally, I told her that unfortunately I was already engaged the next day but that I could meet her in the evening—calculating the end of my shift—at about this same time. "If," I added, "you feel that an evening meeting would be proper."

She smiled just a hint, at least in part I suspect because my French was not up to the task—I intended to say "proper," but whatever word I used, who knows what it actually meant? Anyway, that may not have been the main reason she smiled—as I came to learn, it was a smile that often contained any number of parts.

"Bienséances?" she replied, using a word for properness that I thought beautiful but did not know the meaning of until I went into a bookshop and found it in a French-German dictionary. "Well, that is not something to bother us, do you think?"

Not understanding the key word bienséances did not trouble me for a second. Because her final words were all that mattered. You see, Maître, she had suddenly switched to the familiar "tu," which caught me by surprise, a sudden turn. The first of many by Genève. My cheeks felt hot.

She got up, told me that we could meet at six the following

evening at the Alsace pâtisserie she had mentioned, if that was all right. Of course, I said. She smiled and shook my hand—the feel of which doubled the heat in my cheeks—and said, Until tomorrow, then crossed the enormous hall to find her singer friends.

When I got back to Rue Martel that night, I sorted through my few clothes to figure out something other than the heavy wool suit, which Abraham had made for me and that I had been wearing that day, which was anyway miserable in the heat, to wear for meeting her the next evening, but something that would not give away how rough I was living. Several months before, Maison Albert had an order to produce men's shirts for some large atelier or department store, and Tante Chawa had arranged for an extra shirt to fall off the table for me. She had specially trimmed and tucked it to fit me, and I had saved it to wear only on special occasions. Which had been none. So, I laid out this shirt with my one pair of passable trousers and the shoes I had been given for serving at Bernard's party, to bring it all along with me to work the following day, planning to change at the dormitory at the end of my shift.

It was more arranging than I needed. When I reported for work the next morning, they turned me away. I had no papers, the day's foreman said. I had been given work only because I had a friend in a foreign section, and what did that mean to him anymore? "There are Frenchmen who need work," he said. And to make certain I understood to not bother coming back, he added, "Every day they need work."

I looked around for Rose but did not see her. The few people there who were in Henri's foreign section kept well away from where I was standing with the foreman.

A Party man, the foreman.

Since you asked, Maître.

Yours,
Herschel

Maître,

I do not know how she found the strength to do so much—she fasted every other day, Sainte Geneviève. The real saint, I mean. To atone for her sins, I suppose—although no one ever told me what they were. And on the other days she ate only beans and barley bread. I told Sam about this one time and he just snorted. I know lots of people in Belleville who only eat every other day, he said, but I never heard them call it fasting.

Still, it made an impression to me, this way of her atoning. Also, she drank no wine—and she was French. Thinking back on her this past week—I always do some thinking before I write to you, Maître, even more so lately—I decided that on my own fasting days, like her I also would keep working. I mean writing. Which I did not do when I fasted before. I feel quite weak when I fast, you see, so the effort to work on those days has always seemed too great. But perhaps that is the point. The difficulty of it. Also, there is a strange sense at the top of my head when I fast, an airy feeling, but I never considered before that perhaps this might be a clearing of the mind, which would allow me to think more truly, with sharper outlines, instead of all the clutter and contraries I usually have to sort through. Though I must say, Maître, that during this first attempt to write on a fasting day I am feeling even more strange than I expected.

She was an outsider in Paris, Sainte Geneviève—French, yes, but not a Parisian. And like me came to Paris alone, about my same age. Which was one of the things about this Sainte Geneviève that so much captured Genève, this idea of a girl on her own doing marvelous things. Though I could never sort out exactly what parts of the saint's story went into these strong feelings Genève had about her—because certainly there were things about the saint that Genève had to ignore. Of course, the two of them shared their given name, Geneviève, I suppose it began with that, and from some paintings I saw of the saint when she was a girl, the same slim frame and hair not unlike Genève's. But mostly I think it was this idea of Sainte Geneviève as an outsider. I do not mean geography, Maître, not exactly foreignness, but someone who does things against what is expected. And suffers for it. But in the end is proved right. And then is adored.

It was during an ancient siege of Paris—in the 400s or 500s, something like that. The people were dying of starving and disease, and the women of the city were gathering their children, preparing to flee, willing to risk capture and death by the enemy rather than slow certain death behind the city walls. But young Geneviève told the women not to leave and instead to stay and pray with her. Then she managed to break the blockade, bringing in bread for the people, while herself refusing to eat, and the city survived. Parisians saw her as a savior— excuse me, Maître, perhaps that word is specially reserved—or whatever they called someone like this before they call her a saint.

There had also been an earlier time. When the army of Attila was preparing to attack Paris. Then also Geneviève had told the people not to flee but to stay with her, and to fast and help her pray for the city. That first time, though, most of the people had rejected the girl. Some had even wanted to kill her. But when at the last moment Attila turned away from Paris and went back across the Rhine, Parisians kissed her feet for having saved them from the Huns.

The Huns. This was one part of the saint's story that was a problem for Genève. Because you see the French—I mean nowadays—they speak of Germans as Huns. And Genève was pulled so strongly by Germany, planning visits, wanting to learn the language, so excited by what she imagined of life in Berlin, especially night life. So, here she was deeply attracted by the saint who defended Paris against the Huns, but at the same time also attracted by the Huns themselves. Genève never talked to me about this part of the Sainte Geneviève tale—too many contradictings. Not only that, but I was German. At least to her. And to many other French. There were also other things about the saint's life that Genève never mentioned, such as the original Geneviève becoming a nun. Which Genève definitely was not.

I am sorry if some of this is confusing, Maître, but to have a clear picture of Genève you must allow for some confusing, does that make sense? I am having difficulty following my own thinking today and perhaps it is best if I do not try and instead just let my mind go wherever it wants to then write what it tells me. Without thinking it over again I mean. As I usually do. My head hurts badly. At least my stomach is quiet.

I had to stop writing and lie down for a while—the fasting, perhaps. For a few hours maybe. I am not certain. I will try again now.

The Panthéon was the first place she took me, Genève. It is a huge building on top of a hill, Maître, in the 5th arrondissement on the left side of the river, a hall and a monument and a church though not exactly a church anymore, with Roman type columns inside and out and an enormous dome ceiling. The history of the place was complicated and I never got it sorted—partly because Genève told it during her German lessons with me and mostly I did not bother to correct her or even figure out exactly what she was trying to say. Just enough to let her think that she was learning. Anyway it seems there was once a very old church on the spot dedicated to Sainte Geneviève even with her bones kept there and then one of the France kings—I think it was a Louis, they mostly seemed to be Louis—decided to build this huge new church building also dedicated to Geneviève because praying to her had cured him of some terrible disease or her bones had but then the revolution came and they did not like churches so they changed it to a place with tombs—I forget their word—for France's famous dead people but then it was changed back to a church and then back again to a monument that felt like a church but they said was not and now that I think back on it I do not remember ever seeing any priests there. Anyway the reason Genève took me there and the main reason she loved going was that it had been built to honor her Sainte Geneviève—although the saint's bones had been moved in and out over the years and finally over to the great Notre Dame church, which is another story, the bones—and despite all the changes the walls were still covered right on the walls I mean with enormous beautiful paintings of the saint at all the parts of her life and all around the Pantheon monument were other places named for Sainte Geneviève and even the hill itself where the great building stood.

It was close to the pâtisserie café where I went to meet Genève that first time—the Alsace place she liked, where they let her speak to them in her awful German and were very friendly to her she had been going there for some time she told me and even though she ate very little she always ordered the most expensive pastries which I am sure did not hurt their friendliness but when I spoke to him in German the patron turned cold. Perhaps it was my northern accent him being Alsacien or perhaps it was something else about me I noticed that no one else there ordered tea.

The bones. They seem to love tombs and crypts and bones and such the Catholics have you noticed that Maître? Or maybe you are also a Catholic—I had never thought of that. But anyway not a French Catholic, there must be a difference. Is there? I am sorry if I have offended. Anyway, Parisians would carry the saint's bones—I never asked, but in a coffin or box or something I hope—around the church and later the Notre Dame cathedral every year on the anniversary of the time she had saved the city from starvation and over the centuries also they paraded the bones around the streets when Paris was in danger from invaders or plagues and in those times the bones were carried by the city's best families Genève said—How did they decide that? I wondered, but did not ask—walking barefoot in white linen robes with attendants to hold up the hems and others to sweep the streets in front. All very dramatic it sounded. I think Genève imagined herself taking part one day. And just a year ago when the new Huns the Wehrmacht were about to enter Paris they paraded the bones again. I was in jail then and so did not get to see it and anyway that time the bones certainly did not keep out the Huns, did they Maître. I never got the chance to ask Genève what she thought about that.

During the two weeks before Genève left for her first visit to Berlin we spent several hours together almost every day and again during the two weeks after she returned when she was full of excitement about the life she had seen there and more eager still to learn German until she left again for her boarding school for what was to be her last year there. For me each visit with her meant I could count on a good meal and I always ate hearty, which meant that I did not need to think about food the rest of the day and also helped me hold onto the little money I had saved from my work at the Foire. Genève herself ate very little, and I wondered if that was to be like the saint or just to stay slim, which was the fashion then with the Paris girls, but perhaps both, which would be convenient. They always seemed to me so delicious the restaurants and cafés she knew with things to eat that I had never experienced before not fancy but odd very Paris little places that I would not ever have known about or afforded or been comfortable going into even if I did.

She was always delicate about leaving money on the tables to pay for our meals and coffees and pastries without ever mentioning it and at the end of each day together without any fuss she would hand me the 20 francs fee for the German lesson that was the amount she had proposed, which was a lot of money to me and which I was carefully saving. Mostly we spent our time wandering around the left side of the river where she tried to use her German to tell me about Paris though each time after a couple of hours we always wound up sliding back into French. Months later we did more different things a lot of it at night but that first summer our visits were mostly just a midday meal and an afternoon walk ending with a coffee and pastry at least for me a pastry. We were careful not to ask many questions about each other but I did eventually learn why she had been dancing at the Expo with the group of girls from the Auvergne because her family has a country house there, in a part called the Allier—I actually saw the place three years later Maître an enormous place a chateau that her mother's family had owned for generations where Genève had passed each summer growing up and her parents had wanted her to spend time with the local families at least the best of them and not to be just the Parisian visitor there and so since she was very young she had known many of the girls of the area and had become part of the local girls singing and dancing groups. Authentique.

Genève asked very little about me which was typical of her Paris type not needing to know about people on a lower ladder but I think it was also a way for her not to find out anything that might spoil our arrangement. I did tell her that I was from Hannover and she asked about the city but nothing about my life there or my family and she never asked what I was doing in Paris—I think she did not expect a person to be doing anything in particular—or even where I lived and at first I was relieved that I did not have to answer questions did not have to weave a cloth of lies but after a while Maître I found that I wanted her to ask about me wanted her to want to know so I began offering little bits and pieces such as I had also gone to boarding school meaning my year at yeshiva which I described part of but disguising it and how that also allowed me to know the great city of Frankfurt which I told her she must see sometime and also that I knew Brussels. I wanted her to wonder about me but not too much. After a while I sometimes tried to say things to her so that she would believe me but not quite believe me at the same time. I do not know how else to describe it Maître.

It is tomorrow. I was so cold last night. I could not stop shaking I put on all my clothes but it did not stop until all of a sudden it did and now I am burning up and I will ask the guards if I can miss my job this morning bringing around the food to the cells or maybe I have already missed it. I had no idea that writing on a fasting day could be this much trouble for my body which must mean that I am doing something right working hard would you say so Maître? It has been so long since I have seen you. Anyone.

Genève. I do not remember why I am telling you about her but she is now very much in the front of my mind just behind my eyes between the pain and the back of my eyes so I will go on and why not? Churches. We so often wound up in churches when we were together there was something about them that made her very calm but not me I was always nervous inside them nervous they would know I was not one of them and the blood of Jesus what was I supposed to do and then what would happen because they think we killed Christian children to take their blood for Passover. One time it was a small church where they were giving out food and Genève helped them she went there once a week to give out bread and soup to the poor just like her beloved saint and I stood to the side thinking about the Sportclub Aurore where it was me in the queue for the soup in the winter but this is summer and what am I doing here now in this church on the giving away side of the line and my clothes these clothes I have on they are not clean not proper and what if Sam walks in to get his food and sees me here? It is summer and the soup pot is boiling and I am hot Maître so very dizzy and hot

Genève Genève
one night there was a night we went to a church it was also an enormous place like the Pantheon but still a church the Madeleine on a hill on the right side of the river and in ancient days there was a synagogue there she told me but how did she know that and why did she say it we were there to hear music with a chorus which was part of what she wanted to hear because of her own singing in a chorus but also it was Beethoven Maître German music that she loved because it was Beethoven but also because it was German and we climbed up to the high balconies to sit above the musicians and the singers and looking down on them now like we are in the heavens and she is right it is joyous that is the word she keeps saying in French joyeux joyeux and it is true joyeux to be with her all day and into the evening this evening to be with her near to her because I am a boy Maître after all do you remember I am a boy they all thought of me as history when I was in jail in Paris wanted me to be history the committees the newspapers the lawyers but I am not history yes I am but also a boy a person a human a boy

perfidis judeas they keep repeating in this church here I do not know why my pallet is here in the church but I have to kneel on the floor like everyone else they keep getting up and down and amen and amen when the priest says different things different prayers they are in Latin I can only write when we are all kneeling and the paper is on my pallet we all kneel during each of the prayers it is Holy Friday they call it and all the prayers we kneel except not during perfidis judeas a prayer they say and it is the only prayer when they do not kneel or say amen and Genève will not look at me she looks only at the priest even though she is so warm next to me it is so warm in here and the smells the flowers but also the hogs and the chimney and they say it over and over perfidis judeas and what if Genève says my name they will know even though I asked her to call me Hersch or H but she likes to say Herschel and she will not look at me and what if she calls me Herschel they will know because names here in Paris names are so much who you are and what about you Maître what about you Herr Rosenhaus in Hannover I know families Rosenstein and Rosenberg so what kind of name is Rosenhaus and what if someone asks you or me or you or me

Honorable Maître Herr Rosenhaus,

This place Moabit is so much different from Sachsenhausen. The feel of it, I mean. At least compared to the bunker, the special prisoners place where they kept me there. Of course, some of this you know, since you have visited me here. I did not ask whether you had ever been here before. Such a cold stone place, this prison. I have been given no work here as I had in the bunker, so I am in my cell almost all the day, this cell that is so much smaller and darker than my cell, my room, at Sachsenhausen—which when I think back on it was bigger than almost any of the rooms where I ever stayed in Paris. At least I am allowed to the eating hall here, and an outside exercise yard each day, so I can see other humans, though it is strictly forbidden for any of the other prisoners to talk to me—even from cell to cell. Anyway, the cells on each side and across from me are kept empty. Or the jailers either, to speak with me. Officially I am Schneider, Otto—the same as before. The long days and nights alone in my cell here are much like the Gestapo jail, where you first came to meet me. A year ago now.

As you can see, the writing paper and your envelopes finally arrived. And I am feeling much better than when you were here. Your visit was brief, as I remember it—I suppose because you were considering of my condition, my weak health. I do recall you told me that I was moved here for my protection after being so ill, because the camp fever is still raging at Sachsenhausen, and the possibility to treat people there so poor. As I found out. The camp fever—typhus, the name of it I learned while I was in the hospital, the Berlin hospital, I mean, not the camp building they called a hospital, the place where they treat the guards. And special prisoners. Well, me at least. But you also said that this place, this Moabit jail, is where I have been brought to prepare for my trial, the place where prisoners for the special Berlin court are held to be readied for their trials. And during their trials. Which gives me quite some hope. That at last my time is coming.

I think when you were here we did not speak much about my journey through the fevers these past weeks, and so I do not know how much of it all you have been told. You said that you had seen me in the hospital here in Berlin, yes? I am sorry I cannot remember that visit, Maître. Perhaps I was still too much in deliriums. Or perhaps you saw me but we did not actually speak at the hospital, I do not know. Anyway, you have asked me to write that I am up to health again, and that I have been treated well. So I will, as best I can, because much of what happened at Sachsenhausen and after, once the fevers took hold of me, I do not recall.

I remember finding myself in the camp hospital—the one used for the SS guards, in one of their brick blockhouses. There were no other prisoners there. I do not remember how I got there or how long I was ill before they moved me from the bunker, or much else about my time there. I do recall that the camp doctor was unhappy. About me being there. He would not actually come near to me, would instead give instructions to assistants about me while he stood several meters away. The only other thing I remember strongly, very strongly, was waking to see a camp guard, a healthy one, I mean, in uniform—the guards who were patients were all well away from me, in beds on the far side of the large room—coming toward me with a pistol in his hand but then several others guards were also suddenly in the room and there was loud talking and I remember no more. Though I admit about this memory—since I suppose you may ask—that I had much wild imagining while I suffered the fevers, so yes perhaps the moment with this guard was just another of my terrible fever dreams.

I have only small and confused pictures in my head of moving from the camp infirmary to the hospital in Berlin. It was night and raining and I was in the back of a closed small truck or van but somehow the rain was on me or for some other reason I was soaking wet all over I remember. Or think I do. Then later I was in a large room with many beds and everything very white and many people like sister nurses and others like that who cleaned me I remember and moved me around on the bed but never spoke. And later in a small room by myself—Is that where you saw me, Maître?—also very white, which is something that sticks in my mind because now that I think back on it I have not seen anything white, pure white, since I was put in the Gestapo cells in Berlin more than a year ago now. The snow at Sachsenhausen was always grey.

I have better recalling of a later time in the hospital room where they put me by myself as the fevers began to cool down. There was a strange contraption next to the bed with a long tube which led from a bag of liquid and into my arm through a needle that stayed there, but did not hurt very much, I was surprised. The doctors seemed to look in on me often, although I have never stayed in a real hospital before, except the one short time when I was brought to a different hospital by the Gestapo, for my stomach, so I do not know what is normal there. They did not ask anything about me, the doctors, but at least at the hospital, this real Berlin hospital, they came right up to me in the bed and talked to me in a regular sort of way. The sisters, though, they still did not speak to me. The doctors told me that I was being given a new and special medicine that some Reich laboratory had just produced, and sure enough after a week or so I was feeling a bit better. German technology, Maître—I had often told about it to my friends in Paris but they did not want to listen.

So. Slowly I began to improve, with a clearer head and some appetite—they fed me well at the hospital, and I did not continue my fasting or worry myself about what the food was made from, Torah says it is allowed if life is in danger, did you know that? Which is also why I did not pay much attention to such things when I was in Paris those years. People often believe something but do another. Mostly, I think, because they believe different things at the same time. Whether they say so or not. Or even realize it. What they say to themselves is something else. Humans.

Well, as I recovered my strength I began preparing my mind to return to Sachsenhausen. But day after day went by after they had taken out the needle from my arm and had stopped giving me the medicine, and I went nowhere. By now a policeman of some kind sat outside my door, day and night. People I had never seen before came in with doctors to look at me. I have no idea who they were. The only thing I can tell you about them is that they made the doctors nervous.

Finally I was moved here to the prison, to Moabit. Which I only know why because of what you have told me. But that was two different things, the reasons you gave me. I mean no offense, Maître. Because it does not have to be that only one thing is true. Especially about reasons.

Yours,
Herschel

Maître,

The winter was bitter. And long. There seemed to be no autumn that year, 1937. And no spring in '38. Paris became endlessly cold and wet as soon as Genève left for Switzerland. Or perhaps I just felt it more. Because I not only had to look for new work but also a place to sleep. Which made me wonder whether God had overheard me just then, during my last conversation with Genève. Or maybe even had been spying on me. And had one hand free.

You see, Maître, when Genève and I parted that last afternoon before she left for Switzerland, she asked how she could find me again—to continue her German lessons, she said—when she was back in Paris. How much she intended to, I could not tell from her manner. She was very good at that. But I certainly wanted to make sure she could do so easily, if she decided to. For the money I might earn, I mean. Until that last day, she had never bothered to ask me where I stayed or how she could get in touch with me—at the end of each of our meetings we had simply made an appointment for our next. She had given me the telephone number at her parents' home, on a fancy printed visiting card, to leave a message in case I could not make our next rendezvous, or for me to be given a message if she had not appeared, but I had never had to use it. Now, though, she did not know exactly when she would be in Paris again or for how long, and so asked for some way of making contact with me. Which I realized was a good idea, since I could not just telephone her home time and again over the next months—I knew now that she was a Lazare, and so from the garden party I had an idea what that home was like—and expect that someone there would tell me where she was or when she was returning to Paris. Thinking back on it now, Genève must have had the same thought. So, she asked where she could post me a message to tell me when she would again be in the city.

I had thought about this problem ahead of time. Yes, problem. You see, Genève and I performed a sort of theater with each other—I mean, we both understood that our time together was partly pretend. We just neither of us knew exactly which parts. My role was young Mitteleuropa traveler, somewhat mysterious I hoped, who had landed in Paris to explore its offerings and who for a time was enjoying the company of this equally mysterious Parisienne, but who might anytime suddenly disappear for places and reasons not revealed. Giving Genève the address of Abraham and Chawa's fifth-floor tailoring workshop—Maison Albert rather than Maison Abraham not being nearly enough of a disguise—simply did not fit what I hoped Genève thought of me, though I had no clear idea what that was. So, I had already built a plan.

I went to see Bernard, at the atelier above his high fashion boutique, the Au Courant Dame. We had not seen each other for months, not since he had given me the message that I was wanted to work at the Lazare garden party. Apparently whatever word got back to him about my satisfactory behavior there—or more likely not any word at all—meant that he was almost polite to me when I showed up at the atelier unrequested and unannounced. Polite for Bernard, at least. Though still very cautious, since he realized after a few moments that I was likely there to ask him for something. But when I mentioned the Lazare name, I had his full attention.

Asking that Au Courant Dame receive mail for me from Genève was not what I was after. Even a fancy boutique like that was not the kind of address I hoped to give Genève—she always pronounced the word "shopkeeper" with a particular unpleasant flavor, no matter how chic or expensive the items being sold. And anyway, I knew from before that Bernard did not want my name and unlegal status directly connected to his business. So I now offered Bernard more detail and less truth—that when I had finished at the Lazare party, their head staff man had said that the Lazares might want my German-speaking services again in the autumn—not true—and had asked could they reach me through Monsieur Blucher—Bernard, that is—and that I had said yes. I had forgotten to mention it to Bernard at the time, I continued the lie, but since autumn was coming I wanted to do the courtesy of advising him that a message for me from the Lazares might arrive sometime at his and Elsa's apartment. Bernard sputtered when I mentioned his home and me in the same sentence but, as I had hoped, he could not bring himself to refuse something he believed the Lazares had requested. And when I asked him for nothing else—no money, no work, no help getting papers—he relaxed a bit and even offhanded asked me how I had been keeping busy that summer. As if I was some kind of student on holiday. Without thinking, I boasted a bit that I had worked at the Foire de Paris. He was quite surprised and I am sure would have asked more but—realizing my mistake, that I could not tell him I got the work through the foreign section, those Reds—I quickly thought to say that I had an important appointment and could not stay any longer. My earlier mention of the Lazares may have given some weight to my word "important" and made Bernard hesitate. Hiding my pleasure that my story had got me what I came for, I thanked him and left.

What I came for, Maître—the use of his address, his home address, in the posh 16th arrondissement. And his name, Blucher, his French-sounding name. A proper place that I could give Genève, for her to get in touch with me.

Well, my meetings with Genève—I know I have told you some about that. But with my fevers and the moves from camp to hospital to the prison here I have lost much sense of what I have actually written down and what I have only said inside my head. I hope that what I write now will make sense to you, Maître. That you will know what I mean. Though of course why should reading me be the same as knowing me?

So. In my last meeting with Genève before she left for her boarding school, I told her she could contact me through the Bluchers. Old acquaintances of my family, I said. I reminded her to put her own family name on the outside of any envelope she sent, so the Bluchers would know it was something of importance. And why would I need to receive mail there instead of where I was staying?—which she did not ask but anyway I felt I should explain. Because, I told her, the hotel where I had been stopping was proving unsatisfactory and I had decided to move, but I had not yet found lodgings that met with my approval. She seemed to accept this as completely normal, without any interest in the details, and said she would contact me through the Bluchers when she was next going to be in Paris for any length of time. To continue her lessons.

You see, Maître, that is why I wondered whether God had been spying on me. And did not like what He heard. Because I had lied to her, about having to change where I was staying. Yet that is exactly what happened. Later the very same day.

When I got back to Rue Martel that evening, Madame Corbin the concierge came out of her loge to speak with me in the courtyard. She told me that the following week a family would be renting the chambre de bonne where I had been staying most recently, and that there were no other empty maid's rooms. She said this with the same straightaheadness as she had always shown me—many kindnesses without ever hinting that she was doing anything special, and bad news now without apology. Renting the chambres de bonne was part of her job. And a family that would cram themselves into such a tiny room was probably more in need than I was—at least I had Uncle Abraham and Aunt Chawa for food and a roof when there was none elsewhere.

But now Abraham and Chawa's was also a problem. Of course they took me in again, as always. But to stay there for more than a night or two was now more difficult than it had been the year before. Their apartment workshop on Rue Martel was larger than the one at Bastille where I had stayed with them for several months when I first arrived in Paris, but now the three small rooms were more crowded than the old two rooms had ever been. Their hope when they moved to Rue Martel—that they would attract more personal clients and particularly French ones—had not proved out. Instead, they had to take on even more piecework to keep up with the added cost of these rooms, and also to make up for the lower piecework pay they were now getting. You see, the bigger ateliers, like Bernard's, by now had so many desperate workers to choose from that they could get away with paying them even less than before. The large stores and designer houses knew this and took advantage by paying less per piece to the workshops. There were again strikes against the big ateliers but, after the fall of the Popular Front and the confederation's turnabout against foreigners, there was not much support behind the clothing workers—or the hatters, or furniture makers, or glove makers, or any of the other trades where most of the workers were not real Frenchmen—and so the low piecework pay remained. Now, every space in Abraham and Chawa's rooms was piled with clothing material and batting and boxes of ribbon and edging and thread and cut and sewn pieces at various stages of finish for the mounds of piecework they had to turn out. They also had to make sure that an area could easily and quickly be cleared and curtained for the personal clients, few as they were, to be fitted in private. All in all, there was no place for another sleeping pallet, and for my few clothes and other small things. Also, their work now began earlier in the morning and continued well into the night, with Abraham at the cutting table and Chawa at the finishing table and their machiniste Sidney and seamstress Berenice all putting in long extra time, with Chawa moving over to the machine and carrying on for hours more after Sidney finally left for the day. Me being at Maison Albert meant being seriously in their way.

It was Sam who came to the rescue. Or his sister, actually. Though she was only trying to rescue herself. Did I tell you, Maître, that Sam had a sister? Rachel? Who for two years had been out of touch with Sam and their mother Rina. She was small and lean like Sam, with the same light skin and hair. A dancer's wiry strong body, Sam told me. Though not anymore. When she reappeared at Rina and Sam's door, she was stick thin and sickly—apparently absinthe and cocaine for two years had been the main parts of her diet. I did not actually see her until two weeks or so after her return, and even by then she had not recovered much. At least the broken nose and ribs that Sam told me about had mostly healed, the bruises and swelling of her face almost disappeared. The emptiness in her eyes had not.

Sam learned only slowly, and he suspected only very partly, what

Rachel's life had been since she had left home and dropped contact with him and their mother. Two years before, when she was 16, Rachel had met a woman in Belleville who told her that with her looks she could be an artist's model. Desperate to leave the shabby little room she shared with Sam and Rina, and her hand to mouth days helping with Rina's colporteuse cart, she went with this "finder" to Montparnasse. There the woman introduced Rachel to some painters. Have you heard of it, Maître? Montparnasse? I knew nothing about it, but it seems almost everyone else in Paris did, a district of artists and their strange types, some of them famous it seems, gathering in ateliers and galleries and cafés and bars and nightclubs there. Anyway, Rachel started to model for some painters—as Rachel Polonskaya, exotic Slavic beauty, an idea the artists seemed to love—and began to earn a bit of money. Also for a few sculptors. And later photographers. It was only small amounts—one reason the artists were keen to have foreigner models was they did not have to pay them much—but it seemed a marvel to Rachel who before this had never had any money of her own. Rachel did not say so, but Sam understood that this modeling included being in the natural, as the French say it. Immediately some of the men had tried to push themselves on her, she told Sam, but she was able to hold them away. At least, that was what she told Sam. I got the feeling he did not believe her.

After her first taste of Montparnasse, Rachel began to spend more and more time there, and after not too long she disappeared altogether from Belleville, from Sam and Rina, moving in with a painter in his studio, a Frenchman. This painter was jealous of Rachel being with other artists and demanded that she pose only for him. Which was all right with Rachel, since in exchange he not only gave her a place to live but also dressed her in French clothes and fed her, without her having to shop for and prepare food for them—when they had an actual meal together, which was only so often, they ate in a local bistro, because early on when Rachel had made food for him in the studio, in the ways she had learned from her mother, the painter had called it eastern slop and refused to eat it. He also gave her a little spending money, so she no longer had to pose for anyone else, or do anything at all except clean up a bit around the studio and keep this man happy. Which after half a year she was no longer able to do.

One evening this painter took her to visit another Frenchman artist and after several bottles of wine the first painter told Rachel that he was leaving and that she should stay there instead of returning with him to his studio. This second painter had always fancied Rachel, so the first painter simply handed her on, now that he had tired of her. What Rachel felt about this Sam could not tell from either her words or her face—since she had returned to Sam and Rina she spoke so flatly, looked so blank, that Sam could not be sure she felt anything.

Rachel stayed with the second painter for several months before he passed her to a third. When that man ended the arrangement a couple of months later, Rachel had no one to provide for her, so she returned to hiring herself out as a model. She had now spent enough time in Montparnasse artist circles to be well known, but that was also a problem—she found that the painters there no longer wanted to use her as a model because she was too familiar to them all. Plus there was a sense among them that the alcohol and drugs, the all-nights life in cafés and bars and studios, had dulled her beauty, her freshness. She was used goods. She was 17 years old.

So, to support herself Rachel had to widen the kinds of people who might hire her. This meant other painters and sculptors, over in Montmartre, Saint Germain, Pigalle. And then photographers. Who led her into more and more uncomfortable things. Rachel did not give Sam details, but we both knew the type of photos that were sold under the covers at many book and art stalls along the Seine. How far she went to support herself I did not ask, and Sam, if he knew, did not volunteer.

22 October

Rachel had come to France very young and spoke the language like a born Parisienne, but somehow still the Montparnasse locals could tell she was not truly French, which was part of the reason she right away took on the character of the mysterious Slav. Knowing she was foreign, though, meant that some of the Frenchmen artists treated her worse—refused to pay her, physically roughed her—than they did French girls. These men knew that there was likely no family who would complain, and no worry about the police making a fuss about a foreigner. Also, Rachel said, there was not a blink of disapproving about such treatment from the other Frenchmen—painters, poets, theater and film people—who spent their nights in the Montparnasse cafés. So, between the struggle to find enough work, the sorriness of the work itself, the nastiness she often received, and the diet of wine and absinthe, more and more she found herself exhausted, often ill, and—left out of the social company of the real French girls in Montparnasse—alone.

She was first saved, then damned—These are not words I ever would have used before my time in France, Maître, is that something to my credit?—by de Guise. He called himself a painter. He had lots of money and charm but not much talent or ideas, Rachel said, and spent little time at his easel. He was suffered by the others in the artist set because he was a good storyteller, regularly paid the whole table's bill at the cafés and bars, and often held parties at his large studio. Rachel and de Guise had seen each other around Montparnasse for a while, but he only took a special interest in her when he watched her during a photography modeling session. Rachel did not know why de Guise and three other men were allowed to be there while she was put through a series of extreme poses, but she needed the work badly so she did not complain. Afterward, de Guise invited her for a proper meal—something else she needed badly—and told her that he would like her to model for him also. One thing led to another, she told Sam, and soon de Guise had set her up in a room of her own. Since he did not actually paint that much, he had little use for her at his studio, and anyway he did not want her living there because that would interfere with his freedom to entertain others. Which suited her fine, Rachel said, because even at the beginning she did not truly like him very much.

So, an arrangement of convenience. De Guise paid for her clothes and drink and her own room in the 15th, on the far side of the Gare

Montparnasse train station, toward the Foire de Paris where Sam and I had worked in the dormitories—some distance from the center of Montparnasse itself, so she would not be too close unless he wanted to see her. He also gave her a bit of spending money—she was even able to send a banknote to her mother once in a while, though she put no return address on the envelope. Rachel's part of the bargain was to keep herself available to model—for others that de Guise "loaned" her to, more than for himself—and to accompany him once in a while when he felt like having someone on his arm during a night in the cafés and bars, or at a gathering in another artist's studio. And available in her room. When he wanted. And was able. Which due to the alcohol and drugs he took, Rachel said, was not very often.

Now I am getting to the point of telling you all this, Maître—Rachel's room, that de Guise paid for.

Most of the time de Guise was quite decent to her, Rachel said, not only out in public and but also in her room when he made his private visits. But de Guise loved his wine and absinthe, and was also very fond of the cocaine drug, and he sometimes suffered from what Sam called beaujolâche. Meaning that when de Guise took too much beaujolais wine or absinthe or whatever else, he became lâche—loose, soft. Down there. So he could not perform what he wanted with Rachel. And it raged him.

Usually when this happened, de Guise just growled and cursed and shoved her away, Rachel said, then banged out of her room. One time he broke into tears, then passed out. But in the weeks before she returned to her family in Belleville, de Guise had become violent when he suffered his beaujolâche. One time he had pushed her against the wall, though he apologized soon after. Another time he had lashed out with the back of his hand and bloodied her lip. But the last time he had punched her full in the face, breaking her nose and knocking her out of the bed, then kicked at her wildly, cracking her ribs. As she lay on the floor he called her vile names and said that if she told anyone—she did not know whether he meant about the beatings or about his beaujolâche—he would kill her, but he had not tried to stop her when she ran from the room and out of the building in her nightclothes. She had gone to the nearby room of a girl she knew, another artist model, who let Rachel spend the rest of the night there but hurried her out the door at first light. At least she gave Rachel a dress and some shoes to wear. But in great pain, hungry, cold, without any money, Rachel could think of no one who would take her in. So, after two years gone, she went back to Rina and Sam.

It was a week after Rachel had returned to Belleville—and two days after I had lost the chambre de bonne at Rue Martel—that Sam told me all this, as he and I made our way across the city toward Rachel's room in the 15th. Because she had run out in the middle of the night, she had left behind all of her things—her clothes, her trinkets of jewelry and purses and little boxes and such, and a few sketches and small paintings that different artists had given her. She had accumulated a fair amount over the two years—no one item worth much but still things that could be sold to help support herself and her mother, the clothes in particular, she thought, because they were Montparnasse art stylish and so could fetch good prices even secondhand. She feared that de Guise had thrown it all into the street, but she thought there was a chance he felt bad enough that he had given her things to the concierge, to keep in the cellar if Rachel should return for them.

Rachel herself did not want to show up there, in case de Guise came around or had instructed the concierge to contact him if Rachel appeared—his studio, close by in the center of Montparnasse, had its own telephone, she told us. So Sam volunteered to go see if he could retrieve some things for her. He also hoped he would run into de Guise and take some revenge. But when Sam muttered something about this, Rachel begged him to avoid any trouble with de Guise because then for certain she would never get back her things. So, unhappily, Sam agreed and decided to bring along someone else, figuring that having another person there—as backup, or as witness—might make a bad collision with de Guise less likely. And if by chance things worked out, he would have someone there to help him carry things back to Belleville. Someone. Me.

We went in the morning, when Rachel said de Guise, who was almost always up all night, was usually dead asleep in his studio.

Rachel's building was four floors surrounding a small courtyard, a bit shabby but still far nicer than the awful old ruin in Belleville where Sam and Rina had their little room. Our first task, Rachel had warned, would be to get past the concierge, Madame Barras. Sure enough, we had not taken more than three or four steps into the courtyard when a grey-haired little woman wearing a baggy old black dress, drooping stockings that her bony legs could not hold up, and—as if her face belonged to another person entirely—enough rouge on her sunken cheeks to pass for a circus clown, came scuttling out crying "Who are you and what do you want?"

Sam was prepared. We had worn our best and cleanest clothes. And now in his most formal French Sam told her that he was the brother of Mademoiselle Rachel, who was on holiday in the south— Perhaps Madame had noticed that Mademoiselle had been away for a time?—and that she had decided to stay there longer, so we had come by to collect a few things that Rachel had asked him to send her. Sam held up a key to Rachel's room, which he told the concierge his sister had left with him. In fact, it was just a key that looked similar—we still had to get to the real key, an extra one that Rachel kept hidden behind a drain pipe by the stairway. Sam then produced a letter that he and Rachel had made up, with the southern city of Avignon noted at the top and My Dearest Brother as the greeting, speaking of the fine weather in the south and asking that he send her some things— naming some clothes and jewelry—from her room, because she had decided to extend her holiday.

Madame Barras took a long time looking at this short note. I was beginning to wonder if she could read at all, when she finally raised her head and said, "La Jude?" Sam was startled by the insulting slang, but before he could reply, Madame Barras shoved the letter back at him and waved her hand toward her shoulder, saying "Je m'en fous"—"What do I care?"—and went back through her door, shutting it behind her.

Sam stood there without moving, stung by the French slap of "la Jude." I tugged him toward the stairway before he could do or say something that would spoil the plan. Sam quickly found the key where

Rachel told him she had hidden it behind the pipe, and we went up to the room on the third floor.

"Je m'en fous," the concierge had said. What was it, exactly, that she did not care about? Us going up to the room? De Guise giving Rachel such a beating? Anything at all to do with la Jude?

At the room, Sam and I found the door unlocked, and the place seeming to be exactly as Rachel had left it—blood-spotted bedcovers on the floor, a turned-over chair, half-full absinthe and wine bottles and glasses, some of them toppled on a table, a fancy-shaded electric lamp still glowing by the bedside. Rachel's things there, untouched. It seemed de Guise had fled the room right after Rachel had run off and not been back. Too shamed to show his face? Or holding the strange hope that, if he kept away, Rachel might return? And stay? How did people like this think? Who knew?

We straightened up the room a bit. It was large—three or four times the size of Sam and Rina's room in Belleville—with its own water tap and a cooker as well as a large coal-burning heating stove. Most amazing to me, it had its own toilet and another sink and even a zinc bathtub in a separate water closet that was itself larger than the chambres de bonne where I sometimes slept at Rue Martel. There were paintings and a tapestry, and two brocade sitting chairs next to a small round table by the stove, plus a heavy wood eating table with its own chairs. Rachel had not exaggerated—de Guise had money. We gathered the few things that Rachel had listed in her pretend letter and stuffed a few more items into our pockets. We did not try to take away too much, in case the concierge was watching from behind closed doors when we crossed the courtyard.

I did not go up to Belleville with Sam when we got back to the east—Rachel was still too shaky to see anyone, he said. But when I met him the next day, Sam told me that having some of her own things again had made Rachel smile, a little, for the first time since she had returned. Sam wanted to go back to Saint Lambert—the district in the 15th where Rachel's room was—to get more things. And he had a plan. If the concierge tried to stop us from going in again, he said, we would just charge in and grab as much as we could, then dash away. If instead we got past the concierge with no trouble, we would bring out only a small amount of stuff, in case she was keeping an eye on us. After that, he said, we could return late at night, when the concierge was asleep, because Rachel had told him where in the room to find a key to the courtyard door, which was locked after dark. That way, eventually we could collect all of Rachel's things, most of which Rina could sell from her cart, and maybe we would grab a few of the more easily moveable pieces—lamps, drinking goblets, cookery utensils—that de Guise had bought to furnish the room and that Rina could also sell. Unless the concierge spotted us and put a stop to it. Or rang the police. Sam grinned—this was serious business, getting a hold of things they could sell to feed and keep their family, the three of them now, but he was also enjoying the game of it. So, did I want to come along? He did not have to coax.

We again put on our respectable clothes and rode two buses to Saint Lambert, strolling into the building's courtyard as if we were regulars there. The concierge was immediately out her door, but as she crossed the courtyard toward us, saying "Just a moment, just a moment," she slowed, recognized us, and with a toss of her hand—a "Je m'en fous" gesture—turned and went back into her loge.

In the room, Sam and I felt a bit more comfortable than we had on our first visit, and took a closer look around, discussing the various things that would be useful to carry away. There were all the clothes that Rachel's different men friends had bought her, which was quite a collection—I had never seen so many clothes for one person, and most of them very stylish, at least Montparnasse artist style. There was also her jewelry—fantasy jewelry, as the French call it, not real, but still worth a bit—and scarves and hats and handbags and such. As well as several small drawings and paintings, plus an old hanging tapestry that seemed quite fancy. And all over the room were tchotchkes—little statuettes of animals and naked people, candleholders, match-strikers—that could easily be taken away to sell. Plus a brocade bedcover and very nice bed clothes on a double wide real mattress and a high wooden bed frame, plus spare bedding in the large mirror wardrobe. Then there were all the cooking and eating and drinking utensils, and in another cupboard by the cooker a few tins of fish and under the sink a dozen or so bottles of wine. With labels on them. If our middle of the night plan worked, there could be quite a haul—Sam and I never bothered to discuss how much of it actually belonged to Rachel and how much to de Guise. Sam said that selling these things could help keep the family for months to come. And those months to come would be winter, he reminded me, when there was much less chance to sell things on the streets, so he was anxious that we begin our night raids soon. This time we took just a few more items of clothing, and some of the fake jewelry in our pockets, and headed down the stairs. I am certain that the concierge was watching us from behind her window, but she let us pass without bother.

By the time we got back to the edge of Bastille—our usual separating point, him up to Belleville, me over to Faubourg Saint Denis—that afternoon, Sam and I had planned a return to Saint Lambert that very night. Sam headed up the hill to deliver the things to Rachel and without thinking I began to trudge toward Rue Martel. But I soon realized that there was no reason for me to be there. I no longer had a room to go to, and I should not bother Abraham and Chawa at that hour—Maison Albert was in the middle of its work day. Then I thought of Henri. I had not seen him for weeks, since a few days before I had lost my work at the Foire dormitories, and here I was in Bastille, just a short walk to the foreign section's Paris east bureau near the Gare de Lyon. The idea of seeing Henri suddenly cheered me, as did being in Bastille where the streets, like Henri, now seemed like old friends. Probably my great relief at having got past Rachel's concierge was also a boost—as long as I did not think about the risks of returning that night.

I had no idea whether Henri would be at the bureau. But he might, and anyway just saying Henri's name out loud there and perhaps hearing something about him, made my walk there a pleasure. In a few minutes I reached the bureau. Henri was not there. The foreign section workers were not there. The bureau was not there. The storefront was boarded up. On the boards someone had painted "One for all and all for one." In red.

Sam and I met at a café in Bastille at midnight. He rode up on a bicycle with a large wheeled basket connected to the back. I had seen these bike taxis before—on nice days, people with money would hire them and sit in the basket while the rider pedaled them from place to place, or simply took them on a turn around the Bois de Boulogne or some other park. Sam had borrowed this one from a friend who earned his keep that way. Sam explained to me that if we got things—more than a few clothes, that is—out of Rachel's room, we would need a way to get them back across the city. It was a long way, and in the middle of the night the buses did not run. Also, carrying big full sacks on the street late in the night was an invitation to be stopped by the police. With the bike taxi, though, we would both have a ride to Saint Lambert, saving us the bus fare, and we could stash in the basket—big enough to carry two people—whatever we took from Rachel's room. Sam had brought burlap sacks to fill and an oilcloth and some rope to cover the basket and protect it from the rain. And from prying eyes.

At Rachel's building we quietly opened the courtyard door and put the bike taxi against a wall inside. We made our way up to Rachel's room without any sign of life from the concierge. Once inside, we gathered up the particular things Rachel had asked us to get first—a certain painting, a small statue, some carved wooden boxes, a three-branched candlestick, a fine wool coat. When we had it all collected, Sam looked around and said, "You know, that ride made me hungry."—Of course, we were almost constantly hungry.—"I wonder what there is?"

He looked in the cupboard and in a wire mesh coolbox sitting in the window, and found a large piece of hard cheese and two untouched dried sausages. The cheese had gone bad on the outside, but Sam trimmed it with a funny-looking curved little knife he found there—a special cheese knife, he explained, the French were very keen on them—leaving a sizeable good piece, part of which he sliced for us. He tried to use the little knife on the sausage also, but it would not cut through. "Must be a milchedik knife," he said. I laughed and felt myself relax a bit. "Better not ask," he said, when with his own knife he sliced off a little piece of the sausage and offered it to me—meaning, Maître, that it was probably made of pork. He also picked up one of the dozen or so bottles of labeled wine that lay in a pyramid under the sink, seemed to think about it for a moment—weighing his thirst against the bottle's reselling value, I imagine—then opened it and poured us each a glass. We toasted. "To art," he said, gesturing grandly around the room. "See how it lifts the spirit?"

I am sorry, Maître, milchedik—anything made with milk. The ancient food laws, to never mix meat things and milk things. And for some orthodox even separate utensils for each. So, the special cheese knife, not being able to cut sausage with it—Sam's joke. Not important.

We ate and drank slowly, without speaking, me on a chair at the table, Sam lounging on the big bed. It was wonderful to be warm, put something in our stomachs, and not feel as though at any minute we had to move on. In fact, Sam nestled further into the bed and said, "You know, if we go back anytime soon, we will have to figure out where to spend the rest of the night. And it sounds like it has started to rain. So, how about this? We rest up a bit here, and leave close to sunup. I will take the first snooze," he continued, not waiting for my opinion of this idea, "and you wake me in an hour,"—he handed me his battered old pocket watch—"then you take a turn." And with that he closed his eyes. Within what seemed like only a few moments, he was snoring.

I can tell you, Maître, that despite the late hour staying awake was not difficult for me. I was quite nervous that someone might come storming through the door—the concierge, the police, this wild man de Guise. I did not actually think through the likelihood of any of them, but suffered from a muddled up fear of them all. So, nervously I kept nibbling the sausage and cheese. And sipping the wine. Which is when, for the first time, I understood why people liked it so much. Because the more I sipped, the less I worried about where we were and what might happen, until the next thing I knew Sam was shaking me and offering the bed. Barely opening one eye I moved over and settled into the soft coziness that Sam's warmth had left there. But before I could fall asleep again Sam looked out the window and said he thought he could see a bit of light behind the rain, and we had better get out before the concierge was awake. So, we filled the sacks with the things we had gathered for Rachel, and tiptoed down the stairs. All was still and silent. Quietly we put the sacks into the basket and threw the oilcloth over it, wheeled the bike out onto the street, then took turns riding it on the long trip back across the city while the other walked beside. By the time we got to Bastille we were in high spirits from our successful raid, plus our unplanned late night meal and nap, despite being cold and soaked from the rainy trip back. We decided to go again as soon as possible and agreed to meet at the Bastille café as soon as there was a night that promised no rain.

"Next time," Sam said, "I will bring a loaf of bread."

26 October

Two midnights later I went with Sam and his borrowed bike taxi back to Saint Lambert. There were still plenty of people on the streets as we passed through Montparnasse, whose cafés and bars never shut down. But it was quiet at Rachel's building in Saint Lambert, the concierge's loge was dark and she made no appearance when we entered the court-yard. We found Rachel's room just as we had left it. This time Sam went straightaway for the cheese and sausage and a tin of fish from the cup-board and pulled a half-round of bread from one of the sacks he had brought. I followed his lead, retrieving the bottle of wine that we had opened the last time. We began eating immediately, without saying anything about how the room's food supply seemed to have become the center of our attention. Only when we had finished our meal did we begin to look around for the things Rachel had put on a list for us.

When we were done making a pile of what could fit in the bike taxi, Sam looked at me kind of sideways, with the expression of a child who is slightly naughty but also knows he is the favorite. "You did not get much of a chance last time," he said, "but this bed is very comfort-able." It was after two in the morning, and if we left Saint Lambert then, neither of us would have a place to go—Sam was taking turns with Rachel using the second pallet in the room in Belleville, and I was again staying at Maison Albert but would not disturb Abraham and Chawa in the middle of the night. So, we would have to spend four or five hours out on the cold wet streets, unless we found an all-night bar, which for a couple of small young men could be risky, especially trying also to guard the bike taxi, and where in any event we would have to spend money, which Sam in particular did not want to do. "And," he added, "I have the bike until eight."

He was right—the bed was very comfortable. I had not slept on an actual mattress since I left Hannover more than a year before. He gave me the first sleep while he sat in one of the brocade chairs, then woke me after a couple of hours and took the bed while I sat up, keeping an eye on his pocket watch. I woke him at five, when it was still dark. We quietly carried Rachel's things downstairs and slipped out of the courtyard with the bike.

Twice over the next week, on the only nights when there was no rain, we exactly repeated this outing—except for the labeled wine, which Sam realized was worth more to him to sell than to drink. He reported to me that a few of the things we had retrieved had cheered Rachel a bit, and Rina had already been able to sell some pieces from her cart, a couple of them fetching more than she sometimes made in several days worth of hawking her usual cheap items. Also, we went to the room a bit earlier these next two visits, and so were each able to get longer sleeps there. We even figured out how to use the heating stove, though there was just a little coal left and it only really began to warm the big room just about the time we had to leave.

As we came into the courtyard on our fourth night there, I thought there was a rustling of the concierge's curtain. Upstairs I mentioned it to Sam. He did not say anything but I could see that he took it under advisement. Under advisement—I learned that from the magistrate in Paris, Maître, who seemed to say it every time we appeared in his chambers and my great fierce lawyer Maître de Moro-Giafferi would bring up another legal argument about why there should be no further delay of my trial. Of course, nothing ever happened. Under advisement.

With Sam, though, something did happen. We talked about it as we rode and walked the bike back across the city early the next morning. Sam was now worried that Madame Barras the concierge might be sniffing something wrong. Also, he said, he wondered how much longer the room was paid for—he would ask Rachel later that day—which might also be a reason we needed to finish up our job in a hurry. We decided to meet again that evening to decide on the next move.

As so often for me in Paris, without having work I did not know how I was going to pass the day. But the zinc bathtub in Rachel's rooms had stuck in my mind. Between my earnings from the Foire, the pay Genève had given me for her German lessons, and the money that had come from my parents, I had the most in my pockets since I had come to Paris, so I felt that I could spend a bit of it and decided to go to the public baths. When I was staying in a chambre de bonne at Rue Martel or sleeping in Abraham and Chawa's rooms, every week or so I would wash myself at their tap, early in the morning before Sidney and Berenice arrived, or late at night. But there was also a public baths nearby, where you could not only stand under a warm stream of water but also spend time—more than needed for drying off and getting dressed, they did not hurry you out—in the changing cubicles. Because it cost more at those baths than at other baths across the canal in Belleville or down in Bastille, it was less crowded. I was not the only person who snuck in some sleep there, especially on cold rainy days.

When I met up with Sam that evening, he told me Rachel said the rent for her room was paid to Madame Barras—de Guise would just leave an envelope for Rachel—at the first of each month. Which was just four days away. So, Sam had convinced Rachel that she needed to go back to the room herself, right away, to decide which of her things were the most valuable or important to her, so we could at least get those out before the concierge took back the room. Rachel was still deeply frightened of de Guise but agreed to go if Sam and I went with her. We made a rendezvous for the next day.

The three of us met outside the Gare d'Austerlitz in the morning.

This was my first time seeing Rachel—she was still awfully thin and pale. She managed a smile but there was not much to it, and Thank you was all she said to me, though she seemed to mean it strongly. She did not speak as we rode the bus across to Saint Lambert. Mostly she looked into her lap and played nervously with her hands.

She became even more nervous as we neared her building. A block away, she hesitated. Sam took her elbow and led her on. She kept her head down as we approached the doorway, but every few seconds she darted looks toward the streets around.

We crossed the courtyard and had almost reached the stairway when we heard a noise behind us. Madame Barras. We stopped. The concierge looked back and forth between Rachel and Sam.

"Hah," she laughed, "so you really are his brother." Then she turned and went back into her loge.

I looked at them standing next to each other, Sam and Rachel, and it was true they looked very much alike. Then I thought about what Madame Barras had just said, what it meant—that when we had shown up before, she had not particularly believed that Sam was Rachel's brother but had let us go into the room anyway. "La Jude. Je m'en fous."

When we entered the room, Rachel drew in her breath—not at anything specific, I do not think, since we had cleaned up the mess from the night of de Guise's rage—and she did not seem fully to breathe out again the entire time we were there. Which was not very long. Whether it was because she feared that de Guise might show up or she simply felt too much the unhappiness of her life in this room, Rachel could not wait to get out again. Shaking, she quickly went through her clothes and around the room picking out items of value she thought could be sold, dropped them onto the bed and the table, stuffed a few things into her bag, grabbed a coat, and hurried out, Sam and me close behind.

The night of the next day, Sam again borrowed the bike taxi and we went back to Saint Lambert to collect the things Rachel had selected. It would take at least two trips, maybe three. We still had three nights before the end of the month, but Sam did not want to risk running into de Guise, who might be coming to collect his own things before turning the place back to the concierge. Also, it was raining almost every day, so on this one clear night Sam decided we would make two or even three trips back and forth to clear out the room. We got through the courtyard and up to the room without any problem. Under the door was a note.

It was from de Guise. To Rachel. He hoped she had a good holiday in the south—Madame Barras must have passed on to him Sam and Rachel's little story, Sam guessing that de Guise had given the concierge a few francs tip to bring him any news of Rachel. A holiday is just what she needed, he wrote. And he was so happy that she had decided to return to the room—the concierge must have also told him about Rachel's appearance at the room the day before.

But that was not all. He was sorry, he wrote, terribly sorry, but she must be assured that their unfortunate moments—that is how de Guise put it, Sam translating into Yiddish for me—were only the result of the poisons that had entered their bodies and were no part of his true feelings for her. Or something like that. Still, de Guise wrote, he understood that she might not be ready yet to see him. So, she should take her time. He would keep paying the room rent, had arranged for a coal delivery the following Monday, and would wait to hear from her that he could visit her again. Until then, he would not disturb her. He signed it, "With affection and respect." Respect, Maître! There was 100 francs in the envelope.

Blood money, Rachel called it when Sam got back with the note. She refused to take it and told Sam to return it, through the concierge. Which caused a big row between them, he told me. For them it was a very large amount, a month's rent and food for all three, and medicine for Rina—they needed it, Sam insisted. Rachel argued back that needing it did not make it righteous to keep it. "You certainly pick your spots about when to be righteous," Sam sneered, and Rachel stormed away. They had barely spoken since. He kept the money, he later told me, and gave it to their mother on the quiet.

Sam was still furious with Rachel three or four nights later when we made our next trip with the bike taxi. The more so because Rachel also insisted that Sam return to the room a lamp he had taken the previous time—it was not among the things she had picked out for us, Rachel told him, and belonged to de Guise.

Going to the room was more relaxed this time—we wanted to avoid the concierge making trouble if she saw us taking away things, but otherwise we had understood that she did not care at all what went on in the rooms of la Jude. Also, after the letter from de Guise it seemed that he would not be making any unannounced appearances and that the room would be paid for, so we no longer had to finish our job in such a hurry.

We were so much more relaxed, in fact, that Sam immediately plopped down on the bed and announced that before he would do anything for anyone he was going to take a rest. It sounded as if this was out of spite at Rachel—and at de Guise and Madame Barras and the whole rotten story—but I could tell that it was also because he was exhausted. With Rachel spending almost all her days and nights caving herself away in their room in Belleville, and his mother Rina also in the room most of the time now with her health getting worse and the weather so bad, it was difficult for Sam to be there as well. So, he had been outdoors even more than usual and had been getting very little sleep. I had no reason to object about staying—after all, where did I have to go? So, Sam stretched out and was soon asleep. I got out the last of the sausage we had been working on, found in a sack the bread that Sam had brought, and had myself a small meal. When I had finished eating I poked around the room, looking at things more closely than I had on any of the earlier trips, especially the strange paintings of people who did not look very much like real people. It was getting quite cold, so I dug into one of the coal bags that had been delivered, as de Guise had promised in his note, and lit a fire in the stove. After a few minutes I settled into one of the brocade-covered chairs and soon I was also asleep.

I have no idea how long I slept—since we were not worried about the time, Sam had not bothered to give me his watch—but when I woke the whole room was as warm as an early morning bed. I put a bit more coal in the stove and then went in to use the toilet. It was warm in there also. I actually sat without shivering—what pleasure, Maître. I was looking at the zinc bathtub when I noticed Sam standing in the doorway, smiling. "Why not give it a try?" he said. I must have had an unbelieving face because he said, "Well, why not? The stove is going, we can heat up some water. And someone ought to use it. Right?"

So we did. I took the first bath. It was a dream. There were even clean towels, three or four of them. I headed straight for the bed when I had dried off, but not before I noticed, when he undressed for his turn in the tub, the scabies that had again attacked Sam, not just up his arm but all across one side of his body. Seeing it, I was glad I had the first turn in the tub. Only after that did I feel bad for my friend. I do not know whether those thoughts would have come in the same order before I had spent that past year in Paris.

I woke a while later to find Sam asleep next to me on the big bed. I remember the relief I immediately felt to see that he had put on his shirt, that the scabies was covered, and that the bed was large enough that we each had a side of it without disturbing the other. In a few minutes Sam also was awake.

"Look," he said, sitting up, "when I was in the bath I was thinking. Where can I be? Or you? To sleep. All right, yes we both know places to sleep in the day, but I mean at night, someplace to be out of the cold, now that winter is coming on?"

There was a comfortable bed big enough for two, plenty of covers and a stove with a supply of coal. It had running water and its very own indoor toilet. Even a bathtub. Who ever had a bathtub? And most of all, we did not have to pay a thing. There was nothing to stop us.

Well, actually there was. When and how Madame Barras might make trouble for us hung over our heads. Not to mention de Guise. And if that trouble led to the police, I was in more danger than Sam, who at least had a permis de séjour, a French residence permit. Sam knew my situation. And saw it on my face. We will be careful to come and go only during the night, he said, when the old vulture is less likely to see us. And even if she does spot us once in a while, he reminded me, she has told us more than once that she could not care less what happens in the room of la Jude, as long as de Guise pays the rent, which he wrote that he would do. Also, Sam said he would have Rachel come by once in a while, to show herself to the concierge, which would keep up the appearance that she was back living there. He had worked it all out, he told me. A bathtub is a remarkable place for thinking, he said.

So that was how it happened. Within two weeks of losing the chambre de bonne at Rue Martel, I was able to get out of Abraham and Chawa's way by moving myself and my few things into Rachel's former room, sharing it with Sam. From the difficult kindness of Abraham and Chawa to the unknowing hospitality of de Guise. From nowhere to luxury. Not to mention fame—artists, poets, even cinema stars all around in that district, Maître. And me—H of Montparnasse.

Yours sincerely,
Herschel

Maître Herr Rosenhaus,

Treason? Against the Reich? But the Reich itself, and however many people in Paris, never failed to tell me that I am not German. Not legally. So—legally—how could I commit treason against my country if it is not my country?

The indictment. I am relieved it has finally happened, Maître. You said in your note that I am given a copy because the law requires it. And I am most satisfied to have it, to study it. But you said little else that helps me. Especially about when exactly the trial will be. Perhaps January or February, you wrote. That seems very far off. And the "perhaps" part makes me nervous.

So, treason against the Reich, it charges me. Instead of murder. "To interfere with actions of the Führer and the state." Well, that seems not far from correct. Although bringing the world's attention and actually interfering are not exactly the same thing, are they? Is that a distinction? At the time, it certainly felt like one. My Uncle Abraham in Paris always talked about distinctions. And Parisians seemed to love them. Officials, most especially. But so did my Paris lawyer, de Moro-Giafferi. You see, he discussed with me this treason business. And other ideas of defense. If I chose them.

De Moro-Giafferi spoke to me about treason very early in my case. Because soon after the shooting, the Reich asked the French court to return me to Germany, to stand trial here instead of in France. Maître Moro explained to me that the Reich could not get me sent to Germany because French law did not allow extraditing for the charge of murder if the act took place in France. The Reich knew this, of course, so instead it requested to the French court that I be extradited for treason. Moro was prepared for that also, saying to the Paris magistrate that since I was not a Reich citizen, legally speaking I could not commit treason to Germany. The Reich lawyers argued to the judge that I was born and spent my whole life in Germany, but Maître Moro simply repeated, holding one finger in the air, "Mais pas citoyen"— "But not a citizen." The judge quickly agreed with him—legally the matter was quite clear. Citoyen—it was one of the only times in France I ever heard that word without feeling sick in my stomach.

I also reminded the jailers in Toulouse about these extraditing rules—in July 1940, when I had made it all the way to the south of France, ahead of the Wehrmacht. And again in Moulins, to the French police there, when they were about to hand me over to the Gestapo. But somehow these rules no longer seemed to matter to them. At least, not about me. Though just before that, I must say, other French jailers, in other prisons, had seen and done things very differently.

So, now again the Reich wants to charge treason. Perhaps so that the extraditing of me from France will seem lawful? But Maître, some things have not changed—I am still not a Reich citizen. Which becomes something for us to say at trial, no? Not because I believe it will matter to the court. But because the press will be there, and so the world will be listening.

I have been thinking, Maître, that perhaps there is also some other good in this. The treason charge, I mean. Because it puts right to the center of the trial the question of why. "With intent to interfere." Which means what was in my mind. Just what we have been hard working on all these months, you and I. So, this is a good thing, Maître. Do you think so? I certainly hope.

Sincerely,
Herschel

Maître Rosenhaus,

So, Saint Lambert, the edge of Montparnasse. Rachel's room there, sharing it with Sam. Though soon I saw very little of him. Except when he was asleep.

I still had some money left from my work at the Foire and Genève's German lessons, plus what my parents had managed to send me. Spending it only very lightly I stretched it through the autumn months. But for Sam, as always, finding food and figuring out how to come up with a few francs to help his mother Rina was a weight on him every day. The cold rain that had set in early that autumn did not let up and cut short Sam's outdoors work—not only helping Rina with her colporteuse cart but also his food scavenging rounds and some of his schemes for coming up with things to sell.

Rachel was now doing more of the helping with Rina's cart. In fact, Rachel was doing almost all of it herself. Her mother did not much come out from their room now. Sam would not pronounce the word, but finally they realized that what Rina had long been suffering, and recently become worse, was consumption. Either Rachel or Sam now had to take over most of the cart work, and since Rachel was the one staying with Rina in Belleville, the cart fell more directly to her. Which left Sam freer to latch onto things for Rachel to sell, or to come up with money some other way. This dividing of the work also let them mostly stay out of each other's way. They still did not fully trust each other after their argument over whether to keep de Guise's "blood money." I saw Rachel only a few times during those autumn and winter months. She seemed honestly pleased that I had found a roof for myself in her Saint Lambert room, and that in the bargain Sam and I were pulling the wool over de Guise. Still, Sam sleeping in the comfort that she had paid for with her many inflictions in Montparnasse, while she spent every night tending her mother in the tiny Belleville room, was a splinter under her skin.

Sam now spent most of his time around Montparnasse—it took too long and too much walking effort, especially in the bad weather, or too much money by bus or Métro, to travel very often across the city to the east and back again. So he gave up his food gathering at Bastille and other east Paris neighborhoods and began trying to do the same in the districts near Rachel's room. Not easy. He had no network of bakeries and restaurants over there in Saint Lambert or Montparnasse as he did in the east where he knew how to catch a bit of backdoor food. Also, at the street markets in these new districts he did not know the locals, either the sellers or the other food-gatherers. On top of this, the chance for anyone to snatch food after the outdoor markets was much shorter in the early darkening rainy days. I went with Sam the first few times he tried to work these local markets but we did very poorly—at two different places we were chased away by rough Frenchmen. Though Sam did not say so, I could tell that my being there only got in his way. From then on, I let him go alone.

Since it turned out to be difficult for him to gather decent food, Sam turned to things that would bring in cash, which anyway he needed to help with Rina's rent and medicines. Trapping cats was out—it would have meant schlepping all the way over to Bastille and Belleville, where he knew the territory, for the very little money it brought him, and also the weather now would have made that slow cold work even more miserable. Picking up things outside the discount department stores, for Rina or Rachel to sell from the cart, was also off—the rain now made these things useless unless you snatched them within moments of being dumped, and the growing numbers of people without work who were also scavenging now made for very long odds of collecting a good share of anything that could be sold. Also, the other schemes Sam had always managed to come up with—a box of goods to sell that had fallen off the back of a lorry, copper wire or machine parts to be salvaged from some workshop that had gone out of business but had not yet been cleared—seemed to start with one or another character he knew over in the east, so removing himself from his usual daily rounds over there left him without those contacts.

For several years, though, Sam had from time to time during spring and summer gone from the east over to Montparnasse to perform somersaults and other tricks on the pavements outside its famous café terraces, picking up tips from the many tourists who came there, and sometimes going off with one of them to serve for a few hours as a tour guide or translator, or something, where he might make extra money. And now here he was, staying near to these very same cafés. So, he began again to work the Montparnasse terraces. Tourist season was over, though, and the cold and rain kept the few daytime patrons inside the cafés, so Sam started going over there at night instead, when the regulars gathered and the cafés still had sizable crowds. It was almost impossible to do any of his gymnastics inside the cafés, and the waiters would have thrown him out if he had tried. So, instead he started doing small magic tricks—with cards and such—as he moved around the tables. But this was not bringing him much, and soon he came up with another scheme. He got in touch with a certain colporteur he knew, who supplied him on credit with special kinds of little books and photo postcards to sell under the café tables.

He was out quite late nearly every night now, and slept in the room during the day, so I had hardly any time with him to talk about how he was managing. Also, there seemed to be little he wanted to say—for the first time since I had known him.

In the early weeks of our stay in Saint Lambert, when Sam was doing poorly on his daytime rounds, I would buy a bit of food for both of us and not exactly offer it to him but leave it out on the table—a bread that I would break open, a piece of cheese that I would cut and leave the funny little curved knife sticking in, a few apples with a half left open, a plate with my crumbs and rind on it and a second, clean plate next to it—that sort of thing. But he would not touch the food unless I directly offered him, which anyway he mostly refused. Except on those days when he had eaten nothing at all. I even tried buying some cheap things I saw in the food stalls—leeks, dried beans, beef innards—and fussed with them at the cooker until in a frustrated voice I would ask for Sam's help. It worked a couple of times and we shared some hot food, but soon he was hardly ever in the room when I was, and when we were there together one of us was usually asleep, or on the way out.

One evening I came in as Sam was dressing for his night work at the cafés. I sat at the table while he cleaned himself at the sink in the water closet. There had been no food in the room when I had left that morning, so I had brought back some cheese, butter, bread. I hoped he might eat some before he went out, so I quickly spread the food on the table and cut into both the bread and the cheese, making a small plate for each of us. I was careful not to disturb the small stack there of booklets and postcards that he would try to sell at the cafés that night. I must admit, Maître, I was curious to look at these things he sold. The reading booklets I could never get much sense of—they were in French, which I still read very poorly, and anyway did not know many of the words that seemed to be important, and a few of them were in English. But the drawings or photos in some of the books, and the photos on the postcards, were plain enough for anyone. At least most of them were—a few I had a hard time understanding what exactly the people were doing. I did not want to ask Sam. He did not hide these books and photos from me but neither did he offer to show them. And he never spoke about them.

That particular evening it seemed a new batch, and I was certainly tempted to peek, but I did not want him to see me pawing his goods. And anyway, I would likely have a chance to look through them at some point in the following days, when Sam was asleep. He did not sell them very quickly.

When he came into the room after washing he noticed the plate of food but did not sit down to it. He put on his jacket—the one with the huge pockets where he carried his goods—and I could see that he was getting ready to leave, so I went into the washroom and began my own cleaning at the sink, hoping that he would use those moments alone to eat a bit of the food before he left. I heard the chair scrape the floor as he sat at the table, so I dawdled at the sink, running the water much longer than I needed. When I turned the water off, it was completely silent out in the room. Then came a groan, or cry, or combination of both, I do not know what to call it, Maître, and at the same moment Sam's fist slamming on the table. My first reaction was to rush out to see what had happened but another part of me warned me to stay away and I stopped in the doorway between the washing closet and the room. Sam's head was thrown back and his eyes closed, his hands laid flat on top of the books and postcards he had been sorting. Suddenly he sat upright, then jerked back his chair and stood, gathered up the booklets and shoved them into his jacket pockets, roughly snatched the postcards and went over and jammed them under his extra shirt sitting on a shelf, then hurried out the door as if he could not wait to get out of the room. Of course he saw me standing in the entry to the washroom, but did not actually notice me—if that makes sense.

I did not wait long before I went over to look at these postcards he had stuffed away on the shelf. I do not want to describe them, Maître, but like the others he had been selling they were scenes of a woman, or a woman with a man, or two, and a few of just women or just men. Sam called them érotisme raffiné, though I never understood what was refined about them, except for the rich bedroom settings, I suppose. Anyway, this new group of photo cards was shocking but no more so than the ones Sam had sold before and I did not see why these in particular should have caused him such pain, until I came to two cards, each with the same woman. As in many of the photos, the woman in these two was painted with lip and cheek rouge and color on her eyes, but after a few moments there was no mistaking who she was. Sam's sister Rachel.

4 November

Things were not the same with Sam after that night. Even before then he had begun to keep a distance from me, as I told you, but I had thought of that as mostly just the difference between my days and his. Or, my days and his nights. Now, on the not very often times that we were in the room together and both awake, he barely spoke and

291

avoided even looking at me. Also, I noticed his habits were changing—I mean, how he prepared himself to face the outside world, and how he recovered from it when he returned to the room. He was staying out not just late but the whole night, almost every night, and before going out would pay close attention to what he wore and how he looked. He seemed to be making a bit more money, and even bought food that he left in the room and obviously meant for me to share, though he never said anything about it. One day when Rachel came to the room—she did not like to do it, but Sam had convinced her to come by for a brief stop once a week or so, just to show her face to the concierge—she mentioned that Sam had been buying new, more expensive medicines for their mother, and wondered how he was getting the money. I had no idea. Also, Sam started to appear with new clothes, in Montparnasse style, replacing his few old scruffy things from Belleville. He even started wearing gloves. Not that gloves were unusual in Paris and made good sense those wet and freezing winter nights—it was December by then. But these gloves were soft, fine leather, not the cheap wool ones that most people wore—or mittens of unnamed fur—and they just did not match the Sam I knew.

Another strange thing was that he now took a long soak in the bath as soon as he got back from his night in Montparnasse. Every dark early morning when he crept in, often stinking of alcohol and sometimes other odd smells, Sam would stoke the coal stove and put on it two large basins of water. When the water was hot, he would fill the zinc tub in the washroom and climb in. Usually he just soaked quietly for a long time but sometimes I would hear him scouring himself furiously. Once I heard him in there sobbing. Yes, Sam.

I did not ask what was happening to him. I knew that things were different, in some serious way, but I no longer felt close enough to him—though for an hour or two some mornings we shared the same bed—to mention it. Except one morning. He came in as usual, quietly—both of us pretending I did not hear him through my sleep—and without taking off his coat he put the water basins on the stove, then dropped exhausted onto one of the brocade chairs. After just a moment, though, he rushed into the washing closet. And retched into the toilet. When he came out after a few minutes he took the water off the stove but did not fill the tub. He very slowly got undressed, as if it was a great effort, and climbed into the bed, facing away, being careful not to disturb me.

The painful retching sounds, and his weariness that could not even manage the tub that otherwise seemed to have become so important to him, disturbed me enough that I broke the pact of silence between us.

"Are you all right?"

For a few moments he did not answer. When he did, it was without turning to face me and in a rough voice I did not recognize, as if something had broken in his throat.

"Of course." There was a scold in his tone. "We have food. A room, with no rent. Coal for the stove. Our own toilet, for God's sake. What could be bad?"

His voice crumbled even further with these last words, and I said nothing more.

5 November

But me. After that difficult early morning I realized that I had attached myself to Sam, that during that autumn into winter I had been waiting for him. To continue. He had led me to Saint Lambert, first to the adventure of rescuing Rachel's things, then to making the room our own. And I expected, without actually thinking about it, that whatever happened next would also come from Sam. Which it did. A whole new way of being, it seemed. Some sort of Montparnasse way. But whatever it was, it did not include me.

Earlier—after I had stopped trying to scavenge the local markets with Sam but before I felt him move so distant from me—I spent some days wandering around Saint Lambert, trying to get to know that part of the city, so that perhaps I could contribute something to Sam's and my new life there. Other parts of the 15th were not entirely new to me—I had been before along its far edge, by the Seine, where the foreign section's main bureau was, and the vélodrome where Henri and I had gone roller skating. In fact one day I hiked over to the vélo-drome, thinking I would treat myself and spend an hour skating, but it was closed to prepare it for some kind of large meeting there that night. I did not go near the foreign section bureau.

But I had no experience of Saint Lambert itself, and it felt somehow deeply different from the districts I had come to know—Bastille and Belleville, Faubourg Saint Denis around Rue Martel, and the old Pletzl neighborhood in the center, where the Sportclub Aurore was. Most streets in Saint Lambert are plain and poor, but another sort of plain and poor from the streets I knew. It is a crowded district, Saint Lambert, yet did not feel as much so as those other neighborhoods. I could sense but not quite recognize a difference. Until I went back to the east. You see, Maître, the streets of Bastille, Belleville, Faubourg Saint Denis, they were all mixed in with people like me. But Saint Lambert was French.

So I began spending more of my days again in the old neighbor-hoods. At first I told myself that I was going back there only because I had reasons. To deliver something from Sam or from the Saint Lambert room to Rachel—Sam was still avoiding her. To have supper with Abraham and Chawa on Friday nights. To drop by for some event at the Aurore. And once to locate the rooming house near Place de la République where Henri had said he was staying, though it turned out to be a big busy place, young serious people coming in and out, and at the last minute I lost my nerve and walked past. Soon I found myself traveling over to the old neighborhoods every day. I just felt more at ease there. Well, not exactly at ease. But at least more familiar.

Abraham and Chawa were worried about where I was staying and how I was getting along. They were relieved to hear that I was sharing a room with Sam, someone they had met several times and came from a world they understood. When they wondered about the cost, I explained that the room belonged to Sam's older sister, who had moved back in for a while with their mother to help care for her, so we were actually splitting the rent among three of us, which made it only a small expense for each. Again, this was a story they liked—a daughter caring for her mother, a brother and sister sharing, a friend helping a friend in need. They were relaxing more with each answer, until they asked where the room was. Though I knew the district was famous, I had no sense at the time that the image of the place was built on types like de Guise, so I rather proudly pronounced the name Montparnasse. You would have thought I said Gomorrah. Or Leningrad. Chawa covered her eyes. Abraham turned red and howled What? What?

Quickly I retreated, saying "No, not actually Montparnasse, but past the train station there, in Saint Lambert, the 15th, I only said Montparnasse because I thought that way you would recognize the direction, the area of the city, but that is not really where I am, not Montparnasse, no, no, no."

They calmed down, but were never comfortable as long as I stayed in Rachel's room. Then again, in those days what meant comfortable?

As the weeks passed deep into December, I could see that not too far into the new year of '38 my money would run out. I had earned nothing since Genève had left for Switzerland, and traveling back and forth between Saint Lambert and the east, plus food when I was away from the room, was costing me daily. That winter I was also spending afternoons at the cinema, to have somewhere to get out of the cold without just heading back to the room where Sam would still be sleeping. In the afternoons the cinemas charged less, and I could stay for hours before they cleared the seats for the evening shows, but even the reduced-price admissions mounted up over the weeks. As always, Abraham or Chawa would slip a few francs into my hand as I left them after Sabbath dinner each week, but they had very little to give and not enough to keep me from spending down the money I had saved. In the back of my mind I was still counting on Sam to somehow include me in one of his schemes, but more and more I realized that he was entirely taken over by his new life in Montparnasse and that this life, whatever it was, would have nothing in it for me. That is, except for the food he was now bringing to the room, which I took occasional small portions of when he was asleep in the morning or out at night— reversing our ritual from the month before, when it was me who had a bit of money and he had none.

I did not want to. But I had nothing else. No one else. I went to see Bernard.

I showed up without an appointment at the atelier above his Au Courant Dame boutique. Bernard had been considerably more agreeable to me the last time I had seen him, after I had become attached in his mind to the Lazare name, so I hoped for a decent reception this time as well. When I arrived, he was yelling at two people, workers of his I suppose but with coats and hats on, so I waited just inside the doorway until he had finished with them. Instead of joining the others at the machines and work tables, these two turned for the door, their heads down as they passed me out onto the stairs. They were both boys about my age.

Bernard was still angry when he motioned me into his bureau, but soon calmed himself and seemed almost pleased to see me. He asked how I was getting along. I said fine, and did not mention Montparnasse, then asked whether by any chance he had received a message for me from the Lazares. I sensed a ripple of interest from him when I said the name, but I did not really expect that there would be a letter from Genève—if there had been, I was sure that Bernard would have gotten word to me right away through Abraham and Chawa. Of course, there was always the chance that something had come through the post from her since I had last been at Maison Albert the previous Friday evening. But mostly I mentioned the Lazares simply to remind Bernard about their good opinion of me, or what Bernard thought was their opinion of me based on the tale I had told him that last time I had seen him. Because now I was about to do what he had made clear, over the past year and a half I had been in Paris, he did not want me to do. Ask him for work.

I tried to bring in the subject through a side door, saying that since my French was now improved and I was comfortable moving around Paris, I thought it was time to make myself useful to him, as I casually phrased it in my carefully prepared French. Abraham and Chawa had such a small operation—I said this almost with pity in my voice, flinching when I heard myself—that there was nothing for me to do for Maison Albert. But Bernard's businesses were so large and important,

I said, that I thought perhaps there might be something I could do for him. Bernard knew that I was asking for my own sake, not his, he was no fool, but neither did he mind the flattery. Especially the distinction I made between him and Abraham and Chawa. Distinctions, Maître.

"Well," Bernard said slowly, looking and thinking me over, "I could certainly use someone who can handle responsibility. For a change." His eyes flicked out toward the big workroom, and I realized that he meant the two boys he had just bellowed at in front of the other workers and had sent away. But Bernard then said that for a couple of weeks things would be slow at all his ateliers—it was Christmas in two days, then the French would celebrate New Year with their families, he told me, with factory orders very slow and many of his associates and biggest clients leaving Paris for their countryside homes, so during that time little business was done. Soon after, though, it would pick up again and I should come see him. In the new year, he said, perhaps things will be different.

6 November

Three years ago tomorrow, Maître. The shots. I have decided to begin fasting. And will continue three days until Sunday, the day of Kristallnacht. Also, as you know, I fast every Monday, my own personal day of atoning, which will make one day more.

Three years that I have been in jail. Yes, you have told me January, February or so for the trial, but with all due respect, Maître, "or so" offers me little confidence.

I do not know when I will again have the strength to write.

Yours sincerely,
H.

Maître,

Yes I agree, it is important that I return to my writing, the work I have committed to do. Committed to myself, I mean. Because that is how I think of it, Maître—not labor for the court, but work for myself. Another distinction I learned in Paris, labor and work. From Henri. All except the rich have to labor, he said, but real work—something that contributes, or interests—matters more. Of course for so many people, labor leaves no time or room for work. So, as Henri put it, work has become a luxury. Strange how it is only now, in the Reich's prisons, that I have found real work—my writing. I wonder what would Henri make of that.

Luxury—at the end of 1937 I thought that was the coal stove, big bed, bath and toilet in the Saint Lambert room. It was far more comfort than I had known anywhere else in Paris. Or at home in Hannover, for that matter. Comfort, except for the distance Sam had put between us. But even that did not concern me much. I felt sure it was only a matter of time. Which it turned out to be. New Year's Eve, to be exact.

It was clear of rain that holiday night but very cold. For the celebrations in Montparnasse, Sam put on his best new outfit under a new topcoat and slouch hat. He had mentioned that all the Montparnasse bars and cafés together would become one big carnival that night but he did not invite me to join him, so as he dressed to go out we said almost nothing to each other. I was curious about this carnival, though, and decided I would go look for myself. I also wanted to watch the fireworks over the Seine that would shoot off at midnight. So as soon as Sam was gone I put on layers of clothes—both my pairs of socks, both my undervests, my shirt with no collar under my collared one, my pullover vest on top of that—and finished off with the jacket from the suit Abraham had made me. I also decided to wear the shoes that had been made for me for Bernard's party—they were thin and already falling apart though I had hardly worn them, but they were shiny black and fancy and seemed right for New Year's Eve. As I headed out the door I grabbed one of Sam's scarves, his wooly one. He did not wear it any more, had replaced it with silk ones. I considered my tabby earmuffs, but they seemed too young, or maybe just too poor, for New Year's Eve in Montparnasse. I still had no hat.

It was almost 11 when I reached the center of Montparnasse. The crowds got thicker the nearer I got to the main crossroads along Boulevard du Montparnasse, with people dressed in all kinds of finery and fancy, from formal dress suits and gowns to guignol and clown costumes, and many of them wearing half-masks like bandits. They were drinking and singing and dancing, not only in the bars and cafés but also, despite the cold, in the streets where the music blaring out one door would meet and mangle with different music coming from the next. As I neared the most crowded part of the boulevard I realized that I did not know what I would do if I went inside one of these places, and also had no idea what it might cost. I also thought that I did not want to run into Sam—however unlikely that was among the thousands of people. So, I backed away and headed up some winding streets to the top of a small hill where it was high and dark enough that I could hope to see the midnight fireworks over the river.

I stopped at a spot where two narrow streets meet and the intersection widens slightly to form a tiny square. There was a small bar on the corner, full up and loud, with a few people also outside drinking and laughing. After a few minutes of leaning against a wall on the other side from the bar, trying to stay still and dark enough to avoid the celebrators until the fireworks began, a couple staggered over and tried to drag me into their party. I held back, so instead they pushed on me an open bottle of bubbly wine—champagne I suppose, or something like it. I do not know the difference. Not wanting to seem too difficult, I took a small drink then handed it back. They passed the bottle between them then gave it back to me and this time I took a bigger gulp. This pleased the woman of the couple so much that she put her arms around me and gave me a kiss. On the mouth. All kinds of things would happen to me that night, Maître, yet I remember that so clearly. Who knows how such things work?

It struck midnight and everyone broke out in cheers and song, the couple turned away from me to join the others, and the fireworks began over the Seine. I watched it with people who streamed out of the bar to fill the little square, taking another couple of drinks from different bottles that were offered to me.

By the time the sky show was over my hands and feet and ears were frozen and I was more than a little uncomfortable in both head and gut from the alcohol, which I was not used to, so I headed back to Saint Lambert. The room was very cold when I returned, so instead of undressing and getting into bed I stoked the stove and sat at the table, leaving on my suit jacket and pullover, while the fire slowly dulled the room's chill.

I broke off a crust of bread and cut some cheese to try to soak up the wine that was souring my stomach. The building was quiet, but then loud voices, singing and shouting, came from the court-yard. Rachel's room was at the back of the building, so I could not tell exactly what was going on, but the voices and clamoring got louder, climbing the stairs that led up to the room. Suddenly I picked out one gut-punching word from among all the rowdying—"Rachel!"—and then more clearly someone howling as he came closer, "Rachel, come dance with us," and other voices laughing, then "Let me in, Rachel!" and a bang on the door as if someone had thrown his whole body—or fallen—against it. The other voices laughed again, then a fist pounded on the door, "Rachel, this is me, your de Guise! Your one and only!" Which brought out still harder laughter from the others. Then the voice quieted and I heard him cursing, there was a fumbling in the lock, and the door burst open. Three men lurched in, each of the two in back carrying an open bottle of wine and cheering and the large one in front, wearing one of the bandit half-masks, raising his arms as if he had just crossed the finish line of a bicycle race.

I jumped to my feet, and just inside the door de Guise stopped at the sight of me as the other two spread out and filled the room with their drunken laughter.

"Who are you?" de Guise bellowed, facing me only two meters away and what seemed like a meter above me. He was broad as well as tall, with long wild flowing hair framing his half-masked face. I stood where I was, unable to move, staring at his horrid twisting mouth. "And what is this?" he roared, tearing off the mask and looking around the room—for signs of Rachel, I suppose, most of which by then had been removed to Belleville, her clothes, rouges, perfumes and such, her tchotchkes and her canvases, and replaced by my clothes and Sam's—and then "Where is she?" When I did not answer, he shook his head like a wet dog and shouted "No, forget her, she is a whore. But you, who are you?" and he lunged at me, knocking us both crashing on top of the table. The other two men laughed again as de Guise, alcohol stinking in my face, tried to regain his balance and at the same time hold onto me, jerking me upright.

In other times, Maître, I am certain I would have fought hard, delivered some blows, as I had to do often against the schoolboys my last two years in Hannover. But something made me hold back. I suppose because I knew he was right, that the room was his and that I was the intruder. Also, Maître, we were in Saint Lambert—not Paris east but Paris profond—and de Guise was French. So, instead of hitting I just pushed him off me. A mistake. Though in the end I cannot say whether it would have made a difference. He struck me a terrible blow with his elbow against my cheek, knocking me back down onto the table, struck me again in the face two or three more times, then grabbed me by the throat and began choking. I remember glimpsing the other two men behind him, now baring their teeth. De Guise was choking me harder, his weight too much to push off, and a terror seized me that I was going to die. I felt a knife under me on the table, got hold of it and managed to slash it down the side of de Guise's head, slicing into his ear and sending blood spurting over his neck, the table, me.

De Guise cried out and let go of me, staggering away. The other two also backed up as I waved the knife in front of them. I cannot tell you, Maître, whether I would have dared to use it again—I was stunned and terrified by the cutting of flesh and the sight and feel and smell, yes even smell, of the blood. For a moment the two men and I stood motionless as de Guise stumbled backwards holding his ear, blood pouring down his neck, and staring at me as if he could not believe I was real. I rushed for the open door. One of the men lunged at me, but after I made it to the stairs I heard nothing behind me except de Guise howling, then just the sound of my own pounding feet as I rushed through the courtyard and into the streets of what was by then New Year's Day, 1938.

16 November

I slept under a bridge. Well, not slept, but huddled there against the cold, holding my head full of pain and trying to keep my nose from starting again to bleed. I had run blindly for several blocks and when finally I was sure no one was chasing me I had begun walking toward Faubourg Saint Denis, to Abraham and Chawa's. But soon I got lost in the dark unfamiliar streets and when finally I came out onto the river, I could not get my bearings. I was too tired and hurting to go further, and each time I made a hard step the blood from my nose would begin again, so I fumbled my way down some damp stairs to the river and found myself a place out of the wind.

When it was light, I saw that I had already made a good part of the way back toward Faubourg Saint Denis, and started walking that direction. I knew my face must look a mess, not just by the pain and huge swelling I could feel but also by the stares I got from people along the way. The blood had stopped flowing from my nose but I could see a lot of it dried on my jacket and pullover and shirt—I wondered how much of it was mine, how much de Guise's. I realized that I would frighten Uncle Abraham and Tante Chawa if I showed up this way, but I had nowhere else to go. I certainly could not go back to the Saint Lambert room. How badly had I injured de Guise? The police most likely would have been called, and might be there still. Which made me think about how I could warn Sam. But I had no way to find him unless I walked all the way back there and waited in the street nearby, hoping to catch him on his way to the room, without being spotted by the police or de Guise and his friends, or that awful concierge. But I could barely walk for the pain in my head, it was already well into the morning and Sam probably already had made his way back there, so I carried on dragging myself toward Maison Albert. As for Sam, I could only hope.

When I neared Rue Martel I began to think about what to tell Abraham and Chawa. I certainly did not want to explain about Rachel and de Guise, so I decided just to say that an old boyfriend of Rachel's had come to the room and mistaken me for a rival. When I finally dragged myself up to Maison Albert, though, and Abraham and Chawa had recovered from the initial shock of seeing me—I looked in a mirror there and did not recognize myself, my face was so swollen and misshapen—and they asked what had happened, I found that forming words was difficult with a battered cheek and jaw. "Frenchman," was all I managed. They had lived in Paris for many years, Abraham and Chawa. As foreigners. Of a certain kind. They asked nothing more.

It was a holiday, New Year's Day, and while that did not stop Abraham and Chawa from working, they had given the day off to Sidney and Berenice their machiniste and finisher, and anyway Maison Albert had little work, so Abraham and Chawa put me in their bed and spent the day tending to me, and the next day, a Sunday, as well.

In the time between sipping soup and sleeping, I began to think about all that had now been lost. Not only the room itself—which Sam and I always knew would only last so long—but also the rest of my clothes and my one decent pair of shoes left behind there, plus the blood-ruined suit jacket, sweater vest, and shirt that I had been wearing. Most important, I had now lost all the money I had remaining from my work that summer at the Foire, from my German sessions with Genève, and from what my parents had sent me. You see, because of the possibility always of trouble when I was out on the street, not to mention pickpockets, I left my savings stashed in the room, taking with me when I went out only what I allowed myself to spend that day. Now it was all gone. At least I had my papers—my passport and expired visa and the receipt from the Paris police for my refugee application—which I always carried with me.

Thinking of my papers made me worry about whether there was anything in the room that had my name on it, something the police, or de Guise, could follow up. I went over it in my mind but did not remember anything, and for a few moments was relieved, until I switched my worry to whether there was something there to identify Sam. Had he been carrying all his papers also? Or had he left something in the room they could use to find him? And what of the new clothes he had been buying, and the medicines to treat his scabies that he kept under the water closet sink and now could not go back for? Then there was his money, all the money he seemed to be making over the past weeks. Had he left it somewhere in the room, as I had? But most of all I worried about Sam himself. Had the police taken him when he returned to the room? Or had de Guise and his friends beaten him because of what I had done? Had they hurt him badly? Even worse than me?

I did not have long to find out. Sunday evening, the end of my second day recovering at Maison Albert, Sam came calling. I put it that way because he was so calm and casual when Chawa opened the door to him, looking and sounding like he was paying a holiday social call—nice suit and necktie, silk scarf, topcoat, and stylish slouch hat. Of course, what I knew but Abraham and Chawa did not was that these were the same clothes he had gone out in two nights before, and were probably now the only things he had.

I heard Sam tell Chawa that he had come because he was worried about me, since he had not found me in our room after New Year's Eve. She brought him in to where I was lying on their bed. When he saw the condition of my face, his own face turned dark and angry, the fiery Sam I knew so well, but he quickly recovered a calmer appearance and said simply, "Oh, my goodness." Abraham told him in a severe almost accusing voice that I had been beaten by a Frenchman "over there." Sam replied right away that yes, he and I had realized for a while that it was not for us over there, that he had decided we should come back east, and already he had found a new room, nearby in fact, in the 2nd arrondissement, and I was welcome to share it with him as before, we were so close, we helped each other out, I was in trouble and here he was, and now we would be back on home ground, back and safe. Abraham and Chawa had hated the idea of me over near Montparnasse and their fear for me was now even greater, so I nodded my head at everything Sam was saying. And however little truth there might be in it, after the great distance that had come between Sam and me over the past two months I was thrilled to have him back at my side, saying anything at all.

Sam's little speech had been brilliant. Abraham and Chawa were impressed by this well dressed version of what they had known before only as a scruffy Belleville street boy and they were calmed by his declaring that we were through with Montparnasse and that he had found a nearby room for us. Sam stayed for a while and happily took a bowl of soup but he and I had no chance to speak privately about what had happened to each of us. When Sam got up to leave, he announced that he would be back to fetch me in the morning, to bring me over to our new room. I right away said I would be ready.

18 November

Sam had barely escaped. He had returned to Saint Lambert just after dawn and saw as he approached the building that something was going on—the courtyard's street door was already open, and two men were talking just outside it. As Sam neared, one of the men left, the other went back into the courtyard. The man who left was carrying a small black valise, what Sam thought was a doctor's bag. He had not immediately connected this to me or to Rachel's room, though, since there were many rooms in the building, so he had carried on into the courtyard. A few steps in he stopped short at the sight of a policeman and the concierge, talking at the doorway to the stairs that led up to Rachel's room. The concierge turned, recognized Sam, and screeched "There is one of them!"

Sam knew from long experience in Paris that anything having to do with the police was likely to be big trouble for an allogène like him, never mind his proper residence papers and perfect Paris talk. And the tone of the concierge's cry was more than enough to let the instincts from that experience take over. He ran. He heard the police whistle behind him, but with a bit of a head start and his athlete's legs and backstreet knowhow he was soon able to distance himself from the flic, the cop. When finally he stopped to rest and think over what he had seen, he began to worry that the police and doctor might have been for me. But with the concierge's reaction he knew he could not risk going back, and instead came east, to familiar ground.

I told Sam what had happened with me and de Guise. He listened carefully without speaking, and when I had finished he said quietly "Your face, I am sorry. It should have been me." Then he raised his head and with worry in his eyes he asked "Do you think you killed him?" For a moment I was also frightened, but when I thought back on the moment, on the feel and sound of things, I knew that the knife had not gone deep, and that de Guise had howled with plenty of energy as I ran down the stairs and away. Sam was relieved and said yes, he supposed that if de Guise had died there would have been more police there than just the one flic. But then he frowned again and said, of course there might have been more police or medical people upstairs in the room.

"Listen," I said, "it was only that stupid little French cheese knife." Then I gasped in pretend horror, "Oh, no! De Guise is fleishedik"—made of flesh, Maître, but had I cut him with a knife for cheese. The ancient food rules, you see, not mixing milk utensils and meat. For the first time in a long while we both smiled.

Now Sam spoke of other worries. It was likely a police matter. And even if de Guise was not hurt badly enough for the police to follow it up with much energy, de Guise himself might try to track me down, and Sam as well. So, Sam and I puzzled together about whether there was anything in the room with my name on it or his. I told Sam that I was certain I had not left anything of mine behind. Except my clothes. And my savings. Sam lowered his head and again told me that he was sorry, as if he was somehow to blame. "It should have been me," he said again.

I asked about him, his papers. He said he had them with him, and did not believe there was anything in the room with his name or

306

Belleville address on it. After a moment of shared relief, I asked what he had left behind at the room, what he had now lost.

He waved off the question, "Nothing important, nothing, nothing."

"But your medicines," I reminded him, "for the little bastards"—the scabies. "And what about your money?"

"Hah. I spend everything as soon as I get it," he said almost proudly.

"Yes, so it seemed. But all those nice clothes, gone." I shook my head.

"Not all of them," he smiled and sat up straight—he was still wearing the same stylish suit and shirt he had gone out in New Year's Eve. It was now three days later. "Anyway, what do I need them for around here?" he said, "I have given up all that."

I never knew, Maître—at least not exactly—what the "all that" was that Sam said he had given up. But I certainly knew what he meant by "around here," our new surroundings. The room Sam had found, where we were then sitting, was in a very old and mostly run-down district around the Rue Saint Denis, straddling the 2nd and 3rd arrondissements, a bit closer to the center of the city than Abraham and Chawa's place. The district was known as the chapelet de chair—the rosary of flesh—because its streets and alleys were strung with beads of pleasure for sale. Bordels of all types and costs, Maître, from high-class maisons closes, with fantasy rooms and costume shows they called "living paintings," all the way down to the maisons d'abattage—the slaughterhouses—where men stood in a queue with a five-franc ticket waiting to have 10 minutes with a woman who worked a 12-hour day. There were also the hotels de passe, with officially registered rooms that licensed horizontales, as the women were called, could rent by the hour. And there were clandestins, the small unlicensed bordels that operated behind a local business—a laundry, a shop, a hairdresser—to avoid taxes, and the permits and inspections of the Police de Moeurs—the Morals Police.

Many of these bordels had customers who looked only for one very special kind of pleasure, or for someone who fit a particular description. And that is where Sam and I wound up. Our room was on the floor above and behind a clandestin that itself hid behind a secondhand clothes shop. From some of his gambits Sam knew the man who ran the clothes shop, and when Sam went around to his contacts looking for a place to stay, this man told him that a room upstairs might be available. The clandestin itself was called Miriam's, a very specialized bordel where israélite businessmen—and others who had the same taste—were offered girls who shared their people's bloodlines. Which reminds me, Maître, you are always asking what groups helped me out when I was in Paris. Well, how about Miriam's? I suppose you could call them a group.

I hope it does not offend that I describe such things, Maître, but they are truths of my time in Paris. Anyway, they may not be such a shock to you because I heard while I was staying in the room above Miriam's that Berlin is also known for such specialized places—of course not to suggest, Maître, that you would have personal knowledge.

The room itself barely deserved the name. It was even smaller than the chambres de bonne at Rue Martel, every centimeter taken up by a small cot, a wobbly wooden chair, a low stool that served as a table, and a wardrobe with three legs and no door. There was a sink, but no water from it. And no heat. When Sam and I were both there together, only one of us at a time could stand and move, and to sleep we shared the cot. It took us a while to learn how not to move and jostle each other in the night, and to block out the customers' sounds that came through the floorboards from the factory floor, as the women called it, immediately below us.

To get to this room we had to pass through a corner of Miriam's. On the street next to the secondhand shop was a separate unnumbered doorway. Behind it a narrow staircase led up to a landing with a bright light over a metal door. Clients for Miriam's were previewed first out a window over the street, then again through a slit in the metal door. Once allowed in, the customer was taken either into a little parlor where tea and alcohol could be bought and several women on duty would visit with them for a while or, if the customer preferred, immediately to a private booth behind a curtain, where he could watch a parade of the women, make his choice, and enter one of the chambers all without being seen by other customers. Sam and I also had to pass through the metal door, but we then turned off to another set of stairs to the next floor at the rear of the building. Up there was a narrow corridor with a row of tiny rooms where some of the women—and in honesty I should also say girls, Maître, for some of them were younger than me—rested and chatted with each other when they did not have a customer. None of the women actually lived there, though some would spend days at a time there rather than travel back and forth to some outer shacktown where some of them lived. Even those who lived closer by would stay at Miriam's for a while from time to time when there was trouble at home, or simply too many people in the tiny places they shared with their family. One room at Miriam's the women did not use at all—the smallest and rattiest, at the end of the corridor, with damp stained walls and no window to open to clear out lamp fumes and the smells of the toilet it sat next to. The room where Sam and I landed.

20 November

Rachel wanted to hear from me directly what had happened with de Guise on New Year's Eve, and Sam and I both wanted to talk to her about whether de Guise might know how to find her, and then from her to us. So, a couple of days after I moved in at Miriam's, Sam and I met Rachel at a café near the Bastille market.

I described for her everything that happened with de Guise and his two companions but skipped the details of what he had called her, just mentioning that he had wanted her to join him and his friends that night. Rachel interrupted—"Or, he wanted them all to join me." She was quiet for a moment, then looked at Sam and said in a hard, even voice, "A mensh tracht und Gott lacht"—"A person plans and God laughs." They stared at each other, then she added softly, "No one was tricking me, Sam. I knew what they thought of me. But I did not care. And they had no idea what I thought of them." The words seem to break the spell that had held the two of them apart. Sam hugged her. It was the first time I had seen the two of them touch.

We talked for a while longer about whether there was anything in the Saint Lambert room, or that Rachel had ever told anyone in Montparnasse, that could track her back to Belleville. She said no, that from her first day there two years before she had always been careful to use only the name Rachel Polonskaya, trying not only to create an exotic identity for herself but also to make certain that news of her new life never got back to her mother. The only person who crossed both her worlds—Belleville and Montparnasse—was the "finder" woman who had originally introduced her to the first Montparnasse painter. But Rachel had never seen her again, the woman had not known Rina or the family name, and it had been so long ago now that Rachel was certain the woman would not remember her.

With that we all relaxed a bit, Rachel even gently teasing Sam about his dandy clothes and calling me Cyrano the swordsman. Then she ordered cheap brandies to celebrate our release, the three of us, from Montparnasse. And to toast the New Year. "Things can only get better," she said. It was January 1938.

Yours,
Herschel

Maître,

So, once again I was spending each day just trying to find a way to feed myself and to pay for the room, though Miriam did not ask much for it—and before I got there Sam had arranged with her to clean up and do small jobs around the place as part payment. For food we returned to the Bastille market on Wednesday afternoons, and I also went with Sam to two other street markets. Sam knew these places well, but the pickings in midwinter were small, and the number of other people looking for throwaway food—also at bakery and restaurant back doors—had grown over the past few months. So had the queues for a midday bowl of soup, which itself had become thinner, at the Sportclub Aurore. I could count on Friday night supper at Abraham and Chawa's, and Sam sometimes came along to get himself a rare hot meal—Abraham and Chawa would always gladly stretch the food to include him, may they live to be 100. I also went there sometimes for a midday meal on Sunday when the seamstress and machiniste Berenice and Sydney had the day off, but I did not feel right about stopping in there too often in the evenings just to eat—they had already done so much for me—and who even knew what time they would finally stop working, Abraham and Chawa, to sit for a small bite before dropping exhausted into their bed. So, I needed cash for food as well as for Miriam's room and whatever else I might spend a few sous on now and again—a coffee that would allow me to stay for a while in a café out of the cold, a cheap matinee ticket for a cinema where I could pass afternoon hours and even steal back some of the sleep I usually failed to get at night while lying stretched out stiff and still next to Sam on the single cot. Sam also had to come up with more money now, to help pay for Rina's room and for medicine against the consumption that was eating her away. Rachel was bringing in very little, standing in for Rina with the colporteuse cart, so Sam began once again working his contacts to come up with more goods she could sell. This involved full-on Sam le Gamb trickstery that he did not invite me to join and I did not ask about.

I never told Abraham and Chawa the true story of the Saint Lambert room, either how Rachel came to have it or how de Guise took it back, so they did not know that my clothes and all my money were gone. In fact, I never mentioned money—I knew how little my aunt and uncle had, and the subject had become even more difficult since I had given Abraham such aggravation in the autumn about him not trying to return the funds my parents had sent me, and me then insisting, so angry, that I could well take care of myself. Still, Abraham and Chawa sensed that I was in a bad way, not least because whenever I saw them I was always wearing the same shirt, trousers, and bloodstained jacket. A few clothes, at least, Maison Albert could manage for me without much cost, so over the next weeks Abraham and Chawa made me two shirts, a pair of trousers, and a jacket. That allowed me to wash my other clothes in the sink at the end of the hall at Miriam's, and to let them dry for the many days it took in the winter cold, hanging on nails on a wall of our room.

Abraham and Chawa pressed a few francs in my hand whenever I saw them, but it did not go very far. I had already lost weight over the autumn and early winter in Saint Lambert, and after a few more weeks I must have been nearing down to 40 kilos. I had to do something. Which, I decided, meant Bernard. He had said that after the New Year he might have some kind of work for me, so when my face had finally healed after several weeks—I did not want to show up to Bernard with ugly bruises that I would have to explain—I put on my new set of clothes and went to see him. This time I telephoned in advance from a café, trying to make my visit as welcome as possible. On the telephone Bernard was his usual gruff self but agreed an appointment.

When I showed up at the atelier, Bernard was so pleasant to me that I barely recognized him. He asked how my new year was and how I was keeping myself—"You look a little thin," he said when I took off my jacket and mittens, "but it becomes you." I gave him some pit-pat of an answer, which he paid no attention to anyway, and then I got to the point, reminding him that he said he might have work for me when business picked up in the new year. "Yes, of course," he said, much to my amazement. "Oh, by the way," he added, trying not very successfully to make his expression Oh-by-the-way-ish, "this arrived at the house for you yesterday," and handed me an envelope. The stamp and postmark was Switzerland. The name on the back of the envelope, pre-printed in that fancy way that bumps up from the paper, was G.S. Lazare. It took me a moment to connect the name—Genève.

I was startled, but managed to thank Bernard and put the envelope in my jacket pocket. Bernard said, "No, no, my boy, go ahead, you must be wondering what it is." Meaning, by the way he leaned forward, that he was wondering. So I opened it and found a short note from Genève wishing me a happy new year and saying that she was sorry she would not be able to continue our lessons during her school's winter holiday because instead of her coming home to Paris her parents had gone there to meet her in Switzerland where they were all doing skiing together. She would be in Paris in the spring, she wrote, but she could not be certain that she would have any time for lessons. Still, she hoped to see me again sometime in the coming year. If I was still in Paris.

I was so amazed that she had bothered to write to me, and said she hoped to see me, that it overbalanced the news that it might not be until, well, who knew? I read the note twice before I looked up to find Bernard staring at it. "From the Lazare daughter," I said. "We are friends. Of a sort. I teach her German."

"Yes, good," Bernard replied, though instead of the hungry curiosity he had showed just a few moments before, his face was now disturbed. "But that," he said, pointing to the note, "do you know what that is?"

I repeated that it was not from Monsieur Lazare but only from his daughter, about when we might continue her German lessons.

"No, no. I mean that." I realized he was pointing not at the note but at my hands, one of which was hard at work scratching the other.

"Oh, the rash. I seem to be allergic to my mittens." Sam had brought me a new pair of fur-lined mittens a few days before. You can imagine what kind of fur.

Bernard frowned. "And up your arm?"

I looked at my wrists, which were also now covered with the rash, and then up my sleeves where I found it also on the inside of both my elbows.

"I will tell you what it is," Bernard went on. "The scabies. I know it well because it is a problem for my ateliers. The workers, you see, they bring it in. And the fabric, the clothes we make, no one seems to know how much it travels in clothing, the scabies, but just one case turning up from my workshops could be a ruination. So we check. And sometimes we need to send a worker away. So, get rid of it, boy. All of it. Then come back and perhaps we can try again."

I understood that the discussion of work was now over before it had begun. I put on my jacket and slipped Genève's note into my pocket, during which time Bernard remained silent, his face tight. I started to leave his bureau, to pass through the atelier to the stairs. As I opened his door, Bernard said, "I would appreciate it if you put those on now." He indicated the mittens I was holding in one hand. "They"—he nodded toward the workers—"know we are related."

When I got back to the room at Miriam's, Sam asked how things had gone. I told him that Bernard had nothing for me, though I did not tell him why. A bit later, though, I showed him the rash and asked what he thought it was. "The little bastards," he said, agreeing with Bernard's diagnosis. Sam had seemed to get the scabies under control in Saint Lambert, with the medicines he had spent such money on there, but we both knew without saying that I most likely had picked them up from him, either there or in the little cot we now shared. He lowered his head. "I am sorry," he said softly.

That was the second time within just a few weeks—the first had been about the beating from de Guise and losing my money—that Sam apologized to me for something that was not his fault. Now I felt bad also. Which made things worse. Not because of the feelings themselves, Maître, but because feeling bad gets in the way of whatever has to be done. The same as hope.

Sam showed me how to use sulfur and oil to fight the scabies, since we could not afford the medicines he had bought when for a short time he had money in Saint Lambert. I say "we" because, no surprise, Sam discovered that his own scabies had never altogether left him. We also had the problem of finding a place to give ourselves the sulfur treatment. We could not do it in the room at Miriam's because, like at Bernard's ateliers, the scabies was like the Black Death there—if it was noticed on any of the women, it would scare away customers. The sulfur smell would be a giveaway that we were hosting the little bastards and even if Miriam herself did not discover us, the women upstairs might. They liked us, the girls and women there, liked having us around, but still any one of them might report it to Miriam out of self-protection. And we just could not risk losing our room, the only solid thing we had.

At first we took the sulfur and oil to Rina's and Rachel's room in Belleville, where Rina would get out of her sick bed to help us with the messy treatment. Rina liked being motherly to Sam, which for years she had hardly ever had the chance to do, and was so kind to me as well, but I could see that it was a strain for her and to tell the truth, Maître, when she started her painful coughing I really did not like being there.

After three uncomfortable sulfur sessions at Rina's, I remembered the baths and suggested it to Sam. At first he thought I meant the large baths in Belleville, which he knew well. You see, in different parts of the city, Maître, public baths were the only way for most poor people ever to get properly clean—for those who felt it was worth bothering. So, these baths were heavily used, particularly in the poorest districts, even though any one person might not visit them very often. But that was also the problem with them, at least for what we needed—the cheap public baths in Belleville and la Villette, the ones Sam knew, were so crowded that you only got a minute under the water, and though many of the customers had scabies to deal with, there was no time or space to give yourself a treatment there.

No, the baths I meant was the place I had gone a few times before, when I was staying at Rue Martel. It was west across the canal from Belleville, in the 10th arrondissement, and Sam had never been there— not just because of where it was, Maître, but because it cost twice as much as the baths in Belleville. And that, I explained to Sam, was why it would work for us. Since it was so much more expensive, it was far less crowded than the baths he knew, and they did not push you out after only a few minutes. Also, there were little changing cubicles that were nearly private, so if we kept an eye out for each other, I thought we could wash, treat ourselves with the sulfur and oil, wait there while the sulfur did its work, then have another wash to get rid of the messy, smelly stuff before we returned to the room at Miriam's. Sam immediately said he liked the plan, without giving me his usual grief about something that was not his own idea. Which pleased me more than anything else I could remember—not only was I leading him to something helpful for both of us but for the first time ever he admitted that I knew something about Paris that he did not.

24 November

My baths plan worked. Sam and I went twice a week. But as Sam reminded me, getting rid of the little bastards was a long process. Which meant that, although Sam was managing to come up with a regular supply of the sulfur, paying for the baths was draining our very low funds. Sam was working for Miriam, cleaning up at the bordel, and also had some of his gambits going again, but I was bringing in nothing. Also, I was getting still thinner, the jacket that Abraham and Chawa had just made for me already hanging loose. And my tricky stomach was again a mess, thanks to long stretches of nothing but bread ends and dried-up bits of cheese, and leeks and onions leftover from the street markets, which we boiled in the room on a little spirit stove we borrowed from two women who were our corridor neighbors. I do not know how to explain this—because I do not want to give a false impression, there was never any danger of actual starving—but there was something maddening about always being hungry. I mean that exactly, Maître, mad-making, a constant edge of raging. Even more so, I think, in a city where, in some places at least, the food itself seems more important than eating it.

It was during my next Friday night visit to Maison Albert that I

316

had an idea. When Mirari had left Paris that past summer—Do you remember I told you about her, Maître, the Basque woman with her children, in the chambre de bonne next to the one where I stayed for a while, at Rue Martel? Anyway, when Mirari disappeared she left behind two piles of thick leather sheets, for cutting soles for shoes— her work while she was in Paris. She also left behind a large curved outline knife, a smaller finishing knife, and a sharpening stone. Back then, soon after Mirari left, I had gone down to see Madame Corbin, the concierge, to ask her if there was a place to store the leather, in case Mirari returned for it. I did not really believe she would be back, but immediately dumping it, or giving it to Sam to sell, seemed too cold, too final, as if it would wipe away the fact that Mirari and the children had ever been there. Madame Corbin had first looked at me as if I was cracked in the head, but something in what I said, or the way I said it, seemed to make an impression because after a moment's considering she told me that there was a small storage closet next to the steps down to a cellar off the rear courtyard, and I could put it there. Water got in there, she warned, so I would need to put some bricks or stones under it, and maybe a cover, and there was no lock on the door so who knew how long it would stay, but if I wanted to, there it was. She did not say whether she thought this was a good deed even though mostly hopeless, or entirely a stupidness. As so often with Madame Corbin, she did not feel any need to give me an opinion. Just a helping hand, if she could.

So, I had stored the leather in this cellar, and the knives and sharpening stone at Maison Albert, and soon had forgotten them. But now half a year later as I entered the courtyard heading for Abraham and Chawa's, my eye caught the door to the cellar and I wondered whether the leather was still there. It was, damp around the edges but mostly fine, and it occurred to me that I might salvage it and do some cutting work myself. A few times I had helped Mirari make the soles, so I knew the basics. It was not complicated work, Maître, just slow and hard and dangerous to the hands.

When Sam came back to the room at Miriam's late that night, I told him my idea and asked whether he knew someone who might buy soles from me. He had no direct connections to the shoe leather game but, no surprise, he knew people who did. One of them was a boy I had seen around the Aurore, so it was not too difficult to find him, and from him directions to an atelier that might be willing to use an extra "carver." This atelier was in la Villette, over by the slaughterhouses, a massive place with dozens of workers and clanging machines turning out piles and piles of shoes and boots. The patron there was not interested in me—the boy at the Aurore had warned me that they had endless people without work papers who wanted a chance to do home carving—until I told him that not only did I already know how to carve but that I had my own tools and a supply of good leather. This convinced him to let me try—using my leather, and without any promises—and he gave me a couple of their patterns to follow.

I picked up the carving tools and two sheets of the leather from Rue Martel and carried them over to the room at Miriam's. I began work that afternoon and was very careful to carve and trim the sample pieces exactly, though if you take enough time that is not so difficult. The matter was not whether I could do it but whether I could do it fast enough, without shredding my hands, to make the labor worth the pitiful piecework pay.

Yours sincerely,
Herschel

27 November 1941
Moabit prison, Berlin

Herr Rosenhaus,

I must say that I do not understand your question. Did de Guise's attack on me add to my anger at France? De Guise is not France, Maître, he is French. And why do you even write "anger at France"? It is not something I myself have said. What would it mean anyway? Or matter? Except that, yes, I have heard from you more than once that the France government will send people to speak at my trial. But about what? De Guise and me and anger and France and Germany? And war? All together? When next I see you, Maître, perhaps you can help me make sense of this.

So, the rest of that winter, '37 into '38. What can I tell you? I spent most of my days bundled up as best I could in the room above Miriam's, cutting leather soles while Sam slept in the cot for a few hours in the afternoon, so dead asleep that even the sounds of my sharpening stone and the women around us chattering in their rooms and in the corridor and using the water closet right next to where Sam's head lay on the cot did not stir him because he was again out all night most nights, now working as a server at a nearby fancy bordel called Aux Belles Minettes—The Cute Pussycats—making money to buy medicine for his mother, which is where he spent his mornings, at Rina's in Belleville while Rachel was out working the colporteuse cart, because Rina was so ill and weak now that they did not want to leave her alone for too long. So we each had the cot to ourselves for a few hours, me at night wearing all three of my shirts and piling my other clothes, and Sam's as well, on top of my legs and feet to try to keep off the cold that was so bad in the top-floor room because they had specially isolated the floor below to hold in the heat for them—and also the sounds of Miriam's customers—which meant little of the warmth rose through up to us. Some days that winter even in the daytime I could barely grip the carving knives my hands so cold with cloth gloves clipped off at the fingertips and the cuts to my hands I did not always realize were bad until the blood soaked through the gloves or ran onto the leather and the cuts would not heal because the scabies still had my hands, and my feet and arms, and we did not have enough money now to go to the baths more than once in a fortnight, even though Sam was making much more but it all went for Rina's medicine, and the sulfur and oil that I rubbed in against the scabies would reopen the cuts so they took so long to heal and I always managed to give myself new ones.

The pay I got for the soles was barely more than the cost of the next batch of leather, though at least from the shoe atelier I got a proper pair for myself to replace the thin fancy ones from Bernard's dinner that were the only shoes I had after Saint Lambert and were falling apart so badly in the icy wet streets that I discovered my toes had chilblains on top of the scabies, it was so painful to walk, do you know what it is, Maître, chilblains? Sam had to tell me—he knew from his own feet two winters before. Some afternoons Sam would come out with me to the street markets but usually he was sleeping so I would go on my own and I was never as good at it as Sam. So it was either food or sleep for Sam, or food or leather for me, and for quite a few weeks neither of us had been to the soup queue at the Sportclub Aurore because that was at midday and took too much time away from sleep or work to walk from Saint Denis to the Pletzl and back. Sometimes Sam would stop in Belleville on the way back from Rina's, a landsmanshaft there was giving him sulfur for the scabies and they also gave him a cup of soup sometimes or at least a glass of tea with sugar, he was so often hungry. We both were. We were always cold.

Landsmanshaft—another group for your list, I suppose. Not Sam's, Maître, but a different one that I went to. Landsmanshaften, I do not know exactly how to explain them. They are associations, of a sort, little societies, each one connected to a hometown in the East. They are not anything official with the France government but they are allowed to operate—quietly, without politics or asking anything from the French—helping people mostly from Poland and Russia and Lithuania who are doing poorly in Paris, and also keeping them connected to haimishe things—home things, the way things were done back home. The people who came there, the landsmanshaft put them together with others from the hometown who might help each other in Paris, maybe someone had a little work to give or a place to get medicine or see a doctor, or advice about permits and papers and such, or to help families make arrangements for a marriage, things like that. The landsmanshaften from the bigger places, like Warsaw or Vilna, not only knew about work but even had money they could loan. Also, Maître, and curious to me, every one of these groups offered gravesites, where you could be buried next to your own kind instead of in a Paris paupers cemetery. It seemed such a luxury thing to worry on in those days, but I was 16, what did I know?

I had heard mention of these landsmanshaften, Maître, but I had never given any thought to them for myself—no one had ever mentioned one for Hannover, or for anyplace in Germany, I do not think there were any, only for places further east. But after Sam started going to the landsmanshaft of his small Litvak home region, we talked about whether there might also be one to help me somehow. My parents had come to the Reich from Radomsk—yes, as you know—which was in Russia at the time but then became Poland, which was how all of us in our family came to have Poland passports. I think I told you that as well. Anyway, Poland or Russia is not important, about Radomsk, I mean. Except that later of course it was, with the Poles passing their laws to shut us out—the beginning of the end.

I had never been to Radomsk. But still I thought finding their landsmanshaft was worth a try. The way things were for me, almost anything seemed worth a try. Sam did not know where the Radomsk landsmanshaft was or even if there was one but he said that someone at the Aurore Sportclub was bound to know, so one evening I went over there and sure enough quickly learned the address.

It turned out the Radomsk landsmanshaft was just around the corner from the Aurore club, so I decided to go to there around midday, which would mean that on the same walk from Miriam's I could stop at the Aurore and get a bowl of their soup. I had not been there at lunchtime for several months, so I was surprised by the long queue

I found trailing out the door and along the frozen pavement—plenty of young people had come for the daily soup the year before, when I was going there often, but nothing like that many. So I decided to skip the Aurore—going without food for long stretches was now normal for me—and continued on to the Radomsk place. When I got to the address, though, I found not a bureau but a triperie, a kosher triperie—a shop that sells innards, Maître, animal inside parts, for cooking. I could not locate another building entrance, so I went into the shop and asked if I was in the right place. The butcher said fourth floor and tilted his head toward the rear of the shop. I made my way behind the counter and across the bloody sawdust toward a staircase in a dark corner.

On the fourth landing there was a single door with a small hand-written card which I could barely see in the dim light. Eventually I made out three different letterings, Polish, Russian, and Yiddish, which said—I could read most of the Yiddish—Radomsk Associations of something-or-other, Paris Branch. Despite the triperie downstairs, the dark landing, the peeling paint, and a sickly smell leaking out from under the door, the title impressed me. I knocked.

After a moment a cracked voice spoke in Yiddish and though I could not quite make out the words it seemed like an invitation so I opened the door. The stench stopped me on the spot. The room was tiny and very dark, with a single small window high up that showed only a meter of grey light before another wall appeared. When they saw I was a stranger, the two old men—one tall but stooped and round shouldered, the other no bigger than me—rose together from their low wooden chairs where they were tending a pot balanced on a tiny spirit stove sitting on the floor. I could make out faintly the smell of cabbage, but it was likely something from the shop downstairs that ruled the pot and the entire room and that within moments had turned my stomach. The tall man, with sunken cheeks and eyes and a thin, wrinkled neck, was wearing an old-world heavy black suit at least two sizes too broad for him. The small man had on a shabby dressing gown over several layers of shirts, plus a hat—a shapeless greasy old felt thing—pulled all the way down over his ears. He pulled the hat up slightly when I entered, several stiff gray hairs popping out straight from his temples. They bowed slightly and greeted me.

I apologized for disturbing their meal but they both replied—stepping on each other's words while darting frowns at each other, which was how they carried on most of the conversation—that it was no bother, that I was welcome, and that the meal was not quite ready. I remember wondering whether cooking it more would make the smell better or worse.

They asked how they could help me, calling me "Monsieur" even though we were speaking Yiddish and despite the great difference in our ages. I said that my family was from Radomsk. Ah, come and sit, they said, but we all three realized at the same time that there was no other place except the small cot, so the little man moved over there and offered me his chair. Then I told them that actually it was my parents who were from Radomsk, not me. Strangely, this seemed to confirm something for them, and they said yes, yes, we see.

"You have come to the right place. That is one of the things we can do, sending money."

I was confused. But while explaining that my parents were in Hannover, not Radomsk, it occurred to me that my new French-style suit—the one Abraham had made for me when I returned from Saint Lambert—led them to think of me as French. Not true French, of course, but French compared to them. And so they assumed I was coming to them for help sending money safely to my family in Poland. Once I had finished explaining to them that my parents lived in Germany, had moved from Radomsk many years before, and that I also was from Hannover, I could see it was their turn not to understand, and for a few moments none of us said anything.

The tall man finally spoke, but now with caution in his voice. "So then, what is it we can do for you, Monsieur?" At this point I was almost embarrassed to say—it was obvious they were so deeply poor themselves—but I told them I needed work, adding quietly that I did not have a permit.

The two old men glanced at each other, then the tall one went back to stirring the pot. The little man cleared his throat, then explained, almost apologizing, that there were certain things they could do for people but getting work in Paris was not one of them. Once upon a time, yes, but now, in these days, they were sorry, they had nothing.

At the word "nothing," the little man stopped speaking. I looked around the room. A single cot for the two of them, the small spirit stove, one pot, four plates, four cups, some undergarments hanging on hooks, two pairs of shoes against the wall—I noticed that although they were both fully dressed, they each wore an old pair of carpet slippers. How often, I wondered, did they leave this room?

The one thing they did have was books. Shelves of them. The men saw me glance at them and both at once said brightly, yes, be our guest, take a look, borrow whatever you like. I certainly had not come for reading material, but to make things easier for all of us I got up to see what there was. It was so dark that I had to go close to see the titles—Russian, Polish, Yiddish, even some in French. But no German. I pulled down one of the French books, just to be polite, and returned to my chair. Good, good, the little one said, and the tall one announced that the food was ready and would I do them the kindness—me do them the kindness, Maître—of sharing it with them. The little one slid off the bed and brought over three bowls and handed them to the tall one who began dishing up the foul smelling stuff. The little one then reached into a burlap sack under the sink, pulled out three whole raw onions, and handed one each to me and the tall man. I knew that turning down their offer of a meal—I lied that I had just eaten at the Aurore and also that I must now begin a long walk to an appointment on the far side of Belleville—would be a disappointment to them, not to mention a puzzlement in those days of great hunger for almost everyone they saw, but I simply could not face whatever it was they had boiled up in that pot. The two old men looked at each other and shrugged, and the tall one poured back my bowlful. When I finished making apologies for not joining them, the little man nodded, then took a large bite out of the onion, as if it was an apple, followed by his first mouthful of the food from the pot.

"Please," the tall one said, "keep it." I looked down at the onion in my hand, thanked them and slipped it into my pocket with a rush of warmth toward these two old men. I thanked them also for their time, wished them a good meal and afternoon, and got up to leave. "And a young man like yourself," the tall one added, "come see us if you are looking to marry." I nodded another thanks. "Or if you are going to die," the little one offered to my back as I went out the door. I am certain he meant it to be helpful.

On the way back past the Aurore, the queue outside was gone so I stopped in for some soup. It was finished. I took the onion out of my pocket and gave it to them. For tomorrow's pot, I said.

As I walked back to Miriam's, I wondered whether the old man biting into the raw onion was a Radomsk haimishe custom. Or just a way to prepare for the taste that was to come from the pot.

So, the landsmanshaft, Maître. Of Radomsk. Paris branch. For your list.

28 November

The news from home that winter was bad. Though what means "bad"? What measure? Well, for my family, worse than before. My father's tailoring jobs were even fewer—they only barely got by because Marcus and Bertha scrabbled for part-time work, Marcus as a laborer, Bertha helping out at a Yiddish publisher. Then Bertha lost that work—the publisher's permit was taken away and it closed. Soon after that came the decree about not growing vegetables, do you remember I told you, Maître? Bertha wrote to me that she would not plant our parsley on the windowsill that year, afraid she might go to jail if a neighbor reported her. Her letter was very dark, Maître. Not about the parsley. About the fear.

Despite what they described about home, in Paris I went again to the Reich consulate for a visa to return to Hannover. Yes, Maître, back to Germany. Does that give you an idea how things were for me in France? Of course, the answer from the consulate was No.

Then late that winter came the new law in Poland. Which set everything in motion, everything that happened later, that autumn— my family shipped to Poland, vom Rath, the shots. Though we heard almost nothing about it at the time, this new law about Poland citizenship. It was only the first version of the law, Maître—which was to be pulled so much tighter in the coming October—that if you had lived outside Poland for more than five years, your passport could be revoked. In Poland there was little news about it—the Poland state was not looking to spread the word, since the point was to keep people out, not frighten them back in. Few people in France or Germany knew anything about it for the first few months after it was passed, and since the Poles were doing little to enforce it yet, few of those who knew of it paid it much attention. That summer a few stories were heard about people who tried to return to Poland and were turned away, which caused some confusion for people in Germany who had Poland passports, but they did not really know what to make of it. And people who had managed to get themselves to Paris? They had no intent of going back to Poland anyway, so who cared? In fact, I heard people at the Aurore say that if Poland would no longer let them back in, it might be more difficult for the French to throw them out, so maybe it was even a good thing.

Paris itself, though, was getting worse. Many people from Rumania arrived that winter, driven out by pogroms, then there was the Anschluss, so the Austrians came, and the streets of Paris east grew more crowded, poorer, more desperate. France responded to the misery by giving a new decree—for those caught without proper papers, jail could now stretch to three years. And me, that winter? Still stuck somewhere in between. With a proper temporary receipt. But no papers. In the room above Miriam's. Waiting. I think the Catholics have a word for it.

Then things again turned sideways for me. One afternoon at Miriam's there was a commotion downstairs, banging and running, a screech. There were only a few women in the building and most of them were upstairs where Sam and I were, in their resting rooms—there were always customers at Miriam's during the long French lunchtime but after that there was little call for the women's services until evening, so the afternoon was when most of Miriam's women went home, if they had time to get there and back, or to a café or the shops. When the noise began downstairs, Sam was asleep on the cot in our room and I was in the room next door, taking a break from my leather work and warming my shredded hands over the small brazier the women there had. As I went into the corridor to see what was happening, a young working girl rushed up the stairs, her face full of terror, shouting Police! Police! I panicked, Maître, and without thinking about Sam asleep on the cot—to my everlasting shame—I saw the little window in the water closet, jumped onto the bidet, shoved open the glass, and pulled myself out onto the roof. I scrambled to the next roof and then to the next, where I dove and lay flat behind a large double chimney, hidden from sight of the window where I had climbed out.

I lay there in the cold and wet for a long time, finally getting up the courage to move back to the window at Miriam's. Well to be honest, Maître, it was not courage but just a lack of choices—it had become dark and freezing and I could see no other way down from the roofs. I stuck my head through the little window, saw and heard nothing, and dropped back inside. The whole building was silent, the top floor empty, the women gone. Sam gone. Also gone, I noticed, were my two carving knives. I grabbed my jacket and coat and tiptoed down the stairs. I saw no one as I passed by Miriam's salon.

As always when I had nowhere else to go, I headed to Maison Albert, thinking up a story I would tell my aunt and uncle—Oh, a dispute with the landlord, French people, you never know. And as always, Abraham and Chawa took me in.

A few days later I got up the nerve to return to Miriam's, to find out what I could about Sam and to see about the rest of my clothes and the soles that I had finished carving, which to my surprise were all there in the room, undisturbed. Miriam herself was not interested in talking to me—to her I was just Sam's friend, she did not even remember my name—but two women I had become friendly with and who were now back in their resting room upstairs, told me what they knew. The raid had not been by the Morals Police of the central police judiciaire—who would have shut Miriam down and sent all the women to jail—but by a few local flics. Two of these local cops were already on the take from Miriam, but more cops wanted in on the payoff and anyway a raid was always useful to put fear in the other neighborhood clandestins that would hear about it and be readier with their own payoffs. The police had come in midafternoon when they knew there would be no customers and few women, which would make the whole thing quicker and less messy. The women they had found there were taken to the small local police station but released by nightfall. Except for two women who had no proper papers—they were still in jail, charged with illegally residing in France. Also, two of the younger girls who had not been there at the time of the raid were now too frightened to return. Other than these four girls who were now gone, though, the wider bribes, and the loss of one night's business, Miriam's was already back to normal.

No one there knew anything about Sam. He had been taken away with the women but at the police station he was separated from them and no one had seen him since. I went over to Belleville and eventually found Sam's sister Rachel. She had not seen Sam, and she and their mother Rina were worried. I told Rachel as much as I knew. I expect she told Rina something different.

It was not until more than a month later that I saw Sam again, and heard from him what had happened. The police had roughly hauled him out of the cot in our room but instead of acting ashamed and staying quiet—as a poor foreigner should—Sam had abused them back in his best Paris slang, telling them that he was just staying there on the top floor, he had nothing to do with the business downstairs, that he had his liberté to live where he wanted, they had no cause to bother him, and to get their so-and-so hands off him. Sam knew well that this attitude was not likely to get the best results but, as he explained to me, there are times when something other than your head makes the decisions. The police had been disappointed when they saw that Sam's residence papers were in order but they noticed the leather and the carving knives on the stool next to the cot, and asked Sam for his work papers. Sam did not have any—perhaps you remember me telling you, Maître. He told the police that the leather and knives were not his, that they belonged to a boy named Ahmed who used the room sometimes as a workplace, Sam did not know where he lived. The police checked with Miriam and she said that it was true, Sam just rented the room and did not work for her, and that yes, there was another boy who also used the room, she did not remember his name but he—meaning me, Maître—was small and dark, yes, it might be an Ahmed.

So, it turned out that everything Sam told them—including Ahmed, who he made up on the spot—checked out. They took him to jail anyway. He was not French. He was not meek. That was enough.

At the jail they roughed him some more and tried to get him to admit that he had been working the leather without a permit. When he would not budge, they changed tactics. Well then, they said, if this—waving the curved carving knife at him—is not to cut leather, then it is some kind of weapon, a dangerous one—a foreign one—and so a crime. Take your choice, they said and left him alone in a cell. When they returned a while later they asked him again if he had been working the leather. Sam had thought it over. Having a knife was normal in poor neighborhoods, with Frenchmen and foreigners alike. In all his years in Paris he had never heard of anyone spending much time in jail for having a knife, unless he had used it on someone. And most important, a knife concerned only the local police, not the foreigners' bureau and its deporting machinery, as working without a permit could. Whatever trouble the knife could get him into, it was not likely to lead anywhere worse than a few days in jail.

And he was right. Mostly. The police quickly lost interest in him. The night of his arrest they charged him at the station with possessing a dangerous weapon and interfering with an officer, then sent him over to the jail at Fresnes—the same jail where I was later, Maître. But they never bothered with any official report or court papers against him and so the jail let him go with a caution—a month later.

29 November

I knew that in January Sam had felt bad, somehow even responsible, about what de Guise had done to me at Saint Lambert, and me losing all my money there. "It should have been me," he had said. This time it was me who felt terrible, about leaving Sam on the cot at Miriam's, and what had happened to him, while I climbed out the window to safety. When I saw him again soon after he came out of jail, I immediately told him how I felt. He said, right away, that such worries were nonsense. I had no residence papers let alone a work permit, Sam reminded me, so likely it would have been far worse for me than for him if the police had found me there—a stretch in prison, the end of any chance at a refugee permit to stay, perhaps even immediate deporting. "You did what you had to," Sam said, "which is all that matters. Besides," he patted his stomach, "I think I put on two or three kilos in jail—the food there is French."

So, in very short order that day we were able to make certain again of our friendship. Still, things were now different for each of us, and over the next months I saw very little of Sam. He was back sleeping afternoons in the room at Miriam's and working all night. He no longer had time to work for Miriam, so he kept his rent down by now sharing the room with a young Algerian nut peddler he knew from Belleville. Sam was in the room during the day to sleep, his peddler friend there at night. Everything Sam did now was about his mother Rina. She was doing poorly with the consumption, so he worked as much as possible at the best paying work he could find, which was at Aux Belles Minettes, the fancy bordel, to try to keep up with the cost of Rina's medicine and food and rent for himself and Rina and Rachel, who was making very little from the colporteuse cart. He had no time to waste on gambits that might not pay off, no time to spend for the poor returns from supplying Rachel's colporteuse cart, no time for the Aurore club or a cinema matinée or a dance at the Eldorado hall or even a sit in a café or a stroll with me or the other boys or girls he knew. About the only time I saw him during those next few months was once in a while after the Bastille street market—getting the leftover market food helped him save more to buy Rina medicine.

As for me, I was back staying at Maison Albert, which caused the same problems as before—there was no space for me and my things in the crowded work and fitting rooms. Within a week of my returning there, though, one of the chambres de bonne became empty again. Madame Corbin the concierge had noticed me back in the building. On the quiet she let Chawa know about the empty room and soon I moved in again to my own tiny space in the building's attic. And that was where I was a week later when a message came to Maison Albert for me to go see Bernard.

Yours,
H.

Maître,

When I went to Bernard again—this was in February or March of '38—I no longer had the leather-carving knives and sharpener. The police had taken them when they raided Miriam's bordel and arrested Sam, I think I told you. Replacing the tools would have taken more than the few francs that Tante Chawa had given me when I returned to Rue Martel—though she did not know it, the only money I had. Also, the piecework payment I had been getting for the shoe soles was so little. And the gouges and slices to my hands had kept me from getting them clear of the scabies. So although I had nothing else, for a time I convinced myself—well, half-convinced—that I could not yet return to the backhunching handcramping paynothing leather work.

All of which meant that as I headed for Bernard's atelier, I allowed myself the hope—which had settled as a familiar ache in my stomach— that finally he would offer me some work. My last time there he had begun considering it, or so it seemed, until at the sight of my scabies he had pushed me out the door. Now I made a point of wearing a short sleeve shirt that Chawa had given me and took off my jacket as soon as I entered Bernard's private bureau, offering him an obvious show of my clear hands and arms. From what I had experienced of Bernard, it seemed that obvious was a good idea, and much better than expecting him to accept the truth of anything I told him.

Barely a moment after his grunt of greeting, Bernard handed me an envelope—again, the Swiss postmark and the fancy raised lettering "G.S. Lazare." He gestured for me to open it and waited, almost on tiptoes, while I read.

Geneviève was coming back to Paris. For a fortnight, on holiday from her Switzerland school. She asked if we could resume her German lessons, and she set a day and time for us to meet at the Alsace pâtisserie, on the left side of the river, where we had gone several times the summer before. If I could not make the appointment, she asked that I leave a message for her there at the pâtisserie. That would have been a normal arrangement for most Parisians, Maître, since so few had a telephone. But her parents' home certainly did, so it registered with me that Genève had not given me the number and offered that I phone her there, which would have been a simpler way to let her know, and ahead of time, if I could not meet the rendezvous, and to make other plans.

Despite that uncomfortable pebble, I was so pleased by the news of her return that I almost forgot Bernard standing there. Waiting. I told him that the letter was from the Lazare girl—which of course he already would have realized—but offered no details, put the note back in the envelope and slipped it into my jacket pocket. Bernard watched it disappear, like a strictly trained dog following only with its eyes the movement of a bone. As I expected, he did not ask me anything directly about the letter—that would have been beneath him. And would have risked the even greater undignifiedness of not getting a proper answer, which would be bad enough from anyone, but from me?

"Well, Uncle," I said, changing the subject at the same time I kept it alive, "my appointments will only occupy me some of the time, so I wonder if"—I hesitated—"I might somehow be useful to you," using the same phrase that seemed to have pleased him the last time I was there. As I spoke, I rearranged my jacket on the back of the chair. The jacket with the letter in the pocket.

"Useful to me," he repeated. "Well, that is an idea. But I am far too busy just now"—whether that was true or just for show, to put me back in my place, I could not tell—"so let me think on it. Next week. Let us say Monday afternoon. Come in and I will see what there might be."

As I headed back from Bernard's toward Rue Martel, I was tumbling over in my head what had just happened. Genève's return to Paris—I would see her again, but I wondered what that would mean. Bernard's almost positiveness about finding work for me—but with nothing more than yet another come-back-later. I took Genève's note out of my jacket and began rereading it as I walked, trying to see whether there was something I could spot between the words if I just studied the French carefully enough. Head down I tramped along, eyes glued to the letter, until I smacked straight into someone—not just a jostled elbow but a full-on body collision, my shoulders grabbed and then a big laugh.

"Well, H, when I saw you coming I wondered if you would even recognize me. But there is no way to do that unless at least you see me." Henri. My friend Henri.

The feeling was goosebumping, Maître, seeing him so unexpected, and after so long. One winter when I was a small child, three or four years old, my mother took me and Berthe to the center of Hannover, for some visit or errand, and returning in the early evening we waited for a bus on the icy dark pavement crowded with shoppers and store clerks and office workers on their way home. Suddenly I found myself alone in a forest of knees and bags and heavy woolen coats and I could not see my mother or hear her, the noise of the people and the traffic, and I did not know which way was the street with the terrible danger of autos and trams that she had frightened me about before we left home, or which way was back toward the buildings that I could not see because I was too small in the jostling crowd, and within a moment I was terrified, frozen to the spot, unable to make a sound. I do not know how long it was, Maître, no more than half a minute I suppose, then from out of the dark behind me I was swept up and smothered with hugs, it was my mother, and she was kissing me and squeezing me and rubbing my hair, then tears came to her eyes, and I felt so warm and relieved. And so loved. Seeing Henri again, it was something like that.

I had looked for him during the winter—three or four times I stopped by the rooming house near République where he had told me he stayed, and once I even traveled across the city to the nearly deserted foreign section bureau. But I had never managed to spot him and had felt too awkward to ask someone if they knew him and could I leave a message. And now, after half a year, here he was. Grinning at me. Calling me H.

He was passing out leaflets—no surprise. Spain, this time.

Alongside loving or hating the Communists, fear of foreigners stealing French jobs and daughters, and worry about war with the Reich, the subject most heard in Paris those days was whether France should help in the civil war of Spain. I knew little about it except that many French people wanted to stay out of it all, but that in Paris at least there were also many who wanted France to help the Spanish republicans fight against the fascists there, who were being given airplanes and guns by Mussolini and the Reich. Well, Maître, all that I suppose you know. But what I learned from Henri the next morning, traveling with him across the city to the huge Citroën auto factories at Javel, was that the Spain arguments had become tangled up with the latest syndicat battle, between the metal workers and the automobile and airplane companies. For Henri, this was the best of worlds—workers against the bosses and the fascists rolled into one. And maybe most important, it was action—Henri's favorite word.

Javel, Maître. It is an enormous factories area on the river in the bottom left corner of the city—bottom left, I am sorry, I always think of Paris directions as I saw them on the maps posted outside the bus and Métro stops. Javel was near the area where Henri's foreign section bureau had been, and not far from the Foire de Paris where I had worked in the dormitories the summer before. The Citroën factories filled massive smokestack building after building there, and on the river side there were covered holding lots with lines of shining new autos and lorries and army vehicles, waiting to roll onto rail cars and barges. Some of the autos were the Traction Avant, Maître, Citroën's brilliant new machine. Even during the strike I heard workers there speak proudly about it, with its new front-wheel traction. I wanted to be an engineer, did I tell you? Once upon a time. They truly were amazing machines, the new Citroëns. And so comfortable—like sitting in one of the stuffed chairs in Bernard's apartment. You see, I got behind the wheel one day at Javel. Though not to drive. Actually, not even ride—none of the autos were allowed to move during the strike. Which was a disappointment to me. Because you see, Maître, I had never in my life had a ride in an automobile. Though two summers later I got my first chance. That was a most interesting ride—also in a new Citroën—somewhere in the middle of the chaos countryside, July 1940, during the huge and terrible fleeing south ahead of the Wehrmacht. Well, and before that, my ride out of Bourges. Though I suppose that does not count—it was on a tank.

Now that I think of it, there were also the autos of the French police, which were like private autos. I mean private for me. Going from the local police station to the police judiciaire right after the shooting, and later on that day from there to jail. Then several times from jail to court, in an auto instead of the normal saladier—the salad bowl, they call it, the police van—because I was a special prisoner. Yes, an auto just for me. And again from the train station in Moulins, the summer of 1940, my own special French police car, delivering me to the Gestapo. Well, and yes also in the Gestapo's own, in France and again here in Berlin, their Mercedes, handsome autos they are, taking me to and from the hospitals and interrogatings and such. Plus a very fine SS auto, transferring me to Sachsenhausen. Then another again here to Moabit. Oh, and the airplane, the special plane of the Gestapo, that took me from France back to Berlin. Luxury, every one of them. For me. After the shooting.

My apologies, Maître. For all this babbling about automobiles. You see, there is nothing here but the walls. The hours are enormous. So I have come to depend entirely on remembering, and have developed the habit of letting myself recall as much as will come. Wherever it takes me. Which allows what has been to take the place of what is.

Just the opposite of life outside. With its endless forgetting. Have you ever realized? Of feelings, especially—embarrassment, unhappiness, fear. The daily renewness of waking up and having forgotten how something truly felt. Which allows everyone to keep going. Unless a time arrives when you are unable to forget. A madness, I would say.

2 December

Henri said he did not know what to expect when we arrived at Javel. Since his and all the other foreign sections had lost their support from the labor confederation the summer before, Henri had been disconnected from the workings of the syndicats. He had hardly even bothered to visit the foreign section bureau in the months since then, there was so little going on there. Still, whatever was happening now at Javel, Henri said, he wanted to be part of it.

On the way over, he told me as much as he knew. The metal workers—who built not only cars but also military vehicles and airplanes—had not had a pay raise in two years while the cost of living had gone up by half. That was easy enough for me to understand—I bought almost nothing, but even I had seen that things had become far more expensive since I had first come to Paris. I had just never thought about how that must hurt actual French people also. The factory owners had now offered the metal workers only a crumb of a pay raise, so the syndicat had threatened a strike.

But according to Henri it was more complicated than that. Much more. He tried to explain, but between what he did not know, and what I did not understand of what he said, and what now almost three years later I have mixed up or cannot recall, I hope you will forgive me if what I tell you is more than a little muddy. I only bother trying at all because it was these complications that led to what finally happened with Henri. And also because Communists were in the middle of it, which means you would be sure to ask me anyway.

So, yes, many of the metal workers were Communists, and the metal worker syndicat's Paris central bureau was the Party's dancing partner, as Henri put it. A new France government was just then being formed—which seemed to happen every few months—and the Communists wanted to be part of it, as they had been in the Popular Front two years before. They also wanted the new government to open the border with Spain, to send arms to the fighters there against the fascists. And the Party was trying to use the metal workers—most of them also wanted to help arm the Spanish fighters—to get what it wanted. You see, the auto and airplane factories were not only a big part of the France economy but also of the country's preparations for war against the Reich, which everyone knew might be coming soon. So, any stopping of the factories would be a blow to the government itself and, knowing that, the Party hoped that the metal workers threatening a strike would force the government to give in to them. On the other hand—and here is where I started to get lost, Maître—Henri said he did not think the Communists truly wanted a strike, or at least not much of one, because that might anger too many people against the Party and wind up keeping them out of the government. Also, the main Party in Moscow wanted France to prepare for war, so that France would be able to join Russia in the expected fight against the Reich. And that meant the Moscow Party wanted French factories to keep working. So, Henri said, the Party wanted a strike and at the same time did not want one.

Does all this make sense, Maître? I do not see how it could.

Anyway, it turned out that the actual metal workers at Citroën Javel had their own ideas, and had gone on strike without any official blessing from their syndicat central bureau or the Party. And not a usual walk-out strike but actually occupying the factories, to make sure that no work was done by anyone.

Citroën Javel—dozens of factory buildings packed together over an enormous area, hectares of it, almost a city of its own. When Henri and I arrived there that morning, many areas on the factory grounds looked like street festivals. Red flags and banners were hanging from factory fences, entryways, and windows, and in a large concrete space in front of the particular building that Henri headed to, hundreds of workers were gathered in a horseshoe around two men playing a bouncy tune—on accordions, unfortunately—and a dozen or so workers were clumsy dancing from one foot to the other, twirling around without any pattern I could see, sort of like traveling carnival bears. Despite the morning hour, wine bottles were passing among the dancers and the crowd, hundreds of workers were leaning out the factory windows shouting encouragement to the dancers, and through the large open entryway into the building I could see hundreds more inside.

I followed Henri as he moved toward a fence gate that separated the grounds from the pavement outside, a half dozen burly workers standing at each gatepost. They were keeping watchful eyes on the streets and anyone who approached, but paid little attention to Henri and me—I suppose we did not look very threatening. Still, Henri knew enough not to try just strolling through the gate without an invitation and stopped a few meters short. We stood there watching the scene in the yard, then Henri spotted someone he knew and called to him through the fence. The man came to the gate and Henri stepped forward to talk with him. The man seemed in high spirits, laughing and waving toward the crowd. They talked for a couple of minutes, then the man pointed somewhere far away on the factory grounds, shook hands with Henri, and returned to the crowd.

I went with Henri around to another part of the grounds—the site so large that it took us a quarter hour to walk there—where we approached a gate next to a wide, covered storage lot holding rows of new vehicles. Henri spoke to several men who were leaning weary against the inside of the gate. One of these men went off and into a rear door of the closest factory building. He reappeared a few minutes later with someone else, who came half-way toward the gate, recognized Henri, waved to him, then spoke to the first man and turned back into the building. The first man returned to the gate, opened it up and let us inside the fence.

"And him?" the man asked about me as soon as we were inside.

"He is good," Henri said. "A chômeur."

The man gave me a quick look up and down, without much concern—I suppose a very short, very thin 16-year-old was not of much interest to him, good or bad.

No, Maître, come to think of it, actually I was 17. My birthday the week before. I remember that Tante Chawa had made tzimis for me, on the Friday night, when I usually had a warm meal with them. One of my favorite things, tzimis—a kind of carrot and sweet potato stew. And just like my mother did on occasions like a birthday, Chawa made it this time with a mutton bone. So, we had a dinner that night, tzimis for my birthday, very special, Chawa and Abraham and me, a family dinner in Paris. Just the three of us. Well, that was all we were.

So, this striker at the rear gate, he gave us a job. To look for trouble. Most likely from the Doriots, he told us. At first I thought he meant some kind of dories, a French word I knew, the little boats tied up everywhere along the river. But that did not make much sense—Was the factory going to be attacked by people coming from the river? In rowboats? And why then was he telling us to check the nearby bars and cafés? So I thought I must be wrong, that the word was probably slang, some workers word I did not know. I decided to wait and ask Henri when we were alone, and I started concentrating again on the man's instructions to us. We were to make rounds of the streets to the immediate north of the factories—an area near Henri's foreign section bureau, he knew it well—stopping at the local bars and cafés to have a look and listen. Other friends of the strikers would be doing the same thing in different areas all around the Javel district. We were not to ask questions or appear too nosey, just keep our eyes and ears open. The fact that we were both so young meant that we could walk around without too much worry that anyone would bother us. If there was any sign of these Doriots, we were to directly return and report what we had seen.

Doriots. Henri explained as we started our rounds. It meant people of a France fascist party—which by the way had a few syndicat workers of its own, Henri said—led by someone named Jean Doriot, who raged against Communists and foreigners with equal hatred, calling to lock up any Communists who were French and to kick all the foreigners out of the country. No, it was Jacques, not Jean. Anyway Doriot—a name I was to hear more than enough.

Since the beginning of the factory occupations there had been rumors that the Doriots were planning some kind of actions against the strike. So, the metal workers wanted to keep an eye on the area around, to get some warning if Doriots or others were gathering and to get an idea of what they were up to. There were thousands of striking workers at Citroën, so they could have easily sent out some of their own to keep an eye on the streets. But if actual syndicat men patrolled outside, there was a good chance that eventually there would be a major colliding with Doriots or their like. Normally the syndicat men would have been more than willing for a fight in the streets. But this time the politics of it all was so tottering that the syndicat headquarters and the Party had demanded that the workers avoid anything ugly in public. The Citroën workers were not taking many orders from their central bureau or the Party, but they had been told that if they ever hoped to get bureau or Party support for the factory occupations, they absolutely had to avoid street battles, especially anything that might bring the police. Also, there was so much disagreement among the workers themselves about their demands and all the maneuverings of the strike that there were constant meetings and debates and votes in the factories, and workers did not want to miss any crucial decisions by being away from the factory for any length of time.

There was also something else, Henri tried to explain. Because it was an occupying, there was an almost magical line around the factory's perimeter, a line none of the occupiers wanted to cross for any reason. When the strike was first called, many workers had refused to occupy and had simply left the grounds. Others left over the following days. For those who remained, though, staying inside the factory property—at all times, at all costs, for as long as it took, never taking a break to see their families or have a proper meal—seemed to have the power of a spell.

So, the striking workers decided to call on supporters—particularly youngsters who were less likely to be taken for metal workers—to act as scouts for them out in the streets. Like Henri. And as it turned out, me.

It was exciting, my first day with Henri walking around the streets of Javel, sharp on the lookout and not a little nervous about running into trouble. Henri and I got a chance to talk with each other—well, Henri did most of the talking, a lot of it about the Spain war, which was as much on his mind as the strike. And every hour or two we stopped in at one or another of the district's worker bars and cafés, some of them Henri already knew from his days with the foreign section. Since we had to spend a bit of time in each place to see who was there and what was going on but did not want to stand out as snoops, we would have a coffee or glass of wine, and twice during the day a meal. The man at the factory gate had given Henri a few francs to cover the cost. I had not eaten so well since the brief time when Sam had a little money in Saint Lambert, months before. At the end of the day, I told Henri that I could get used to this kind of work. Not him, he said—it felt too much like being a cop.

The next day they switched us to night patrol, when I must say the nervous excitement of the first day felt much more like fear. The streets were mostly empty and without lamps, and the late night worker bars rough—the looks I got there I felt in a paining stomach. Also, as the nights went on and we saw no one on the streets to report, my mind created stranger and stronger images of what these mysterious Doriots must look like—creatures out of the Brothers Grimm. I suppose the wine we drank in the bars, which I was not used to, did not help. And it was tiring, these hours of walking, more so I think with the tensions of nighttime. We talked less, Henri and I. Also the mood at the factories had been changing, the high spirits of the first few days sagging under the workers' frustration and exhaustion. When we returned to the factory at dawn on the third morning, two workers just inside the rear gate were yelling at each other and hurling foul curses. Four other workers stood near them, not bothering to watch or listen. The change was wearing on Henri, I could see it.

Part of the reason the workers were souring, Henri told me, was that although the strikes and occupations were spreading to other factories around the city, the central syndicat bureau and the Party were still not backing up the strikers. They even told the newspapers that they did not support the occupations, which confused and pained the workers. And to further cover their tracks, neither the bureau or the Party would meet with the strikers, or advise them about the syndicat's negotiations with the owners, or pay the workers anything out of a strike fund, or even get them any food. Which turned out to be the next job for Henri and me.

3 December

The workers inside the factories had to make their own arrangements. So, when Henri and I arrived at Javel on our fourth night, we were asked to end our patrolling at three a.m. and head over to a bakery

342

just past the Pont Mirabeau, a bridge over the Seine. We were met at the rear of the place by a baker who had come in before midnight to make extra bread, which was waiting for us on cooling racks in the back. We loaded the loaves onto a hand cart that stood outside the rear door and covered the huge stack with a blanket, then hauled the cart down to the factory, about two kilometers away. At the gate we saw more carts arriving.

After the workers unloaded the bread, they asked us to take the cart to a street market on Place Violet, over toward the Saint Lambert district where Sam and I had stayed in Rachel's room. It was quite a hike, especially pulling the heavy wooden cart over old streets, many of them cobbled stones. It was still dark when we arrived but the food sellers had already set up their stalls and early customers were moving around the square. We found our contact man—there were also four other boys sent there from the factories, each pair with a hand cart—who organized for us cheeses, cherries, dried sausage, onions, and sacks and sacks of potatoes. He was a large, fearsome, gruff-speaking man but he both helped and encouraged us in loading the food, calling us comrades. I did not tell Henri that he was the same man who had chased Sam and me away from that very same market, cursing us "sales métèques"—"dirty wogs"—just a few months before.

So, that was our job. The first part of each night was nerve-making—walking the dark streets and forcing down drinks in the scary bars, looking for signs of the mysterious Doriots. The later part of the night was less stressing but still exhausting, hauling first bread and then potatoes and onions and such in a heavy cart over rough streets to the factories, from different locations across the bottom left corner of the city, then returning the cart to wherever we had started, and finally in the morning riding a bus back across the city to the east and our beds. At least I was getting plenty of filling food. Also two francs for my pocket from the strikers at the end of each night—not a lot, but more than anyone was giving them. Most of all, I was spending time with Henri, and around something he cared about. Cared hard.

My own feelings about these things—which I suppose you may be more interested in, Maître—were not very clear. I was certainly more comfortable in the company of these factory men than I was with the people at Bernard's party, for example, or at the Consistoire. On the other hand, with these French workmen there was always a distance that I did not feel around, say, Berenice and Sidney—Maison Albert's seamstress and machiniste—or the young people at the Sportclub Aurore. Or even most of the men and women of the foreign section I had worked with at the Foire the summer before. And now I had to think about just how much this all mattered to me, the strike and Henri both. Because the following day I was supposed to return to Bernard's atelier. And three days after that I was meant to meet Genève. Each appointment was in the afternoon, and since I was now working at night in Javel, I could have grabbed a couple of hours sleep on each of those mornings and still made it to both rendezvous. But complicating things was the hope—yes, Maître, even then—that at least one of the three would lead me to something more. Regular work from Bernard. More connections to real France from Henri. And from Genève—well, I did not know what. So before deciding what to do, I had to think in a longer way.

The idea of work from Bernard—if ever it actually happened— was a great pull. He had business all over the city, and if I could get into his circuits I might finally get myself beyond the daily scrambling to nowhere that had been my nearly two years in Paris. But time with Henri had already meant actual work—at the Foire and now at Javel—and food as well. As did my outings with Genève—it was hard to imagine an easier job than her German lessons, or better food than our restaurant meals.

Also, the more I thought about things, the more I felt about them. Does that make sense, Maître? Let me say it this way. Since Sam and I had gone our separate ways, my days had a different hole than just the one in my stomach. A hole that Henri filled. And Genève might. But Bernard?

The morning of the day I was meant to go to Bernard's atelier, I went to a tabac and phoned him. I would not be able to see him that afternoon, I told him. Something had come up.

"What do you mean?" he growled.

"The Lazares," I said. He went quiet. He did not ask whether I meant her parents or just Genève. But I do not believe he had enough imagination to think I was lying.

4 December

That night I saw my first Doriot. More than one. It was not a surprise. Well, not the first sight of them, anyway. Because when Henri and I arrived at Javel to begin our street patrolling, we were told the Doriots had staged rallies outside several of the factory buildings that day, and afterward marched around handing out leaflets against the strike. Then after dark they drove motor vans around the outside of the occupied buildings, blaring messages over loudspeakers. We saw the leaflets—they were scattered all over the streets—and heard one of the loudspeaker vans. I did not understand much of what was written and said, but I had no trouble recognizing certain words they kept repeating—"Bolsheviks!"—"Work Is Liberty!"—"France for French!"

As Henri and I made our rounds that night we saw a few more people on the streets, and going in and out of certain bars and cafés, than on previous nights. And about two in the morning—an hour when a few bars were open but all the cafés were normally shut—at one large café the lights were on and several people were standing outside the door. Henri and I went over to take a look. Through the windows we could see some sort of meeting going on inside, dozens of people crowded around the café tables and a man standing in front of them talking and gesturing strongly. Before we got very close, though, two men came up and asked what we were doing. Henri quickly said that we were just on our way to work, at a bakery, that we always walked by there but had never seen the café open at this hour, so we just came over to see what was going on. The man said they were PPF—Doriot's party—and did we want to come in and learn something. I was frightened, Maître—I did not want to go inside and perhaps be discovered if my accent spilled out, but I also worried what would happen if we refused. Fortunately, Henri was up to it. He brightened and said something as if he was quite interested to hear about the PPF, then quickly changed to say that well, no, after all, we had better not be late to our work, a Frenchman needs his baguette in the morning, and workers need to keep working, France has to depend on something in these times. The man humphed at this but the words France and Frenchmen seemed to drop a protecting cloak over our shoulders and we headed away without any trouble. Though not before I noticed that a man standing next to the café door had a revolver in his belt.

Henri thought we should report what we had seen before going to the bakery, so we hurried back to the factory. The strikers already knew that the Doriots were holding meetings near the factories, trying to coax in and organize workers who did not support the strike, or who had originally supported a strike but not the occupations and who now wanted to get back to their jobs, and also to attract people who just wanted a crack at the Reds. There had already been some small fights that night between Doriots and members of another syndicat who had come to Javel to support the metal workers. And yes, they knew about the pistols, though the Doriots had not used them yet.

The strikers thanked us for our good work—they had not known about that particular café—then sent us back out on the second half of our duties, to collect another load of bread and later to a street food market. They told us not to poke around at any bars or cafés on the way—it was now just too dangerous. I was proud to hear their praise but also greatly relieved at our release from detective duties.

The bakery this time was near the Quai de Grenelle, further up the Seine. Henri did not know the streets around there and we took a little time finding the place, so on our return with the bread we decided to bring the cart straight down along the river, then head in to the factory from the back side. We were within sight of the smoke-stacks when they jumped us. Six of them? Eight? In the dark, we heard but never saw them coming. I think it was one of the loudspeaker vans, but afterward it was all too blurry for me to be sure—a van of some kind, anyway. It came up behind us, with no running lights, and swerved in front of the cart. The men leaped out of the back and ran at us, three or four against each of us, shouting "Bolshies! Bolshies!"

346

and knocking us to the pavement, punching and kicking us, and finally pushing us over the bank, down to the river.

We were lucky. The riverbank there is not nearly as steep as in the center of Paris, and not paved or bricked. The dirt and weeds slowed my tumbling fall and I came to rest just short of the water, my head banging against a small boat—a dory, I suppose. I lay stunned, waiting for my body tell me if anything was broken and hoping that the men would not come down the bank to continue the beating. It was too dark to see but I could hear them above, laughing and grunting as they pushed the cart and sent it rolling then crashing down the bank and into the water. Then more laughing as they got into the van and drove off. I managed to sit up and though I was beginning to feel bruises at various places on my body, I did not seem to have any serious damage except for a big gash in my brow that was filling my eye and covering my face with blood.

After a minute I heard "H," Henri calling "H," and I said "Yes, over here" and got to my feet. He appeared out of the dark, asking if I was all right. He did not look so great himself, wet and half-covered in mud. He had fallen all the way into the edge of the river but it was not too deep there and he had managed to scramble out, soaked and badly bruised. We climbed back up the bank together and took stock of ourselves. Henri had a kerchief in his back pocket, soaked with river water, that he used to wipe the blood from my brow and eye and that I then pressed against my forehead to stop the bleeding. I brushed some of the dirt and sand off myself and out of my hair but there was not much we could do about Henri's wet muddy clothes.

"The cart," he finally said, and we carefully made our way back down the riverbank. It was lying upside down, half in the shallow water. After some struggle we managed to pull it out and set it upright. We could make out mashed and broken loaves on the bank and in the mud where the cart had come to rest. The rest of the bread was floating away in the river.

There was no way we could get the cart back up the bank, so we left it and trudged back to the factory. The men at the gate brought us inside the nearest building and into a small room next to the canteen. Soon two more people came in and began seriously tending to my face and checking Henri. Several other workers crowded the doorway to have a look at us and to hear what had happened. At first, because of all the blood, they feared that I had been badly hurt. But when these two medic people got my face and the wound cleaned up, they announced that my swollen shut eye itself was not damaged, and handily set about covering the forehead wound with gauze and tape. Everyone in the room relaxed and the people in the doorway drifted away, which I must admit, Maître, disappointed me a little.

They produced some dry clothes for Henri and brought us bowls of hot coffee. Henri told the tale now in detail to several strikers, who thanked us for our courage and contribution. I was thinking that we had not had any chance for courage and that our contribution had been to lose both the cart and the bread, but I was anyway gladdened by their words. We warmed up and rested for a few minutes and regained our nerves—well, I regained mine, I do not think Henri ever lost his. Then someone said that if we were going to leave now, they could escort us to the far edge of Javel. Or, the man said, they could find something for us to do inside the fences. Henri looked at me. I said, "Action." He smiled and told the man that we would stay.

Straight through until dawn, Henri and I helped bring in the food that others were delivering to the gates, and distributed it to canteens in different factory buildings. I got to see more of the enormous Citroën complex, but just as impressive as the buildings and machinery was the many hundreds of men and women sleeping on the factory floors and benches and canteen tables, and the groups—in every hall of every building—of talking, arguing, arm-waving strikers carrying on their debates all through the night.

I was filthy and jumpy and exhausted from it all as Henri and I made our way to an early morning bus, to take us back to the east. Also quite dizzy from the crack to my head—I had to stop and lean against a wall, my head throbbing badly and the sight fuzzy out of my one open eye. Henri checked that my wound had not reopened, and after a minute or two we carried on. My head pained me for days to come, but every time I touched the bandage above my eye, so expertly applied by the strikers' medics, the hurt softened a bit.

The next night Henri and I were met with hearty salutes and slaps on the back from the men at the gate—they were pleased that we had returned despite the beating. After a medic checked on my wound and changed the gauze and plaster, the strikers gave us work inside the perimeter, patrolling the storage yards and cleaning soot off the rows of new autos—my chance to sit behind the wheel of a Traction Avant—then later helping to unload and deliver bread and other food from the gates to the factory canteens.

It was toward the end of our deliveries, sometime near dawn, when we saw her. As we were about to enter one of the canteens with our factory trolley piled with bread and potatoes and such, from inside we heard an extraordinary voice, a woman's voice, crackling across the room and echoing off the concrete walls. Meetings and arguments were normal at any hour and in any corner of any building, so we carried on, pushing through the doors with our trolley. The room was packed to the edges with women, all women, wearing the smocks that announced them as workers, few of them young and those that were had faces marked by their time in the factories. They were all focused on a broad, fierce woman who stood on a table in the middle of the room, her head almost banging one of the many low-hanging pipes, the sleeves of her dress and smock pushed up to her elbows giving freedom to her muscled arms that gestured toward the factory floor, veins standing out in her neck as she urged at the women with every ounce of her heart. It was Rose—Henri's friend who had given me work at the Foire dormitories the summer before. One of the leaders of the syndicat confederation. Do you remember me telling you, Maître?

Henri and I stopped just inside the door, halted by the thick pack of bodies, by the tenseness in the room, and by the sight and sound of Rose. We looked around for a spot to drop off the food, but every table surface was covered by the women and no one made a move to open up space. Only a few near the door even glanced at us. Outside again, after we had retreated with the full trolley, I asked Henri whether he thought Rose had recognized or even noticed us. "Usually there is little she misses," he said. "But we are very little. And this is not usually."

I will end this now. The guard will be coming soon with my evening food, and the evening guard is the one who is permitted to collect my letters to you. God gives us routines, Maître.

Yours,
H

5 December 1941
Moabit

Maître,

Right in the middle of all our Citroën Javel doings was my appointment with Geneviève. When I received her letter, I set aside my best shirt—I had three altogether—for the occasion, and during those next two weeks did not wear my one extra trousers and jacket, which were mostly clean. But after the Doriot beating and my unplanned gymnastics down the riverbank, plus several nights of food deliveries around the occupied buildings, my personal self was filthy, my scalp still crusted with sand. I badly needed to wash myself before seeing her. Normally I washed at the sink at Chawa and Abraham's—Did I tell you that they had their own water tap in their Rue Martel rooms? As often as once a week, Maître—staying clean seemed important to me, one of the few things I had at least some control of. Actually, it is the same in jail. But by the time I could cross the city from Javel back to Rue Martel that morning, Maison Albert would already be busy and crowded—the machiniste and seamstress working alongside Chawa and Abraham, and perhaps even an early client—and I did not want to barge in on them, especially with the amount of scrubbing I had to do and a forehead bandage I had no wish to invent a story for. I thought about going to the public baths where Sam and I had sulfured the scabies, but that would eat up most of the little money I had, and I did not want to go with empty pockets to my afternoon—and perhaps evening—with Geneviève, just in case. Also, instead of spending all the time it would take to get to and through and back from the baths, I needed to try for some sleep. So before leaving Javel after my night's work, I found one of the striker medics to change the bandage on my head, then I cleaned myself as best I could in a factory washroom. Is all this more than you want to know, Maître? But these were the kinds of things that swallowed the hours and energies of every day during my time in Paris, these weighings, balancings, tactics of living.

Paying pained attention, every moment, to everything and everyone around me.

I also snuck out from a factory canteen two hunks of bread and a piece of dry cheese in my jacket pocket—Sam would have been proud—so that I could eat something later on and not be jittery with hunger when I first saw Genève again. Though it turned out I was jittery anyway. When I got back to the attic room at Rue Martel that morning I lay down and closed my eyes but barely dozed—I feared sleeping straight through the appointment time—and when I went out again late that afternoon I had altogether slept very little over the previous several days, and I was exhausted. As I neared the rendezvous spot at the Alsace pâtisserie, though, the ethers in my body took over—Is that what they are called?—and I was surging wide awake.

Genève was there ahead of me. I thought that was a good sign. Then immediately doubted it—I suppose that was my jitters. Also, when I approached the table I had a panic about whether to offer a handshake or that French not-quite-kissing thing. Why had I not thought of these things before I arrived? Genève rose and gave me the double cheek brushing. Did that mean something? It felt wonderful. I was a wreck.

She had cut her hair, her wavy flowing red-hinting hair. Short. Shorter than mine, though my length was mostly from lack of attention—Tante Chawa was my haircutter, and I did not like to bother her for it too often. Genève could see that I was startled by her haircut, and as I sat down she rubbed her hand back over her head and said, "I was in Berlin again. Our class at school made a trip there. I did not get to do much, the schoolmistresses and chaperones and rules and all that. But while I was there I saw an advert for a nightclub—and next time I will get to that club, no matter what—and the two women in the advert photo, well, this was their style."

I was not unhappy to listen about hair. Part of my nerves had been that I did not know what we would talk about, what I would say about myself if she asked. She did not. Except about my bandaged forehead. "A small collision," I said and shrugged, "with a dory." Then added quickly, "Boating, you know."

"Boating," she repeated. And must have been satisfied with whatever notion that brought her because she said, "Yes, we sail during the summers, in the Allier," and asked me no more about it. "Well," she said, "shall we continue in German? I have been studying."

It had not helped, not her accent or the twisted shapes of her sentences. Though she did seem to know more words. She greeted the café owner and ordered her coffee in German—he smiled on her as if she was reciting perfect Goethe—but she did not ask for a pastry, as she usually did there. Our meeting was late in the afternoon, we were alone in the place, perhaps it was no longer a proper time for pastry with the French. So neither did I order any, despite being tortured by the gorgeous smell in there. I did order coffee—I had moved on from tea.

She had a plan for us. The first part was to stop at the Panthéon—though she called it the cathedral of Sainte Geneviève—where she had taken me on our first day together the summer before. Did I tell you about this place, Maître? I have the sense that I did but I do not remember for certain. Forgive me if I repeat some things, but we have been talking for more than a year, you and I. And now the trial coming, January or February, I cannot worry about repeating.

She told me that it calmed her, the Panthéon. There were things there that "spoke" to her, she said. I do not know what they spoke about because she did not finish the sentence. Or perhaps she did finish. In either language, with Genève I was never sure.

We walked the short distance from the pâtisserie to the Montagne de Sainte Geneviève—the hill topped by the Panthéon—with Genève trying in German to describe her visit in Berlin, the fashions there, the music halls and nightclubs she heard about and saw advertised and wanted so badly to experience. Despite her German being crooked and full of holes, she spoke it as quickly and confidently as her French, so I could understand only about half of what she said—it was like those moments in a cinema when the film slips on the sprockets of the projector, Maître, do you know what I mean? But it did not bother me much and she seemed not to realize it. Or maybe she realized but simply did not care.

Just inside the great domed Panthéon building I stopped short at the sudden sight of the huge archways and columns and statutes and paintings, and every centimeter of the high, high walls covered with carvings and murals, all of it framed by the black and white patterned marble floor that was a wonder in itself, and by the enormous central dome painted with angels and saints and such who all look down on you whether or not you look up at them. Our school once visited the opera house in Hannover, Maître, to hear Beethoven performed. Well, walking into the Panthéon seemed like being dropped into the middle of that orchestra pit with every instrument playing the finale at top volume, so how all this could be calming for Genève I did not understand. Not until later, anyway, when I had experienced more of her great skill at ignoring things around her.

She went ahead of me, directly to a side wall where she stopped and stood very still in front of a wide set of murals. They were all of Sainte Geneviève—one panel of her childhood in the countryside, another one of her praying, another of her bringing grain to the starving people of Paris, and some others. On our earlier visit there Genève had shown me these Sainte Genevièves but she had also taken me all around the great building and told me about the Jeanne d'Arc murals and the Saint this-or-that paintings and the King so-and-so panels, and statue after statue the size of giraffes. Not this time—it was straightaway and only Sainte Geneviève. She said nothing, Genève, just stood still and looked at the murals for the longest time. I stayed behind her, out of her eye. Finally she turned to me, smiled, and led me out.

She was quiet now—no more chatter about Berlin and night-clubs and haircuts—and what little she said was in French. The sun was going down as we walked to a nearby side street where people were crowding into a small church. Genève led me into a plain two story building just next to it. She did not say why. Inside it felt like a large cold house. There were priests bustling around, preparing themselves with special cloaks and such, and nuns, or sisters—Is it the same, Maître? Being so close to these church people made me squirmish. I had never been around them, and there was always something about their faces when they looked at you on the street in Paris, some-thing with their eyes and mouths, that told you they knew you were wrong. Somehow wrong. I had not seen nearly as many of them in Germany when I was growing up but even those few had frightened me. I remember waiting at a bus stop in Hannover with my mother, I must have been about five, when an old lady nun in her black costume and pinched-up face came and stood near us. I began to tremble. "Is she a witch?" I finally managed to ask my mother. The nun heard me, and from her look I could tell that she did not think kindly of me. Or of my mother.

The priests and nuns in this building where Genève brought me did not look kindly either. Not at the people who later came out the side door of the church. And certainly not at me, though I think Genève was trying to save me—and perhaps also herself—from a harsher judg-ment when she introduced me not as Monsieur Grynszpan but as Monsieur H. Anyway, for Genève they had smiles, the priests and nuns there. Half-smiles, at least. They all knew her. She visited often when she was in Paris, I learned from her later, both the church itself and this building next to it where the priests and nuns stayed—or maybe only one or the other actually lived there. Would they live in the same house, Maître? I wondered about that when I was there, but I did not ask. Strange, the thoughts I had sometimes. Maybe it was being with Genève. Or maybe not so strange.

We went into a large kitchen area at the rear of the building where two nuns were setting out stacks of long breads and arranging several huge rounds of cheese onto wooden planks. There was also the smell of leeks and turnips or some other root like that, cooking in an oven. The kitchen nuns greeted Genève and thanked her for coming, then asked if we would take on the bread and cheese chores while they set up the courtyard behind the—well, whatever the building was called, some catholique word. The bread was to be sawed into sections, and portions were to be carved out of the cheeses with one of those special curved knives. Genève said yes, of course, that was why we were there—which was news to me—and took off her scarf and stylish long jacket, almost like a man's—Berlin fashion, I guessed. She did not ask me if I minded that we help with this kitchen work but simply turned a smile on me, which she probably knew was enough. She did ask if she should show me how to work with the special cheese knife but I told her I knew how—thinking back to the one I had used on de Guise's ear. As we set to our tasks, I was a bit disturbed that Genève had asked me about the cheese knife, thinking of me as coming from some world where I had never used such a thing. And though it was true, I wondered what world she imagined that was.

While we worked in the kitchen, one or another of the nuns and priests would stop to chat with Genève about the lovely spring evening and the church services that special holy week before Easter and how Genève was getting on at school and would they see more of her in the coming summer? Thankfully, they said almost nothing to me—I had come in with Genève, but they all somehow sensed that they need not act the same toward me—so I was able to avoid giving away my accent or saying some accidental strangeness about one of the catholique things they talked about. After a few minutes all the nuns and priests had disappeared except for the two nuns who were working in the courtyard behind the kitchen, and I heard the beginnings of a service in the church next door. With the help of a hunched old man who appeared from I do not know where, the nuns outside set up a small low table they covered with a white cloth, a few steps from a side door of the church, and next to it two higher, slightly larger tables. On the other side of the courtyard they arranged three long wooden trestles end to end, and benches running the length on both sides.

In a half-hour or so Genève and I had finished up our kitchen work and a priest in ceremony costume came from the building out into the courtyard and stood behind the small covered table, placing on it a silver cross and a little bowl, I think, and a few other trinkets I did not know. Soon after, we could hear much shuffling and bustling inside the church, then its side door opened onto the courtyard. People crowded there, waiting to come out of the church, but did not yet move through the doorway. I helped the old man carry out the wooden planks with the cut bread and cheese and four huge oven dishes full of cooked vegetables and put them on the two tables next to the priest's, who then signaled for the people to begin coming out of the church. One by one they went first to the priest, who said some Latin words over them, and they repeated several phrases. They then bowed their heads as the priest crossed them—Is that the right way to say it, Maître?—after which they slid over to the first food table. There a nun placed a portion of cheese on a torn sheet of newspaper and handed it to them with a few mumbled words and, for every one of them it seemed, an expression like a parent slightly disappointed in a child. Another nun dished up a lump of the leeks and roots, then Genève gave a chunk of bread and finally each person moved over to the long trestle tables and sat down on a bench. No one yet took a bite of their food.

I did not know what to do with myself. I had no task in the court-yard but I was not about to go back into that nuns and priests house, not without Genève. I did not want to stare at the people in the food queue but neither did I want to make a point of looking away. So, I stood there behind Genève, listening to the small exchanges between her and the people receiving the bread, forcing a smile at the ones who glanced at me—most of them did not smile back—and remember-ing how often I myself had stood in the soup queue at the Sportclub Aurore, or with Sam had scrounged food scraps at the Bastille street market. Yet I felt quite clear that the people here were different from me and Sam and the young men and women in the food queue at the Aurore, even though they had the same red hands and hungry eyes and rough clothes. Because these people were French, Maître. True French. And yet here they were, heads down and voices low, having to wait for bread. I must say, watching it, from the outside so to say, was a bit of a shock.

When all the people who had come out the side door of the church—40 or 50 of them, counting children—were sitting at the long tables, the priest said a few more words, a kind of blessing I suppose, and they finally dug into their food. The priest disappeared into the building but four of the nuns stood together looking over the eaters. I remember how it made me crazy, Maître, when the guard used to stand in my cell and watch me while I ate. When I first was in the Gestapo jail. Until you arranged for them to leave me be, do you remember? I wondered how the people in the churchyard felt.

Genève and I stood a couple of meters behind the nuns. Genève tilted her head toward the long tables and said to me in French, "The scene." She looked for my agreement, I think, but I did not know what she meant. She repeated, "The scene," and when I still did not react she whispered in German, "The Last Supper." I knew what that was, sort of—one of those important things with Jesus—but I had no idea why Genève was saying it. "Holy Thursday," she said to me, in French again. "This evening, in churches, the scene." I did not know whether she was talking about the service that had been held next door, or the row of people eating at the tables, or what.

I think the nuns overheard Genève and half-turned in our direction with expressions that were, well, nunnishe. Genève noticed and with a confident smile and her most well-spoken high-style language announced that we had to be leaving but that she looked forward to seeing them tomorrow. The nuns made polite smiles back at her, then nodded slightly to me, though without the smiles. To my relief, Genève headed for the courtyard gate onto the street instead of going back through the building.

It had now turned to evening. On one hand, I hoped we would go for food—I had missed the pastry I expected at the Alsace place, and then for two hours watched and smelled all that bread and cheese and oniony stew. If we went together then for supper, I knew I would eat not only plenty but well—I always did with Genève. And which she always paid for, without a mention. But I also now imagined that joining us at a meal would be all these church doings, to talk about, and it was all such a confusion to me, Maître. Why bring me to a church? Was this a normal thing for a French girl to do? And what did this little church mean to her, being so welcome there but at the same time so clearly somewhere outside of it? Above it, I suppose you could say.

These things had time to roll around in my head as I went back to Rue Martel, to change my clothes and head for Javel later in the night, because there was no meal with Genève that evening. It turned out she had to return home for a family gathering. Maybe they were having a celebration or ceremony for this Holy Thursday thing—Do people have a Last Supper of their own, Maître? I did not ask her that, and she did not say.

When we were parting she held out some money, carefully enclosed by her hand as she always made a point to do, in payment for her language lesson. I would not take it, though, telling her that we had not really done any work on her German. And added that for me it had anyway been a most worthwhile afternoon. Of course, the money was hard to resist, it was always 20 francs, just imagine me passing up such a sum, but whatever good it would have done me, turning it down did me more. Genève shrugged and immediately put the money away—I suppose I hoped she would press it on me, but that was not her way and she said nothing about it, including my "worthwhile afternoon" remark. Still, from the way her eyes remained on mine an extra moment, I think it pleased her, my turning it down. She asked if we might rendezvous again the next the afternoon, later than usual and skipping the pâtisserie, at this same church. "Holy Friday," she said to me and raised her eyebrows in what seemed like pleasure at some private idea.

6 December

The mood at Javel that night was nervous, quiet, waiting. Since I had not known where I would be at the end of my visit with Genève, or when, I had told Henri that I would meet him at the factories rather than travel together from the east as we usually did. When I got to Javel, though, I did not find him at the gate where we entered each night. I asked a couple of the people we worked with. They had seen him earlier but did not know where he was then. I did not want to bother anyone else, so I spent the first part of the night wiping down the autos on the storage lots, work I chose because it put me in contact with the fewest people.

After a while I returned to the gate where they organized the arriving food to bring into the factory canteens. Still no sign of Henri. Early loads were already waiting so I decided to start without him, though I was nervous that I might be asked to go into the factory buildings on my own. Then I spotted him, standing in a doorway. Speaking to him was an older man with a quietly serious face. And behind the man, Rose. Henri put up his hand for me to stay where I was—to wait for him, or perhaps to come no closer, I could not tell—and after another few words with the man Henri came over. Rose nodded at me but there was no hint of her usual big energy.

As we began our food delivery rounds together, Henri told me that the strike was at a very difficult moment. The syndicat central bureau, backed or ordered—depending on who you asked—by the Party, had made a deal with the government and the companies to end the strike at the aviation factories, and the occupying workers at Citroën were now trying to sort out what that might mean for them. Henri said that there were terrible arguments and accusings going on in the factories that night, with different striker sections fighting among themselves about who had said and done what, and what should happen from there on. The stitches that had been holding them all together were stretching wide.

"And Rose?" As soon as the words were out of my mouth I wanted them back—I had no right to ask.

Henri stopped and looked at me, though with no disapproval. Just weariness.

"Things are difficult." And after a moment added, "But she is still Rose."

I asked no more about it and we spoke very little as we went through our deliveries the rest of that tense and restless night.

After a few hours sleep back at Rue Martel, I put on my clean clothes, slipped a note under the door of Maison Albert saying that I would not be there for our usual Friday night supper, and headed out for my next rendezvous with Genève. I wore a necktie, which seemed right for meeting her at the church, but carried my jacket instead of putting it on, hoping with those small changes that it would not be obvious to her that I was wearing exactly the same things—my only clean things—as the day before.

She was waiting at the edge of a crowd that was working its way into the little church. Her outfit immediately struck me—twill trousers, a long, tight-fitting man's style black suit jacket, a white collared shirt, and a dark blue scarf tied in a knot like a necktie. All beautifully tailored, of course. It was striking on Genève, especially with her very short hair then. But it was also curious and certainly not what I had seen on any other woman in Paris, even in the advertisements for fancy autos and perfumes and such. I thought perhaps it was something special for the holy day, but then I saw that of all the other women heading into the little church, there was not a single pair of trousers. And then I thought, well, Berlin style, it must be Berlin.

There was no cheek brushing or other greeting when I reached her. "Just do what I do," she said and looked at the jacket in my hand. I put it on and followed her in.

It was uncomfortable and nerve-making for me, Maître. I had never before been in a Catholic church, in Hannover or Paris, let alone during an actual ceremony or service or whatever they call it, and this one so important to everyone, it seemed, this Holy Friday just before Easter, the rows tightly packed, and all of the doings so complicated. First a priest—I suppose that was what he was—all dressed in black appeared at a doorway up at the far front of the church and everyone went silent. Then a line of priests and maybe junior priests or something came in also all in black, went to spots around the altar place and kneeled, then actually lay face first on the ground—it looked so strange, from what I had seen of the way priests acted on the streets I never could have imagined such a thing—and after that there was all this Latin preaching or praying and the people in the rows kneeling and mumbling and standing up and then kneeling again, over and over, and saying things together with the priests, and the candles burning, and the smells, Maître, I remember the smells of the place were so different from what I knew. The whole time my mind and body were racing together to keep pace, to kneel down or get up when the others did, to pretend to speak when they spoke, it went on and on, and Genève next to me in perfect time with all the rest but completely unbothered, it seemed, whether or not I did things right. I thought it would never end.

In fact, I do not know when it ended. Because at a certain point there was another total silence in the church, then a large wooden cross was brought out and laid on a piece of satin at the altar place, and all the people began to sing, then very orderly left their bench rows and single file headed toward the priests and the cross, which one by one the people bent and kissed. As the rows emptied in front of us I became terrified that I would also have to go up there, and what terrible mistake would I make in front of all the French people? But we were in the far back row—I realized afterward that Geneève must have planned it that way—and as the people next to us moved out of the row, Geneève took my hand and led me not to the front of the church but to the rear door and into the street.

Outside she let go of my hand—which certainly made it easier for me to pay attention—and faced me. She nodded back toward the church and with a softish sweet smile, definitely not her usual, she said, "Je l'adore"—"I love it." That was all. Then she touched my elbow in that way she had of guiding me without saying anything, and headed us back toward the Panthéon. But we went past the great monument building and into some narrow side streets, which strangely seemed familiar to me, then kept going partway down the hill until we reached a restaurant which I recognized she had taken me to the past summer. There is something calming about returning someplace, almost anyplace, where you have been before, and as soon as we stepped inside the restaurant I felt a soothing of my stomach that had been paining me the entire time we were in the church. It was a small space, this restaurant, crowded with eight or ten tables covered by oilcloths and an unmarked bottle of red wine sitting in the middle of each. There was a chalkboard menu but I did not bother trying to figure it out—these were anyway always difficult for me, since I could not read very well the peculiar handwriting script the French use, and even if I could read it I mostly had no idea what the names of the dishes meant—because I remembered that the other time we had been there Geneève had introduced me to a wondrous stew of giant white beans and duck something-or-other, which she told me was a specialty of the restaurant, from some south part of the country. Well, yes, with sausage also, Maître, which was maybe pork, but I had not asked what it was the first time we were there and definitely did not worry about it this time—the only meat I had eaten in the past several weeks was small bits from the mutton bone that flavored the tzimis Tante Chawa had made for my birthday.

There were people at only one other table when we arrived and from behind the bar the restaurant patronne indicated that we could sit where we liked. When finally she came over to us, Geneviève ordered a light meal, which was usual for her. For appearance sake I looked over the chalkboard menu but after this pretend decisioning shook my head no, then confidently ordered the stew—the name of which I cannot recall now but which I was able to repeat because it was painted on the outside of the restaurant window—even though I did not see it listed on the chalkboard. The patronne opened her mouth slightly but said nothing, an uncomfort dropping over her face. She looked at Geneviève, who after a moment spoke rapidly, jokingly, with the patronne, the only word I understood being "visitor." The patronne nodded and went off to the kitchen. When she had gone, Geneviève said to me, "But it is still Lent. Until tomorrow." And when I looked at her blankly she said, "No meat." I still said nothing, and she added, trying to be helpful, I think, "Not here, anyway." She could tell I was not only confused but embarrassed. Her face softened and she said kindly, "Yes, of course. How difficult. Keeping track. Crossing borders. So exciting. But yes, difficult. I can only imagine."

7 December

Geneviève and I passed our suppertime in the nearly empty restaurant speaking German when the patronne was not within hearing, Geneviève trying again to describe where she had gone and what she had seen in Berlin. By the way, Maître, a place I have never been, Berlin. I mean, before now. Though I never said so to Geneviève. And she never asked—I was German, which she seemed to think meant that I must know Berlin, where else was there? The conversation had to keep switching between German and French, depending on when the patronne was near and also whether Genève could make herself understood to me, and finally we switched permanently to French when some people sat at a table near us. With the jumping back and forth between languages, and the topic of nightclubs and fashions and famous Berlin sights, we began enjoying ourselves, laughing together at her nonsense words and upside down sentences, and her poking at my funny ways of pronouncing French. By the time we left the restaurant we were both more relaxed in each other's company than any time before.

"I want to take you somewhere," she said when we were outside. This was a surprise because in the summer our visits together had always ended after an evening meal, with Genève getting into a taxi going back to the 16th and me gesturing vaguely that I was headed in another direction. "A very different Paris," she added about our destination that evening, with a hint of mystery and sparkle. It occurred to me that scrounging for food at the Bastille street market and staying above Miriam's bordel and climbing over rooftops to escape the police were already plenty enough different for me, but I did not say that to Genève.

She led me back up the hill to the neighborhood of steep narrow streets we had passed through on our way from the church to the restaurant. It was dark now, the lights on in the little bars that dotted the streets, and that was what made it more familiar, what helped me remember. That this was the district where I had gone with Henri and his friends from the foreign section that first night after I had met him, to the tiny bal musette music bar, where I had made the blunder of offering a drink to the girl I danced with, and wound up fleeing out the door. Genève and I passed by that very place, I think, but she was headed a few streets away.

Where she took us was a music bar something like the one that I had been in with Henri but with a different feel, larger but darker, more upper style—no lights strung across the ceiling, no cheap papier-mâché decorations. There was a bandstand but no musicians yet—it was still early in the evening for Paris nightlife—and only one couple standing at the bar, a few others sitting at tables, talking quietly, having drinks. When we settled at a table, Genève looked around the room and said that she had been told that everything in this place happened late. I resisted asking what she meant by "everything" and instead said, "You know, I have a little experience of these places myself." She leaned closer, her eyes widening. "Not this place," I continued, "but another, nearby." "Where?" she wanted to know. "Which one?" I told her I did not know the name but it had java music and a packed crowd of dancers. She looked at me from a different angle, then said maybe we should order a drink. I said, "Fine. But who is buying?" She sat upright and seemed ready to be offended, until I said in a serious voice, "Well, I happen to know that in these places buying someone a drink means you want something from them." She stared at me—with what thoughts and feelings I had no idea. "But," I said with a sudden smile, "we make our own rules. Right?"

I went to get us drinks. There was something about the woman working behind the bar. She had hair almost as short as Genève's, combed straight backwards and held in place with pomade, and wore a collared white shirt and dark necktie. She gave me a bit of a cautious look-over, and stared across the room at Genève, then seemed to decide something and loosened, asking what I would like. I ordered the cocktails that Genève had named and paid for them with money she had just given me, which was a good thing because just the two drinks cost more than all I had.

When we had taken a sip of the drinks, Genève looked around the room and asked what I thought. I could not tell what about the place she meant, but I peered through the dark at the stylish leather booths and barstools, the soft electric lights behind shell-shaped glass mounted high up on the walls, and at the other people, who were far better and more stylishly dressed than where Henri had taken me— dark smooth suits and silky dresses instead of rough jackets and print smocks. All the men wore neckties but none of them wore a hat. As I adjusted to the dark, my eyes kept returning to a young man at a far table, who finally I realized was actually a young woman, with short hair and a dark man's jacket not unlike Genève's Berlin style. It was strange for me to realize—and perhaps what Genève was hoping for when she asked what I thought—but she and I, together, seemed to fit in this place, this dark drinking place on the left side of the river. Not something I had experienced very often in Paris, fitting in. What an odd place for it.

Very nice, I told her, and she sat back satisfied. Or maybe relieved. She suggested that we work more on her German, which she reminded me we had been neglecting. That caused me to look around the room again. "As long as there are so few people," she said, then added, "anyway, in here I do not think they would mind." I had no idea why not—after all, this was still Paris, and a Paris fearing war from the Reich—but there was no one near us so we began speaking German again. This time I acted more like a teacher, asking her to describe her Switzerland school—as an exercise, I told her. At first she liked the idea and we began to have one of our zig-zag conversations, with her trying to express herself in German and me asking questions about what she meant to say. But soon she lost her good mood, no longer wanted to talk about the school, it was boring, she said, of no interest, already the past—she had only two months more there before she would leave the place for good. So I found myself telling her instead about my own boarding school—the yeshiva in Frankfurt, Maître, though I did not say that, and invented details about the place as I went along, making it sound like some German boys' version of her Swiss place for rich girls. Telling her these tales was partly to give her the sense that we shared something. Other than our same height. And build. And at that point, the length of our hair. But thinking back on it now, it was also because of the relief, the release, of the first time saying more than a few words about myself—even if only half true—to Genève. To anyone, actually. Since I had been in Paris. Going on two years.

After a while Genève looked around at the people who had slowly begun to fill the room, then turned back to me and said it was now late enough and there was somewhere else she wanted us to go. At that point I probably would have agreed to go anyplace with her— except perhaps another church—despite the late hour. But that was also the problem, the hour. Because I was due soon to meet Henri at Citroën Javel for our night of delivering food. And I still had to travel half way across the city to get there. Of course, the strikers who handled the food could get on just fine without me. They would not even notice whether I was there. But Henri would. And that mattered. So after a brief moment, not so much weighing my thoughts as reading the feelings in my body, I told Genève that I was sorry but I had an appointment.

"An appointment? So late?" she wondered out loud, and I could see on her face that she immediately regretted this failure to remain, what, Not bothered? Sophisticated? Without knowing whether I was saying it for her advantage or mine, I answered with something very much like what she had said earlier—"Well, things happen late in Paris." She regained her balance and said, Yes, the place where she wanted to take me did not even open until late, which was why we had come to this other place first. Also, she said, she had wanted to make sure things would be all right with me in such a place.

I could see that she was disappointed and maybe even a bit put off at my leaving her, but that was tamped down, I think, by what I sensed was a new respect for me—that I had been before to a bal musette and even knew their code of drink buying—and an almost jealous curiosity that I now had somewhere to go, without her, at such a late hour.

"What about tomorrow?" I asked, thinking that later that night I could let Henri know that I would miss the following night's Citroën work.

She thought for a moment, then made a sharp intake of her breath that by then I knew meant a negative. "This is the last night," she said. "Then Easter."

"Well, maybe next week?"

"I will be back in Switzerland," she reminded me in a cool, slightly scolding voice, then turned to squarely face me, as if we were in some kind of contest. I did not know what to say, or whether I wanted to win or lose.

"Alors, Hersch," she finally broke the spell, "à la prochaine"—"until next time." One of those many French ways to say goodbye. But one that at least gives an expecting that there will be a next time. Or so I believed. Hoped. I remember, because I thought about it all the way over to the Citroën factories.

I got to Javel a bit earlier than the usual time and waited for Henri by the bus stop a few blocks from the edge of the factories. He arrived soon after, wearing the same worried face I had left him with that morning. When he saw me, though, he stepped out of his darkness long enough to tease me about my handsome clothes. And my necktie, that I had forgotten to take off. I quickly stuffed it into my pocket.

When we turned the last corner and the factory buildings came into view, we both stopped. The gates were all wide open, no strikers standing guard. There were only a few people in the yards outside the buildings, moving slowly and each seeming unconnected to any of the others. Here and there workers carrying small bundles were trickling out of buildings and, without looking around or talking, heading to the nearest gate and out into the night. One torn red flag dangled from a pipe high up on the nearest building. All the other flags and banners had disappeared.

Henri showed no change in expression. "As I heard," he said, and we walked onto the factory grounds.

Just inside we saw Morel, one of the workers Henri had known before and who had been friendly to both of us—especially after our beating from the Doriots—as we worked with him distributing food. We went over and greeted him.

Morel did not return our greeting, just said, "So, you know?"

Henri told him that there was word on the street that some deal had been made with all the auto companies, but no one outside seemed to know the details.

"Or in here, either," Morel snarled. "Because the great shits refuse to tell us."

Excuse my language, Maître, but that was the sort of word he used—not meaning the auto companies or the government but his own syndicat. And the Party.

Morel did not exactly explain what had happened—and anyway I could not follow much of his choppy worker French—as much as he cursed at bits and pieces of it. When he left us after a few minutes, Henri said, "It is worse than I thought," then explained to me the main things Morel had told him. The central syndicat bureau, under pressure from the Party, had made a deal with all the auto companies and the government to end the strike, but without asking the workers themselves. There was to be only a sliver of a wage raise, and the local syndicat men would no longer have any say about work conditions on the factory floor. Also no more 40 hours week, which was the most important thing workers had won during the huge strikes of '36 and the Front Populaire. During this strike that had just ended, Henri told me, the metal workers had offered to go past the 40 hour limit if the work was for national defense and if at least some small armaments would go to the Spanish republicans. But the deal between the central syndicat bureau and the companies had turned this completely on its head—now workers would have to put in more than 40 hours in any factory that did any defense work, anytime the owners decided, but with no mention of Spain, and even if the extra work itself had nothing to do with defense. So for example, Henri explained, a small part of these Javel Citroën factories made special army vehicles—defense work. So under this new contract, Citroën could order any of the factory's workers to put in over 40 hours even if all their hours were spent producing the fancy Traction Avant autos which the factory also made, and which by the way none of the workers themselves could afford. The worst of it all, though—as Morel had kept repeating—was that the syndicat and the Party had done of all of this behind the strikers' backs. "Salauds!"—"Bastards!"—Morel had finally spat.

"There is someone I need to talk with," Henri said. "Come on." We went into the building where I had spotted Henri coming out the night before. There were only a few people inside, and no one paid us any mind. We walked down a long side corridor that led to some stairs, then up two floors to a landing with a series of small rooms closed off from the factory floor below. The door was open to one of the rooms. Inside was the older man I had seen talking to Henri the night before, along with another man. And Rose. They saw us and, after a few words among the three of them, waved for us to come in. Or at least, for Henri to. But Henri said, "Here we go," and we both went in.

Henri sat down at a table across from the two men. Rose was

sitting slightly off to the side and behind the men. I leaned against the wall by the door.

"So, have you decided?" the older man asked Henri, looking at me for just a second before choosing to ignore me.

"First, is it true?" Henri's question carried an accusing tone.

The older man—who was the head metal workers syndicat official for all of the Citroën Javel factories, Henri told me later—glanced at the other man, who was there from the Party, then over at Rose, who I knew from the summer before was important with the confederation of syndicats. First moving his head side to side as if he was not certain he would answer, the older man went into an explanation about the whats and whys of ending the strike, which sounded like a prepared speech but which was too fast and full of words I did not know, and after the first few bits of it I did not try to follow. Mostly I watched Henri and occasionally peeked at Rose. She said nothing during the older man's tale about the strike deal, her face a mask. Neither did the Party man speak, though his expression was clear, a defying challenge.

After the syndicat man finished his speech about the strike, he answered—or from what I could read in Henri's following words and tone, responded to without answering—several questions from Henri. Then there were a few moments silence, and the older man said to Henri, "So, I ask again. Have you decided?"

They were offering Henri to be an official member of the metal workers syndicat. It had come on Rose's recommendation, it seemed, based on Henri's work with the foreign section during the Expo labor wars, and with support from the metal workers who got to know Henri during this Citroën strike, particularly his return to the streets again after the Doriots had thrown him into the Seine. It was a great opening for Henri, a chance to be an official part of this powerful syndicat—not just in some foreigners' section hoping to cling onto its side—and nearly a guarantee of skilled well-paid work for life. Getting into the syndicat was extremely difficult unless you were born to a family that was already part of it. Henri's parents, I think I told you, were not originally from France, so even though Henri was born in Paris, this was a rare thing he was being offered. It came, though, with another attachment—he would have to join the Party, whose section of the metal workers syndicat was the one opening this door and which was the reason the other man was there.

All this I learned from Henri on our way back east that night. But the final part of the meeting I heard and understood for myself. During the syndicat man's speech and his sort of discussion with Henri, my thoughts had drifted off. First back to Genève. Then to the warm company of Abraham and Chawa at their Friday night meal—so different from the cold calculatings of these men—that I had skipped that night. Then to my parents, and my brother and sister, who were especially in my mind every Friday night, and that night even more so—it was the first night of the Passover holiday, Maître, a time of special family closeness when I was growing up. But I was snapped back to the room when I heard Henri say, "And what about him?" as he turned and looked me in the eye for a moment. "What do you have for him?"

Rose shifted uncomfortably—she still had not said a word—and the syndicat man went into a roundabout explanation, a lot of "Well" and "You see," and finally "That is something quite different."

Henri interrupted, telling the man that I had done the same work as him, had been just as devoted to the strike, and on top of that was as clever as anyone he knew. "Ask Rose," he said, putting her on a spot that I could see she did not want.

The syndicat man did not bother to look at Rose but started into another blather.

Henri interrupted. "And that?" he turned and pointed at the gash on my brow. "This far from losing an eye. Or worse. For the strike. So, what is that worth? Not a place in the syndicat itself, yes of course I know. But something. In this huge place, surely something."

"Alors"—"Well"—the syndicat man raised his hands, palms up, as if he was helpless.

"And I understand he has no papers," the Party man put in.

"No, but you could do something about that," Henri insisted. "If you wanted."

Now the syndicat man had enough. "Enfin, mon ami, il n'est pas des nôtres," he said, glancing at me—"In the end, my friend, he is not one of ours."

And to make it stronger, it seemed, the Party man put it slightly different, his stress on the last word. "Il n'est pas nous."—"He is not us."

Henri again began to protest but the Party man cut him off. "Get it in your head, comrade," he said, leaning forward and punching his thick forefinger onto the table top with every phrase. "There are only so many places here. This is not some sewing shop." His eyes darted toward me as he said this, then looked back at Henri. "This is Citroën. We are Citroën. Which means we are France."

8 December

I could not sleep when I returned to Rue Martel late that night and as soon as it was light I went out again. I wandered around for a few hours, then headed to the Pletzl to get some soup at the Sportclub Aurore but there was no midday food because they would be having a Passover holiday meal that evening instead. I was too tired and unspirited to wait there all afternoon, so I headed back toward Faubourg Saint Denis. On the way, I took a detour over to Miriam's place to see Sam but found that he had just left, I guessed to begin his work at Aux Belles Minettes, the fancy bordel—Lent did not matter there, I suppose. I did not know the people over there, had never been there, and so decided not to disturb Sam in case that would be a mistake they would mark against him. I wandered around a bit more, then in the late afternoon finally went back to Rue Martel, climbed the six flights of stairs to the attic, and fell asleep with my clothes on.

I heard voices in the night and got up to look in the hallway. It turned out to be people getting ready and leaving for church, Easter mass, which was held late at night, I do not know why—perhaps you do, Maître. I fell back to sleep but was wakened again sometime later by more noise in the hallway. I turned over to go back to sleep but then heard the noise more clearly, someone loud-whispering, "H? H, are you there?" It was Henri, who knew where I was staying but not exactly which of the unmarked doors under the eaves. I let him in.

He had come to say goodbye. He was leaving for the Spanish war. He did not know where, exactly, or who with, but said it did not matter. He would sort it out when he got there.

I received several letters from Henri when I was in the Paris jail, Maître, after the shooting—he had learned from the newspapers where to find me—so I knew that he had survived his time in Spain. And I know from his final letter to me that he was still free in '39 after the French police had rounded up his parents, along with many other Red or sort-of-Red foreigners, and sent them to the French camps. But whether he remained free I do not know, or where he is now. That night before he left for Spain, sitting next to me on my pallet at Rue Martel, was the last time I ever saw him.

Yours sincerely,
Herschel

P.S. Citroën, Maître. I happened to mention it to Uncle Abraham one time—the auto, I mean, not what had happened to me there.

"Yes, it was founded by a Levy," he told me. "Whose mother was a Kleinmann. From Warsaw. Did you know?"

9 December 1941
Moabit

Maître,

The news from home that spring and summer kept getting worse. I suppose that comes as no surprise to you.

In their letters my parents mostly just sent their love and did not complain. But my sister Berthe also wrote to me and told me things that my parents would not, about how my father's work had become less and less and how his few customers could afford to pay so little. Then there were the Reich decrees. My father became terribly worried by a new law that demanded all non-Aryans to register their assets with the authorities, which for him meant his sewing machine. He feared it would mean a new tax, or even that his machine would be taken away, but he did his duty and went to the police station to report it. They laughed at him—it turned out that only assets worth more than 5,000 Reichsmarks had to be registered. Then they stopped laughing, accused him of mocking the law, and threw him out onto the pavement. The fall broke his arm. He could not work for weeks.

From then on things went downward quickly. For a long time my family knew that just being on the streets in the wrong district of the city could be a problem, depending on how you looked and sounded, but now such troubles were coming to them in their own neighborhood. Local shops, and the people in them, were being attacked, windows broken, curse words and pictures of men hanging by ropes were painted on the buildings. In Munich, the great synagogue was burned. Then the police began to arrest people—thousands, so it said in the Paris Yiddish newspapers—for "race pollution," which had something to do with non-Aryans and Aryans mixing together but people did not know what this meant exactly, the news reports were uncertain and no one was ever properly told, but anyway it landed these polluting people in prison camps. Well, the non-Aryans, at least.

Soon after came the most terrifying for my family—the Social

Action law. Was that the name? Anyway, a new law that said any non-Aryan—or perhaps it said anyone with a not-German passport, I am not certain—who ever had even the slightest police trouble could now again be picked up and sent to prison. And from then on my family lived in awful fear for my brother Marcus. Five years before, you see, when he was a boy still in school, he and some friends had been caught in a biergarten, drinking up the dregs left in the bottom of steins. The biergarten people had not made a big fuss, had just kicked them out, but there happened to be two policeman outside and they took down the names of all the boys before letting them go. Except for Marcus. Because his name was Grynszpan, they brought him to the police station to check his papers. They held him there, overnight, until they got around to notifying my worried parents, who went to collect him. And were told by the police that they had registered Marcus in their criminal records. At age 14. For sneaking sips of beer, Maître. In Germany.

Well, still, this was nearly nothing, and it was years ago, the family had almost forgotten it. Except when Berthe and my mother saw what happened to old Herr Abramowitz, a neighbor on Burgstrasse, a widower who lived alone in a tiny room. And who had one time complained—two years or so earlier, just before I had left home—about a tram fare collector who had given him short change and then called him names when Abramowitz protested. Abramowitz had refused to leave it alone, and a few stops down the line had seen a policeman and called to him. The policeman listened to them both, then arrested Abramowitz—for insulting the municipality, or something like that—and he had to pay a fine. Then, in that spring of '38 two years later, they came for him. Two policemen went to his room. Berthe and my mother were coming home just then and saw them dragging the old man out of his building. When Berthe asked what was happening, one of the policeman said, "Enemy of the Reich," then put his hand on his baton, adding, "And you?" Berthe said nothing more and they left her alone. But took Abramowitz away. Which made the family recall Marcus and the biergarten. And to imagine the worst.

Berthe told me that my mother was even planning a trip to Poland, to Radomsk, to see relatives there and to find out if it might be possible for them all to move there, to the only place their passports might allow them to go. My mother did finally visit there later that summer, but learned that there would be little chance for my father to find work there and even less so for Berthe and Marcus, who spoke no Polish. There were also the pogroms, which the Poles were again becoming so fond of.

And no, Maître, before you ask, I do not know what relatives she visited in Radomsk. Other than the ones where the Reich has already searched.

All of these fears and sorrows were pressing on me as well, Maître—built up from the weeks and months of my parents' cautious letters and Berthe's censored but still plainer speaking ones. Also from the Paris newspaper reports that filled in some of the blank spots, and from the worrying stories that were spreading by mouth through Paris east. It was all burrowing under my skin like the scabies, and multiplying there with my own Paris struggle that seemed to have no movement, or direction. Only weight.

10 December

For me the rest of that spring of '38 and into the summer was a blank of waiting. For something to happen, anything, but most of all for papers. Abraham had helped me applicate for them more than a year before but still the papers did not, would not, come. They might have been at Quai d'Orsay or Hôtel de Beauvau or Quai des Orfèvres—the different ministries, Maître, great mysterious names that imagined to me Mount Olympus and the pyramids. Or perhaps the papers were at the giant central Préfecture de Police where Abraham and I had gone when I first arrived in Paris. And that was part of the worry that ate at my insides. Who was deciding? What mattered? Who even knew? Not that it would have made any difference. We had no connections—Bernard's favorite word—there was nothing we could do. But it was a special misery of its own, the not knowing where or what or who was holding my life off the ground.

Twice that spring I went with Uncle Abraham back to the Valley of Tears—the entrance courtyard to the préfecture—to try to learn something. We first chose a Saturday morning, when we thought the crowds might be less because of the Sabbath—not Sabbath for the French, Maître, but for most of those we imagined were bringing their pleas there. We were wrong. We got there at eight in the morning and the queue already stretched across the entire courtyard, the sounds of Italian and Spanish burbling far more than Yiddish among the crowd. We never even reached the first information counter before the doors shut at noon, not to open again until Monday afternoon. It rained on us the whole time.

Later we went to the préfecture on a weekday and queued before dawn. We finally got to the first counter in midmorning, and to the desk at a particular bureau by four in the afternoon, only to be told that any decision would come to us not from there but through the 10th arrondissement, which was the residence district of Uncle Abraham, my "person of responsibility." So, a week later Abraham took more unaffordable time away from his work and we went to the marie—the mayor's hall—for the 10th. After a two-hour wait, which by then seemed positively speeding, we were told that to learn of any decision we would have to go to the police there in the 10th, to one of their local stations. Which was in a small street nearby, Passage du Désir. As I write that name, Maître, I wonder if you will believe me.

From then on we checked regularly at this little police station. Into the early summer they still gave us no news.

I had returned to making leather soles in the attic at Rue Martel—each day alone in the dark little room, hour after hour, but I had nothing else—when I heard from Bernard. He told me he had finally sorted out a way for me to be useful to him—without bringing himself too much risk, which was the part he did not say. You see, Maître, this was a time of great fear and confusion in Paris, that spring and summer of '38. The French were passing new decrees faster than anyone could keep track, and now people who were irrégulier—without a proper visa or residence papers, or at least papers in process, like me—were being picked off the streets, jailed, and deported. If there was nowhere to send them, they simply stayed in prison, or were put in one of the camps the French had built around the country, mostly in the south. Also, anyone caught working without the proper permit got the same treatment—arrest and deporting or jailing—even if they had France residence papers. And for many there was the endless bad dream called, upsidedownly, horribly, "sursis"—"reprieve." It began with arrest and then, if there was nowhere to deport after weeks or months in jail, a temporary release—the reprieve—with orders to leave the country. But of course the arrest itself meant that a proper visa to go anywhere else—already little more than a fantasy—would be impossible. So, then it was a matter of trying to survive in hiding until hunger or a police informer or the crazedness of staying in a tiny room with five or ten other people drove a reprieved person onto the streets again and oftentimes quickly to another arrest—the police were by then constantly checking papers of anyone on the streets they thought did not look and sound true French—followed by more time in jail before another sursis and then the whole awful circle going round and round without end. Except for suicide, Maître. Which broke the circle for more than a few that spring and summer.

All this also made difficulties for the many workshop owners like Bernard who used mostly foreign workers. Under the new decrees, employers themselves were breaking the law if they hired people without proper papers. Of course, the real French were not worried about that, no one was going to arrest them. I was not certain whether that included Bernard. Neither was he. Bernard took precautions, I think I told you, so that he was not officially the owner of the two large piecework ateliers he ran near the Gare de l'Est train station, the ones crammed with recent arrivals, almost none of them with work papers. But even for the owners who had no real fear of their own arrest, the jailing of so many workers was causing serious problems. On any given day the workshops could not tell how many empty stools there would be, how many silent machines, because of arrests during the night, or workers having just escaped arrest and gone into hiding. Even in the main atelier directly above his fancy Au Courant Dame shop, where he checked that his workers had permits, Bernard was losing high quality tailors—a work permit might not be renewed, a permit or visa might expire or be revoked or was never truly proper in the first place, or a worker's papers might be in order but not a husband's or a wife's, and suddenly someone would disappear. So, Bernard was now struggling not only to keep the big piecework ateliers running, filling his orders and making his deadlines, but also to manage at the main atelier, above Au Courant Dame, where the tailors made his high fashion things, and his reputation.

And that was where he finally found me useful. When there was a rare work opening at Bernard's high-end atelier, he filled it by promoting someone from one of the other workshops, someone who had not only shown top skills and proper documents but also the passable basic French he required of all the workers there. Did I tell you Bernard insisted that his workers, almost all of them foreigners, must speak only French at the Au Courant Dame atelier? So, when considering new people for work there, Bernard would interview them in French. And sometimes for going deeper into their backgrounds he would call on his rusty Yiddish, which he could understand better than he could speak. There were plenty of Spanish and Italian tailors he could have chosen from also, Paris was full of them fleeing the Spain war or Mussolini, but he did not trust them, Bernard—all the Spaniards and Italians who had come to France were Reds, according to him. You see, Maître, ever since the strikes of '36, Bernard had more carefully chosen the people who worked at the main atelier, questioning them closely about their backgrounds and their attitudes. If they had politics, Maître, any politics, he did not want them there.

And so. That spring Bernard needed to fill several spots in his high quality atelier, but with the rope tightening for foreigners it was more difficult than usual. The two tailors Bernard wanted most to bring over from the other workshops were German. And Gentiles. You see, all kinds of people were fleeing the Reich by then—communists and socialists and syndicalists and democrats. Also types with odd views or different ways of living. Well, I suppose you know that. Anyway, since these two tailors spoke only very simple French, and of course no Yiddish, Bernard wanted someone to translate the questions he would put to them, and especially their answers. Someone Bernard could trust. He decided that was me. God gives a fool legs, and lets him run.

The first tailor Bernard and I spoke to was from Berlin. He was a young man, maybe late 20s, long straight blond hair swept back from a long thin face on top of a long, thin body, and wearing a beautifully tailored jacket of a quality I am sure Bernard noticed, a very stylish but completely different cut from what I saw in Paris—a recent Berlin style, I suppose. It reminded me of the jacket Genève had worn that last day I had seen her.

The man said that he had worked as a costume designer for a famous stage theater in Berlin, as well as for a certain cabaret, where he also was a singer. The young man spoke some French but immediately there were many words he could not find, so he gave me the German and I translated for Bernard into French, or Yiddish when I did not know the French. From those jobs, the man explained, he had learned to make everything, from high fashion gowns to easy-off costumes—which took me several more questions to understand was for some kind of burlesque which involved men, but which I translated for Bernard as "clown acts." Bernard seemed satisfied with all this, even impressed, I thought—though he tried not to show it—by mention of the Berlin theater, a name Bernard seemed to know. He had already seen the man's high quality skills from his work at one of the piecework ateliers, which was why Bernard was considering him in the first place, so he quickly moved on to the other kinds of things he wanted to know. Had the man been in any labor syndicats in Berlin, any politics?

"Politics?" the man said immediately, raising his brow. "Who do you think would have wanted me?"

I translated and, although it puzzled me, Bernard seemed to like the answer. I do not think he expected completely truthful replies from the man, or from anyone he interviewed—though Bernard can be blind, he is certainly not stupid. But still he wanted to hear what the man would say for himself, and to watch him closely as he said it. Then Bernard asked an even more direct question. So, if he had no politics, why had he left Germany?

The man's forehead wrinkled and his eyes narrowed as if to get a clearer view of the person who could ask such a thing. "But, the way things had become," he shook his head. "The theater said it no longer needed me. And the cabaret, my cabaret, the Reich stamped it immoral and closed it down. So, there was nowhere for me to be."

I translated as, "There was no longer enough theater work there, and work is all I want."

Bernard nodded at these words, and at the suddenly very serious face of the young Berliner. He started work right away above Au Courant Dame. And had a smile for me when afterward I passed through the atelier a few times on my way to see Bernard.

Later that day Bernard and I met with the second German tailor, a very different sort. He was middle age, with a hard face over a square jaw and thick neck, his dark eyes in a permanent squint, and wearing a rough brown jacket and trousers that were no one's idea of style. He had tailored for years in a factory that made both men's and women's clothing, not high fashion but very good quality. Bernard knew the company name, knew that the man was telling the truth about the workmanship there.

Then Bernard began his more difficult questions—Had the man belonged to any labor syndicats, and what did he think of them? I repeated this in German but added at the end, as if it was still part of the question, "Be careful how you answer." The man looked in my eyes, trying quickly to read me, then replied, "Until a few years ago, every one of us in the factory was part of the syndicat. But all that is over. At least, for now."

I translated loosely for Bernard, changing "a few years" ago to "many years," and saying that in those days everyone in the factory had been required to be in the syndicat, but not any longer. I left out the "At least, for now."

Bernard then asked the same kind of question he had earlier asked the young man—So, if you had a good job in a good factory, why did you leave Germany?

The man hesitated, again trying to read what he could from my face, then answered. "The factory now makes uniforms for the army.

And the Wehrmacht decided that certain of us were not wanted anymore. After that, it was the same answer everywhere else I tried—the list of forbidden names moved faster than I did."

I translated this for Bernard as "The army took over the factory to make uniforms, they had no need to pay high skill tailors, and other places had no jobs."

The tale of the Wehrmacht struck a note with Bernard—he was no admirer of the growing Reich army—and he needed this German man's skills, so despite the man's very limited French and his past in the syndicat, Bernard surprised me by giving him the job. After the man had left the interview, Bernard said to me, "Well, he speaks no Yiddish and his French is poor, so how much harm can he do me?"

Bernard gave me good money for my translating that day—25 francs, if I remember—but in the months that followed I heard nothing more from him, despite the fact that the new decrees were disappearing people from his big piecework ateliers so fast that he constantly needed to fill spots. You see, Maître, Bernard already had Yiddish speaking "greeters" working for him at the train stations—Gare du Nord and Gare de l'Est, where most new immigrants from the east arrived—sniffing out people who had tailoring skills and who could be put to work for long hours and little pay in these big ateliers that were located, not accidentally, right there by the stations. And since there was no shortage of Yiddish-speaking tailors staggering their way into Paris, Bernard had no particular need for me and my German language—"unfortunately," he would say to me when from time to time I would go to see him, with a tilt of his head that was supposed to show his regret.

So, in the end, speaking with those two German tailors was the only time Bernard called on me for translating. Or for any other work. Later I wondered whether perhaps he had understood some of the German after all.

Yours truthfully,
Herschel

11 December 1941
Moabit prison

Maître,
   Things suddenly changed again. Not for the better.
   This was how it happened. How it often happened. Sometime that June, Sidney disappeared. Sidney the cutter and machiniste, who had worked five years for Abraham and Chawa. He left Maison Albert in the middle of the day to pick up some fabric. And did not return. After two days Berenice the seamstress went out to Clichy, a low rents district at the north edge of Paris where Sidney lived with his wife Lili and two young children. Berenice found Lili and the children huddled in their small room, red-eyed and terrified. Sidney had not come home, Lili did not know where he was, she had heard nothing, knew nothing. The logical thing was to check with the police but the most logical also seemed the most dangerous. You see, Maître, Sidney had certainly not just run off, but if they had arrested him for being irregular—he had a temporary visa that he kept managing to get renewed, but Abraham and Chawa had not asked him about it for a long time—did that mean they would also lock up his wife and children? Might the police—Lili asked Berenice, the only person she had seen since Sidney disappeared—even come looking for them? Should they leave their room and stay somewhere else? If they could find someone to take them in?
   Berenice had full proper France residence and work papers, so she decided to brave the local police station and ask there about Sidney. He was registered as resident of the district, so perhaps they would have been notified if something official had happened to him. But the police there knew nothing. So they said. Though they now knew Berenice—they made a record of her name and address, as a person who had inquired about Sidney. Just procedure, they told her.
   Berenice reported all this to Chawa and Abraham, who in the meantime had checked with the place where Sidney had gone to fetch

the fabric. Yes, they told Abraham, Sidney had been there, nothing seemed out of the ordinary, he had chatted for a minute then left, to return to Maison Albert as far as they knew. Without having to be asked, they told Abraham that if somehow the police came there asking questions, of course they would not mention Maison Albert.

Abraham went around the neighborhood and spoke to a few people he felt comfortable with. Eventually he heard from a street vendor that she had seen a man picked off the street by the police on that afternoon several days before, when Sidney had disappeared, and that the man had been carrying a large package. But this woman could not describe either the man or his package—these arrests were by then so common that people paid little attention unless it was someone they knew.

While Abraham was out, Chawa brought me down from the attic to sit with her and Berenice and tell me what had happened. We waited for Abraham with ants in our legs, as the French say, not only to find out about Sidney but also in worry that, under the newest decrees, Sydney's trouble with the police might also come back to Maison Albert. Abraham returned and told us what he had heard, and we talked over what we would say if the police arrived and questioned us—that yes, Abraham and Chawa knew Sidney, once in a while he sold fabric to Maison Albert, but no, he did not work here. It was a story to protect not only Abraham and Chawa but also Sidney himself, in case they were accusing him of working without a proper fiche.

A day or two later Abraham said that he was going to the local police station there in the 10th, to learn what he could. But Chawa stopped him, reminding him what had happened to Berenice at the Clichy station—the police would connect Sidney to Maison Albert simply through Abraham's inquiring. It was too much risk. We would just have to wait. And not know. Which by then was the way of things.

Abraham now had to take up all of the work that Sidney used to do, on top of the marking and stitching and finishing he and Chawa and Berenice had always done. I helped them, not with the tailoring itself, which I did not have the skills for, but with other things. I appeared at Maison Albert each morning and they gave me simple errands they no longer had time for, such as going to the bakery and greengrocer and bateau-lavoir—the laundry boat on the river. But they also gave me more important things that Sidney had done, such as making client deliveries and picking up fabrics, which not only took more learning but was what Sidney was doing on the day he disappeared, and so was somewhat nerve making for me. Abraham and Chawa schooled me not only on the tasks but also on what to tell the police if they stopped me while I was carrying materials back to the workshop, or finished pieces to customers. I was not working, I was to tell them, just helping family—the uncle who was my "person of responsibility" as it said right there on my police receipt paper, which I always carried with me. And even though this was the truth, each time before they let me go out on workshop business Abraham and Chawa would drill me on exactly what to say and how to say it.

One morning about two weeks after Sidney disappeared, Chawa asked me to go to the crémerie for her. She gave me some money and told me what she wanted, then put a few more francs in my other hand. Without her saying so, I knew this other money was for me. Part of me did not want to take it—things had been very difficult for them for a while, and more so now that Sidney was gone, they were working much harder for less. But with me running errands and doing chores for them, I could do less of the shoe leather work, which was no longer paying me much of anything, and so I almost never had more than a few sous in my pocket. Also by then I had figured that my parents would be able to send me nothing more. Nor did I want them to. Instead I should be sending them money, I thought, because who knew how bad things really were for them? So, I took the money from Chawa. It made her happy. But me it pained, each time.

Chawa then handed me an envelope and asked if later that day I would take it to Sidney's wife Lili, in Clichy. The envelope was closed but I was almost certain from the feel that it held franc notes. It contained a short letter to Lili, Chawa told me, saying that she should contact Chawa and Abraham if she heard anything about Sidney, and that they would do whatever they could to help. The letter also said that the money was Sidney's earnings and that his work—though to be safe, she did not use the words "earnings" and "work" so plainly in the note, she told me—would be waiting for him when he returned.

Berenice gave me instructions on how to find the place in Clichy, and after a long Métro ride plus a sizeable walk I reached Sidney's room at the back of a shabby building in a warehouse district. I heard voices behind the door, but as soon as I knocked there was silence. I realized then that a surprise knock, without word that it was a neighbor or friend come to visit, could be a thing of terror, the very thing Lili must have been fearing since Sidney had gone missing. So I explained through the door who I was, and after a few moments of whispering, Lili opened it. She was a very thin, pale woman who I suppose was young—I remember Chawa teasing Sidney earlier that year when he turned 30—but who looked to be almost any age. Behind her in the dark room, two small children tried to hide themselves among the bedclothes of the room's one mattress.

Despite thinking of almost nothing else all the way over to Clichy, I did not know what to do or say when Lili opened the door, so from the hallway I just stuck out my hand with the envelope and said simply that it was from Chawa. Lili took it and opened it. Still in the doorway, she took out the folded letter and saw the francs inside. For several long moments she stared at the money in her hand, and at the unread note from Chawa, and silently began to weep. Standing there in the hallway I felt there was too much in her weeping for me to understand—or perhaps I just did not want to—and I hurried away down the stairs.

It was difficult when I told Chawa what had happened, what I had done, not even asking Lili if she had heard any word about Sidney. But Chawa did not scold. She kissed me on the forehead—just as my mother used to do—and said I had done fine.

Two weeks later Chawa again asked me to take an envelope to Clichy. This time she asked me to explain to Lili that the money in it was an advance on Sidney's work, for when he returned. And made it sound as if this was a perfectly normal thing that someone would do. That someone should do. My Tante Chawa, Maître.

In Clichy, Lili opened the door for me and with wide eyes but no words stepped aside for me to enter. Immediately she pulled a letter out of the pocket in her dress. It was from Sidney, in a France prison camp somewhere I had never heard of. The writing was very small, on a single sheet of paper, with some parts scratched out—I suppose by whatever police had read it before allowing it to be sent. I could barely make it out in the dim room, but he wrote that he had been arrested because his visa had expired and for working without a proper fiche, even though he had explained to the police that he did not have a job but merely bought fabric from barrow sellers, then used his tailor skills to make clothes that he sold at street markets. In the letter he asked Lili if she could send him some of his own clothes and some food that would survive travel through the post. No one, he wrote, had told him what would happen next.

"So," I managed to say and tried for a smile, "he is alive and well"— though of course nowhere did it say that he was well. "And this," I handed her the envelope of francs, "will help you send him something good." As I said it, I glanced around the tiny room—one small window black with soot, one oil lamp, no heat, no water, the smell of mold, kerosene, and a chamber pot, a room in Clichy like so many I had seen in Paris east—and realized that whatever small amount was in the envelope, it could not possibly be enough to send much to Sidney and also to feed Lili and her children for long. So to bring the only other hopefulness I could think of, I added the message from Chawa that Sidney's job would be waiting for him when he returned. Lili bowed her head—in thanks, or perhaps in doubt about my mention of Sidney's return—then quietly asked me if Abraham and Chawa were well, and Berenice, and when I told her yes, she answered good, good, and her voice faded away. We stood without speaking, and it was only then I noticed that she was holding my hand. She also noticed and, slowly, let go.

When I told Chawa and Abraham about the letter from Sidney, Abraham said that it was much as he expected. At least they had let him write to Lili, Chawa added. And to us, Abraham said. Chawa nodded. I did not understand, though, so Abraham explained.

Sidney's bothering to put in the letter what he had told the police—about buying fabric from unnamed barrow men and then selling homemade clothes at street markets—was a message to Abraham and Chawa that he had not told the police about Maison Albert, or about the people where Sidney had picked up the fabric. Which meant that the police would not be bothering any of them on Sidney's account. Abraham sent me right away to give the news to the fabric supplier. They should not carry the worry of a police visit because of Sidney, he said, even a minute longer than they need to.

Your note has just been given to me, Maître. I must say that it surprises me. Yes of course I am aware that the trial will soon be upon us, what do you think? We need to speed up, you say. To stay on the point, the why, of what I did. Tell all, you have always instructed me—but now hurry, you say. Neither one is simple, Maître. And leave no one out, you remind me. But most in particular, make certain to answer these questions, this typewritten list of questions, that you are asking. Or someone is asking.

Tomorrow, Maître. I am tired, it is night, I have finished my evening food. I need to sleep. I have nothing to do but think and sleep and write, but many days and nights I do not manage to sleep much, and when I do not, I cannot remember clearly and so cannot write clearly. But I will try again tomorrow. When I have rested. And had time to think. About what you are asking.

12 December

Did I ever work again for the Party, after the strike at Citroën Javel? The first question on your list. Well, your list, someone's list, whichever. The answer, Maître, is that I never worked for the Party. Not at Javel or anywhere else. I never said that I did. Those are your words, someone's words, not mine.

Then these questions about Henri. I believe I already told you that I do not know where he is. His rooming house at République? Well, I am sorry, Maître, but the address I cannot recall. It was not actually on Place République but behind it by a couple of blocks. Or more. Which street or direction, though, I do not remember. Besides, I do not know whether he lived there again after he returned from the Spain war. And Vladin? Is that how I spelled Henri's family name? Well, I suppose I might have gotten that wrong. With an F, perhaps? And an r in there somewhere, but not an l? Or another vowel? You see, Maître, Henri and I did not use family names between us when we spoke. And I had no occasion to see his name written. So, perhaps it should not be a great surprise if I have it wrong—after all, it has been three years now. Some details, surely you can understand, I might have difficulty recalling. Accurately, anyway. And I never was very good at spelling.

Next on the list—Did I have more contact with the Lazares? Does this mean the parents? Or the daughter? Well in fact, yes, both. I will tell you.

In late June of '38 Genève returned from Switzerland. Just in time. For me, I mean—the money she paid me for her lessons. She had written to me a few weeks earlier that when she got back to Paris she would again be keen to work on her German.

She set a meeting at the usual Alsace pâtisserie rendezvous spot and on that day, still with the very short hair, she walked in with a big smile and bouncing step. I might have told myself that it was because of seeing me again but I think it was mostly about her final release from prison, as she called her boarding school.

Earlier in the spring she had always been the one to choose where we spent our time together, but on this day I decided to surprise her with a plan of my own—which not accidentally would head off what I feared might be an immediate trip to some church or other. But I would not tell her what the plan was, and while we ate our pastries I said she should use her German to coax out of me where we would be going. I made a game of it—like the one parents play with bored children, with questions that begin "Is it animal, vegetable, or mineral?" It was good language training for her but soon she was beginning to get irritated. It was not the guessing itself that bothered her, I think, but the not knowing. I used her poor German to stretch out the questions and answers, but she ate her pastry quickly so that we could end the game and be on our way.

To travel west across Paris I led her to a bus, which I was used to instead of the more expensive Métro. As we got on, I got the sense that she had never been on a bus before. But she seemed to enjoy it, not only the view of the streets from higher up than in a taxi or private auto but also the casual bodies and conversations of the types who sat around us. And we were speaking French again—German in the crowd would not have been a good idea—which seemed to relax her. As we passed through Montparnasse, I pointed out and told her a bit about the famous cafés and bars I had come to know there, or at least know of from Sam, during my time living with him in Rachel's Saint Lambert room. Just as on the evening in the bar some months before, when I had told Genève that I had experience of the bals musettes, this description from me of these night spots was a surprise to her. Maybe impressed her a little. Which yes, was the idea.

When we got off the bus next to the Tour Eiffel her shoulders drooped in disappointment that the tourist tower should be our destination. I said nothing as I walked her straight past the tower heading south, then laughed when she looked back at it over her shoulder, wondering. She laughed also, realizing her mistake about what we were doing.

We continued south along the river until I knew we were only one street away, then I asked her whether she was good skater. She looked at me with a puzzled expression that made me a bit nervous—Did she think it silly? For children? Low class? But within a moment she grinned and said, "Is that what we are doing?" We rounded a corner and I said "Voila" and gestured toward the Vélodrome d'Hiver, where Henri and I had such a good time rollering the summer before.

"Oh, yes," Genève said, "some of the girls from the Allier, they did this last year, when they were here for the Exposition, my dancing troupe, do you remember? They said they had a wonderful time."

People were gathered around the building entrance but as we got closer I realized that these were not young people in high spirits who had come to skate but an older crowd, mostly men wearing collars and neckties and serious faces. Grim faces. Angry. At first I thought perhaps there might be a boxing match but when we reached the front I saw large posters that told me who they actually were. Doriots. A rally, with Jacques Doriot the man himself to be speaking. They had taken over the entire place for the day.

I groaned and said, "Not my favorites."

"Yes," she said, "petit bourgeois, the lot of them."

It was a phrase—petit bourgeois—I had first heard from Henri. And from both of them, Genève and Henri, in a voice full of—well, what exactly? Something not very kindly, to be sure, by either of them. But Henri and Genève seemed to me about as far apart as two young people could be—two French people, that is. So, I thought, did they even mean the same thing when they said it? And then I questioned to myself whether I understood what either of them meant. Which made me uncomfortably wonder again, as I walked alongside her, about who or what Genève thought I was.

We went a few blocks without speaking, to put some distance between us and the ugly crowd outside the Vel d'Hiv. Finally Genève stopped and turned, with what I can only describe as the most open face she had ever showed me.

"Écoute," she said—"Listen"—and immediately I pretend-scolded her to use her German. She smiled but continued in French.

"I did not know whether you would be there to meet me today," she said. "And even if you came, I was not certain how you would feel. About continuing. Not just the lessons, I mean, but the moving around Paris that we have done. The different kinds of Paris. So, in my doubt, I did not leave the whole evening free today—I am supposed to be back at my parents house for a supper. But now, well, can we make another rendezvous? Since it seems that you are pleased enough to see me." She smiled openly again, and then I realized what she truly meant—that until she had actually seen me again, she was the one uncertain about continuing.

We made an appointment for the coming Saturday, and she said that then it would be her turn for a surprise. She asked me to wear a collar and necktie, and instead of our usual afternoon time she set our meeting for eight in the evening, at a restaurant she named in the 5th, on the left side of the river. I took all this in without speaking, but I suppose with an uncomfortable look on my face because she laughed and told me not to worry, it most definitely was not going to be a church.

13 December

Restaurant de la Rive, or something like that. On Rue de Seine. A handsome place, at least compared to where I had ever been. And Genève being there made it more so. She had combed her short hair straight back from her forehead quite the way I did my own, and had on a wonderfully tailored, slightly cutaway long jacket, like a man's morning coat—finer fabric but nearly the identical blue-black color as the jacket I always wore when I saw her, the only decent one I had, which Abraham had made me. With it she wore a white shirt with a soft collar and a dark silk man's necktie. And trousers. Dark, striped trousers, Maître. Altogether it looked like what my lawyers wore under their robes when they appeared with me, later that year, in the Paris court. People stared at her on the street. She looked so different. And to my eyes, superb.

It was the most difficult meal of my life. Well, at least until I was in the Gestapo prison. Not because of Genève—she was in good spirits, and my problems at the table made her even more merry. I mean the meal itself was difficult. The actual food. I suppose you might be experienced in handling a whole artichoke, Maître. Well, not me. And escargots? Do you know what they are?

I saw the word artichoke on the menu and remembered it from the Lazares' garden party. So, I ordered it at the restaurant, thinking that it must be a high class sort of thing. And when Genève said that the restaurant prepared escargots beautifully and perhaps we should order some, I said yes of course, it sounds wonderful, why not—though I had no idea what they were.

It turned out that the artichoke in the restaurant was not the little cut up marinated pieces they had served in the Lazares' garden but the whole vegetable or whatever it is, cut lengthwise down the middle, a horrible green and purple thing with sharp pointy leaves, and what was I supposed to do with that? I could feel the sweat gathering under my arms as I stared at it and Genève chattered on about, well, I could not possibly remember now, something about Berlin and cabarets, no doubt. She was beginning to eat her own food and I heard just enough of what she said to make occasional small noises in reply, because I was fixed on the untouched artichoke that sat there getting stranger looking and uglier by the moment, until I was saved—or thought I was—by seeing a woman across the room also being served an artichoke and watching as she picked off a leaf with a tiny fork that I also had next to my plate, and dipped the leaf in a sauce they had served with it. I had the first leaf in my mouth, chewing it and beginning to gag, when I noticed that the woman at the other table had not actually put the whole leaf in her mouth but had just bitten into it, then put it down. Which I relievedly did with the horrible green lump that had formed in my mouth. Then I saw that Genève was staring at me with her own mouth open. Our eyes met and she laughed.

Just the fleshy part on the bottom of the leaf, she explained. Embarrassment flushed my face but then I realized she was not making fun of me but simply enjoying the fact that she had introduced me to a new experience. She said, "Yes, I can imagine these are strange if you are not used to them," and I was relaxed by her kindness. No, not kindness, Maître, not exactly, but an understanding that I was different, and a difference that did not offput or anger her but instead made her interested. At least, some part of it.

She happily instructed me through the rest of the artichoke eating—it got complicated again when I reached the insides, with one part you could eat but not another part, and anyway it does not fill you up, so I cannot understand why they bother. And not long after they cleared away that long struggle, the escargots arrived. Now I was completely befumbled. When I first saw them on the plate, I thought they were some kind of seafood, and it is against the ancient diet laws to eat fish that live in shells. Then I looked closer and realized actually what they were. So, what were the rules, I wondered, about something you cannot even imagine eating? I decided quickly that I could not be breaking a rule if I did not know that it existed—just as I had convinced myself about the saucissons, the cheap dried sausage, that everyone ate in Paris and that I knew very well was usually pork but not always, and so any particular time if I did not ask, I did not know, and so I ate it. My experience of those endless yeshiva debates turned out quite useful to me after all. Though not, I suppose, what they had in mind.

Food rules, though, was just the beginning of my escargot problem. Once I had decided to eat them, how was I supposed to do it? I watched Genève pick up a strange contraption the restaurant gave—it worked sort of like pliers, except backwards. She captured one of the shells with this gadget, then used a tiny fork to pull out the snail. Well, at least now I knew what to do. But knowing is not doing. My first try sent a slippery shell skidding off the plate toward me and over the edge of the table. Genève was working on a shell of her own and I think did not notice. I did not look around to find out if anyone else had seen. I managed to wrestle with the other escargots, and got through the rest of the meal without any more accidents. But I sat for an hour and a half with a snail in my lap, covered with my napkin.

Why am I telling you about all this food nonsense? Because you asked about the Lazares. Or, the list of questions asked about the Lazares. And to understand what happened with the Lazares and me—when I myself tried to understand—it seems these little bits and pieces added up.

It turned out that the next part of the night was Genève's true purpose. Yes, we had continued her lessons during our dinner, quietly speaking German until people sat at the table next to us. And we spoke German again as she walked me up the hill, the Montagne Sainte Geneviève, and into the back streets behind the Panthéon where we had gone to the strange dark little bar the last night I had seen her earlier that spring. This night, though, she led me to a different place. Even stranger than the other one. It had musicians and dancing but very different from the bal musette where I had gone with Henri and his friends the year before.

Before we went in, Geneve moved me a few meters away from the entrance and pulled from her jacket pocket a fine silk necktie similar to the one she was wearing, in the same blue-black colors as both our jackets. I did not know what to say—or feel. She gently pushed up my chin, then lifted my collar and removed the thick, old-world tie I had around my neck and replaced it with the new slim silken one, tying it in a narrow shapely knot like her own. "From Berlin," she said.

The bar had a small entryway which was separated from the main room by a dark curtain, and in front of the curtain a man who acted as a sort of concierge. He did not say anything to us when Geneve and I stepped through the door but he did not step aside to let us pass until he had given us a long look. Geneve had placed her arm through mine, and in a mirror just inside the main room I saw the two of us standing against one another and noticed, as perhaps the doorman had—with Geneve's short hair combed back and no lip rouge or powder, and her man's outfit, and both of us now in the same color jackets and silk neckties—how very much alike we looked, simply light and dark versions of the same small, slight, young nightpeople of a certain style. A style that apparently was welcome in this bar.

As we made our way over to a small table I could see that ours was not the bar's only style. There were older people and young, men and women, expensively dressed and ready-made, high fashion and plain, though everyone seemed to be sporting their best. Such different types in the same place was not something I had seen before in Paris, and there was something else about the room, something odd in another way, that I felt but could not identify.

The musicians were taking their places as Geneve went to the bar, and soon after she returned with funny colored drinks they began to play, not a fast and rowdy java as in the bal musette—and, thankfully, no accordion—but slow, on a guitar, drums, and a horn with a strange cap on the end. "Le jazz," Geneve said. "Je l'adore." Couples took the floor to dance together close, and it was only then that I realized what it was about the place. The couples were men, Maître. Or women. And some who might have been either but I could not tell—which, I realized, was perhaps what the others now saw when they looked at

Genève and me. I peeked to see her reaction. She had put on a very serious—I suppose it was meant to be sophisticated—face, but at the corners of her mouth I saw the outside edges of delight.

Yours sincerely,
Herschel Grynszpan

Maître Herr Rosenhaus,

I was very much not certain what I thought about it all. Or felt. Genève and the strange jazzy bar, I mean. We had danced close, pressed together by all the others on the floor, and that alone was enough to keep me confused in the days that followed. But I also wondered what was attracting to her about the place, those people. And in the end, I was not certain how much she had brought me along for any reason other than for the way we looked together, a way for her to be allowed in.

Within moments of leaving the place late that night Genève was making another rendezvous with me for the following Friday. She told me there was a cabaret—just like they have in Berlin, she had heard—where she very much wanted to go. "You must wear your new necktie again," she said, as if I had been the one to choose it and she was complimenting me. And she asked if I had a black shirt, which she said would be so much "avante vogue." I have the oddest rememberings, Maître.

But other things happened in the meantime. One thing especially. The following Monday Uncle Abraham got a notice from the police that we should appear at their local bureau. Passage du Désir. My papers. Finally. Almost two years after Abraham and I had applied for them.

As you might imagine, I did not sleep the night before but anyway was bright awake with excitement when we presented ourselves in the little police bureau at exactly eight in the morning.

"As you might imagine"—well no, Maître, I suppose that is likely not so.

We had learned on earlier visits that there was a separated spot at the end of the counter where foreigners had to make their inquirings regarding papers, and there was already a queue there. But it did not take long. Most exchanges with the clerk were over quickly, like the man just in front of us who was simply told there was no news—that special kind of miserableness I had lived with for two long years until that morning. Then Uncle Abraham and I stepped up and presented the notice for us to appear. The clerk asked for my papers and I handed over my Poland passport, which by then had expired, and my police receipt—that almost holy paper I had held onto so dearly since that day it had been issued to me over a year before. The clerk disappeared into a back room. His blank expression when he returned was no different than when he had left. He handed back my papers. I expected some new document but there was none. The clerk said nothing, just looked at us with dead eyes. Then I saw that the receipt had a new mark on it. An official stamp. "Residence—Denied." I opened the passport. It had the same stamp.

I became dizzy, Maître, clung onto the counter, but managed to say "This cannot be!" or something like that, then Uncle Abraham saw the stamp and asked the clerk what this meant and what the reasons were. The clerk barely shrugged and said he knew nothing of that. Abraham began to protest, said all our papers were in order, that he was a legal resident and my sponsor, I had been in no trouble, he was responsible for me, I was a minor, alone, a refugee, entitled to asylum under the laws of France, there was no reason, not even to give a temporary visa, a child had a right to protection, the League of Nations, a refugee, a refugee, there must be some mistake. Abraham got more and more agitated until the clerk turned away and looked to a policeman in uniform at a desk behind, who moved to the counter, put up his hand to stop Abraham, and said firmly, "It has nothing to do with us." The clerk then looked past Abraham and me to the people behind us in the queue. "Next," he announced.

Abraham was right. Everything had been in order—he was a relative and a proper France resident, he was sponsoring me, a minor alone, coming from the Reich where France knew well by then what was happening, I had all the qualifyings as a refugee even under their strictest new France rules, there was no reason—no proper reason—to turn me away. And so we were completely unprepared. They had even refused me a simple identity card.

In the alleyway outside I tried to get a breath while looking to Abraham for some explanation. Some solution. God's other hand. Abraham said nothing, holding a tight grimness on his face. I was nearly doubling over from pain in my stomach as he brought me down into the Métro and over to the refugee bureau past the Gare de Lyon, where we had filled out the refugee request papers two years before. There were hundreds of people jamming the place and we had to push and struggle our way in and toward the counters, but especially with how weak and pained I was we could make no headway. Abraham said he would come back by himself, and we returned to Rue Martel.

He was gone almost the entire next day. I lay waiting and tossing on my pallet in the attic room, the pain in my gut unsoothed by the soup Tante Chawa brought me. When Abraham finally returned in the evening, I came down to Maison Albert and the three of us sat at the little kitchen table. Abraham had brought back a paper, a single paper, from the refugee bureau but I saw on it only his own handwriting. The refugee bureau people had given him directions to the particular section of the Interior Ministry that accepted refugee appeals and suggested some things to include in a letter asking for review of my case. But there was no actual state paperwork for this, no formal process of appeal they could advise him about, and nothing they could do to help. Still, I was lucky, they had said—the rejecting of my papers had not come with an order immediately expelling me from France, as often happened. Because if it had, the people at the refugee bureau told Abraham, I would not have made it out of Passage du Désir.

We spent the next three evenings composing a letter to the ministry, though there was nothing to say except the same things we had put on our original applying papers, plus telling them that I now had no valid passport—my Poland passport had expired in January—so there was nowhere for me to go. Partly it took us so long to compose because although Abraham and Chawa had lived in France for many years, they did not write very often in French, and then it was usually just short notes having to do with their business. They knew that there was a special kind of official written language that sounded different from what people spoke on the streets, even real French people, and from what was in the newspapers and such. But neither Abraham or Chawa knew how to make that language on paper. We thought about asking for Bernard's help with the writing, but within a few moments of mentioning the idea we all let it drop without needing to say why. Bernard was why.

By the third day we decided we should get the letter to the ministry soon, because there might be some time limit, who knew? Abraham said we would go the next day. That would mean him taking yet another day away from his work, so I said I would go on my own. But Chawa said no, I should not go at all. Because what if there was now an expelling order? They might arrest me on the spot. So Abraham went by himself, before dawn the next day. He got to the correct bureau by late morning and, a bit to his surprise, they took the letter without a fuss. Though when Abraham asked what would happen next, the clerk there did not reply.

Sam. I needed to see Sam. I did not have any idea what he could do to help me, but other than Henri, who had gone off to the Spain war, Sam was the person I knew who best understood Paris, especially the Paris of outsiders. It had been many weeks since I had seen him, back when we had been staying together in the room above Miriam's bordel. I went over to Miriam's the next morning, thinking that was when I was most likely to catch him there, but there was no sign of him. I mean not at all—some other person's things were in the little alcove room we had shared. I found one of the women there who had been friendly with Sam and me, and she told me that Sam had moved out weeks before, she had no idea where.

I knew where Sam had been working—at Aux Belles Minettes, the fancy bordel. But I did not know the properness—bordel properness, I mean—of going to visit him there, so instead I went to the room up in Belleville where his mother Rina and sister Rachel stayed. I tapped softly on the door, hoping not to disturb his mother who was so ill all the time. Rachel opened, then stepped out onto the dark little landing to speak with me in a whisper. She told me that I could find Sam there every afternoon, staying with their mother while Rachel was out working Rina's old colporteuse cart. Sam would bring Rina medicine, make her soup, and sit with her for a few hours before he went to his night work. But Rachel also told me that Sam had taken a room of his own close by, to more easily help care for Rina, who now oftentimes could not manage even to get out of bed. Rachel gave me the address, which was just around the corner.

It was another shabby Belleville building, but the room itself was at least bigger than the tiny alcove we had shared above Miriam's bordel, and nicer—it had its own running water tap, and a real bed. There was also a wooden wardrobe with a mirror. The wardrobe door was open—Sam had just gotten out of bed and was dressing—and I noticed what seemed like some niceish clothes hanging there. More like the things Sam had worn in his Montparnasse days than when I had first met him as a cat-trapper, or when we were staying at Miriam's.

Sam was happy to see me but pale, nervous, his eyes darting around while we spoke. He told me that over the past weeks he had again been able to afford medicine for his mother but she was anyway getting worse, he did not know what to do, Rachel thought they should take her to the Hôtel-Dieu, the poor people's hospital, but he was afraid to, there were so many terrible tales of people going into that place and never coming out, and for a foreigner like his mother, well, he did not like to think. I had never seen him look so poorly, Maître, and I felt uneasy about mentioning my own troubles. But eventually he realized that with all his frantics about his mother he had not thought to ask how I was, and when he did the whole tale about my papers came rushing out of me. When finally I stopped, we sat facing each other, silent, Sam on the edge of his bed, me on the one wooden chair.

He drew a deep breath, thought for a few moments. Then slowly he began to offer me advice. It was all about the police and how to avoid them—a series of scenes he described, with dangers and defenses and tricks that went on and on, in the thinking and telling of it Sam slowly rocking back and forth on the bed, his eyes closing and fluttering open and closing again, as if he was speaking from inside a trance. The total of all the things he said about slipping the police was an amazement to me, both impressing and frightening. And no doubt useful. But when he had finished I realized that he had said nothing, knew nothing, about the one thing I had come to him for—some lawful way to stay.

15 December

The following day Friday I was supposed to meet Genève again for an evening meal and then to the Berlin-style cabaret she had said she was keen for. But I was so ill in heart and stomach about the rejecting of my France refugee papers that there was no way I could play catabouts with her at some nightclub. I thought to telephone her at her parents' house to cancel our meeting but I did not know whether contacting her there was something she would appreciate. Then I thought I might leave her a note at the restaurant where we were to meet. But what would I say? And in which language? As the evening approached, I found that I could not face sitting with Abraham and Chawa at our usual Friday night supper, the three of us staring at each other with nothing to say about the one thing most on our minds, so I went to the rendezvous to see Genève in person.

She could tell right away, by the look on my face and the way I was not dressed up as she had expected, that something was wrong. I had rehearsed what to tell her, which I hoped would sound mysterious but just came out fuzzy and full of doubt. I might be moving on from Paris, I told her, though I did not know exactly when, and in reply to her question I could not say to where, trying and failing to make it sound like I was deciding among tempting choices. Things were moving quickly, I said, so I would not be able to accompany her to the cabaret that night and would have to get in touch with her later—perhaps in a few days, perhaps longer, I did not know—to tell her when I could see her next. What would be the best way to do that?

She said that I could send a message to her at her parents' house, and gave me the address—not having any idea that I already knew it from being a server at their garden party the summer before. She also asked where she could get in touch with me—Was it still best to write via M. Blucher? I had not thought about that, but quickly decided that I could not stand to face Bernard just now. I had very low energy for tactics that night, so I simply wrote down for her the name and address of Maison Albert. Acquaintances of my family, I told her, and attached to their business they have living quarters for visitors, which they had put at my disposing.

Genève would likely know immediately—even without seeing the faded building or Abraham and Chawa's little rooms there—the difference between Bernard's address in the 16th arrondissement and Rue Martel in the 10th. But her expression gave no hint of a comment. Which I appreciated. Our meal that followed was quiet, with small talk in German so that we could pretend she was having a lesson, and it finished quickly. I told her I would send her a message as soon as things had become clearer.

To my surprise, the very next afternoon a note in the familiar envelope with the raised lettering arrived for me at Maison Albert, by special messenger. When Tante Chawa came up to the attic to give it to me she seemed impressed—by the Lazare name or by the messenger or perhaps just by the envelope's high style. She knew that recently I had been dressing up sometimes to go out but she had no idea what I was doing or who I was seeing, and she asked nothing now.

Genève wrote that her parents had decided that the family would be going in just a few days to their house in the countryside, in the Allier, and Genève wondered if she could see me before she left—to discuss continuing our work together, as she put it. The following day, Sunday, would be best, in the afternoon. She gave the telephone number for me to reply.

I was not feeling any better when I got this note on Saturday than I had been on Friday, and I did not expect Sunday to be any different. But now Genève was leaving Paris, and I did not know when I might see her again. Ever, it passed my mind. Any arrangement we could make, even if in the end I could not meet it, seemed better than none at all. So I went to the corner tabac and telephoned. I think it was Monsieur Philippe the head staff man who answered, and I flustered, mangling my words. But perhaps Genève had warned him I might call because he immediately asked me to wait.

She came to the telephone and told me that she was sorry for the short notice about her leaving. She had hoped to remain in Paris for a while when her parents left for their house in the Allier, but with all that had been going on—Was I supposed to know what that meant? I wondered—they insisted she go with them. So, could we meet the following day, in the afternoon? I said that yes I suppose I could, trying not to sound too free or too eager—though at that point I do not know why I bothered trying anything. Fine, she said, if I would come to the house we could have our visit there.

"Your house?"

"If you would not mind," she said.

This inviting seemed to break the unspoken rules we had set for ourselves—of keeping a certain mystery, and safety zone, between us—but my head was still fogged from the disaster with my papers and so I simply said yes I would be there.

When I peered through the gate in the high walls around the house grounds, I felt very small. And alone. Even more than usual. The gardens and walkways were empty, the separate service building dark, the whole place silent and still in the heavy afternoon heat of July. I crunched up the drive path to the front of the house and sensed that few people ever arrived that way. On foot to the front door, I mean. I rang the bell and was surprised to be greeted after not too long by Genève herself, without any sign of the house staff I had nervously readied myself for. There was no cheek brushing—Genève shook my hand and led me into a grand entrance hall, open two stories high and centered by a huge staircase that led up to a landing where it turned to climb further into the unseen upper floors. She took me into a small parlor just off the hallway, where a silvery setting of coffee and tea and cakes was laid out on a low, finely polished table.

Genève looked different. She was wearing trousers but otherwise there was nothing about her of the avante vogue, as she had called it. I do not know what I expected, but I was not prepared for the young-ness, and the ordinariness, of who she was that day, a teenage girl moving cautiously under the watch of her parents somewhere in the house above her.

She made only a bit of small talk—Did I locate the house all right?

Would I like tea?—before asking whether I was really leaving Paris, as if it was something she had not been able to understand. I had not made up any new story to tell her—I was too downspirited even to try—and just said that I still had not decided. She told me that she and her parents were heading to their Allier country house in two days time and would be there through August. If I left Paris while they were away, she said, I must write to her from wherever I went, because now that she was finished with school she planned to travel quite a lot and might very well visit me almost anywhere.

It was difficult by then to keep up my end of our bargain—the pretending that I was a young man of some means and status, adventuring around Europe—but I managed to say that I would make certain to stay in touch with her. She brightened and said that if I did remain in Paris I would surely want to get out of the city during the August heat, and perhaps I would come stay for a few days at their house in the Allier. She had even mentioned the possibility to her parents. She did not say what their reaction had been.

The thought that she had said anything about me to her parents came as a shock. I do not remember now whether it disturbed or pleased me. Probably both. As well as this idea that I would travel to visit her in the wilds of the countryside where there was no one but Frenchmen. She spoke a bit more about their house in the Allier—I still had no idea where that was—where she had spent every summer all her life, about the farms and forests and lakes around it, the grand Cher river that passed not far from the house and the neighboring little town—Champs-Lévy—where a small spur railroad made a stop. I could train from Paris to the nearby city of Montluçon, then take this local train to the town. Or if I came by car—Did she actually imagine that?—I could ask anyone in the town for directions to the house. As if all this was so simple.

"Come with me to my father's library," she then said, "and I will write these things down for you." It was easier for me to go along with this fancy that I might visit her in the countryside than to think up pretend reasons to tell her why not, so I said nothing and followed her into the entrance hall. We were headed for another doorway across the way when she looked up. Just reaching the landing of the grand staircase was her father. We stopped. He looked over the banister down onto us some five meters below. When Genève realized that he was staying on the landing, she introduced me to him right there.

"It is a great pleasure to meet you," I said up to him in what I thought was excellent, respectful French.

He did not respond right away, then said slowly, in a deep, quiet, and slightly challenging voice, "How do you know that?"

After a few stunned seconds I babbled something about meeting him at least being better than not meeting him. He said "Hmm"—still not moving from his spot above us—as if he was actually considering my reply, then Genève jumped in and said that we were just going into the library for her to write down how I could contact her in the Allier.

"I see," he said. "Well, carry on," and I followed Genève through a door on the other side of the entranceway.

This room was paneled in dark wood, reminding me of the bureau at the Consistoire where Bernard and I had gone the year before. It had a stone fireplace, a delicate writing table in the room's center, and shelves built into the walls on three sides and reaching to the ceiling, full of leather-cover books.

Genève went to a side table and took a sheet of paper from a drawer, then sat at the desk and wrote for me the telephone number at the country house and the name of the small nearby town, Champs-Lévy—Lévy Fields. She looked up to tell me that the house and the town both bore the name of her mother's family, which had built the house there two centuries before, at the center of their farmland, with the little town growing up nearby.

Her father came into the room. Genève picked up the paper and got up from the desk as he moved over to it and sat down.

"I understand, Herr Grynszpan, that you may be leaving us." I remember, Maître, that he called me Herr, not Monsieur. It sounded so strange in his French voice.

"Well, yes, that is possible."

He was already taking a fresh sheet of paper out of the drawer. He dipped a pen and began to write, not looking up as we spoke.

"And I also understand you are having some difficulties."

"Difficulties?"

"About where it is you will go."

"Well, yes, I have not yet decided. Or whether I will go at all."

"Ah." He looked up for a moment and glanced first at Genève, then at me, before writing again. "Of course these things can be quite troublesome," he said as he continued writing, "so I have heard." He finished, folded the paper into one of the special Lazare name printed envelopes, and wrote something on the outside. Then he rose and came and stood next to the chair I was sitting in, which I took for a sign that I was supposed to get to my feet also. He handed me the envelope and said, "This may give you another choice. Who knows, Herr Grynszpan, perhaps much the best one you have."

I looked at the envelope but the name and address on it meant nothing to me.

"I suppose," he continued, "I could have sent this around to Maison—What was the name?" He looked at Genève.

"Albert?" she finished for him, glancing at me to make certain she had it right.

"But this way we have had a chance to get to know each other." He smiled at me and gestured slightly, but clearly, toward the door.

"Oh, and Champs-Lévy," Genève said, handing me the paper with the country house information.

"Yes. Do stay in touch," her father said. "If you are at liberty."

I went into the entryway with Genève. Monsieur Lazare remained in the library and closed the door behind us. It was clear that my visit was over. That it was meant to be over. Genève took my arm and led me—in that same light touch way she had guided me to restaurants, nightclubs, monuments, churches—toward the front door. Out of the corner of my eye I saw Monsieur Philippe, the head man, standing in the shadow behind a doorway to another part of the house, watching.

At the door Genève shook my hand and said, "A bientôt, Hersch"— "Soon." I could not tell if she believed it.

I waited until I was out of sight of the house before I looked at the letter Monsieur Lazare had given me. It was addressed to a Madame

Milhaud at something called the Aliya de Paris. The name Aliya was nearly familiar to me but I could not place it, and Monsieur Lazare's letter inside did not help. It seemed to give me an introduction to this Madame Milhaud and to ask if her organization might be able to help find me a place—that was as much as I could translate the French.

Neither Abraham or Chawa knew what this Aliya place or group was, so that evening I went to find out. It did not take me long. Madame Corbin the concierge, an ocean of Paris knowledge, had never heard of it but Millstein, a tailor originally from Germany who lived across the road, knew the basics. It was an organization that helped German emigré youths in Paris, Millstein told me, training them in farming or craft skills, teaching them Hebrew, and in the end sending them to live in Palestine. Aliya—it was the French spelling of the Hebrew word that meant moving to Zion.

So, Monsieur Lazare must have put together the pieces about me, from things Genève had told him—the dark boy afloat in Paris, the boy named Grynszpan who said he was German, the boy who knew nothing about what to do in a church or how to eat things that came in shells—and decided to place me with Aliya. Genève's father was not trying to help me stay in France, Maître. He was trying to get me to leave it.

Palestine. I had given up any idea of going there ever since the miserable experiences my father and I had with the Zion groups in Hannover. And why should I now think that one of these groups in Paris would want me anymore than the others had? Anyway, truth be told I could not imagine myself there. Even compared to my scratching bare survival in Paris the past two years, the thought of digging wells in the desert and living with the types who had interviewed me in Hannover made me shiver.

There was something else that puzzled me that night as I tried for sleep in the Rue Martel attic. Why would Monsieur Lazare have entrance to such a group, this Aliya? Of course, someone as rich and important as him might be connected to all kinds of people, all over Paris—I remembered the top treatment he had been shown at the Reich consulate the summer before, when I had seen Genève collecting the visa for her first visit to Berlin. But as I lay awake I began to realize that there was more to it than just his importance, his connections. More to the whole Lazare family. Such as Genève's visits to the little church, on the holy days before Easter. Why was she not in some much higher fashion church, one that fit her family station? Why was she there alone on such important church days, instead of with her parents? And why on that Holy Friday did she leave the church, just when everyone else went forward, deeper, into the service. Then I thought back about when Bernard had first mentioned the Lazares—important people in "the community," he had called them. What community? And just that afternoon, Champs-Lévy, the town in the Allier—her mother's family name, Genève had said. Lévy. And finally the light went on. Not Lazare the saint but Lazare—Eleazar—of the desert, of the wilderness. Son of Aaron. Nephew of Moses. They were israélite, the Lazares. Or rather, français d'origine sémitique. Which must be something you already know, Maître. Because why else would they be on your list? Why else would you keep asking me about a young French girl who loved church on holy days? Why else would you keep asking me about a French girl whose given name was the adored Catholic saint of Paris? Why else would you keep asking me, Maître, about a slip-thin French schoolgirl with gray-green eyes, pale skin, and freckles?

Yours sincerely,
Herschel

Maître,

At least they had not arrested me that day in the Passage du Désir. And I held onto some small hope that the letter of appeal Abraham had given at the ministry might one day bring relief—after all, I met all of France's official qualifyings to be a refugee, and no one had given us a reason, not a single reason, why I had been denied. So, during that July and into August of '38 I still had a sort of liberté, though thinner and more foreign-feeling than ever, and I drifted through the days in a trembly sleepwalk. When I was not doing small tasks for Abraham and Chawa I wandered around Paris east—if nothing else, to get out of the sweatbox that was the Rue Martel attic room in summer. Sometimes I ran into boys I knew in Bastille and Belleville, sometimes I escaped the long afternoon heat in a cheap cinema, sometimes I headed over to the Sportclub Aurore. Mostly I have no idea what I did.

Then the other boot fell. Early one morning in the middle of August the police showed up at the door of Maison Albert. With a refus de séjour—an official paper that expelled me from France. It gave me four days to leave the country.

The police were not meant to arrest me until those four days were up, so they did not actually need to deliver the document in person. They did anyway—big men in uniform banging on the door at seven in the morning can leave an impression, which I imagine is what they intended. When they had gone and Abraham came to the attic to tell me, I could see from his eyes that the impression had been made well enough.

Abraham, Chawa, and Berenice the seamstress sat with me around the empty cutting table at Maison Albert—the table where Sydney had worked, before they had taken him away. Tante Chawa, who had opened the door to the police a few minutes before, was still shaking. Berenice was weeping softly—she had walked in while the police were there, they had demanded her papers and though everything was in order they had threatened her roughly, with insulting crude words. Now we all stared at the expelling order that lay on the table like a house rat we were told had died from the plague. I was numb. None of us spoke. After a few minutes I could not stand the silence and said I was going out. Abraham started to speak but could not come up with a clear enough thought to put in words. I kissed my Tante Chawa and left.

I was amazed to see people outside bustling about in their normal routines, getting on and off buses, going in and out of buildings and courtyards and shops. The smell of croissants, coffee, and cheap brandy drifted out of open café doorways. As if nothing had changed. I staggered around the streets for a while until late in the morning I found myself heading over to Belleville. To Sam's. I did not have anything particular in my mind about going there. I simply did not know what else to do.

Sam was not happy about being woken at what was for him, with his night work, still early, but he stopped grumbling as soon as he got a good look at my face. When I told him what had happened, he put his head under the water tap, shook himself like a dog, sat back on the bed, and set to thinking. First, he warned, I had to get out of Rue Martel right away—the police often come to arrest as soon as the voluntary leaving period is up. And if they do not find me on their first try they are likely to show up several times more in the following weeks. After a while, Sam said, they will probably lose interest and simply wait for one of their street sweeps, or a word from a helpful French citoyen, to get their hands on me. But for a couple of months at least I had to stay away from the building. Even in the middle of the night, because after the latest decrees the police were allowed to search for foreigners at any hour. And from reports around Belleville, Sam said, they seemed to enjoy the extra terror they caused with raids in the dark. Sam paused for a moment, but only a moment, then announced, "So, you will stay here." As if it was a fact, not an offer. "I am gone every night," he said, "and what is the point of an empty bed? Often I do not return until after it is light but make sure to get your sleep by three or four," he warned, "because sometimes I get back earlier and will be in no mood for company in the bed. After my work," he added, "I am quite nasty."

In the past, a smile would have followed such a remark, but my situation, or perhaps his, kept the usual smirk off his face.

I went to get my few things from Rue Martel. Sam told me not to bring much—not that I had much—in one go, because carrying a valise or clothes and other personal things through the streets was one of the many tip-offs to the police that someone was on the move and likely an irrégulier, and I might be followed right to Sam's door. Also, he said, he did not want people in his building to get nosy. There was a concierge, he said, though I had not seen her on either of my visits to his place. Sam explained that she was too busy with cheap rum and two small children to bother much about who came and went. And he gifted her with a bottle of spirits once a week or so, to stay on her good side, so if she happened to stop me it would likely be no problem once I told her I was just a visitor for Sam. But the tenants, Sam said, some of them were actual French, and if they saw me carrying in things, well, you never know.

When I got back to Rue Martel I told Abraham and Chawa of my plan to stay at Sam's. They were not happy about it but could see why it made sense. I told them that in an emergency they could find me there nighttimes. Abraham began to note down the address but Chawa warned him to write only the number, not the street, in case the police came back looking for me and searched through Abraham and Chawa's papers. I would post them an unsigned card once a week, I told them, to let them know I was all right.

By the time I got back to Sam's room he had gone off to sit with his mother for a few hours as he did every afternoon while his sister Rachel was out peddling with the colporteuse cart and before he went to his night's work at the bordel. He left me a note saying there was some cheese and bread in a tin box, and that I should help myself. The box top—for some reason I can still see it—was painted with the flag of France.

So, for a third time I found myself settling into a room with Sam. Well, sort of with him. Sort of settling. At least I had a place to get a few hours sleep each night. But I was down to my last few francs. Over the weeks before, a cinema matinee once in a while or a coffee with one of the boys had emptied my small reserve, and there was nothing now to replace it—the money my parents had sent was long gone, Henri with his syndicat connections was off in Spain, Genève's German lessons were over, and for a while at least I could not risk visiting Abraham and Chawa who, as always, would give me a few francs now and then. Also, now I could no longer go there for Friday night supper, the one true meal I had always been able to count on. From my time with Sam the past two years I knew how to scrabble up food in Paris east—scraps from street markets, midday cabbage soup at the Sportclub Aurore, and in the evenings at a warehouse kitchen opened for refugees, no questions asked and supposedly no police, on the other side of Gare de Lyon, though I would only go there once in a while because it was an hour's walk and by summer '38 you can imagine how long the queues—so that before the expelling order I had not gone hungry for too much of a stretch. But now they got longer, the stretches. With all the refugees then crowding into Paris it was harder than ever, for all of us. And both the Aurore Club and the street markets were now dangerous for me because of so many police sweeps, checking papers. In the evenings there was also the Salvation Army barge in the Seine, but I had gone there once and the Christian ceremonies they made you go through in order to get a bowl of porridge was more than I could stand, not to mention the nasty porridge itself, and anyway I got the uncomfortable feeling that they wanted French people only. Also, why an army?

So by the end of most days I found myself with an aching empty stomach, waiting to scrounge a bit of bread and cheese or dry sausage from Sam's tin box, just enough to let me fall asleep, and I am certain that Sam kept the food there for me as much as for himself. Still, slipping into the building after dark, as he told me was safest, and raiding his food box, then sneaking out again before dawn, made me feel like a thief in the night. So after a week of one-foodscrap-to-the-next days, one-sneaking-in-and-out-of-his-building-to-the-next nights, I decided to have a talk with him. Somehow, I told him, I badly needed to make some money. He stared at me hard for a moment, then said, "How badly?" I did not know what to answer, and after a few more moments he told me he would think on it.

The next night when I slipped into Sam's room there was a note from him, telling me to wait there in the morning. He did not get back until well after dawn, and looked none too cheerful, but told me he had some news that might help me out. He said "might" in a strange way, but I was too caught up in the "help me" part to think about it.

It was Aux Belles Minettes, the fancy bordel where Sam had been working the past few months. He had spoken to the patronne there, Madame Claudette, describing me and telling her that I was experienced as a server to the bourgeoisie, who made up the clientele for this very expensive place. Sam told me that the Belles, as they called it, was about to expand the tableaux vivants—the live scenes— they put on and maybe could use another server who brought champagne and other fancy drinks to the rich clients as they watched these shows. Madame had told Sam to bring me around to meet her. "But the police?" I said, remembering the raid at Miriam's bordel. Sam explained that it was not a problem. Unlike Miriam's clandestin, Aux Belles Minettes was legal, actually licensed by the police, who visited with a doctor two afternoons a week to check the women's papers and inspect them for diseases. Sam himself had no work permit—I think I told you—but the police did not bother with him or the few other boys there because the boys did not provide the house's official services. As for surprise police visits, Sam said not to worry—the clientele was too well-born for the police to disturb.

I wandered around while Sam slept for a few hours, then when I knew it was the time when he usually left to tend to his mother, I returned to the room to clean myself at the water tap. Sam collected me in the early evening and we went together to the Belles, which was in a small street near Rue Saint Denis in the 10th.

It was a remarkable place, Maître. From the outside, a plain four story building with no sign or name but just an oversized street number fashioned from red and white tiles. In the large entryway, red and white polished stones made a complicated design on the floor and a handsome iron stairway curved up to another door. At the base of the stairs two giant men in formal black suits sat in leather chairs, a large leather-bound book and a telephone on a small table between them. The men said a friendly hello to Sam and waved us up the stairs. One of the men pressed a button, opening the door at the top.

Immediately inside on the next floor was a salon that looked like something from a picture book of ancient Rome, or perhaps the Arabian Nights—the walls painted from floor to ceiling with soft blue and pink scenes of angels among the clouds, water nymphs around ponds, dancers in circles, slave girls in harems, and more of I do not know what. Except that whatever the figures were, they were all naked. Around the room were divans with large soft cushions in darker shades of the same tones as the walls.

The room was empty—it was before opening hours. Sam told me to wait. He went through a door and returned a few moments later following a large and very homely woman with an equally homely but I suppose stylish curled hairdo and wearing—as she always did, I later learned—a high-fashion black beaded silk dress and a long pearl necklace. Madame Claudette, patronne of the house. She greeted me formally but kindly, as if she was a school friend's mother I was meeting for the first time. A Gentile friend. In my early school years in Hannover, I had a few.

We sat on one of the divans. Madame asked me about my serving experience and I exaggerated about fancy dinners and garden parties in the 16th and 17th. She seemed to watch more than listen to me, then asked me to move around the room from sofa to sofa as if I was serving people there. I ended by going through the niceties of pretending to ask Sam and her what they would like to drink. In French, of course. She nodded and said to Sam, "Dark. And delicate, as you said. He will do."

Madame explained that they had themes for their tableaux vivants—the live scenes that men and couples watched from special viewing rooms before, and sometimes instead of, going further upstairs to even more private rooms. While the clients watched, they were brought drinks by servers dressed in costumes that matched that tableau's theme. The house already had a Hindu scene, Madame told me, and was adding an Alhambra one—my eastern "look" would work well in both of them, she said. She would only need me on Saturday and Sunday nights—it was August, and much of her clientele were away at their country homes outside Paris. I would be paid 10 francs for a night's work but I could expect to receive extras directly from some of the clients. If they were pleased by my service. I snuck a peek at Sam. His face gave away nothing.

17 December

Life had shrunk very small. Every night I hid away in Sam's room, except weekends when I worked at the bordel. But I had to leave his room before dawn and stay out through the afternoon so he could get some sleep before he headed over to care for his mother and then on to the Belles. Also just to let him be alone, which in those days he seemed to need as much as sleep.

What I needed was ways to be invisible during the long hours I was out of the room. I could be sure of very few places. There were the low-price cinemas in the afternoon, and the big public baths in Belleville, but I had to be careful with the little money I was now making at the bordel because it also had to feed me—scrapping at the street markets had become very risky, with the police stopping people all over the east, and some of the real French helping to point out suspicious foreigners. So I began spending days in the posh neighborhoods of the west, in their parks and public gardens. That part of the city was especially quiet in August when the people who lived there had gone to their country homes, and it remained quiet even well into September that year, before Munich, when fear of war with the Reich and bombs falling on Paris extended those people's summer in the countryside. In that part of Paris, you see, a decently dressed boy—I still had the nice suit Uncle Abraham had made for me, which Sam had advised me to wear always, and with a necktie, to soothe the eyes of any passing police—strolling during the daytime did not raise suspicion. But even so I was always on my nerves—unlike in the east, which by then I knew well and where the crowded streets and alleys made it easier to disappear, in the west I would have a hard time slipping away if a policeman happened to show any interest. So, by the end of every afternoon I was exhausted and stomach pained from having spent all the day looking over my shoulder, and was desperate to get behind the walls of Sam's building in Belleville. Though even there I was never totally comfortable because going in I sometimes had to remind the rummy concierge who I was, and also pass by the eyes of neighbors. The only time I truly felt safe was weekend nights. At the bordel.

I do not know what to say to you about the Belles, Maître. I do not want to hide things but neither do I want to offend. Anyway, what matter is it to the things we are concerned about? Except, I suppose, that what went on there did not help my state of mind. Which everyone in the jails and courts has always been so interested in, my mind, and which as I have always told you was a mix of confusions that autumn. Right up to the day I walked into the Reich embassy. With the gun in my pocket.

Let me just say that I saw things at the Belles that I could not have imagined. Of course, I knew what the business had been at Miriam's, the clandestin where Sam and I had shared a little top-floor room and could not help but hear things from the floors below us. But I did not actually have to see anything there. At the Belles, though, so much was so open. On display. Which was part of what they offered. The Alhambra scene, where I served drinks in the viewing room? Naked harem girls would wash each other, touching every part, while an older woman would bring one girl at a time up close for inspection by the pasha—which actually meant a client who was watching through one of the wall openings while lounging on a sofa in a darkened side room. And the clients themselves, Maître—some were couples whose hands wandered all over each other, even opening each other's clothing. Meanwhile I would walk among them in puffed out Arabian pants, my top naked except for an open-front satin vest, taking their orders and serving them drinks. Some of them said things to me. Some of them gave me tips. Some of them even tried to touch me, though I was always able to slip away. Or the pirate scene which I also worked,

Maître—naked girls tied up as if they were captives on a ship while other women wore pirate hats, though little else, and pretended to whip the captives and prod them and do other things to them. I tried my best not to look.

Women playacted all the parts in these tableaux. There were no men. But sometimes there were boys. Sam served drinks as I did, in one or another of the viewing rooms. But he also appeared in the actual tableaux. I watched him fanning and drying off the naked harem girls. Not wearing much clothing himself. In another tableau he was something like an altar boy, among young nuns in training. And those were just the ones I saw. Sam did not talk to me about that part of his work. Except to tell me that it made him extra money. Which he was using to keep his mother alive.

Sam was not the only one with a mother on his mind. Of course big news about Germany—meaning, would there be war with France—filled the Paris newspapers every day that September. But those papers said nothing about people's lives there. Still, certain bits got through to me. I heard things from a boy Jacob who lived near Sam—his family had come from Hamburg to Paris when he was young and they kept in touch with relatives back there. Also I saw items in the Yiddish papers when I risked going to the Aurore, and in certain cafés in the east where you could look at newspapers for a few minutes without having to order a drink. So I managed to learn things about life at home. Which yes, home, I mean Germany. Special identity cards issued, synagogues burned, beatings on the streets. I do not imagine this is news to you, Maître. I mention these things only so you will know what I was hearing in those days.

Then in early September I read about a Reich announcement from a few weeks before that gave me a terrible chill. It said that for all foreigners in Germany, residence visas had to be renewed by the end of the year. All foreigners, Maître. My parents. My brother and sister. With Poland passports. Approval would be given, the report said, only for those the Reich decided were worthy.

Now I just had to see Abraham and Chawa, to learn whatever

news they had from my parents. So I went to Rue Martel on a Friday night. From the other side of the street I watched the building entrance for a while, trying to make sure there were no police about, then finally I went in. As I passed through the big double coach doors into the courtyard, I looked up at the first-floor loge of Madame Corbin the concierge. The window was open to let in the evening air and I could see that she had noticed me. She did not lean out and speak to me— neighbors might have heard—but just nodded to me that yes, it was safe, I could go on up to my uncle and aunt.

It was a night full of news. Which left me knowing less than before. Is that possible, Maître? Well, understanding less, anyway.

Abraham and Chawa were relieved to see me but frightened for me to be there. The police had come twice, they told me, the first time a week after the expelling order, then again a week later in the middle of the night. The first time there were four of them. Two had taken Abraham and Chawa and Berenice the seamstress one at a time into the kitchen to question. They all said they had not seen me and did not know where I was but the police had followed the questioning by turning the rooms upside down looking for any hint of me—or else just for the doing of it. The police had also questioned Madame Corbin who also said I was no longer staying at Maison Albert. As I later learned, she never mentioned the attic room. Even when the second search late at night turned up no sign of me, Abraham and Chawa had the impression that the police would be back.

When I asked if there was any word from my parents, Chawa brought out a card from my sister, which gave the usual small news, and another card from my mother—cards came much quicker than letters, which had to wait for the censors to open, read and put back together. My mother's card was dated two days after the foreign registration law had been announced but said little except that they hoped to send me a gift parcel. As I looked up, Chawa placed in front of me a small stack of franc banknotes. A packet of Reichsmarks had been delivered to Rue Martel by someone who was able to travel without problems between Germany and France. Excuse me, Maître, if I do not identify the person, who anyway I did not know and did not see deliver the money, which means, I suppose I need not tell you, a lawyer yourself, that legally I would not be a trustworthy court witness to the fact—one of the things my great Paris lawyer Maître de Moro-Giafferi discussed with me. One of many things. So there is no reason to ask me further.

It was a large amount, at least to me. French money had dropped in value by more than half over the past year, my uncle explained, so that when he immediately exchanged the money—he did not want Reichsmarks in the rooms if the police came again—it had translated to almost 3,000 francs, which was two or three months earnings for Abraham and Chawa. I had never seen such an amount. But even before I could think about what it could do for me, I wondered how my parents could afford to send it. Were they trying to get what little they had out of Germany? What did they know, to make them do so? Or was it to send me as much as possible because they did not know if or when they could send money again? And which of their few possessions did they have to sell to get the money? What did this money tell me?

Of course the idea of having something to spend on myself was for a moment a tremendous excitement. First, it meant that I would not have to scramble for food all the time. But just as I began to picture things to eat, Abraham said quietly that I needed to make the money last, that he and Chawa could no longer afford to give me much of anything. They even had to leave Rue Martel, he told me. Business at Maison Albert had never increased as they had hoped when they moved two years before from the little place in Bastille to these larger, more costly rooms. In fact, over the past year things had become worse, and they simply could no longer afford to stay there. They had found another place nearby, they told me, smaller and cheaper, two top-floor garret rooms. They would be moving in October, less than two weeks away. Worse still, they no longer had enough work for Berenice. Their seamstress. Their friend. The three of them had been together, 10 or 12 hours a day, nearly every day, for seven years.

I had a hard time taking in all of this. Even when I was not staying there, Rue Martel had been the center of my life in Paris, a place I could always come to when I was in trouble, or needed a meal, or a few francs, or the smell of my Tante Chawa when she hugged and kissed me. Of course, they were not disappearing, Abraham and Chawa, they would still be there, just a few streets away. But from their faces and voices as much as from what they said I knew it would be different in this next place, these new times. For me as well as for them.

I offered to help them with the move but they said that it would be too dangerous, they expected the police again anytime. They gave me the new address, on Rue des Petites Écuries, and we agreed on a date in a few weeks when we would next meet, in a neighborhood café. In the meantime, we decided that since I had no safe place to keep this money my parents had sent, Abraham and Chawa would hold onto most of it for me.

Just as I was about to leave, Tante Chawa remembered something and asked me to wait. She went to a drawer, brought out a stack of papers—orders and receipts and bills and such—and from the middle of it pulled an envelope. From Genève.

18 December

She was back in Paris, Genève, and asked if we might meet. But the letter, which she had posted from the Allier, had been sitting at Rue Martel for two weeks—with me out of touch, plus the police raids and their own great troubles, getting me this note from some French girl, which was all they knew of Genève, had not been high in Abraham and Chawa's thoughts. The rendezvous the note proposed had passed two days before, to my surprising great distress. Surprising to me that I should be so bothered, I mean. Because it was not over missing the money she might have paid me—people were expecting war with the Reich at any moment, so I certainly did not imagine that Genève would again be looking for German lessons. In fact, in the note she had made no mention of lessons. Yet there it was—she still wanted to see me. And I had missed the chance.

In my mind I prepared an explanation about why I had not made the rendezvous or even let her know that I could not. I had been away from Paris and out of contact, I would tell her, on matters I would be importantly vague about, and so had not received the note until too late. On the following day I went to a café that had a closed telephone cabinet and rang her house. I think it was Monsieur Philippe the head man who answered. I gave my name and asked for Genève and he left the telephone for a long time. When he returned, he said that Mademoiselle was not at home. I asked when she was expected and after a short pause he said that he did not know—in a voice that did not convince me. And did not seem to try. I telephoned again the next day. I got the same reply. And sensed that I always would.

I decided to write to her instead, to say—without actually saying much—that I had been away on matters of some importance, to offer regrets about missing the rendezvous, and to propose a new one. But I wanted to phrase things just right, and how could I do that? Up to then I had never written anything in French and had no confidence that I could choose, let alone spell, the right words. But I did not want to use German because I was sure she would only get the roughest idea of what I said. Also, I wanted the address on the envelope to be in a French hand, those odd curling letters they make. Because if it looked like a German hand, well what was to say that the letter would reach her any better than my telephone calls had? I decided to consult Sam. I knew there were scribes all around Paris east, people who could speak and write many languages, real scholars some of them, people who used to be school teachers and even university professors wherever they had come from, who made their living now writing letters for people who needed to go from one language to another. Or who could not write at all.

With a bit of my new cash I bought some nice writing paper and Sam put me in touch with one of the scribes, a distinguished-looking gentleman in a well cut waistcoat suit who told me that he had been a teacher of philosophy. He shared a single room with several adults and children, though there was space only for two beds and two small chairs. His tiny writing table was hanging on the wall, his pen and ink wrapped in a cloth under a bed. In Yiddish I explained a bit about my situation with Genève and he immediately suggested some proper language, then wrote in a beautiful French-type script just like I had seen on chalkboards in the restaurants where Genève had taken me. The scribe looked at me a little strange, though, when I told him what to write on the envelope—I could not tell whether it was the Lazare name or simply the 16th arrondissement address—but he did not say anything. Nor when I told him not to put on any sender's name or address, which I hoped would raise the odds of it getting to Genève.

I set the rendezvous for the second week of October, after our high holy days had finished, which I hoped would give time for the letter to reach her and for her to make arrangements to be free. But almost as soon as I had posted it I began to fret. Would her father let the letter through to her? What if she could not make the rendezvous and had to change it? How could she get a message to me now that Abraham and Chawa were moving Maison Albert out of Rue Martel, the only address she had for me? The next evening I went over there. I knew Abraham and Chawa would be concerned to see me there again, worried about the police, and certainly not happy that I should take the risk of coming there about nothing more than a letter from some French girl. So, I did not go up to their rooms. Instead, I went to see Madame Corbin, the concierge, who first received and distributed all letters for the tenants. I told her that an important letter might be arriving for me there, and asked if she would hold it for me rather than give it to Abraham and Chawa, either before or after they moved. She looked at me with some concern, so I added, "From a girl." She gave a small smile, nodded, and said that she would take care of it. She knew my situation with the police, of course, and that me coming into the building day after day to check for a letter was not a good idea, so she offered a solution. She picked up a small colored-glass candleholder—I think it was one of those Virgin Mary scenes, they were everywhere—and told me that if a letter came for me, she would light the candle in the evening and put the red-glowing glass in the window that faced the street, so that I could check just by passing by. Me, waiting to see the Virgin.

But I could not stop chewing on the doubt that Genève would even get my letter, so I decided to try to see her. I knew I could not just appear at her house. But our high holidays began in just a couple of days, and I had heard that the old French families had their own particular grand synagogue, which made me wonder whether perhaps the Lazares would be there, and that somehow I might catch Genève's eye and manage to speak with her. So, on the first day of Rosh Hashanah—our New Year holiday—I put on the handsome new topcoat I had just bought with some of the money from my parents. I needed a coat for the coming winter, you see, and a fine shop of men's clothing, where I had made some deliveries for Abraham and Chawa, gave me a friend-in-the-business discount down to almost just their cost. It was a fine-cut fawn color topcoat, waterproofed even, that had specially caught my eye. The same coat I was wearing the day of the shooting, its fine style and quality that helped me get into the embassy that morning, I am sure. You can see it in all the newspaper photos. Anyway, the coat also helped me get into the grand synagogue for the New Year services. Along with mentioning the Lazare name.

And I was right, Genève did turn up, with her parents. Have I told you about going to this synagogue, Maître? The things I heard them say there? It feels that I have, but never mind that now. Neither the coat or mention of the Lazare name, though, got me anywhere close to Genève. The place is enormous, Maître, and as a nobody-special I was herded up into one of the balconies. I could see Genève and her parents far below, in one of the front rows, but she never saw me. And when the service was over I could not get down through the crowd—they held the balcony people back until everyone on the main floor had left—in time to see her before she and her parents rode away.

So, I was back to waiting. For her. And everything else. I was still working at the Belles, and there I was

19 December

I am sorry, Maître, if I did not say much when you suddenly appeared as I was writing last night. Though perhaps you did not mind. I had not seen you for so long, you see, and had no idea you were going to visit. But yes, I appreciate very much that you came in person to let me know that I would not hear from you during your holidays, the Christmas and New Year, which I must say I had not been thinking about. I hope you will enjoy the visit to your hometown. Which I am sorry I did not ask the name. Mine is Hannover. I would love to see Hannover again.

And warning me—well, so it sounded—that after the holidays we will work at a harder pace, to prepare for the trial, which will come soon in the new year. And that I need to concentrate my thoughts, and my writing, on the days and weeks just before the shooting. Because that is what they want to hear more about from me. They?

Also that until then I should use the time to explain about the summer of 1940, which I have not spoken about at all. You almost made it sound like I have been hiding about it, but Maître I would say that there has been plenty enough else to keep my writing occupied. Anyway, to explain how I managed to get from Paris all the way south across the country—a question from the list. That they want to know about—who helped me. Still looking for secret groups, Maître? Kabbalah networks? Communist cells?

Well, all right. I will gather myself for that. Since they want to know. And as part of it, you said to me last night, the why. When I was free in the countryside, why go on my own to a French prison—three different times in fact, yes—to turn myself in? That is not part of the question on the written list, Maître. Is it your own?

Yours sincerely,
Herschel F. Grynszpan

Honorable Maître,

It was 3 June that the bombs began to fall on Paris. Or 4 June. Well, the Luftwaffe can tell you better than my memory can. If comparing what I write is something you might do. Or someone else. Perhaps it has been always.

The French called it la Pagaille—the Great Chaos. First the Hollanders and Belgiums, then the north French, then Parisians and the France government and the France army and everyone else. Including courts and jails and prisoners—at least some of us special prisoners. All on the move, jumbled and jammed together. Heading where? Of course rich Parisians had their country homes to go to, and many others had family to reach for. But for most it was just south. Away. The Wehrmacht was coming fast from the north. So, anywhere south. June 1940, France.

Since early May, from radio and newspaper reports about the Wehrmacht moving so quickly across Holland and Belgium and the people there fleeing south into France, many French people already believed, even where I was, in the Fresnes prison—or especially there, where prisoners do not suffer hope—that it would all reach Paris soon. Even though the France government kept saying that it would not. The bombs settled the question. Fresnes prison is not in central Paris, Maître, it is a few kilometers south, but it was the south of the city— the factory areas, Billancourt and Javel—that the planes first attacked, close enough to the prison that we not only heard the bombs but felt them. Smelled the burning.

A few nights after the first attacks, the prison turned upside down. Police from outside filled the place, we were all told to collect our things, then one by one they took us out of our cells. I did not know what to bring, I had been there for so long and had collected so much, all the legal papers, and the newspaper and magazine articles about me, and the letters and photos people had sent me from all over. Also, changes of clothes the other boys did not have, good clothes that Abraham and Chawa had themselves made for me at Maison Albert and sent in to me, which was allowed, you see, as well as special food, my stomach, there was money for it, the Defense Fund, the money from America, I think I told you. Later, on the roads, I saw many people who wore several layers of clothes on top of each other, even in the awful summer heat, so that they would not have to carry them, with so many other things they were already dragging along. But I did not think of that at the moment when suddenly they were hurrying us out of Fresnes. It was difficult to think at all, with everyone shouting and banging and running around. And think of what? Since I had no idea what was happening. So, I took only a few of the newspaper clippings from just after the shooting, along with some papers from my lawyers and two letters from my parents that they had managed to send from Zbonszyn, the place where the Reich had dumped them on the Poland border, before they disappeared deeper into the East. I also grabbed my dictionary. And my coat, my fine fawn-color topcoat, which I had not worn for so long—not since the past winter, in my cell to stay warm—because there had been no court appearings for months.

In the prison's juveniles section, I was the last to be let out. I did not know where the rest of the boys had been taken and I was led alone to the central courtyard. Many adult prisoners from their much larger section of the huge jail were already standing there in several groups of 20 or 30 each. The guard who brought me out announced a number to a policeman in the yard, and he directed us to one of the waiting groups, where the guard deposited me. From the jail's offices people were carrying out dossiers and registers and all manner of paperwork, loading them into police vans parked inside the courtyard. At the final outer gate beyond the vans, in the faint light of daybreak I could just make out boys from the juveniles section and many adult prisoners being released on their own into the streets.

As we waited in the courtyard, a light rain began. I put on my topcoat—it was waterproofed, did I tell you that, Maître? But after a minute I looked around and saw that few of the other prisoners had any kind of coat, and certainly none of them a fine one like mine. A nearby prisoner was staring at me, a cold and nasty glare, and I realized that the coat set me apart—something I had enjoyed among the boys in the juvenile part of the jail but which now suddenly seemed a very bad idea. Also the rain was full of oily soot from the bombing fires still burning, and was turning the coat a dirty gray. Then I saw that this same man was now staring at my hands. Which held some papers and extra clothes. And my dictionary. With "German-French" printed large on the cover. I turned away, took off my coat and wrapped it around my other things, tying the arms around the bundle to make it a rain-protection carryall. And to cover the dictionary title.

The outer gates were now opened wide and several buses, regular city buses, were driven into the courtyard. There was a lot of shouting and bustling around by guards and police who herded our group onto one of the buses, about 25 of us, checking off our names as we entered. I did not look at any of the others when they pronounced Grynszpan but I was relieved also to hear a couple of Poland-sounding names. Catholic Poland names, I mean. But anyway not French, so at least I was not the only foreigner. We were all handcuffed to the seat bars. Some men from the jail offices came onto the bus carrying piles of dossiers and within a few minutes we were on our way.

It turned out that our group was bound for Orléans. I knew nothing about the place and so could not imagine what direction—except not north—or how long it would take or what would be at the other end. Once we got moving I was surprised to see that the bus was headed along the same route as when I had been taken, from time to time over the past year and a half, to the central Paris court—what I mean is, due north into the city. The black rain on the bus windows made it difficult to see but as we rode along I got a first sense of la Pagaille. Going in the other direction the roads were crammed with humans and vehicles of every kind, heading out of the city. There were some big expensive autos, most of them full of passengers though not otherwise different from how they would normally look. But there were also many other autos and delivery vans and small lorries and such, with bags and boxes and birdcages crushed in with the people, many with mattresses and bedding piled on the roof, and even furniture on top of that. Some had thought to cover these with oilcloth but much was getting soaked and filthy from the soot-filled rain. Mixed in with the autos and vans I was amazed to see now and then a large wagon pulled by a tractor or horse or mule and filled with furniture and farm tools and barrels and live chickens and ducks, what seemed like the entire households of the farmers who rode in or walked beside the wagons, French but obviously not Paris people and who were passing through the great city without stopping or even looking around them, its only importance to them as a place on the map to get beyond. Refugees, Maître. Though I doubt they would have used the word themselves.

Alongside this strange queue of vehicles was a second flow of people, half on the pavement, half in the road, walking and pushing bicycles or carts or baby prams or anything else with wheels that could carry house goods, or family members too young or too old or too ill to walk. At least it was orderly, vehicles and walkers both. People were able slowly but steadily to keep moving. It was to be much worse just a few days later, further south.

As our bus crossed into Paris itself it stopped at a large crossroads. Signs pointing opposite to our direction marked the way out of the city. Down on the pavement I saw an old couple dressed in their Sunday clothes, sitting in the rain on pasteboard valises tied with rope, one of the bags soaked through and broken, clothes fallen into an oily puddle, the woman waving her arm weakly at passing vehicles in hope of a ride, the old man just staring down at his soaking shoes, the stream of walkers parting to go around them. Our bus sat there for a moment and I realized something strange—that despite the huge exodus, the roadway was almost totally silent. The walkers were moving steadily but stiffly, staring straight ahead, without talking or looking around, and the autos and vans and trucks and wagons moved in a perfect slow straight line as if on a tow-rope, with the low hum of motors but without the sounds of brakes or shifting gears or tires turning corners or the usual Paris horns, and as background the soft putt-putt-putt of a couple of tractors. Even the animals made no sounds. It was like watching a silent film, Maître. Except without the music.

The bus turned off the route I was familiar with and into a district of large homes and big leafy trees. There were a few expensive automobiles moving south but otherwise there the streets were empty, most shops closed, cafés shuttered. Almost the only people to be seen were policemen, patrolling the streets and checking that windows were closed, doors locked. As we rolled toward a large fenced park, laughter came from the men in the front of the bus. In a moment I saw why. There in the middle of the perfectly groomed garden square was a large flock of sheep, grazing on the thick well-tended grass. Two policeman were standing in the middle of the flock arguing with the shepherd, whose family was calmly having a meal spread out on a park bench, two oversize umbrellas propped over them. As the bus moved past, I noticed a large sign on the pavement behind the heads of the arguing policemen. It advertised the Comédie Française, one of the biggest theaters in Paris. The show was called, as best I can remember to spell it, "On Ne Sait Penser à Tout"—"You Cannot Think of Everything."

We rolled on into a much poorer district with buses and delivery vans and horse wagons but few private autos and the streets crowded with people, some carrying baggage and seeming to be leaving but most just standing outside shops or huddled in doorways talking in small worried groups. "No way to leave," a prisoner behind me said. "Or nowhere to go," someone added.

Soon the streets became familiar to me and I realized that we were close to the Gare d'Austerlitz, the train station where I had gone often to catch a cross-city bus. Our prisoner bus turned a corner and we could see the glass roof and iron columns of the station building but not the entrance because it was blocked by thousands of humans packed and raging in front. A madhouse. People carrying all manner of parcels and luggage, many of them trying to hang onto children and each other, plus hired porters pushing handcarts piled with impossible numbers of bags, all shoving and shouting and going nowhere—over their heads I could see that the entrance gates were shut. The streets were backed up in every direction, autos and vans and taxis and city buses stuck in the midst of the crowd, trying to edge forward or go around and getting nowhere in any direction, all the while honking their horns. Our own driver stopped before getting caught in the mess, then one of the policemen riding with us told him something and he turned the bus and went down a different street headed away from the station entrance. Even the side streets were crowded but within a few minutes the driver managed to get the bus several blocks down to a gate in the wall somewhere along the station's side tracks. Two policemen got off the bus and went into a small building, then came out with a man who opened the gate there. The bus drove in, the man quickly closed and locked the gate behind, then the bus followed him through a jumble of tracks and disconnected train cars. We finally stopped close to a lone train car sitting by itself on a side track. It had a number chalked on the side. Its windows were painted black.

The guards unlocked us from our seats and told us to come out. When we had first got on the bus and sat down I had put my bundle of clothes and papers under the seat. As we readied to get off, I slipped out the German dictionary. And left it there.

They cuffed us in pairs and led us off the bus toward the train car. The rain had stopped but the ground was oily and muddy. I stepped down carefully holding my bundle in my uncuffed arm, but the large man I was hooked to slipped and as he steadied himself, his weight pulled me down instead. I fell to a knee, jerking the cuff hard on both our wrists. I expected a complaint or even a blow from the big man, but instead he helped me up. He gave me a few moments to gather myself and to try to wipe some of the oily mud off my trousers, but a policeman came over and poked me hard with his baton, telling me to get moving. The large man reached out with his free hand and grabbed the policeman's stick. "Alors," he growled at the cop, "there is a war. Things have changed." Another policeman stepped in and told us keep moving. As we turned, the cop who had struck me said to the big man's back, "Not for long."

21 December

Orléans was not far—only 100 kilometers or so, someone said. But the trip took ages. First we sat for hours on a side track at the Austerlitz station, the car being moved twice before actually hooking up to a train. Then the train sat for hours. We could not see la Pagaille outside but we could hear it—whistles, shrieking loudspeakers, bells on baggage carts, children crying, people shouting and shouting, several times horrid crazed screaming, and every once in a while a train engine starting, belching out a huge blast of steam that seeped through cracks atop our old car's mostly closed, blackened windows.

We were given a bit of water but no food. A few of the prisoners, though, had brought some with them from their cells—a piece of hard cheese, a bit of dry sausage—and after a few hours, when it was clear that no one was going to feed us, they shared it around all the other prisoners. So I had two bites of cheese to go with my few sips of water. And that was it for the morning, the rest of that day, and that night. It was the beginning of weeks of hunger. Again. You never get used to it, Maître.

When finally our train moved it was only a few hundred meters, to let some other train pass, and we waited again for an hour or more before we actually left the station. The whole journey was like that, stopping, sitting still for long stretches, moving slowly, stopping again, all without anyone telling us what was happening and without being able to see out the painted windows. We had left the Fresnes prison shortly after dawn. It was June and stayed light until nearly 11 at night but it was dark again by the time we pulled into the Orléans station. Which was packed, even at that hour, people standing and fussing about, or sitting on their bags, waiting, some of them camped out asleep on the platforms. Though it was not as crowded or frantic as what we had left at the station in Paris. And nothing like what we would see right there in Orléans just a few days later.

We walked to the prison, quite close. After the massive buildings of Fresnes, the Orléans jail seemed like a toy. They brought us into the mess hall and registered us there, matching us with our dossiers that the guards had brought from Paris. There were not enough empty double cells to house all of us just arrived so they looked through the dossiers of the new prisoners, deciding which cells to put them in. When they checked my dossier, the chief guard who had come with us from Fresnes spoke with the Orléans guard who was distributing us new prisoners. I was given my own cell.

Nothing happened during the week I was in the Orléans jail. Nothing to me, I mean. But outside it was all collapsing. Soon after we arrived we heard a radio broadcast by the France premier, or prime minister, or whatever they call him, who said that the France army would make a stand against the Reich army at the edge of Paris, and if need be defend the beloved City of Light block by block. Two days later the government left Paris. Four days later the Wehrmacht marched in.

Late on the morning after the Wehrmacht had reached Paris, and following a dawn bombing raid on Orléans that had struck close to the jail, they brought all the prisoners to the yard—about 100 of us plus 15 or so guards. Some of the local Orléans prisoners were set free, then the jail director told the rest of us we were being moved by special train to Bourges, another 100 kilometers south. The journey should take no more than two hours, he said. And while in transport, we and the guards would be under the protection and command of the France army. Then he rose and began singing the France national song. Two jail office workers joined him. Some of the guards sang also, but most barely moved their lips or just looked down. Only two or three prisoners joined, the others silent or cursing, shaking their heads, some close to laughing. When the song was finished, the director said he was now officially handing authority over us to the army, and from a corner of the yard a little middle age pot belly fellow in a badly fitting uniform stepped forward. Sergeant Xavier Brodard or something like that. Sergeant X we soon called him, or just X. And that was it. That was our army. The jail guards looked around, wondering what was going on, but before anyone could say anything the director announced "Dismissed," and went back into his office.

So, Maître, the list you gave me, it asks about groups that helped me escape across France. Well, that was one—the France army.

Sergeant X immediately began barking—well, more like squeaking, since his voice cracked every time he raised it—orders to the guards and prisoners in army language that I did not understand and it seemed few other prisoners or guards did either. Finally he got us all to line up in what he called "marching form," which was simply two rows next to each other with guards front, behind, and beside. There were not enough handcuffs or leg chains for all of us, so they hooked us together with a combination—some of us with one type, some with the other, still others by rope around the waist. The early morning bombs had fallen close to the jail, so none of us was unhappy about leaving the place though we had no idea what waited for us outside the prison walls.

It was the train station that the Luftwaffe had targeted. The station itself had not been hit but buildings around it had been smashed, train cars knocked onto their side, tracks destroyed. Some trains were still standing and their cars remained full to the brim with people who refused to give up their places even though they were now going nowhere because of the ruined tracks, and the platforms were swarming, not only with local people and their baggage but also with many others who had staggered into Orléans from days on the roads to the north, desperate to get off their feet and now stunned with despair that having finally reached a sizable city with a station, there were no trains out.

Sergeant X halted us at the edge of the crowd—actually the pack of the crowd halted us at the edge of the crowd—and looked over the situation. Calling out "Armée de Terre Française!"—"The Army of France!"—he began pushing his way forward. A few people backed up when they heard this cry and saw the uniform but most—including several ragged soldiers mixed in the crowd—ignored the little sergeant and after a few moments he returned, red in the face. "We march!" he called out to us. One of the guards said, "All the way to Bourges?" and Sergeant X replied, to all of us, "Our orders are Bourges, so that is where we go." And off we went. In marching rows. Cuffed and shackled. With no food and little water. Already by ten o'clock in the morning the sun was brutal.

We made our way south through the small city. The going was slow, not only because of our cuffs and leg irons, plus the fact that for months, some even for years, most of us prisoners had not walked more than a few steps at a time, but also because there were so many people and vehicles on the roads. All going in the same direction. When things backed up because of a broken wagon or an auto out of petrol or a balky mule or a child gone missing, Sergeant X would wave his arms and cry, "Clear the way! L'Armée de Terre Française!" People paid little attention, and as the days wore on we heard it from him less and less.

After a short time we came to a bridge over a wide river. During my two years in Paris, Maître, before jail I mean, I had often seen advertisements for summer holidays on the Loire. Sometimes I had daydreamed what it would be like. Maybe with Geneviève. At Orléans that day I can remember thinking, as we marched across and I saw a sign with the river's name, "Well, here it is summer. I made it after all."

South of Orléans the road narrowed and everyone had to move at the same pace—autos and lorries and vans slowing to the speed of tractors and horse or mule wagons and the thick crowd of walkers, including here and there a solitary soldier, dazed and lost and weary from it all, and who Sergeant X would sneer at but chose—or perhaps dared—not to speak to. Since we prisoners were marching two-across with guards at our sides, we took up most of the road. When one of us stumbled and fell, as often happened, and our whole chained group had to stop, an angry driver behind us would shout or sound his horn to get us to move aside but Sergeant X would show his uniform and shout back, and we would hold our place until we could plod on. Sometimes autos would go around us, over the side skirting of dirt and grass that usually fell away into a ditch separating road from fields, but often they could not pass us because of the line of abandoned wagons and autos that had broken down or run out of petrol—people fleeing south had jammed the roads like this for two weeks already, one of the guards said—or families resting there, or animals allowed to stop and graze the grass.

Finally, as if on a word from God, the road suddenly opened up—within no more than a few minutes almost all the autos, vans, carts, wagons, cycles, and walkers had moved to the side and stopped. People set up little tables or spread blankets, brought out bread, fruit, dry sausage, cheese. And wine. But it was not God speaking, Maître.

It was France. It was noon. Which meant lunch. A proper sitting down meal. Nearly everyone on the road. Except us prisoners, because the guards had brought no food for us. Or for themselves. So, Sergeant X made the best of it. At least in his mind. Instead of trying to find us something to eat, he decided we should keep marching and make good time—well, better time anyway—while the road was more open. On we went.

By nightfall we were exhausted, insect bitten, parched, weak with hunger, our hatless heads sunbeaten, our prison-pale faces burned, our feet raw and blistered—most of the men did not have decent shoes, and none of us was used to long tramping on a country road—and the skin torn and bloody on our wrists or ankles or hips, depending on whether a prisoner wore cuffs, leg chains, or waist ropes, and on how many falls he had taken during the day. As it got dark, traveling families staked out patches of roadside grass or spread out in fields to spend the night, and our guards did not poke or even bark when a few prisoners called out for us to stop as well. Sergeant X pushed on without looking back, though, until at a small crossroads he finally stopped, pointed to a recently harvested patch of land and said the name of someone it belonged to, which somehow he knew, and announced that was where we would spend the night. As we moved across the roadside ditch and collapsed into the stubbly field, the Sergeant told two of the guards to collect the water canteens and to head over to some trees on the other side of the field where he said they would find a farm animals drinking hole. Then he headed off down a small side road. Word eventually made its way to us from the guards that we were close to X's home village, which was why he knew the field and the water hole. X returned later in the night, rousing us with bread loaves he had collected in his village. It was thick. Brown. Wonderful.

We slept both heavily and terribly, the rough ground and the cuffs or chains competing all night with our exhaustedness. When we managed at dawn to get into our marching rows to start off again, we saw a road sign facing the other direction: Orléans 25. Which meant that in 12 or so hours of miserable marching the day before, we had only covered 25 kilometers. Some of us could do the math in our head—at our steadily slowing rate, it was four or five more days of this before we would reach Bourges.

We had not been walking long that morning when we crossed a stone bridge over a stream and heard a droning in the distance behind us. It was new to us prisoners, the sound, but not to most of the people around us who had been on the move for days or weeks and who immediately showed panic and scrambled off the road, huddling against trees or diving into the roadside ditch and flattening themselves, leaving their autos and wagons and carts and prams and cycles and all their baggage behind them. Just a few instants after we heard the sound, we understood it—they were over us, Luftwaffe planes, shooting their rapidfire guns. We prisoners all tried to jump off the road but our shackles made sudden movement nearly impossible. Finally we all made it into the ditch and flattened ourselves as best we could. I was twisted up like a pretzel, my arm turned behind me, the man I was cuffed to laying on top of me, my face pushed into the mud at the bottom of the ditch.

I do not know why I remember this, Maître, but even with the terrible noise and fear and pain, and half my face buried, just centimeters in front of my nose I noticed a snail, calmly moving through the wet grass. It sent me back to my dinner with Genève and the escargots, and as I watched this one crawl past me, uncuffed, unchained, free to go where he wanted, I wondered if someday someone would eat him.

22 December

None of us prisoners had been hit. The planes seemed to have been most interested in shooting at vehicles and bombing the bridge. As we climbed back up to the road, we saw that the bridge had been badly damaged, a tractor in the middle and many autos and wagons on both sides of it hit and crumpled, two horses shot and down. We picked our way around the vehicles that could no longer move, including a large new auto with two mattresses piled on top, thicker than I had ever seen and with beautiful blue satin comforter quilts. There were four people in it. On one side, the two passengers in front and rear seemed not to have been touched—they were staring straight ahead, their heads moving slightly forward and back, their mouths open but no sounds coming out. On the other side, the rear passenger and the driver were slumped forward. Dead. The bullets had come right through the mattresses and the roof. The top of the driver's head was gone. It was the first time I had ever seen anyone shot, Maître. I was sick.

Well yes of course, it was the second time. Vom Rath. Strange, but I remember so well those two people killed in the auto on the road. And vom Rath before the shots, I also remember well. But not after.

There was now a huge roadblock behind us, the bridge torn up and autos and the tractor on it smashed. In front of us also the road was cluttered with ruined wagons and autos, now added to the ones that had been left on the sides of the road in the days before. As we prisoners began to gather again, two guards from Orléans went up to Sergeant X. They argued. Then two guards who had come with us from Fresnes joined in. Finally X stomped away and the guards returned to our marching rows and told the other guards to unlock us. We will get to Bourges two days sooner this way, one of them said. Which meant two days less of being shot at.

Our group marched on through a tunnel of broken wagons and empty-tank autos and abandoned furniture and baggage that lined both sides of the road, every once in a while passing a person or a family sitting to the side, exhausted, empty-eyed, unable to go further. We made it through the rest of that day without being shot at again but by late evening when we stopped at a small town we had reached our limit—we had not eaten anything since the small portions of bread the night before, we had long since drunk all the water we carried, and we had been blasted by the summer sun for a second straight 12-hour day on dead legs and sore and blistered feet. We settled against a long wall just outside the town—far enough off the road so as not to be hit by autos running without their lights—while Sergeant X and two guards went to look for food.

A while later X and the two guards returned with water and three sacks holding an odd collection of onions, potatoes, unripe apples hard as rocks, and a few rounds of bread. The guards cut up the food and passed it out but there was enough only for a few bites apiece and within moments there was a commotion a few meters down the wall from where I sat. It was the two Polish prisoners being beaten and their food taken away by four other prisoners. The guards did nothing. It was over quickly.

Because we had dumped the shackles that morning, Sergeant X decided that we would spend the night behind the walls we were resting against—which turned out to be the town cemetery. He and the guards led us in and told us to settle down among the gravestones. Once we were all inside, he used a pair of handcuffs to lock the gate. It was a very strange night, Maître. Despite being so tired, I stayed mostly awake, my gut badly paining, listening to some of the other prisoners vomiting from the raw onion or potato or unripe apple on their empty stomachs, and shifting around trying to avoid the shadows of gravestone crosses that the moving moonlight kept passing over me.

In the early morning when we formed our rows it was obvious that something was different. A count soon showed that during the night 10 prisoners had escaped over the cemetery wall. Sergeant X was furious but none of the guards seemed the least interested, and we set off again. A signpost told us that we were still 70 kilometers from Bourges. Weaker than the day before, even without the shackles we marched slowly, and every once in a while a prisoner would stumble and fall, or simply sit down and refuse to move. People on the road behind us complained, but the sight of nearly 100 men and armed guards kept them from getting too close. The guards were also suffering and in no hurry to get into arguments with difficult prisoners, so it usually took a visit from Sergeant X before the guards would bother, grumbling and moving slow, to roust a prisoner to his feet and get us all moving again.

We had not gone far when we saw a group of France soldiers, perhaps 20 of them, standing at the side of the road as if in a meeting. When we reached them X stopped our march so that he could speak with them, but just then the soldiers began to move into a field where there was an empty tumbled-down farmhouse. X managed to catch the group's sergeant and as they spoke we could see X getting agitated. When the other sergeant turned and walked away, X shouted at him, "Let me speak to your officers!" The other sergeant stopped. "Officers?" he yelled back, "They left three days ago." The soldiers reached the old farmhouse, put all their rifles in a pile next to it and began to strip off their helmets, cartridge belts, and other gear, dumping it next to the old walls. Most of them also took off their uniform shirts, and some reached down to pull out the bottoms of their uniform trousers from inside their boots. Then they shook hands with each other and moved off in all directions, some across the fields, some back to the road south toward Bourges, others to the road but going north. Sergeant X returned to us, embarrassed and furious, and yelled at us to start marching again, despite which—or perhaps because of which—we took our time.

In the afternoon the Luftwaffe showed up again. This time it was worse. Three of our men were hit but still alive. Other people were not so lucky—we saw several bodies shot dead in the field, several more on the edge of the road, three others in the front seat of a van they had not got out of in time. Though this van was now ripped to pieces, from its black paint, dark tinted windows, and special large rear door it was easy to tell that it had been a funeral carriage. As we walked by it, we could see through the shattered side that six or eight people were packed into the place where the coffin usually rode. All shot to bits. Some of them children.

After the attack, it took people a while to get moving again. Families had to pull together their scattered and sometimes shattered belongings. Some tended to their wounded or mourned their dead, a number of them in the middle of the road. Other travelers moved around these desperate families, giving them wide space, even if that meant rolling their own autos or wagons dangerously close to the roadside ditch, and a few stopped to offer help. But there was no such patience for damaged vehicles blocking the way—people would band together to shove unmoving carts and autos off to the side, often crashing them down into a ditch or field, some with people still in them. Punches were thrown, but there were always many more who wanted to clear the road than those whose vehicle had broken down, so the outcome of these fights was never in doubt and they took little time. Once in a while a gun appeared, a warning shot sometimes fired in the air, though I did not actually see a traveler shoot at another one. Not then, anyway.

The guards tended to our three wounded men as best they could, then they argued with Sergeant X about how these three could continue. Someone suggested that we repair a damaged cart to carry them. One of the prisoners was a wheelwright, and he pointed to a small wagon he said he could fix with parts from others left along the roadside.

In an hour or so they had the wagon patched and we marched on, stopping only to rummage through other abandoned wagons in search of food left behind, finding an occasional sack of potatoes or onions and eating them raw. We passed several homesteads where farmers were selling food and water, but we had no money. The guards bought themselves a small bite to eat and drink but not much at the prices the farmers were charging, and they were not about to spend anything on us. So, in the early evening when we passed through a village with a water pump in the square, we prisoners fell upon it to drink and to soak our burning heads. The guards did not try to stop us and even X himself said nothing about the delay. As each of us finished at the pump we moved over to a grassy area next to the village church and collapsed. Though there was still an hour or two left of daylight, it was clear that no one would move again that evening. X did not bother to try.

In the morning there were only about 20 of us prisoners left. The rest had all slipped away in the night. Including the guards. All of them. None of us mentioned it, not even X. Of course, what was there to say? X announced that we would continue to Bourges, which he expected we would make in half a day's march, as soon as he got some provisions—for us all, he made a point of saying—from a little village shop on the square. He returned in a few minutes, empty-handed. The shop had been out of food for two days, they told him. But never mind, he said to us, at Bourges in just a few hours we will all fill our stomachs. While X had been in the shop, though, some of the prisoners had talked among themselves, and they now spread themselves facing him in a three-quarter arc that announced, without words, that they were not going. By their posture and expressions they also made it clear that if X reached for his revolver they would quickly close in.

"Where do you think you can go?" X said to the group, gesturing toward the jumble of humans and animals and vehicles packing the road. "Who do you think will feed you? Care your wounds?" he directed at the three prisoners who had been shot during the airplane attack. "All right, I am leaving. I have orders. And in Bourges I will have a meal, and hot water to soak my feet, and tonight a bed."

Then X surprised me by coming over to where I was sitting, off to the side of the others. "You," he snarled, "I had special instructions about you. To protect you—from them, mostly," he tilted his head toward the other prisoners. "So good luck with that now," he snorted. "And if the Bosch catch up with you, they will shoot you as soon as they know who you are. At Bourges you would have the army of France around you. But suit yourself. Which seems to be what you have always done."

I mumbled something about being too tired, unable to move, but that I would show up at Bourges as soon I as I could manage. "Je m'en fous"—"I could not care less"—he said, then turned and joined the crowd on the road heading south.

The other prisoners talked for a while. They did not invite me to join them. I sat there beside the church, thinking about what X had said about the Wehrmacht finding me. And about him needing to protect me from the other prisoners. But I was so sore and exhausted and hungry that I could not put together any clear thoughts about what to do. So I just stayed where I was, watching the roadway covered with humans moving south.

After a few minutes the 20 or so prisoners got to their feet. Most of them headed off—alone, in pairs, in small groups, in all directions. Remaining at the edge of the village square were just the three wounded men in the cart, and three others. One of them came over to me.

"We know who you are," were his first words. "We all know." Which gave me a sudden stomach pain on top of my cramping legs and swollen feet and aching head and both wrists so stiff and raw from the cuffs that I could barely hold my little coat-wrapped bundle of clothes. "Some of us think you shooting that German helped get us into this mess," he said, and from the long ugly scar across his face I immediately imagined knives slicing my flesh. Then he went on, "But I say, you killed a Kraut when nobody else was doing nothing. And that makes you okay with me."

Kraut—Please excuse the language, Maître, but I wish to say how it truly was.

He told me the men intended to continue on to Bourges. They knew nothing of the region we were in and no place except Bourges where they might find doctoring for the three wounded, who were friends from the Fresnes jail that the other three would not leave behind. They meant Bourges the city, the man with the scar said, not the prison. And not with Sergeant X. He told me they were going to try to find some food in this village, then eat and rest, and walk again only after the sun had gone down. I could come along with them, he said, if I wanted.

I did not know what I wanted. Except not stay there, alone. What this man said about some of the other prisoners matched what X had warned me—that some of the French would be a danger to me if they knew who I was. Or even if they just knew I was foreign—I had not forgotten what had happened to the two Polish prisoners when things had got difficult about food. Then there was the Wehrmacht, what I feared they would do if they found me. Perhaps I should have known better about that, Maître, realized that the Reich would insist on proper procedures—my trial that is coming soon here—but in the middle of la Pagaille the idea did not enter my head.

So, the only things I knew for certain was that I did not want to be a foreigner with a German accent alone and hungry in the middle of this French nowhere, and that I did not want to meet the Wehrmacht. Which were plenty enough reasons for me to go with the men, helping push the cart carrying the wounded, when they got moving again that evening on the road to Bourges. We rested. And ate—as the men suspected, the village shop was not out of food but was charging sky-high chaos prices which Sergeant X had not been willing to pay to feed us prisoners. Despite the rifle the shopman kept on the counter, the three scary-looking prisoners—who right away told the man they were convicts—quickly convinced him to part with some salt fish, dry cracker bread, and a liter of wine. As a donation, they told him. To the war effort. I stood lookout at the door. I was terrified by the man's gun, but afterward sort of proud.

23 December

We walked for a few hours in the cooler late evening, slept for a while in a field, then continued our tramp at dawn. The men did not speak much—it was too much effort—and when they did it was not to me. By mid-morning we had reached the edge of Bourges. It seemed smaller than Orléans but I could not get a good sense of the place because of the fleeing thousands who had poured into the city ahead of us. Signs on the road into the city directed people to a refugee center. We followed along with almost everyone else. Police and worried local wardens were posted along the way to make sure refugees did not overrun the town itself. The route curled up a hill behind the train station to a flat grassy area and a dirt avenue down the middle lined with broad trees. At the end of the avenue was a large walled chateau or fortress of dark brown brick.

You could see only patches of the grass through all the humans and bags piled on top of it. There was a long queue leading up to large pots of soup and six or eight rough wooden tables where people were eating. Hundreds of people were jammed under several rickety canvas pavilions that had been set up against the walls of the fortress to provide cover from the sun and rain, while the rest camped as best they could under the trees. Our three wounded were all doing poorly, so we continued toward the fortress. When we got to within 50 meters or so of the entrance we could read the sign over the huge, arch-topped double doors. Maison d'Arret de Bourges—Bourges prison. The men stopped and looked at each other with disbelief and disgust. They spoke for a few moments and realized that the wounded men needed help badly, right away, and they knew nowhere else to go. The man with the scarred face turned to me. Good luck, he said, and they left me behind.

I made my way back out to the food queue. When finally I got to the soup pots a woman serving asked for my bowl. I said I had none and she gave me one but also, along with the serving woman next to her, an odd look—my foreignness had been revealed even in the few words we exchanged. I had heard people in the crowd speaking what I suppose was Hollands, and others in an accent that I knew from my time in Paris was Alsace, so I was certainly not the only one around who sounded other than proper French. Still, the look the two women gave me added a new uncomfort and reminded me of Sergeant X's warning about me needing protection. As I ate my soup at one of the tables, I heard talk around me of a radio announcement the France president had made, saying that the France army was going to give up the fight and that the Wehrmacht would soon take control of some of the country but that other parts would remain under the new France government—whatever that was. The French people there were talking about what it all meant, and wondering when the change would come, and what would happen in Bourges, where they thought they had reached safety.

I looked around for a place to settle myself. But what did settle mean? To do what? To wait with my topcoat and my news clippings for the next serving of soup? Then what? The more I thought about the Wehrmacht marching on, and what the scar man had said about people blaming me for the war, and the strange looks from the French women who had served the soup, and the pale soup itself, the more I thought about the prison just a few steps away. You see, Maître, for the entire year and a half I had been in the Fresnes jail, I had been someone special. I had eaten better than any time during the two years before—my experience of liberté—in Paris. I had books and company and visitors in prison. I was warm enough and dry. I could keep myself clean. And most important, in all that time the France government had refused to give me over to the Reich, despite the many lawyers the Reich had sent to the France courts, and all their legal moves, and pressures on the politicians, which my lawyers told me was happening in the back rooms. My thoughts about this were not simple, though—after all, just a few months before the shooting this same France government had denied me papers and looked to throw me out of the country. So, what would they do next? Of course, in the end, hand me to the Reich is what they did. Here I am.

But at that moment in Bourges what was freshest in my mind was that the France prisons had always protected me, had moved me out of Fresnes to keep me away from the Wehrmacht, and again from Orléans toward Bourges. All because they had promised me a France trial. Where I could tell the world why—and which by that point, with everything that had happened in Germany, and the coming of war, I thought the world certainly would be ready to understand. Yes, Maître, even at that moment I wanted to speak. To be heard. And as I have told you many times, still do.

So, after an hour or so of sitting among the crowds, I decided. I went through the gates onto the grounds of the Bourges prison, across a courtyard full of tents and injured people, and up to up to a window in an inner wall. "I am Herschel Grynszpan," I told the guard sitting behind the bars. "I am expected."

24 December

I did not stay long at the Bourges prison. In fact, I never was truly in the Bourges prison. Not officially. The prison director had me brought to his bureau. Sergeant X was there in a corner, though the director paid him no attention. I began to say who I was but the director cut me off, telling me that he already knew, indicating on his desk my Fresnes dossier that X had brought from Orléans. The director—whose hair sticking out and badly wrinkled suit told me that he had likely spent all his recent nights on the cot I could see in an alcove at the rear of his bureau—told me that the new France government had agreed to some kind of surrender but the agreement had not yet been signed, the fighting was still on, and he did not know whether in the end

Bourges would be under France control or the Reich's. The telephone rang and the director spoke to someone about food for the refugees on his prison grounds. Though I could not understand the details, I could tell that he wanted to make certain the refugees got the food, and that the strain on him was great.

"So," the director said after the phone call, not wanting to waste any more time explaining things, "however things work out in the end, believe me that at this moment you do not want to be here. And in this situation, why would we want you?" I peeked at Sergeant X, who looked unhappy but stayed silent. The phone rang and the director said, "Send him up." A large silver-haired man in a nicely cut blue suit came in and exchanged first name greetings with the director. "This is him?" the man said, looking at me, unbelieving. I suppose he was expecting someone who looked more, well, who knows?

He was the state prosecutor for Bourges, or the district magistrate, or some kind of high law official like that. The director told me to wait out in the hallway and dismissed Sergeant X. Even with so much else that was to happen, Maître, the look of disgust X gave me then, maybe hatred, appeared in my dreams for weeks after. They soon brought me back into the bureau and told me that I needed to get out right away—the state lawyer said that the Wehrmacht was only a day or two from Bourges, and not slowing down. The director called in a guard and told him to feed me and let me wash, to see that the cuff wounds on my wrists were tended, then to bring me back in no more than an hour. "And this," the director picked up my dossier and handed it to the guard, "take it to the kitchen and burn it."

When I returned to the director's bureau, the state lawyer told me that there was only one road open out of Bourges, toward Chateauroux—which did not either encourage or discourage me since I did not know where or what that was. He said that a small unit of the France army would be leaving Bourges on that road to join some other soldiers in making a stand at this Chateauroux, and that he had arranged for me to travel there with them. Once I arrived there, the director told me, I could report to the jail, where they would admit me under a false name, "just in case." He had telephoned his colleague there and arranged things. "I explained about you," the director said, "and told him we are on the same side. But I cannot say that Chateauroux will be any safer for you than Bourges. The Germans will occupy much of the country from the north down, but no one knows how far or where exactly, so the further south you go, the better your chances. I have also telephoned the prison director in Toulouse, in the far south, an old friend, and told him about you. In case somehow you manage to get that far. Here," he handed me a road map of the region, and my passport, my long expired Poland passport, which must have been in my dossier. I had not seen it since I had been taken to jail in Paris right after the shooting. "Wherever you wind up," he explained, "you may need this to show who you are. And since you sound German, to show who you are not."

The big lawyer drove me, meter by slow meter, through the old town's narrow streets packed with people on the move. He did not speak—the sight of the refugees and panicking locals needed no comment. In a field on the far side of the city we approached 20 or so soldiers gathered around an army lorry, an auto, and a tank that looked like it had been through several battles and should not have survived. I went with the lawyer over to an officer who greeted him. The officer looked at me and, in almost exactly the same doubting way as the lawyer had a little while before, said, "Is this him?" Before the lawyer left, he gave me some money from his pocket, about 30 francs. Just like that. Not a lot of money for a lawyer, I suppose, but still. Then he shook my hand and wished me luck. He said nothing about what might happen next. I was moving on. He was staying. That was all there was.

So, Maître. Group Two. For the list. Of those who helped me escape across France. A jailer and a court man. Or perhaps just two humans.

It was a mad trip to Chateauroux. Guards were posted at the beginning of the road south out of Bourges, turning back regular people and their vehicles so the army would have a clear path. But people from the area anyway made their way onto this main road from small dirt side roads and paths, and within a few kilometers south of

448

the town it was almost as clogged as the roads further north. Except that we had a tank. I say "we," Maître, because that was how I soon came to feel, part of a struggle between the army and the civilians, and though up to then I had been with the scraggling refugees, I now found I had switched sides. How easily I did is a bit disturbing, now that I think back on it. Anyway, it was not long before I switched again.

So, a tank. Which was how I made the journey, on the front of the tank. The officer had first sent me to the soldiers' lorry but thought better of it when a sergeant screamed at me, "What is this?" and the soldiers themselves turned to look at me. In not a friendly way. So, the officer took me to the tank and showed me a small spot on the front, right under the big gun barrel, where I could wedge myself in and hang on. There were bullet scars all over the metal just where I sat.

The officer's auto—with an empty rear seat in which I would have fit just fine, I noticed—took the lead, followed by the lorry and the tank in the rear. We made good speed for the first few minutes but then bogged down behind fleeing civilians who had made roundabout ways onto the road. The officer ordered the tank to move up front, and the noise it made—at first quite painful to me sitting right on top of the thing, Maître, but I was so amazed at being there and so concentrated just holding on that soon I paid no notice—plus the sight of it charging up from behind sent walkers and drivers scattering off the road. I had quite a view.

The scene we came upon at Chateauroux a few hours later was very strange. A group of about 25 or 30 France soldiers was facing a huge crowd at the crossroads entrance to the city. Behind the crowd, flying from every lamppost, from most of the buildings, and from the remains of ancient city walls, were hundreds of pieces of white fabric. Flags, Maître. White flags. We drove up close. The officer got out of his auto and the arriving 20 soldiers climbed out of the lorry. I crawled down from the tank. At the city entrance, separated from the soldiers by about 10 meters of open ground, was a man in a black formal suit with tails, a wing collar and an ascot tie, with a large medallion hanging from a red, white, and blue ribbon around his neck. He held a scepter in one hand, a white flag on a pole in the other. Behind him was a line of eight or ten men in suits and neckties, all of them also holding white flags. And behind them, several hundred townspeople. Many of them carrying rifles—hunting guns, I suppose. Held at the ready. Up on the old walls I saw other townsmen with rifles. Pointed at the soldiers. Altogether the townspeople with guns must have outnumbered the soldiers five to one.

I circled around to where I could watch the two groups facing off. The chief officer I had arrived with talked briefly with a soldier who was already there, then began speaking to the man with the medallion and scepter—the town's mayor, I heard him addressed. The mayor told the officer to come no closer. The mayor shouted everything, I suppose so the townspeople behind him could hear.

The town did not want the soldiers. And was threatening to keep them out, with their own guns if they had to. I could not understand all of the French and, surprising to me, the mayor told the officer—in what seemed a disrespectful tone—that he had a difficult time understanding him.

I remember Genève once telling me proudly that in the Allier people spoke the purest French. Purest?

"You are not of this region," the mayor challenged. "Where do you come from?" "France," the officer challenged back, and the mayor turned to the crowd behind him and said "Bien sûr"—"Of course." The mayor said to the officer that the Wehrmacht would reach there soon and that the France soldiers could not stop them, so the most important thing was not to have their town shelled and bombed. "It is not worth it," the mayor said. "Then what is?" the officer answered but got no reply.

"Look," the officer kept trying, "the Bosch announced they are only going so far, and if we can make them stop here, your town might just remain in free France."

"Very nice," the mayor responded, "after it is blown to bits?"

It went on and on like this. The last words I heard the mayor say to the townspeople, when the officer turned back to speak with his fellow soldiers, was "It was good enough for Paris, eh?"

By this point, reporting to the city's prison made no sense to me.

If the mayor got his way and the city was just handed over to the Wehrmacht, the prison walls would not protect me. And what were my odds if there was a battle? Though I might have felt different if also I was a soldier. Or at least had a gun. Or was French.

"The further south the better," the Bourges prison director had said. So, I moved away and the next person I saw I asked the way south. He told me the main road south was blocked but pointed to a road at the edge of the town and said that if I followed it I would be heading mostly southeast. That was good enough, and I started walking.

25 December

This road I took out of Chateauroux was quieter than the ones I had been on further north. There were few autos now—I passed through a village where a sign on a petrol pump said none was to be sold except by special permit, by order of the new government. I suppose the road was also quieter because many people had stopped moving, either arriving somewhere or just giving up and staying put at a refugee place like the one outside the Bourges prison, where there was warm food and rumor snips of information and the comfort of being around something official—despite how little anything official seemed to mean anymore. Also, at Bourges I had heard people talking about staying put until they knew more about what the new agreement with the Reich would finally say, hoping that then they could just go home.

It was also quieter because the road was small, so except for locals not many people were likely to know where it went. Unless they had a good map of the area like I did thanks to the Bourges prison director. The map showed that the road headed toward the city of Montluçon, which somehow sounded familiar. There were once in a while signs along the road showing the name of an upcoming village or hamlet, but they did not help me to know where I was because only towns and sizable villages were marked on the map. I kept walking.

For some distance beyond Chateauroux a stream ran near the road so from time to time I was able to stop and drink and wash my face and head. After a few hours, though, the road turned away from the stream. I was afraid to ask any of my fellow walkers for water—there did not seem to be much sharing on the road, and I did not want to share my accent, since just being alone out there was enough to make people look suspicious at me. So, when I passed through a tiny village in the late afternoon and saw a little bar with a shop, or shop with a bar, I decided to stop and use some of the money the Bourges lawyer had given me.

It was a dark low ceiling room, three little tables and a few chairs squeezed into a small corner immediately to the right of the entry, and a zinc bar with a few bottles of spirits behind it. Along the left and back walls were shop counters, shelves, barrels, and in one corner a curtained doorway. A kerosene lamp on the back counter was lit, since the daylight barely made it through the gloomy room's grimed front windows.

There were customers in the shop, a French family, and from the loaded cart outside and their dusty clothing it was obvious that they were people fleeing south. The shop man was taking down from the shelf several tins of sardines while the family's two children chose candies from a box on the counter. The woman asked how much the sardines cost and the shopkeeper said one franc per tin. The husband and wife looked at each other as if that was a high price, but said nothing. "And white wine?" the husband asked. The shopkeeper said they had a local farmer's wine for 10 sous. The woman presented a bottle that the shopkeeper filled from a cask behind the bar.

Besides food, Maître, the bottle interested me most. You see, water in the summer heat was my biggest need, and if I had a bottle with me I could fill it whenever I came upon a stream or a village pump. I had thought earlier in the day about looking for a bottle in an abandoned wagon or cart alongside the road, but I had seen how angry and ready for ugliness travelers had become at the sight of anyone rummaging through other people's things, even if it was clear that the owners were not coming back. So, a bottle. When the French family had gone, I first I asked the shopkeeper for some bread. He said they did not have any—most people made their own bread around there, he said, and the baker's wagon from a nearby town only came through once a day, early in the morning. The shopkeeper was anything but friendly, so I decided to make things as simple as possible and get out of there. I asked for a tin of sardines. Without looking back at the shelf the shopkeeper said they did not have any. "But right there," I said. Without turning he replied, "Those are not sardines. They are"—and he used a word I did not know. "Well, may I please have one tin anyway?" He took a moment to decide, then took down a tin and smacked it onto the counter. It said Sardines right on the top. "And some of your local white wine, please," I said. He asked if I had a bottle and when I said no, he said that would cost extra. He filled a bottle—not all the way full, I noticed—and put it on the counter next to the sardine tin. "Four francs," he said.

I had just heard how much he had charged the French family— less than half that much—and said, "Wait, that cannot be right."

"It is right if I say so. And who are you? Not French, I know that."

"I am from Holland"—advice from the Bourges lawyer, to explain my accent.

"Yes?" he said. "Let me see your papers."

"Papers? Well, who are you?"

"A Frenchman. Which is all you need to know. But as it happens, also mayor of this district. Where we know how to take care of spies."

I became so raged by this man, Maître, on top of my hunger and thirst and exhaustedness, that I cannot say now what I would have done—I have told you before that my temper does not always help me make the best decisions. But just then a voice called from behind the curtained doorway, which made the decision for me. I threw two francs onto the counter, grabbed the bottle and the tin of not-sardine sardines, and ran out the door and back to the road. I wanted to keep running, but running on the road for no obvious reason would be suspicious, so I fell in with the other walkers, waiting for the shopkeeper mayor or a policeman or a soldier or I did not know who to yell for me to stop, or to grab my shoulder from behind, but no one came.

I was parched and starving, but I did not want to stop until I had got some distance from that village mayor. After a while I noticed a large fruit orchard far on the other side of a field, and the combination of the cool shade there and perhaps some of the fruit tempted me off the road. I stopped after 20 meters into the field to pretend that I was passing water, which gave me a chance to see if anyone on the road or in the field or trees was eyeing me. I saw no one and kept going.

The orchard was huge, with rows of trees loaded with apples and pears, separated from the field by a wood fence which I climbed and slipped into the shadows, out of sight from the road. Almost all the fruit was too high for me to reach, but I managed to pull down a few pears. They were nowhere near ripe but I was too weak to look for any softer ones, so I slumped against a tree, broke open the tin, and settled down to my meal of rock hard pears and salted sardines. The salty fish made me even thirstier, and with no water in sight I greedily drank the wine, without even tasting it. Or thinking what I was doing. I leaned back against the tree to rest and within a few minutes the wine and pears and sardines gave me such head and stomach pain I had to lie down. When I next opened my eyes it was dark. I still felt sick, and after a while fell back to sleep.

The sun was up when I woke. Instead of returning to the road right away, I moved parallel to it under the shade of the fruit trees. The orchard went on and on, it must have been a kilometer, until I could see the sky through the branches up ahead. I also could make out a man up in a tree, picking his fruit, or perhaps another fruit stealer like me. Either way, I decided to keep my distance and moved back toward the road. It was only when I was half way across the field that I could see the man in the tree clearly. He was not picking anything. He was hanging. By the neck. There was a large sign pinned to his chest. It said "Bosch."

I went slowly toward the road, moving at an angle backwards so that I would be further away from the hanging man when I rejoined the other travelers, trying to keep them from making any connection between me and him. When I reached a point on the road directly across from the hanging man, though, I had to resist with all my strength the urge to run over and look at him closely. And to do what I knew was unthinkable, Maître—to reach up and pull off his trousers. To see if he was circumcised.

Later that day I saw a road marker that startled me. At the turning to an even smaller road, not much more than a path, it read Champs-Lévy 10. Meaning that 10 kilometers that way was Champs-Lévy—the small town next to Genève's family estate.

Her father had made it clear that he wanted me away from his daughter. And more important, Genève and I had parted on poor terms—I cannot remember, have I written to you about that, Maître? So poor, in fact, that despite no doubt reading all about me in the newspapers after the shooting, she had sent me not a single word during the 20 months I was at Fresnes. Still, this sudden reminder of her, and so close, well, I found myself walking down the path toward Champs-Lévy. With no idea what I would do when I got there.

After a few kilometers the path came out onto an actual road where there was again a stream of people fleeing south, steady but not too thick—a few autos and horse wagons but mostly walkers, some pushing bikes and prams and carts. At this small crossing a man was just banging a road sign into the ground. At his feet lay brushes and two pots of paint. The sign, old but freshly painted, read Champs-Lévis 4. It looked odd somehow, and then I realized why—not Champs-Lévy, Maître, but Champs-Lévis. Which the French would pronounce the same. But which looks much different.

I went along with the other travelers and at the edge of the village another sign also read Champs-Lévis. Under the letters "is" you could just make out the shadow of the "y"—only if you knew to look, I suppose—through a new coat of white paint.

The village had perhaps 100 small houses and shops. Those on the road itself all had their doors and shutters closed and at first it seemed the entire town had evacuated. But soon I noticed some people moving about in the houses behind, in the back lanes. On a little main square was an inn, a bakery, a butcher, a church, all shut, and a squat building that said Mairie—Town Hall. Above the mairie door hung a white flag. Standing in front of the butcher and baker shops were two police of some kind, with a different uniform from the police and gendarmes in Paris and Orléans and Bourges, and black helmets. Every once in a while they would slightly wave their batons, which they held down at their sides, in a gesture to us travelers to keep moving. We did. One of the people in front of me spoke to them—I could not hear what—and a policeman replied something about "grande maison, tout droit"—"the big house, straight ahead."

On the far side of the town I could see, branching off at an angle from the road ahead, a long wide avenue shaded by a row of evenly spaced tall leafy trees on each side. At the end of this avenue were high stone walls, and above them the top floors of an enormous stone and red brick house, surrounded by four or five lower but also large buildings whose pointed grey slate roofs were all I could see. To one side was an orchard and behind that a thick forest. On the other sides, a rolling patchwork of yellow and brown and green fields stretched in every direction. It had to be. There was no one to ask, but it had to be. The great Lévy house. The Lazares.

About half the travelers in front of me were heading down this tree lined avenue while the others stayed on the road that turned away from the big house and continued south. I followed toward the house, and as I got closer I saw a wooden table in front of huge carriage doors in the enclosure wall. People behind the table were scooping out something from wooden baskets and giving it to the refugees who passed in front. Next to the table were several large barrels, and from these there were two women in identical maid outfits filling the travelers' cups and bottles.

As I got closer, I could see that the travelers were being given small red fruit—cherries, I realized, when I saw that a dozen or so of the large orchard trees were full of them. I also saw that standing at the edge of the trees, and another just back in the shadow of an open gateway door, and another up on a ladder atop the enclosure walls, keeping eyes on the hungry travelers, were men with guns.

Taking a beggar's bowl at the Lazare door was a miserable thought, but the cherries were so bright and beautiful, Maître, and I was once again terribly hungry and thirsty. So I started to move forward. But as people moved along in front of the table I saw a figure there, a flash of reddish hair. I stopped. When people moved on I saw her clearly. Her hair was long again. She was wearing not a stylish Paris or Berlin outfit but a shapeless rough cloth dress. Fashion for handouts, I suppose. For saving the starving French from the Huns. Yes, Genève, but as Sainte Geneviève. And after that final meeting in Paris, this version of her, this image, soured my stomach. Suddenly I was not quite so hungry anymore. I curved off and headed back to the main road.

26 December

I found a bit of luck that night. Well, luck—which means what? All things considered.

A few hours after leaving Champs-Lévy—or Lévis—I was able to buy some sort of small potato pie in a village, and to fill my wine bottle with water. I just managed to get out of the village before crossing paths with a policeman checking the papers—I could hear him speaking in an extra loud voice, in that way people do who think you do not understand their language—of a family moving through on the road. Another policeman stood behind, closing them in. It did not look like it would end well.

The same sort of thing in a small town further on that day. There was a little refugee center set up in the town square where families were gathered and given food. But from a spot at the edge of the square I also noticed several policemen, with the odd black helmets I had seen in Champs-Lévis, holding a number of people against a wall and looking at their papers. This was the third time in two days that I had run into papers being the center of attention. I turned and walked back out of the town, through some fields, and around it. I did not want to be sitting in some local jail if the Wehrmacht or Gestapo came through, having to rely on the good will toward foreigners of a France small town mayor or policeman.

Then there were the camps to worry about. The French camps. I knew well that for years the France police had been putting away foreigners they did not like, in camps deep in the countryside. And once the war began, the Yiddish newspapers my lawyers gave me had talked about how anyone caught without proper papers—and anyone German, no matter how proper their papers—was now being sent to one of these faraway places. I was already faraway. Which likely put me close to the camps.

So, staying away from towns and large villages seemed like a good idea, though that also meant staying away from the easiest places to get food and water, either shops or set-ups to help refugees—French refugees, at least. But while I was avoiding these places, where would I go? And anyway where was I headed? The only answer I had for myself was, "south."

I moved to smaller roads, some not much more than paths, and not marked on my map. Nor could I ask for directions from people on the roads because there were none—the little country roads I chose were too far out of the way for most other refugees. Even when I passed through a hamlet or village its name did not usually help me because it was almost always too small to appear on my map and passing through quickly always seemed the best idea. I used the sun to keep myself heading more or less southish.

I saw quite a few farm houses along the way. I was tempted to stop for water and to see if I could buy something to eat but large barking dogs made it impossible at several of them and the others looked shut tight. Anyway, after my experiences on the road, not least the hanging man, I was not certain it would have been a good idea. In the late evening, though, I had that piece of luck. It had been an awfully hot and sticky day and as the sun was going down a thunder storm suddenly blackened the sky and it began to hail. Huge stones, Maître, painful, and the sound incredible. I tried to cover my head with my topcoat but still got a slash on my forehead as I ran toward a huge tree up ahead. Once safely under the tree and its thick canopy of leaves, I watched amazed as the hail shredded a row of small fruit trees, and then saw that I was just 50 meters from a low stone farmhouse. The door was open against the day's heat, a wooden awning keeping out the hail and the heavy rain that soon followed. Eventually I could make out people in the room, looking at me out the doorway.

I could not move from under the tree. Partly because of the pouring rain but mostly I was just too exhausted, my mind as well, empty. I heard voices sent toward me from inside the house but with the rain could not make out the words. Then a woman came out, under an umbrella, and marched over to where I stood. "Come," she said, and there was such kindness in the one word that I followed her without question. "He is just a boy," she said into the room as we entered.

They were the Fabre family. Madame and Monsieur and their daughter and son-in-law. It was a farm and they gave me warm milk. Hung up my jacket and topcoat to dry by the cooking fire, put my wet shoes on a ledge above it. Gave me a plate of food from their supper pot. And later fixed up a straw paillasse for me in a clean part of a barn. In the morning they made me boiled eggs and hot coffee. Gave me bread and their own goat cheese for the road. And drew a hand-made map of a road to take south from there. As I left, Madame brushed my cheeks and wished me luck, using the "tu" form of "you." I was grateful for that as well.

It just occurs to me, Maître. I had arrived in France in the summer of 1936. It was then the summer of 1940. And that was the first time I had been inside the family home of French people. True French, I mean. Unless you count the Lazares.

They asked me nothing, the Fabres, but over my supper plate I gave them a brief story about being a Hollander and going to Paris to visit family, being caught up by the war and separated from my relatives in Orléans, heading on my own for Toulouse where I had an address, then getting lost there in the countryside. They told me what little they knew about the situation, the war. They had no radio—in fact, as I could see, no electricity—but from the region's newspaper and some radio broadcasts in a nearby village café they had a bit of news. The France-Germany agreement had been signed, and the trains and buses would soon run again. But it was now forbidden to move anywhere without special permission, either from the Germans or the new French government, depending on where you, and they, were. And still no one knew where the line between them would be. So when I left the Fabre farm that morning, south was still all that mattered.

Soon I stumbled onto my next piece of fortune—in the end good or bad I cannot judge, even now. The small dirt road was very muddy from the night's heavy rains, and at a bend I came upon an auto, its rear wheels stuck in some deep mud to the side, near it on the ground four large metal canisters, and two men struggling to push the auto back onto drier land. I hesitated—every situation in those days called for thinking before doing. But they paid me no attention—they were two big strong young types, and my 45-kilo figure, or by then more likely 40, gave them no reason to pause. So I continued toward them. Slowly.

I was surprised to see that the auto was a brand new Citroën, a very expensive model whose first small numbers were just being introduced when I was helping Henri and the strikers at the factory in Javel two years before. I was surprised to see the fancy new auto out there in the middle of nowhere, but also because these young men in worker coveralls did not look the part to own such a costly thing. As I edged closer, the two men—brothers Aram and Nikol—managed to get the machine out of the mud. I stopped at a slight distance, still ready to make a run into the nearby trees. The brothers looked at me, at each other, then one of them said simply, "South?" I nodded—I had trained myself to reveal my accent as little as possible—and he said, "Well, come on."

There was a relaxing way about these two young men, and as I helped them put the canisters back into the trunk, I found myself saying that it was too bad they did not have the Traction Avant model, with its front wheel drive, which would have made it much easier to pull out of the mud, and once we were moving one of them wondered how someone like me—a young poor foreigner, they did not have to say—knew about the new Avant. So I told them—cautiously, because of the complicated politics there—that I had worked a little at the Javel factory in '38. Well, this opened up the brothers even more, and joking they called me Comrade Hersch.

They were Arminian Frenchmen, brought over to France by their mother who was fleeing something or other—I did not ask them what exactly, or what had happened to their father—when the brothers were just small. They had grown up in the south port city Marseille, become auto mechanics, and later moved to Paris where the big factories and big politics were. There they had joined the foreign section for Arminians, which like Henri's Poland foreign section was also connected to the confederation. Despite being foreign section organizers, though, they had not been able to get into any of the syndicats—even raised nearly their whole lives in France, they were still considered Arminians—and so could only get poor paid, low skill jobs in the auto factories. But they were talented mechanics, and finally got better jobs in a special garage just outside Citroën Javel, where they worked on new autos that had mechanical problems when they first rolled off the assembly floor. As the Wehrmacht closed in on Paris, the brothers knew they would be in for trouble because of their organizer activities with the foreign section. But they had no money or way to travel, so they had "liberated" one of the autos they were working on and, instead of baggage in the trunk, loaded big canisters full of petrol from the garage and headed for Marseille, making it this far by using the small backcountry roads where they often got lost but where there was little traffic to slow them down, no Luftwaffe attacks, and fewer police to ask for the new travel permit they did not have. At least they had proper French residence papers, plus their Citroën garage identification papers, and a faked work order—an official Citroën form, they showed me, very impressive—for the auto to be delivered by them to Marseille.

27 December

I shared the Fabre family bread and cheese with the brothers, and while it was not much, it allowed us to keep moving all that day without having to stop to look for food in one of the perhaps risky villages. Despite the bumpy back roads, in the afternoon I fell asleep on the rear seat and did not wake until we stopped somewhere after dark for the brothers to fill the tank with petrol from one of the canisters. There was a stream we could see by the light of the stars in an almost moonless sky, more stars than I had ever imagined, Maître, so many stars as to make me think for a moment about the hands of God, about how He went about choosing to use them, and we drank the water and filled our bottles and took off our shirts and splashed our heads and bodies, and ended up laughing, the three of us, yes laughing, until it hurt. Then we switched places in the auto and drove on, Aram now sleeping in the rear and me helping Nikol watch for animals and fallen branches and such on the dark road as we rolled along without headlights.

I did not realize that we stopped again later that night—I had fallen asleep sitting in the passenger seat. When I woke it was light. We were on the side of the road, at the top of a rise overlooking a sizable town, a main road running through it, in a valley below. The brothers had no more spare petrol, which they would need to reach Marseille, and were deciding whether to look for some in the town. If we avoided the town and its police, we would have to look for petrol in some village further on. And in a village, the brothers figured, they were less likely to be asked for one of the new travel fiches. But even if they could find a village pump there might be no petrol, and if there was, maybe no authorities there to prevent thieving high prices—I remembered the village shopkeeper mayor and his triple-price sardines—and the brothers had just enough money to maybe fill the tank at normal petrol prices but not with any refugee multiplier. My few remaining francs, which I immediately offered, would not be enough to help much. From what we could see from above, the town and the main road were swelled with refugees—though not nearly as many as in towns and cities further north. We did not know exactly where we were, but the brothers said we had traveled almost 300 kilometers south, or mostly south, during the previous day and through the night. Finding out where we were, so the brothers could point themselves toward Marseille, was another reason for at least approaching the town and its road signs, so they decided to give it a try.

Aram and Nikol cleaned themselves and changed from their coverall bleus into Sunday suits they had packed in a small valise, to better match them with the car, they told me. The suits were not finely tailored, Maître, but respectable and spotless. I thought to put my fine topcoat over my own filthy clothes, but it would seem strange—and so, perhaps suspicious—in the southern summer heat.

In the part of the town where we entered from the side road we saw no refugees, only locals who were beginning their workday and their shopping. We got some strange looks—Aram said that probably no one there had ever seen one of these brand new Citroëns. As we passed slowly by a bakery, someone coming out shouted, "Cassez-vous!" and another, "Allez en enfer!"—"Get out of here!" and "Go to hell!"

The brothers laughed. "The Citroën," one of the them said. "They think we are rich Parisians."

Further into the town it became more crowded with travelers, and as we got to the edge of a large square we could see a refugee place set up there, with people standing around tables and a kiosk with hundreds of tiny papers stuck on it. And as usual at these places, a number of police. The brothers decided to avoid the square and head to the other side of the town, on the main road, looking for a petrol pump.

At the back end of town we found a place selling petrol, and at close to normal price, but there was a queue of perhaps 50 autos and vans. Even with all the windows open the Citroën was like an oven, so I volunteered to find some water for us, and something to eat with the few francs I had left. I did not find a water tap until all the way back at the town square. After a long wait I filled my bottle and one of theirs but by then I was so nervous about the police on the square that I decided not to get in the food queue there. Returning to the petrol pump I passed several bakeries but the customers all looked like locals, no outsiders, so I did not go in. Finally I found an empty bakery and bought a semi-round of dark country bread. I also found a crémerie with no customers for the moment and with the last of my money got a bit of their cheapest cheese.

When I got back to the petrol pump the brothers were just getting out of the Citroën to speak with two gendarmes who stood at each side of the auto. I edged my way through a crowd that was forming around the scene, but kept a distance. The brothers seemed calm, confident, when the gendarmes asked to see their travel permit. They produced what must have been the form from Citroën. The gendarmes looked it over and discussed it, then one said it was not a normal permit.

"Of course it is not normal," Aram said. "It is special. From Citroën. Official supplier to the army of France. Citroën is the army. Citroën is France."

The two gendarmes were considering this when another flic stepped forward. "No," this other cop put in, "Citroën is Paris. And Paris is not France. Your papers."

The brothers produced their France residence papers. This other policeman looked them over, then asked for the brothers' passports.

"Arminia?" the policeman said. "What is Arminia?"

One of the brothers started to explain but the policeman stopped him. "Not here," he said. "Come with us."

Nikol tensed, I thought he might make a run for it, but instead he allowed one of the gendarmes to take him by the arm. As they took a few steps away, Aram looked back at me. The policeman leading him followed this look but Aram turned away again quickly, and though my filthy clothes and water bottles marked me as a refugee, many others in the crowd were also from the road, and nothing connected small dirty me to the large brothers in clean suits. As they led the brothers away, another policeman took charge of the Citroën and it was only then I remembered that my other clothes were still in the back seat. And my passport, my Poland passport—my only identification. Except for the newspaper clippings in my trousers pocket. I became terribly upset. Though not about the passport, Maître—it had never done me a bit of good. No, it was my topcoat, also now gone. My beautiful Paris topcoat. It made me suddenly miserable. I remember so well how I felt, not my papers but the coat, how awful the feeling, though I could not tell you why. Which seems so often a problem.

The brothers were taken through the crowd. Someone yelled at their backs, "Salauds Parigots!"—"Paris bastards!" I decided to move away. Behind me I heard someone else call "Sales métèques!"—"Dirty wogs!"—and I moved faster.

28 December

A small half of bread. A bit of dry cheese. A wine bottle of water. And south. Keep heading south. These were the only things I knew.

At the crossing out of town I recognized one name on the road signs—Toulouse. It was only 50 kilometers away, probably just two days walking if I did not get lost on the smaller roads which I would take to avoid the police. But what did it mean, Toulouse? What would I do if I got there? Try to find a way to feed myself—with my German accent? Trust myself to the refugee helpers—a foreigner with no papers? And what if the Wehrmacht arrived? Or the Gestapo? As I walked along an empty country road I struggled to imagine someplace else, someplace where I could be small and quiet, and I thought back on the Fabres, the farm family that had been so kind to me a few days earlier. They were hundreds of kilometers north but perhaps I could find another such family, avoid cities and towns altogether, offer to work for my keep. Then I thought, What could I do for a French farmer, 40 kilos of German city boy? Sew their clothes? Grow parsley in window pots? Read to them from Torah?

At midday it started to rain, a thunder and lightning downpour that quickly soaked me, and worse, my bread. Ahead I could see a small stone building with a Christian cross on top, and about 100 meters further the few houses of a hamlet. I hurried up to the little church, at first thinking just to shelter in its covered doorway, but when I heard no sound inside I tried the door. It was unlocked. I took a half-step in and peeked. I saw no one, went in and closed the door behind me. There were a dozen rows of benches and a small very plain altar place, the little room dark and grey and silently serious, though as my eyes adjusted I could see on a side wall the faded colors of a mural painting. It showed a large crowd, ancient days people, going down a road, with one man in the middle dragging a large wooden cross over his shoulder. It reminded me of something, but I could not recall what. I sat on a bench and took off my wet shirt, leaving only my undervest, and ate some cheese and soggy bread. The place was hot and stuffy and somehow cold and draughty at the same time, with odors of mildew and candles and strange things that I had experienced before only in the Paris church where I had gone with Genève and that altogether I had come to think of as the Catholic smell. I lay down, my jacket rolled into a pillow, staring at the wall painting and realizing that what it reminded me of was the roads south of Bourges.

I was woken by a gentle hand. I jerked up in terror and found myself staring into the calm face of a sister. Is that what to call her? A nun? Anyway, a very thin, middle age lady whose black nun outfit was different from any I had ever seen before, with a white bib sort of thing and the most fantastic high white winged headgear, like a futureworld airplane they had showed in the Palais de l'Air at the Paris Expo. "Come," she said, "we do not want to miss it, do we?"

I had no idea what she was talking about. But she looked so kindly on me and said nothing about me sleeping in the church in my under-vest. I certainly did not want to try to explain myself, so I grabbed my jacket and shirt and followed her outside, dressing as we walked. The storm had passed. It was beautifully bright. The sun was high, so I guessed I had not slept for long. The nun wobbled down the road ahead of me, looking back once in a while to see that I was following. We passed through the empty hamlet and continued along the road. It was about 10 minutes later that I realized I had left behind my water and the rest of my cheese and soggy bread under the church bench. I could not think of what to do or say, so I just kept following, a few steps behind.

Ten minutes more of this strange silent walk and we came to a village. Farm carts, wagons, bicycles, tractors, and a few old autos crowded around the edges. The nun turned, gave me a big smile full of pleasure, and said, "I was right, the brocante!" then walked on. A bro-cante, I knew the word from Paris—a jumble shop that sells second-hand things. But we did not stop at any shop and instead walked through the village filled with people—all local, it seemed, I saw no one who looked like a road traveler—coming and going with baskets of fruit and vegetables and odd assortments of farm-looking tools and lamps and utensils and all manner of small things I could not tell what they were. Two or three people said "Bonjour, Marie!" to the nun and smiled at her as she tottered past. But she was concentrating so hard on getting to her destination that she did not return the greetings.

I followed her to the far edge of the village where there was a flat open field that sloped down and then leveled off after about 50 meters. All over the field were dozens of small tables and blankets and piles of farm boxes, some of them heaped with fruits and vegetables like at a Paris street market but others with household goods and farm tools and, well, just tchotchkes—little home and farm things of all sorts—with each separate set-up tended by someone or some family who bargained with the other villagers and farmers stopping to buy. A brocante, Maître, but instead of a shop it was big outdoor market, there must have been 200 or 300 people. Looking over the field of plenty and the relaxed locals I forgot completely the roads full of desperate fleeing refugees. And the war. Although it had not yet quite formed a thought, I began to feel that this might be a place I could stop for a while, where life was, well, normal. Until I noticed, in the shade of a large tree, three young men sitting on stools, hovered over by several women. Two of the young men had bandages covering most of their heads. The third had his shoulder heavily wrapped, above a missing arm.

Sister Marie halted at the sight of the brocante and clapped her hands in joy, then seemed to remember something—me—and turned. "I told you," she smiled, then headed into the crowd. I stuck close to her, feeling that everyone there must realize that I was a refugee—not least by my filthy city clothes—and hoping that being with the nun would somehow shelter me—an outsider, yes, but one who had the church's protection.

The fruits and vegetables and sausages and cheeses all looked so beautiful, but I had no money. I thought about how I had so often scavenged food at the end of the Bastille market, and wondered whether I could do the same here. But it was only the middle of the day, and even if I hid out in the nearby woods, it seemed someone in the village would be sure to spot me if I returned to the field anytime before deep darkness, many long hours from then.

Sister Marie did not buy anything. She moved from set-up to set-up, making happy noises whenever she saw something she liked—which seemed to be almost everything—and to my relief turned to me from time to time to see that I enjoyed what she did, which kept me connected to her in the eyes of the crowd. Or so I hoped.

We made our way down to the bottom of the field where there was a row of six massive covered iron cauldrons, maybe a meter high each—something meaty and strong-smelling cooking in them over wood fires—and nearby a number of canvas sided stalls. The crowd was thickest down there at the bottom, many people queuing up at a table where several women were cutting and selling portions of wrist-thick curled black sausage brought out steaming from the cauldrons. Others were gathered around two stalls, mostly families with children, one for hooking little wooden ducks out of swirling water, the other with some kind of beanbag toss.

A third stall had the largest and loudest crowd, mostly men, a few women watching from the edges. I was curious what was going on there but Sister Marie seemed to flinch at the sounds and did not even look in that direction, remaining at the children's games. As I looked around the field, thinking how I might get my hands on some of the food, someone called out, "Marie! Marie! There you are." It was an older woman, a proper villager—not wearing farm clothes, I mean. She glanced at me but at that point there was enough distance between me and Marie that it was not obvious we were together. Not that we truly were, of course. "We missed you at lunchtime," the woman said to Marie. "I think it would be good if you came back now for a rest." The woman spoke quietly, evenly, as if calming an animal. Sister Marie smiled shyly, then let herself be led by the arm up the slope toward the village. As she moved away, I noticed for the first time that her white headdress was quite soiled at the edges.

A woman nearby called "See you soon, Marie," then caught me watching. "A sister?" I asked in as few syllables as possible, to hide my accent. "Oh, yes," the woman said, "she was once, our Marie. But for years now a débilitée"—feeble minded, Maître. Then doubt crossed the woman's face. "And who are you?"

My mind churned. "Oh, a chômeur," I managed, calling up the word Henri had taught me so long before—someone looking for work.

The woman sniffed. I could not tell what that meant, so I nodded politely and moved away, joining the crowd at the noisy stall. There was a table set up there as a countertop and about five meters away, between a piece of canvas about shoulder height and a large netting behind, a man in a top hat was bobbing up and down, showing his head for a few moments, then ducking again below the canvas. Five sous, a handwritten sign said. For 10 overripe tomatoes. The idea was to throw and hit the man's hat or head, not easy but from the looks of him quite a few people had managed. At first, all I could think of was what might be left of all the thrown tomatoes, for me to gather and eat when the day was over. But as I watched, my attention was caught by how serious, how concentrating, the customers were, how much feeling there was—anger, Maître, maybe even hatred—behind their throws. Slowly I began to piece things together, from what the men said as they threw, from the jeers of the crowd, and from the looks of the man who was the target. Behind the tomato stains I could make out a thick drooping mustache and dark round glasses painted on his face, and a large strung-on nose. And the top hat, Maître, which had been a favorite ridicule at Léon Blum, the former premier, since the night years before when he had showed up at the scene of a Paris riot, coming directly from the opera still wearing his formal silk hat.

A tomato found its mark and the crowd, laughing ugly, cried "Boom Blum! Boom Blum!" As I moved away up the slope another must have hit the target. "Boom Blum!" I heard again, and "Sale Juif! Boom Blum!"

30 December

It is a pink city, Toulouse. I mean the buildings, Maître, so many made of rose pink bricks, and in the morning and evening the low sun making them glow. Even the prison is pink, a castle with square turrets like a big wedding cake in the window of a fancy Paris pâtisserie. The pink made the whole city look soft. Well.

There was a roadblock set up at each entrance from the north into the city. I watched one from a distance. Walkers and vehicles were stopped, questions asked, papers examined. Some travelers were allowed through directly into the city but many were directed to a nearby warehouse. The large doors were open. I could see cots laid out inside, and in one area food being given. It did not look like a jail, and the food was terribly tempting after another day and night with nothing to eat. But I feared any contact with the police, so I walked around the edges of the city until I found an unguarded alleyway and slipped in.

I wandered around, my eyes open for gendarmes, until I came onto a main square. On one side was an outdoor street market, like the one at Place Bastille. Wooden barriers, guarded by police, separated this market area from the other side of the square where a refugee place was set up in front of the city hall, with hundreds of people and their baggage gathered, and the lower part of the walls covered with individual scraps of paper. There was a small food area there, and no one seemed to be asking any questions, so I got in the queue and was given a small portion of bread and soup. I ate quickly, then walked around watching and listening, trying to figure out what was going on. People seemed to be strangely worried about their appearance, parents trying to clean off their children with the little precious water they had, adults trying their best to wipe off the road dirt and to put on whatever clean clothes they had in their valises.

Some kind of announcement was made over a loudspeaker—between the scratchy sound and the southern accent, I could not understand it—and all the refugees smoothed themselves out again and gathered along one wall. Not wanting to stand out alone, I joined them—at one end of the group, near a side street, so that I could make an escape if I had to. I could now read some of the papers on the city hall wall behind me—notices about missing family members, lost children.

Two policemen led about a dozen people into the square, some of them in city clothes, some like farmers. These people walked up and down in front of the waiting refugees, looking them over—like customers at Miriam's bordel—and speaking to refugee individuals or families they picked out. Some seemed to come to an agreement and moved together out of the square. Other refugees made no connection, though, and slunk back against the wall. It was only during the third or fourth round of these encounters that I overheard enough to understand. It was money. In exchange for a place to sleep. The locals picked people whose looks they found acceptable, then questioned them and, if the refugees passed that test, told them what they would charge to house them. If the refugees could pay, and agreed on an amount, they left with the local. If not, they remained in the square and hoped for another chance with the next group of locals to come through. I was a lone young male. Filthy. Dark. No one chose even to talk with me. Anyway, my accent was not likely to pass an interview. And I had no money.

After two hours or so of this, the selecting was over for the day. More than half the refugees who had been there at the beginning were still there when it was over. The official helpers rounded up these remainders and led them all together—many of the refugees seemed to know the routine—out of the square. I was not certain about whether to join them, but I noticed that there were no police— they were guarding the barriers between the refugees and the food market—and I had nowhere else to go, so I trailed along. We walked for a few minutes until we reached an area of large covered open air enclosures. It smelled terrible. When we went through the gates I could see why. On the far end of these enclosures one pen still had sheep in it, and dung was scattered all over. Two of the enclosures had fresh straw on the ground and barrels of water. Some of the refugees immediately set to work fixing a blanket to shelter one corner of an enclosure, for a toilet area. The rest settled into the straw. And that was how we spent the night. Shortly after dawn, the helpers came and rousted us out. The people all picked up their belongings and headed back to the city hall square.

So. At the very best—if I was not plucked up and sent off to a camp in the middle of nowhere—stretching endlessly ahead of me were days of one bowl of thin soup and nights of sheep dung. But I was so weak and the summer heat so smothering that the idea of heading back into the countryside seemed impossible. Anyway, what would I find there? I could barely understand the way these southern people spoke, and I certainly did not want them to hear me, so what chance did I have? My only papers were gone. And my topcoat. I had reached the end, Maître. The only place that made sense, the only place I could imagine myself, was the prison. Where the France court and the special prison police had always held me safe against the Reich. Where I was fed enough. Treated well enough. And most important, Maître, where they had promised me a trial. To tell the world about what I had done. About why.

I got directions, appeared at the prison gate, asked for the director. The guards tried to turn me away. "But I am Herschel Grynszpan," I told them, "wanted by the Reich, sent here from the Paris and Bourges prisons." I pulled the press clippings from my pocket, as soiled and battered from the journey as I was, but my photo still recognizable. And I said the name of the Bourges prison chief. It worked. They spoke to the director, who took me in. I was given a cell to myself. A shower. Food. And I learned that the Wehrmacht would not be entering Toulouse. Keep moving south, the Bourges director had said, and he was right. I was, at last, safe again.

Two weeks later they handed me to the Gestapo.

31 December

So, Maître. You want to know—or they want to know—who helped me reach the south. Well, now they have it. The France army. Some convicts. A prison director and a court man. A kind farm family. And a sort of nun. All of them French. Real French. I suppose this will disappoint.

Oh, yes, and two Arminian Frenchmen.

If you will permit me, Maître, I wish you a Happy New Year.

Yours, H.

Honorable Maître Rosenhaus,

You will excuse me I hope for being nearly silent when Herr Weimann was here with you. It is just that for so long I have not seen anyone but the guards. And you, of course—well, once in a while. So my surprise was so great when Herr Weimann walked in that I simply did not know how to act. And even more surprised when you told me he would be appearing with us in court, another lawyer for me. Until this morning's visit I had no idea there would be someone next to you, next to us, at the trial. Who decides such things? You did not say.

I suppose I should be pleased at being given such extra attention. But I must say, Herr Weimann did not much build my confidence. It seemed he was here just to look at me. Which is part of preparing, certainly. But without actually listening to me? What I have to say? Or even a good sense of how I speak? Maître, he did not ask me a single question. Yes, of course, I realize he is meant to come again, to continue preparing. As you said. But still.

So. The weeks just before the shooting. As you insist.

Alone—what I remember most about those weeks, late October into November. More alone than ever. Abraham and Chawa had moved themselves and their workshop from the three rooms on Rue Martel to two much smaller top-floor rooms, a converted garret, nearby on Rue des Petites Écuries. I took the risk to see them once in a while, though not often, or for long. Yes risk, because in early October the police had again searched for me at Rue Martel, to arrest and deport me—or since there would have been no country to take me, to send me to one of their "camps de concentration," as the French named them. They had found the old Maison Albert empty but soon made another raid at Abraham and Chawa's new address. That was the fourth time they had come looking for me. Most likely they would not bother many more times, but how many more we had no way to know. So I needed still to keep a distance from Abraham and Chawa. For their sake as well—it was a crime, you see, to harbor a personnage clandestine.

So, Abraham and Chawa were nearly off limits. Henri was gone to Spain. Genève was, well, out of reach. And then Sam disappeared. Though I did not realize it for several days.

Maître, I am confused. Will Herr Weimann be reading this? And so, should I try now to explain about Sam? And Henri? And Genève? Everything that came before is part of those final few weeks that you want to hear about now—the whole reason I have written so much to you over all these months—but there is no way now I could possibly go back. Or will he read what I have already written? Perhaps he has already. All along? May I speak with you soon, Maître? Alone. To help me understand.

During that October I was sleeping at Sam's room in Belleville. But I made sure always to leave well before dawn—to avoid the neighbors and the concierge but also to give Sam an empty space to return to after his long nights out. When he woke in the afternoons he would go straight to his mother Rina's bedside—the costly medicines he was buying only barely helped her, he told me, and he needed to be with her as much as he could during the daytime when his sister Rachel was out with their mother's old peddler's cart. With these hours and duties of his, usually I saw him only on weekends, when we both worked at Aux Belles Minettes. And it was at the Belles on a Saturday in middle October that Madame Claudette the patronne asked me if I knew where Sam was, saying he had not shown up for work the past three nights.

So. I had not wanted to write about this, Maître. But I suppose now what difference does it make? To Sam I mean. You see, late nights, after his work at the Belles, Sam had been going sometimes with one or another of the Belle's clients. For private visits. Mostly in hotels de passe though sometimes, he later told me, he also saw the inside of some fine hotels. Even a few private homes. The offers of money from these rich men or women, and sometimes couples, had been so much more than what Madame Claudette paid him at the Belles, and the medicine for his mother so costly, that eventually he had begun to give in.

But one night in October things did not go well. A client refused Sam the amount he had promised, which led to Sam shouting and even smashing a mirror. The clerk of the little hotel had hailed a passing policeman—to the horror of the client. Of course the flic, the policeman, understood immediately that the client was an upper type and that Sam was, well, something other. So, the flic apologized to the client for disturbing him. And dragged Sam off to jail. They kept him locked up for weeks, even though the client and Sam had both been careful not to mention that any exchange of money had been involved. When finally the jail released him in early November, they registered him with the morals police and instructed him to report there for regular examinations. Sam told me he never would, and so he became a clandestin of sorts himself.

His disappearing was a new weight on my mind, Maître. And then when he reappeared just before the shooting, his telling me about what had happened became yet another weight. On top of everything else.

When I heard from the Belle's patronne that Sam had gone missing, I went to see his sister Rachel and mother Rina in the room they shared, but they had no idea where he was. Rina was so weak she could barely open her eyes. She looked terribly old. Her skin was grey. Since Sam had disappeared, she was not getting her medicine—Rachel did not have enough money.

Rina died the day before Sam was released. She was getting a pauper's burial the same morning he was getting out of jail. He knew nothing about it. She was 41 years old.

Yours sincerely,
Herschel F. Grynszpan

16 January 1942
Moabit prison

Honorable Maître Rosenhaus,

It was early that October, the last month of what had passed for my liberté, when the first reports appeared in Paris about the Reich's intendings to get rid of all its Poles. That was the word the Reich used, "Poles"—officially, anyone living in Germany with a Poland passport. But we knew who they meant.

What little news there was about it came from Pariser Haint, the Paris Yiddish newspaper. Not a word in the French papers—it did not affect Frenchmen. Or concern them. Especially not after Munich, the "detente" with the Reich, which had been announced on the first of the month, with Daladier the France prime minister returning to cheering crowds along the Champs Elysées. Next to the Arc de Triomphe.

I did not hear those earliest reports about the Reich's plan because I was staying away from all the places—Abraham and Chawa's, the Sportclub Aurore, cafés in the city's east—where it would have been talked about, or where I would have seen the Pariser Haint paper. I was spending my days walking about in the rich districts of west Paris or passing long afternoon hours in a cheap cinema or the public baths of Saint Denis, all to avoid the police, and weekday nights holed up in Sam's Belleville room. On weekend nights I worked at Aux Belles Minettes, where Polish passports in Germany was certainly not a topic of conversation. But eventually I learned about it, later in the month. Just before seeing Genève again.

When I first heard the reports, I went right away to Abraham and Chawa to find out if they had any word from my parents. Nothing. Abraham tried to make me feel better by saying that the Reich had announced no definite plan, given no official notice to people, there was still plenty of time for Germany and Poland to come to an agreement, he told me, and that was how things worked in those days— right up to the cliff, then settled. After all, he said, look at Munich.

I was not convinced. Neither was he. But we both needed something to hang onto. I do not mean hope, Maître. Something far more bitter. Like what I felt about my letter of appeal to the ministry, asking them to let me stay in France—an ache deep inside a damaged bone, which you want to keep feeling so you know there is still blood flowing there. I immediately sat and wrote a card to my family in Hannover, saying to please give us news. Abraham asked me if I needed more of the money my parents had sent, which he was holding for me. I told him no, thinking without saying so that I still wanted to find a way to send the money back to them.

It was evening and Abraham and Chawa were about to have supper. I had not eaten a warm meal for some weeks—although I had a portion of the money my parents had sent, plus pay from my weekends at the Belles, out of long habit I had spent hardly any of it. Except for my topcoat. But I had already stayed at Abraham and Chawa's longer than we thought was safe, in case there was yet another police raid, so I headed back to Sam's room without having the meal with them. I walked a slightly roundabout way along Rue Martel, checking the street window of Madame Corbin the concierge, as I did every few evenings, and this time there it was—the Virgin Mary candle, the sign she would give if a letter had arrived for me.

It was from Genève, saying nothing except that she would be pleased to see me at the rendezvous I had proposed for the following week. When I looked up from the note I realized my rudeness in tearing it open and reading it immediately, but Madame Corbin just said, "Good news, I hope," and smiled kindly. On my way out, she mentioned that one of the sixth-floor chambres de bonne was again empty. Abraham and Chawa were not tenants there anymore, so I no longer had any proper connection to the building. She told me anyway.

The rush of pleasure when I first read Genève's note had mostly gone by the time I actually saw her. Paris felt impossible. The mood on the streets, except in Paris east, was suddenly so gay, it was unbelieving to me, French people not just relieved but almost agiggle—if that is a word—about the Munich agreement. The French newspapers were cheering. I remember one of them, Maître, for some reason it particularly stuck in my throat—"Goodness, that was close," it said. "We almost became heroes." Street attacks on foreigners picked up pace, as if Munich had sent a message direct to the thugs that the nation was behind them. In the days right before seeing Genève I had been caught up myself in two of those attacks. Did I tell you about them, Maître? I think so, though it is difficult for me to recall sometimes what I have actually written to you and what I have considered writing but did not get around to. Or decided otherwise.

As I readied to meet Genève my energy was also damped by recalling the last time I had seen her, watching from the balcony above as she sat with her parents in the front row of the fancy synagogue, listening to the rabbi warn the Lazares and the other true Frenchmen to keep clear of all the allogènes in Paris, the outsiders. Then on top of the news about the Reich's plans for its "Poles"—and on top of everything else—Sam had gone missing, as I told you. So, to keep my fears and worries and angers from making me completely crazy, I had turned myself numb. Even about seeing this girl. I could not imagine what we even had to say to one another, but still I decided to keep our rendezvous. Because you see, Maître, at that point, other than Abraham and Chawa, who I saw only once in a while and briefly, and sometimes bumping into a few Paris east boys whose talk—Who had been arrested? Disappeared? Suicided?—was often worse than loneliness, Genève was all I had.

After my last visit with her at her parents' house, and her father's sorting out who—or at least what—I was, I doubted that she would still accept my playact role as sophisticated traveler. If she ever had. Still, she wrote that she was pleased to be seeing me. So I wore my new topcoat. Truth be told, Maître, the idea of one day seeing Genève again was part of the reason I had bought it.

She was beaming when she came through the door of the Alsace pâtisserie. But not, I soon understood, because of me. It was Munich. The agreement, she immediately told me, meant that she could now go back to Berlin. As soon as possible.

"And you," she said, switching to her awkward German. "I have you to help me."

I stared at her, trying to let her words reach some part of me that could make sense of them. She continued to smile, as if my silence was the result of so much pleasure at her idea. It was heartscalding, that smile.

"Berlin? Now?" I finally managed to say in German. Then, as my rage rose, without intending to I switched to Yiddish. "Can you not see what is happening? My family, and thousands, what will happen to them? While you drink and dance? And whatever else you want to try in the nightclubs there, your cabarets, your precious avante vogue? Who are you, Genève? What are you?"

Or something like that. Of course I cannot remember exactly what I said. Except the last few words. And the surprise on her face. She told me she did not understand, that I had spoken too fast—she did not realize that it was Yiddish, not German. The Alsace pâtisserie owner did. His expression said he did not like it. I did not care.

Still, Genève had understood something. "Listen," she spoke quietly, seriously. In French. "Of course I have considered things. I realize it is difficult to know what will happen. But I do not believe in choosing only the worst possibilities. You see, in my experience, things work out for the best. But also I want you to know that I have sought guidance. The right or wrong of it. From a priest. At a small church I know. Well, in fact you know it also, a bit. We went there together. On Montaigne Sainte Geneviève. And he agreed with me, the priest, about me going to Berlin. He said that we must find the good things in our neighbors. And that we have so much in common, France and Germany. Besides, if it turns out that I am wrong, there is always forgiveness."

"What?"

"You see, if in the end it turns out to be a mistake, me going to Berlin, even some kind of sin, I can always ask for forgiveness. In the confessional. You are supposed to be official Catholic to do it but, well, at this place, this priest anyway, he lets me in. And always grants it. Forgiveness, I mean. It is a wonderful system they have. You should try it sometime."

It was the last time I ever saw her. At least, up close.

Yours sincerely,
Herschel F. Grynszpan

17 January 1942
Moabit prison

Honorable Maître Rosenhaus,

When Sam disappeared—weeks in jail, as I told you—it seemed too much risk for me to stay in his room since at the time I did not know what had happened to him. So I slipped back to Rue Martel, to the chambre de bonne that Madame Corbin had told me was empty. And except for when I was working weekends at the Belles, I stayed in that tiny room day and night that October, taking up the time by reading, as well as I was able, all the day-old French newspapers I could get my hands on, as well as the Yiddish papers, to try to find out what was happening in the Reich, their plans for "Poles" in Germany, and the latest decrees and police moves against foreigners in Paris. Every few nights I would go out for a short time to snatch up some leftover newspapers and to stop briefly at Abraham and Chawa's to see if there was any word from my parents, or from the ministry about my appeal letter. Nothing. After a while I became so anxious, Maître, so near to panic by the endless stomach paining hours in the small dark space under the eaves, that I felt I was going to choke. I realized that I needed to get out of there at least for a while each day. But I could not face again spending empty time alone in the parks of Paris west, just to keep away from the police, because if I was to stay in Paris what kind of life was that? So on weeknight evenings I began walking around Paris east again, seeing a few boys I knew, since nights were a bit safer than daytime. But also for exactly the opposite reason—I went out because I was beginning not to care anymore. About being arrested, I mean. Because compared to what?

The truth is, Maître, during the long stretches in the little room I had become embarrassed to myself. How foolish I had been about Genève, imagining that I might be allowed into her completely separate Paris. How foolish about waiting for the ministry to wave a magic wand allowing me to stay. Foolish about France making even a small space for me. About anyone even taking notice.

The distance between embarrassment and anger is not very great, Maître. At least not for me. Not then. So that when the news came about my parents, well.

At the end of October appeared some small mentions in the newspapers about the Reich deporting people with Poland passports. First from Berlin and Cologne. Then Munich, Leipzig, Nuremberg. But what means deporting? There was no legal process, no paperwork, nothing—people just pulled from their homes, jammed into locked trains, sent to the Poland border, and dumped. Perhaps you know this, Maître. Though at the beginning no one was speaking the details.

On the last day of the month, a Paris Yiddish newspaper told that 12,000 people had been packed off. But still I had hope—Yes, Maître, hope—because the reports had not mentioned Hannover. For the next days I spent every evening with Abraham and Chawa, going over the day's newspapers and listening to the radio news. Then on 3 November the card arrived from my sister Berthe, sent via the Red Cross from Zbonszyn on the Poland border—they had come in the night, taking them first to the police station, then to the trains. The last words Berthe wrote were "We do not have a penny."

I spent the night on Abraham and Chawa's floor, and in the morning rushed out to get the day's first Yiddish newspaper. It described the miseries at the Zbonszyn border camp where the Reich had dumped these thousands of people. These humans. My family. The people had all been turned out of the trains two or three kilometers short of Poland, their money taken except for 10 Reichsmarks, then driven on foot through fields and woods by the SS, with whips and batons and guns, to the border. There they spent a night in the rain on the open ground until, because they had Poland passports, they were allowed across. Poland troops then herded them into old abandoned barracks and horse stables on a former army post. Those who managed to squeeze into the crumbling buildings slept piled on top of one another. The rest remained out in the mud. Many had been injured or taken sick, there was little food—the Red Cross and some Poland groups sent bread and soup but not nearly enough—and the deep winter cold had begun. The Red Cross helped people send postcards out but, the newspaper said, no letters or packages were getting in.

Now I was frantic. I told Abraham and Chawa that we had to send money to my parents, at least what was left from what they had sent to me the month before and that Abraham was still holding for me. But no letters were getting in to Zbonszyn, Abraham reminded me, scolding. We started to argue but Chawa stepped in and said that I should go out and pick up the latest French newspapers, that she would talk to people in the neighborhood to find out what they knew, that Abraham would go see the Red Cross, and that we should all hold ourselves still until there was more news. I was furious with my uncle. Not because of what he had said, which made sense, but because in that moment he was able still to make sense. Does that make sense to you, Maître? As I have said many times, when I walked into the embassy three mornings later, my mind was in a terrible confusion.

I went out to pick up the morning newspapers. From habit I first moved around the edges of café terraces, trying to scoop up papers that customers had left there, before the waiters collected them. But that was slow, and I was becoming more and more aggravated by the satisfied faces of the Frenchmen all around me who calmly drank their coffees and wines and apéritifs while the world was going to hell. It finally occurred to me that I had money in my pocket—it was a rare enough experience—so I bought several papers. But the afternoon papers were not out yet, and since I was due to work at the Belles that night and the next, I decided to go tell Madame Claudette, the patronne, that I would not be coming in. When I stepped into the front parlor there I was stunned to see Sam, who had been missing for weeks. He and Madame were talking in raised voices, and I heard her say that she did not care why, he had been gone all that time without a word to her, and now he was finished at the Belles. Perhaps I should have waited until later in the day to tell Madame that I could not come to work that night, or perhaps it would not have made any difference when I told her, but I wanted to leave with Sam, to hear what had happened to him, so I told her right then. And she told me, right then, not to come back.

So. Stunned again—just when I wanted most to make some money so that I could send it to my family, I lost my work. Sam and I sat on some crates in an alleyway as I told him what had happened to my family and he told me about how he had been jailed. And about how, without him to get medicine for his mother, she had died. I did not know what to say. And for one of the only times since I had met him, he could think of nothing to say to me. I headed back to Abraham and Chawa's, where Sam said he would later come to see me.

There was almost nothing in the French newspapers about the people at Zbonszyn—a small paragraph here or there said simply that "illegal" Poles had been deported from Germany. There was nothing on the French radio news reports. It was as if the 12,000 people no longer existed. Had never existed.

Chawa had not learned anything in her rounds of the neighborhood. She had even gone to see Bernard. He would look into it, he had told her, reach out to his contacts. We knew how much that meant, how little, and mentioned him no more. When Abraham got back later, he told us he had not done any better. The Paris Red Cross bureau knew nothing about what was going on in Poland. He had waited for several hours while they tried to telephone and teletype elsewhere. In the end they could tell him nothing, but at least they invited him to return the next day, that perhaps they would know more then.

Again I told Abraham and Chawa that we had to send money, even if we did not know whether it would get through. Abraham told me not to be foolish, that we did not have money just to throw away. I became angry, told him that was easy for him to say, sitting safe there in Paris. Abraham turned red with anger and with, well, I am not certain what else, but Chawa quickly edged between us with the idea to ask the Red Cross the next day if there was a way to wire money to one of their offices in Poland, that might then make its way to my parents in Zbonszyn. She made it sound so reasonable that I grabbed on and managed to calm myself. Abraham, though, was still fuming and would not look at me. We lit the candles, the Friday night Sabbath candles, then ate supper in silence. I slept again on their floor. But not much.

The next day started the same, except that it was Saturday, the Sabbath, so there was no Yiddish newspaper. I bought several of the morning French papers and tore through them desperately looking for news, but there was none. Not even little snips like the day before. Already it was forgotten. Yesterday's news. When I got back to Rue des Petites Écuries, Abraham had not yet returned from the Red Cross. Tante Chawa fed me, then as I began to pace around the two little rooms, she instructed me to go to the public baths for a good scrub, then to Rue Martel to fetch my other clothes which she would clean up and press for me. Whatever would happen in the next days, she said—if I should go to the Red Cross myself, or to some other organization or bureau—it was important for me to be as proper and well-groomed as possible. Perhaps she was just trying to get me out for a while, to find a way for me to spend the hours. Or perhaps she sensed something. But either way, she was right. Because you see, Maître, if that morning two days later I had not been so clean and well-dressed in my best suit and tie—and my handsome topcoat, freshly brushed and pressed by Chawa's own hand—they might never have let me into the embassy.

Which brings to my mind something that is troubling me. I have been asking for weeks now to have them cut my hair but the guards do not respond. They used to chop it off regularly, hack it off, as you know from seeing me, but now they have let it grow for months and it is wild and snarled and I cannot imagine how it looks. Also my whiskers, Maître, thin as they are, they have not allowed me to shave for weeks. The trial is coming soon, Maître, and the press, the world press. So when will they allow me to make myself presentable?

Yours,
Herschel

484

19 January 1942
Moabit

Honorable Maître Herr Rosenhaus,

Lawyer Weimann was just here, Maître. Along with two others. Did you know?

He brought with him a newspaper, a Paris newspaper from the early days of November '38. "This communist paper," he called it. He showed me the big headline "Dreyfusards, Réveillez-Vous!"—"Dreyfusards, Wake Up!"—and told me it called on Frenchmen to act against the Reich deportings to Poland. Then he asked if I had read it. No, that is not correct, Maître. He did not ask. He said that I must have read this. Just before the shooting.

It was not an easy thing to do, with him saying this so surely, and the two other men, large men, towering behind him, but I told him no, I had not seen that paper. Believe me, Maître, I would remember. I would remember if I had heard anyone speak up—the confederation, the syndicats, the Consistoire, anyone. Just as none of them spoke up for me after the shooting—they all completely turned their backs. Besides, that was not the real communist paper he showed me. Perhaps communist according to Herr Weimann, but it was not the Party's paper, which I knew from my days around Henri. And which, I remember well, had said not a word against the deportings. All these things I told Herr Weimann. He did not like it.

It was only two days ago I wrote to you about how I had combed the Paris newspapers, looking for news about Zbonszyn, about my family. It seems that Herr Weimann is preparing well.

Yours,
Herschel

20 January 1942
Moabit prison

Maître,

Abraham returned to the Red Cross bureau that Saturday afternoon, to see if he could wire money through them to my parents, but they said it was not possible. The Paris Red Cross people had learned that they had only a small group in Poland to feed and nurse the 12,000 Zbonszyn refugees, and they were struggling just to keep up with the ill and the injured, so providing special deliveries for particular people, out of all those thousands, was not something they could manage.

My afternoon was no better. I went to the baths, as Chawa had urged, then to Rue Martel to get my one good shirt and suit. Madame Corbin the concierge came down to the courtyard as I was leaving. She waved me over and when I saw her face up close I knew. "The room?" I asked, and she nodded. I asked when, and she said the coming Monday. Strangely, Maître, it did not bother me. In the midst of everything else, losing the room seemed completely unimportant. Even somehow as it should be. I managed a smile of thanks to her—for all the things she had done for me, I hoped she could tell—we shook hands and she went back to her loge. Monday? I thought. Why wait? I climbed the six flights of stairs again, put my few other things into the cloth sack that by then had become my regular moving valise, and brought them with me back to Rue des Petites Écuries.

Abraham and Chawa and I talked deep into the night. The next morning we divided up the few straws we had come up with. I went to the refugee bureau near Gare de Lyon. Chawa rang Bernard—she got on better with him than Abraham did. And Abraham went to send telegrams to relatives in Poland, in Radomsk. Well, straws they turned out to be. The refugee bureau was packed with desperate people, it took me hours to get to anyone official, and no one had news about Zbonszyn. Chawa went to see Bernard, but he reminded her that the Consistoire—his supposed important connections—helped only people in France. Bernard did say he would give Chawa 500 francs, but only if she could guaranty it would get into my parents' hands. Chawa did not tell me what she said back to him. Abraham sent telegrams to the relatives in Radomsk—the telegraph could not do Yiddish lettering, so he had to use what little remained of his childhood Polish—but the telegraph people could not say when the messages would be delivered, and anyway the relatives were very old and very poor and Radomsk was hundreds of kilometers from Zbonszyn, so what did we think a telegram would mean?

We met up back at Abraham and Chawa's rooms late in the day. Abraham had a Yiddish newspaper, with another story about Zbonszyn, this time reporting sleet and ice, and diseases spreading quickly. I knew my parents were not strong, Maître—my sister Berthe's postcards over the summer and autumn had told me of their poor health—so now I was desperate. I told Abraham that we had to send my parents the money he was holding for me, even if there was only a small chance they would actually receive it. Abraham reminded me that he was legally responsible for me, that I would need the money myself, and again said—insisted—that until we knew of a reliable way to get the money to my parents, it would be just throwing it away.

How would I now describe Abraham at that moment? Responsible. Sensible. Wise, even. But at the time I could see only a refusal to act, to do anything, and the calmer he remained the wilder I became. It shames me now to recall it, and perhaps it will come as no surprise to you at this point, Maître, but I badly lost my temper, and said things to him I would give anything to have back—that he did not truly care what would happen my parents in the ice and snow of Poland. Or for that matter what would become of me. They were horrible ridiculous things to say, of course, to these two people who had so little themselves but had opened their tiny home to me, fed and clothed and nursed me, and who now risked the police and jail on my account. Which, as you know, in the end is what happened to them, jail, after the shooting.

Well, Abraham had heard enough, and lashed back. "Look at you," he gestured toward my neatly pressed suit and the silk tie Genève had given me. "Claiming to worry so much over your parents at the same time you dandy up yourself." I started to say something back at him, I cannot remember what, but Chawa stepped between us and told Abraham that she had been the one to insist I put on my best clothes, and reminded him that she and Abraham were the ones who had made that very suit and shirt for me in the first place. "Well, and what about that?" Abraham pointed at the topcoat, my fine Paris topcoat, that Chawa had just cleaned and pressed and was hanging spotless on a wall hook like a dignified visitor—a French visitor. "Which cost who knows how much? How does that help his parents? Or us?"

He had touched a raw spot, Maître. He had no idea what it had truly been like for me during my two years in Paris—I had always shielded him and Chawa from most of the ugliness. But still, at that moment, with my clean clothes and my bathed skin, with Chawa's warm food in my stomach and money in my pocket, there was enough truth to what Abraham said—the distance between me in Paris and my parents in the Polish mud—to make it hurt. So much hurt, in fact, that I lunged at him. It makes me ill to think back on it. Chawa, thank God, blocked my way and just then there was a knock on the door. We froze, but it was Sam, not the police. He must have heard on the landing something of what was going on inside because he did not take off his coat but just bade a brief good evening to Abraham and Chawa and right away said to me that we should be going. I was near to doing or saying some kind of horridness, Maître. And near to tears. Sam was giving me a way out and I turned to leave with him. Abraham grabbed my topcoat and thrust it toward Sam. "No doubt he needs it," he said bitterly.

I held back a howl as Sam hustled me out the door. Held it back on the stairs and in the courtyard, so as not to bring the attention of neighbors. Held it back when we reached the street, not wanting to draw notice from any police who might be in the area. Held it back. For one more day.

H.

21 January 1942
Moabit

Honorable Maître Rosenhaus,

I wandered the streets with Sam, sick with unhelpfulness and guilt, sick in my whole being, about my parents and the 12,000. Guilt—a wasteful emotion, Maître. Like hope. But more difficult to let go of. At least for me. In this I do not mean to speak for anyone else.

We were silent as we walked along, going nowhere Sam and I, each carrying the loads of our separate miseries, on top of the ones we shared. For me there was the terrible worry about my parents and brother and sister, but also about myself, with no papers, no place to stay, my name on the police search list. And anger, Maître, a great rising that I was losing control of—at the Reich, of course, for what it had done to my family, but also at Bernard, the Consistoire, Madame at the Belles, the préfecture, the France ministries, Daladier at Munich, the Foire de Paris foreman, the Party, the confederation, the Doriots, Genève, de Guise, and on and on, all of them piled together.

We ran into two boys we knew who said they were headed to a gathering at the Sportclub Aurore. We walked along with them but after a few blocks I could not listen any longer to their talk, their everyday chatter, and realized that I had no mood for a crowd. So I stopped and said I had changed my mind. I could see that Sam understood. He gave me a hug and said we could meet later at the Tout Va Bien, the café where we had often spent time in earlier days. Then he walked on with the boys. It was the last time I saw him. Tout Va Bien—it means All Is Well.

It just happened that we had stopped in front of a gun shop. Which is when the thought began. Not a clear thought, Maître. As I have said many times, it was never a clear thought, right up to the moment I fired the shots. But the spark of it must have struck then, as I glanced through the shutters of A La Fine Lame—The Sharp Blade— the knife and gun shop on Rue du Faubourg Saint Martin.

In fact I did go to the café, the Tout Va Bien, but straightaway, when I knew that Sam and the others would not be there yet, and sat for a while trying to slow down the zig-zag jolts that were storming in my head. After a while some boys and girls I knew showed up, I did not want to talk, so I left. And though I did not start out for it, I soon found myself again outside the gun shop. This time the thought formed itself into the definite shape of a pistol.

I headed to a nearby cinema, where I had often gone before to pass long empty hours, to be alone in the dark. As I approached I saw that above it was a hotel, a small shabby place that I must have known was there but never took any notice of. I realized that I needed a place to spend the night—there was no room for me any longer at Rue Martel, and I refused to go back to Abraham and Chawa's. The posted rates showed that the hotel was cheap, I had money, I went in.

You are supposed to produce papers to stay in a proper hotel, Maître, even a low one like that, and I had nothing but my expired Poland passport. Also I was without a valise to make me look like a true traveler. But I knew that cash was the most important paper in this type hotel, so as I told a story about having left my papers in my bags at the nearby train station, I made a show of my banknotes and suddenly the clerk was very understanding. Especially, I suppose, because I looked so respectable in my clean suit and silk necktie. And my topcoat.

I went up to a room. As I lay on the bed in the dark, the thoughts and feelings of the past few days raced around my head in a struggle with each other, then were joined by all my knocks and tumblings of the past two years in Paris, then back further to my last years in Hannover, and so in the end to my parents, my brother and sister. Which brought me around to imagining them in the cold and mud and hunger of Zbonszyn. It was driving me mad, Maître. I had to do something but there was nothing I could think of. And then the image again, the pistol in the gun shop window.

That was the moment I knew I would go to the gun shop in the morning—if finding that moment interests you as much as it did the Paris lawyers. By why? Since I had no idea at that moment what I would do with a gun if I managed to get one? Except sometime pull the trigger.

In my coat I happened to be carrying a photograph of myself in suit and necktie, that I had taken at a recent street fair and the photo people printed on the front of a postcard. I had intended it for my parents, to show them how well I looked, for them not to worry about me, but I had not known what to write to them those past weeks, and so it had remained blank, waiting. In the hotel room I decided to write, to give them something from my hand before whatever I did with the gun the next day might make that impossible.

I suppose you have already seen the words I wrote on the card—it was in so many of the newspaper stories about me. "My Dear Parents, I must protest so the whole world hears me. I beg your forgiveness. I could not do otherwise."

So, did I know exactly what it meant when I wrote it? And if not then, when? The lawyers and magistrates in Paris, this is what they endlessly wrestled with—When I went to the embassy the next morning, did I already intend to shoot someone? Or was it a last moment decision? Or no decision at all? Had I gone to the embassy thinking just to fire off the gun, to make a big scene? Or did I have intendings of a far greater scene—to shoot myself there?

I told them many times that any of these was possible, that I never knew what it would be. And I still say so. But more important, Maître, what I want to say now is that those are not the right questions. And never were. You see, it does not matter when I decided to shoot vom Rath. Because in the end, I did it. What matters is not when or even what, but why. As you have always rightly sensed. And have urged me to say, to help me prepare for the trial. For my chance, at last, to speak to the world the words that are the other side, the other face, of the gun I fired. And for that, Maître, I am grateful.

Herr Weimann did not tell me exactly when, but it seems that the trial is coming very soon. Maître, when will I see you?

Yours truly,
Herschel

23 January 1942
Moabit prison

Honorable Maître Herr Rosenhaus,

Herr Weimann was just here. Insisting that I speed up. Shorten my telling, I finally understood him to mean. But, Maître, after all this time explaining, what sense does that make? To you and me.

He gave me reasons, sort of. He told me that there is less than three weeks before the trial and that he wants to make certain to hear and understand beforehand what I have to say about that morning of the embassy, what my intendings were. But also he wants me to train myself to quicken my telling because, he said, when actually I speak at the trial about that morning, I will have to be brief. I suppose because there is so much else I have to tell.

But something else seems very strange, Maître—the trial will be seven days, Herr Weimann said. Seven exactly. But how can the Reich know that already? Because one of the things my great Paris lawyer, de Moro-Giafferi, told me—when I would ask about this or that France court hearing, what would be said and how long it would go on and such—was that you never knew until it happened. That was the way of things with courtrooms, Moro said, and with humans. Well this is another reason, Maître, I feel the serious need to talk with you.

So, 7 November 1938. The morning in the hotel, early—I had slept very little. I knew three things. First, I wanted a gun. Second, if I got one, I would go to the embassy to use it, one way or another. And third, I would go straight away, before I lost my nerve. So, I dressed and groomed very carefully, left the hotel and directly walked the few blocks to the gun shop. Madame Carpe—I only learned her name later, of course—was just rolling up the iron shutters and said I could go inside to see her husband. The place was full of all sorts of dangerous-looking things, knives and rifles and pistols of all sorts, boxes of bullets, and I had a hard time not stopping and staring. But I knew what I was after, sort of, and did not want the shop man, Monsieur Carpe, to think that I might

Yes, I am sorry—shorten. Herr Weimann's insistence. And so.

I told Monsieur Carpe that I had to carry cash when I traveled for my father's import business in Poland, and that sometimes in Paris, being so small and on my own, I did not feel safe. Monsieur Carpe said he knew what I meant, especially in that district, with all the métèques—the wogs, Maître, the dark foreigners. He brought out a small revolver that could fit into my suit pocket without much bulge, and the bullets to go with it. He showed me how to load and fire the gun, then gave me the form I was supposed to file at the local police bureau. It was in Passage du Désir, he told me. I said, "Oh, yes, I know it well," and bit my tongue as soon as the words were out. He looked at me a bit strangely but fortunately we were finished and I quickly left the shop.

I went to the Tout Va Bien café, down to their basement toilet, loaded the gun and put it in the inside pocket of my suit jacket. Over my heart. Then I rode the Métro to the 7th arrondissement, the posh area where the embassy is.

Getting into the embassy? And the shooting itself? What can I tell you, Maître? After all, what about these things is truly important? There were many versions from the various people I crossed paths with that morning—the France gendarme at the front gate, the first Reich guard, the Ambassador himself, who happened to be going out for a walk as I was coming in, though I did not know who he was at the time, the two reception people inside the embassy, and finally, vom Rath. Many details from them later, contradicting each other—about what I said, what I did, how I got them to let me inside, how I got to vom Rath. And my own memories of those few minutes so hazy, and confused by what others later said—I was in a state, Maître, doing all I could to hold still my emotions and keep calm my movements, concentrating on getting myself inside and hoping they would not notice what felt like an enormous blaring signal horn in my jacket pocket. But what matter anyway, these details? Because in the end—be brief, Herr Weimann said—I did get in, and I did shoot Third Secretary Ernst vom

Rath. Which was as I had written in the postcard—a cry to the world, to wake and see what the Reich had done. And do something about it.

Maître, what else do you, could you, need to know?

Yours most sincerely,
Herschel

26 January 1942
Moabit

Maître,

Something very strange has happened. Something wrong.

A man came into my cell today—one of the men who had been in before with Herr Weimann, I do not know his name. With him was a tailor, who brought some clothes. The man had me put on these clothes, Maître, told me they were for the trial. They were too big, and the tailor made some markings, to fix them. The man scolded the tailor to hurry up. "Just so it looks like they belong to him," the man said.

But Maître, these clothes. Worn, rough black trousers and black jacket, a black shirt with a frayed collar, and an old shiny black coat, down to my ankles. I have never worn such things in my life. These are clothes like the Hasidim wear, Maître, everything black, and the heavy coat to the ground. Or someone in a shtetl. As if I am from Poland.

Maître, I am from Hannover. And Paris. What is going on?

H.

Honorable Maître,

It is madness.

Confirming. That was Herr Weimann's word here this morning, the center of all his words. At least, the one that remains center in my mind. And has shaken me badly.

He told me that I will have only part of a single day to speak to the court—and so to the press, the world press, which he did not mention but you have many times told me will be there. A single part of a single day? How can that be, Maître? With all there is to say? How can that possibly be?

I was so startled that I barely managed to ask, "But who will speak during the rest of the time, the seven days?" His only answer was, "That is up to the Reich."

While I tried to take this in, he pushed on. Because I will have such a short time to speak, he told me, I will be limited to confirming certain things. He himself, Herr Weimann told me, will be the one asking me at trial for these confirmings.

The first confirming, he said, will be that I shot vom Rath in vengeance against the Reich for my family and my people. "No, not vengeance," I told him, "but to make the world take notice of what the Reich had done."

"Well," he said, "vengeance is close enough."

Next he told me he will ask me to confirm my association with the communists. I started to protest but he cut me off, saying "or fellow travelers" and, looking into a dossier, named in quick order Henri, the foreign section, the confederation syndicats, the Foire de Paris workers, the Citroën strikers, Rose. I became dizzy, Maître, and thought perhaps I was ill, even delirious, that the camp fever had returned.

Also, he said, French bankers and big capitalists. Wait, I

thought—communists and capitalists both? Now it seemed he was the one delirious. And I said so. But my remark did not even slow him down, and he noted from his file my visit to the Consistoire— "that Rothschild place" he called it—and the mansion of "the speculator" Lazare, plus my "relations" with the speculator's daughter. I was startled to think of Genève and almost said, "She loves Berlin," but Weimann was already moving on.

He told me he will be asking me to confirm that, under the influence of these communists and capitalists, I had intended to provoke France to war with the Reich. I told him that I wanted France, and the world, to do something, but I never imagined that a single boy, even with a gun, could start a war. "Well," Weimann replied, as if he had caught me in a schoolchild lie, "it was right after Munich, was it not? And what had these warmongers wanted at Munich?" I said I did not know about such things, I had no idea what made nations go to war— or not. He said fine then, just confirm that you intended for France to take action. Others can tell the court what that would have meant.

"Others?" Maître. What others? What was he talking about?

Then he said I was to confirm my hatred of the French. I replied No, I did not hate the French, and never said I did. And anyway, which French? Which ones did he mean? He brushed that aside, saying all right then, he would simply ask me to confirm particular facts—that France had refused to let me work, had turned me down as a refugee and refused me residence papers, had ordered me out of the country, and had put me on a list to be arrested. What my attitude was to France after that, he said, and so whether I would have had any concern for the consequences on the French of war with the Reich, would be left to the court.

"Finally," Herr Weimann said, "you will be asked to confirm the influence on you of certain criminals and degenerates." I was so stunned now I could not make a sound, just stared at him unbelieving. He calmly listed Sam and his late night engagements, Rachel and her relations in Montparnasse, my living at one brothel and working at another, and my "favoring" of bars where perverts gathered. Even Rose. "Rose?" I croaked. "It says here," he referred again to his papers, "that you admitted she invited you and another man into her bed at the same time."

With that, Herr Weimann snapped shut the dossier. "Now you are prepared," he said. "Now we both are."

I was choking, Maître. As he started to leave, though, I managed to say, "But my parents? When will I describe about my parents? And the 12,000? The roundups, the trains, the misery of Zbonszyn? The actual things that sent me to the embassy that morning?"

"Ah," Weimann said calmly, "you mean how the Poles were returned home to Poland. Well, you were not there, so you have no personal knowledge of the facts about their transfer, or of conditions at Zbonszyn. So you will not be allowed to testify about them—such are the rules of court, there is nothing to be done about it. Anyway," he added, "there will be others at the trial to speak of these things."

Others. Again. This time I managed to ask, "What others?" He said that need not concern me. And left the cell.

Maître, where are you?

Herschel

Honorable Maître Herr Rosenhaus,

I have not seen or heard from Herr Weimann these past few days. Or from you. Which has made things calmer. Made me calmer. And clearer.

Of course I have spent the entire time considering what Herr Weimann told me during his last visit, about the strict limits on what I will have a chance to say at my trial. About what Herr Weimann's questions will try to "confirm" about me. What is to go on during the rest of the trial days, the other six days when I am not speaking, remains a mystery to me. I must tell you, Maître, that this is not the trial I have expected. After all our preparing. But I believe that I have come to understand why it is to be this way. And as Herr Weimann said, it is not something we can control.

So. Things I can control. I must say, Maître, it has occurred to me that I could refuse to participate at all, refuse to answer when Herr Weimann or the court asks me questions—or confirmings. But how would that look? I mean, to the newspaper and radio people gathered there, to the world that has waited these three years to hear from me? Turning down the Reich's offer to speak? Because after all, in the middle of a war it would not be too difficult I suppose for the Reich to be the one refusing, quietly refusing me a trial, since I must admit, after all this time, how much truly would the world care if it never heard from me again? Yet here is the Reich still making the trial happen, and bringing to Berlin all the press. War and all. So I have decided, I will take my part.

Most important, I think you will agree, is what I will say about my reasons. The why. Herr Weimann says he will ask me to confirm that I went to the embassy seeking vengeance, for my family and my people. And I told him No, it was not vengeance but a cry to the world, to wake the world.

Well, Maître, that is not entirely true. Because yes vengeance was a part of it. Just not the kind Herr Weimann was describing. Not vengeance against the Reich, exactly. But personal vengeance. Against vom Rath. Though in those days nothing was only personal.

You see, Maître, he had made me promises, vom Rath. All along he made promises, right up until the last days before the shooting. A promise that he would get me proper papers for France—he was an embassy official, the embassy had connections with the France ministries, he told me, it was something he could do. And most important, a promise that my family would be protected by the Reich. That no harm would come to them, that they could remain at home in Hannover and not be bothered. But he lied. And once I learned that my family had been shipped to Poland I knew that he had lied, that the whole time he had lied. The whole time that he had been using me. For his private purposes. His foul abuses. Yes, vom Rath—this embassy official, this representative of the great nation, whose death sent the German people into the frenzy that was Kristallnacht, who the Führer magically turned into a Reich hero—had used me over and again, under the cover of his lies.

Used me. A boy. A minor. A Jew.

That also the world will hear.

Most assuredly,
Herschel F. Grynszpan

4 February 1942
Moabit prison

Honorable Maître Herr Rosenhaus,

It seemed to me that Herr Weimann's terrible anger this morning was difficult for you. I saw him glance toward you from time to time as he bellowed at me. As if he thought that somehow this has been partly your fault.

But after all, what means fault? The truth is there, you cannot change it, I cannot change it. And Herr Weimann cannot change it—despite all his yelling and accusing and name calling, his red-faced "How dare you!" And most important, the court will not be able to change it. At least, I do not believe. Though I got the sense from Herr Weimann that such is what they will try to do—to deny the truth of what I have to tell about vom Rath. Well, so be it. That is the nature of a trial, is it not, Maître? Different people giving different versions of events. And letting the truth be sorted out. By the judges. And anyone else who might be watching and listening. So I have been told.

Sincerely,
Herschel

6 February 1942
Moabit

Maître,

It has been quiet. No sign of Herr Weimann. Or you. What is happening? We must continue to prepare. I would think.

Well, I should say that not all has been quiet. For the first time in the nearly four months I have been here at Moabit they have moved a prisoner into the cell across from mine. He keeps asking me to talk with him. It makes an interesting change.

Yours,
Herschel

Maître Herr Rosenhaus,

So yes, as you asked, I am prepared to tell you—and others, it now seems clear—how my connection to vom Rath came about. The details. Well, as much as seems necessary. As I will also tell it in the court.

He first noticed me at the bar where I went with Genève, the dark jazzy bar with the men couples and women couples. Do you remember, I told you? Well, vom Rath was there that night and noticed me, followed me when I went to the toilet. He stopped me and said he had heard me speaking German with my friend and asked if I was "free." Or something like that. But I had no interest, Maître, and went past him without replying.

Then it was the baths, some weeks later. As I told you, I went now and then to the public baths in Faubourg Saint Denis and in Belleville, first to rid myself of the scabies, and later in the summer and fall of '38 when I was no longer able to go to Abraham and Chawa's for a wash. Also a safe place in those long afternoons when I had to be out of Sam's room but needed to stay clear of street sweeps by the police. Well, vom Rath spotted me there one day and began talking to me, quickly realizing from my accent that I was German. He invited me for a coffee, saying that he would be glad just for some German-speaking company, that we must have things in common, being Germans in Paris—or perhaps he said, "from Germany"—and that perhaps there were ways we could help each other. It was that last remark that made me curious—I had just received the papers expelling me from France, my situation suddenly desperate. So I went with him to a café where we sat out on a nearly empty terrace, the easier to speak German without offending.

It did not take vom Rath long to tell me that if I spent time with him he would take me to nice places. When I did not reply he added that he would also give me spending money, and I could tell by the way he spoke, his manners, his fine tailored clothes, that he probably had plenty. I want to be truthful with you, Maître—though vom Rath used words like "spend time with him" and "be company for him," I knew what he meant. You see, by then I understood what Sam had been doing those late nights in Montparnasse, and now again with clients from the Belles. Not completely understood, but enough. And I also knew other refugee boys who made money that way. So, I was not entirely surprised by vom Rath's proposings. Still I refused. I could not imagine myself that way. And after all, I had lived for two years in Paris with almost no money, so why should I cross such a line now for a handful of francs? I also recalled the deeply unhappy look on Sam's face when he returned from those nights—it had made an impression on me all its own.

But he kept at me, vom Rath. I suppose someone like him—an embassy official, a fancy "vom" name, connections in the Reich—was used to getting his way. He asked me how long I had been in Paris, where I stayed, where I worked, and from my answers, vague as I made them, he guessed that I had no papers. He did not say anything right away about fixing my situation but the way he looked at me sent a message that the idea was there. Then he asked where my family was, and when I told him Hannover, he said they might benefit from me getting to know him. He could tell that this remark caught my attention but also that I was doubtful, so he showed me his business card, with his official embassy title. All of this he put in terms of helping, of protecting, but somehow behind the words was also a hint, a warning, of what might lay ahead for my family if I did not agree. That was the moment I began to weaken. And to hate him.

It was a Friday and I was due soon at the Belles, where I had just begun as a server. I told vom Rath I had to leave for work and he asked me when he could meet me again. I said I did not know, and I got up to leave. He put money on the table and got up with me. As we walked out together, he handed me several banknotes, saying it was just to thank me for my time. I suppose I could have turned it down. But I took it.

He walked with me as I headed for the Belles, talking in that soft smooth voice of his about how certain he was that he could be helpful to me. And to my family. Several times he mentioned my family. At the corner to the street where the Belles was, I told him I had to leave him but I agreed to meet him the next day at the same time at the café where we had just been. He nodded and smiled and let me go on without him.

When I told him I would meet him again I did not meant it. And I did not show up at the café the next day. But that night there he was at the Belles, sitting in the room where I was serving. He was quiet and smiling, without any hint of upset that I had not met our rendezvous. He gave me a very generous tip when I brought his drink, and another later when I served him again. When I left the Belles that night he was waiting for me outside.

As he walked next to me in the dark streets, he said that in his work he dealt directly with the France ministry for foreign affairs, which he knew had the final word on refugee matters. He had made friends there, he told me. He knew people. Then he asked about my parents, what news I had from them, saying how worrisome it must be for me, with things becoming so difficult in the Reich for certain people, as he put it. And me not being able to help, how frustrating that must be for me. I stopped and turned to him.

"Are you saying that you can help?"

"In Germany, yes, your parents. And you, here, as well."

In the morning, when I was alone again, for the first time in two years I could not quite stop the tears. More in relief for my parents than in sorrow for myself.

H. Grynszpan

10 February 1942
Moabit

Honorable Maître,

Herr Weimann was here again this morning. With two men I have never seen before. They did all the talking, these two men. One of them took notes. Herr Weimann was fuming, but these men did not show me any such attitude. They were cold, formal. And careful with every word.

They asked me to tell them about where vom Rath lived, to describe his rooms. I said I could not because he never took me there, I did not even know where it was. He would always meet me at a café, I told them, and in the first weeks take me for a nice meal, then to one of the bars or nightclubs where men were allowed to be together. One of these was the bar near the Panthéon where I had gone with Genève, the place where vom Rath had first spotted me. Then after a bar or club, each time vom Rath would take me to a hotel de passe, the kind of hotel that rents rooms by the hour. And asks no questions. The two men this morning wanted me to name the hotel and say where it was but I cannot, because they were all different, vom Rath changed them each time, never the same place twice, not even the same neighborhood, and anyway most of them showed no name except Hotel. After a while vom Rath no longer bothered taking me for a meal but almost always, before a hotel, we went to one of these bars or clubs for drinking and dancing, which he seemed to enjoy very much. He especially liked seeing the other men watching me. Which was one reason he wanted me to dress up nicely. Gave me money for clothes. It was vom Rath who told me to buy a stylish coat that autumn. My fine Paris topcoat. I was wearing it the day I shot him. No, that was not something I thought of beforehand. It just happened.

As I tried to describe these bars and clubs to the two men this morning, I said that I had heard there were places like that here in Berlin. "Not anymore," Herr Weimann growled. The other two men did not change expression but stepped outside the cell and conferred for a minute. Then the three of them left without saying any more to me.

Yours,
Herschel

12 February 1942
Moabit prison

Maître,

The two men were back today, with Herr Weimann. The men who were here two days ago. I am sorry I cannot tell you their names— they do not introduce themselves. Well, perhaps you know who they are.

When they were here before they said very little, asking me short questions then letting me speak and noting down what I said. This time, though, they were very rough. In speaking, I mean—they did not touch me.

They called me a liar. About vom Rath.

They repeated what I had said about vom Rath first seeing me at the jazz bar, the night I was there with Genève. Then said it was a lie. Because they found in my writings to you that Genève and I had gone to that bar in June. And vom Rath, they said, was not posted to the Paris embassy until July. Well, Maître, I told them that did not make it a lie. Perhaps I had been mistaken about the date, I told them. Perhaps it was later.

Or perhaps vom Rath was the one who was mistaken. Perhaps it was some other boy he had seen there, some other time. And only later imagined it was me. Vom Rath had a lively imagination, Maître, when it came to boys. Which is something I will also tell the court.

And the coat. My Paris topcoat. I had told the men that I bought it because vom Rath wanted me to, so I would look stylish when he took me into these places. Another lie, the men accused me, because I had written to you some while ago that being with Genève was the reason I bought the coat. But it was true, Maître—seeing Genève again truly was a reason I bought the coat. Just not the only reason.

They refused to believe me, the two men. Over and over, called me a liar.

I said, "Well, I will tell the court about vom Rath, and you can tell the court your doubts, and they will decide."

They snarled a few more awful names at me, and left.

Yours,
Herschel

16 February 1942
Moabit

Maître,

A postponing, the trial. In order to decide things. About vom Rath and me, I suppose, about the things that I have now told. Although you did not exactly say so. But decide what, exactly? Things happened as they happened. They will not be different if the trial comes later on.

I have been digesting this news, this delay. Of course, I am disappointed, as I told you this morning. But thinking back on it, perhaps when you were here I did not show my disappointment very strongly. Surely that is because I have experienced so many delays, since the very beginning in Paris. So many disappointments. And learned how to regain my balance if sometimes briefly I lose it. It was something the great de Moro-Giafferi taught me. Moro, in Paris, my lawyer above all the others. We discussed so many things. Some of which have proved very useful.

You will certainly let me know as soon as the new date is set. So we can begin again to prepare, especially with this new part to the story. Well, newly told.

It looks strange, now that I write it. The word "story," I mean.

Yours sincerely,
Herschel

2 March 1942
Sachsenhausen

Maître Herr Rosenhaus,

Yes, I am back in Sachsenhausen camp. In the bunker again. Perhaps you know. Since I was here last, three more bunker houses have been completed, with special prisoners in each. I have even heard that Schuschnigg is here, the Austria premier—well, former. With his own furniture and books and such. Visits from his family. And his own little garden to tend. Quite some company I am in.

But company is not quite right. Because there is no mixing between the bunkers, and now there are fences between the different bunker buildings, keeping us as much as possible apart. About changes to the rest of the camp I cannot say because there is now a wall between the bunkers and the main camp, so it is only possible for me to see parts of the rest of the camp when I am on the top floor of the bunker during my rounds with the food plates—they have given me again the same work I had when I was here before.

As usual, they told me nothing when they moved me here from Moabit last week. But I now have my paper and pencil again, and your addressed envelopes. The guards here did not give them to me at first. Then it seems they received an order to allow it.

Perhaps you can visit me soon, Maître? To help prepare me to speak at the trial. About vom Rath and me, I mean. Which you and I have never discussed. Also, to tell me when the new trial date will be. If you know. And are permitted to tell me.

Yours sincerely,
Herschel

16 March 1942
Sachsenhausen

Maître Rosenhaus,

Four of them came to see me this afternoon. The two who had come twice to my cell at Moabit with Herr Weimann, plus two I had never seen before.

Just as the last time, one of the men began by saying, almost shouting, that the whole thing was a lie, vom Rath and me. He told me that they had gone over all the witness statements in the Paris court file and that none of the people at the embassy that morning said I had asked for vom Rath by name. So it was nonsense, he said, my claim that I was trying to get to vom Rath in particular. But, Maître, I remember those witness statements, remember them well because my lawyer de Moro-Giafferi and I went over them together many times, and they were all different, and contradicting, about what I said that morning to gain entrance to the embassy. And most important, all of them—the France gendarme, the Reich security guard, the concierge, the receptions clerk—admitted that they did not remember what my exact words were. An uncertainness which de Moro-Giafferi made certain was a part of the official record. "All things to the contrary notwithstanding," Moro liked to say.

I was startled by the man's yelling at me, thrown a bit off my balance by these four large men in their long leather coats and nasty faces surrounding me as I sat on a stool in the bunker's small ground-floor shower room. So, while I was able to say to them that I knew the witness statements were a jumble, I did not manage to tell them what actually happened. Which was that, no, I did not mention vom Rath's name that morning at the embassy. Instead, I told the receptions clerk there that I needed to see the Third Secretary, which I knew was vom Rath's official position. Because you see, it sounded more formal than saying vom Rath's name, more businesslike, since I also said I had important documents to deliver to him in person. Which is what I will say at the trial. And which I ask you to inform the men from this morning. Though perhaps this writing is enough.

Then another of the men took over, saying that in all the papers from my Paris court file there was never a mention of vom Rath and me. Over the months I was in the Paris jail my statements changed in many ways, the man said, whether I was intending to wound, or just to shoot off the gun, or to kill myself, or was in a daze and did not know what I intended. "Typical shiftiness," the man called it. But one thing remained the same in all my statements, he said—that I was acting for my family and my people, the 12,000 dumped to Poland. And the same thing in the postcard, the card to my parents, that they found in my coat pocket. But never once a mention of knowing vom Rath. Which means, the man said, very satisfied with himself, that it was nothing but a lie. A typical lie.

Well, Maître, yes of course it was about my parents and the 12,000. To raise them from the mud of Zbonszyn and into the world's eye. But that does not explain away that it was vom Rath in particular I shot. He had promised to protect them, my family in Hannover. If I allowed him what he wanted. And promised to help with my France papers. But he did nothing, for my parents or me. And never intended to. It was vom Rath who was the liar, Maître, not me. So yes, the shooting was about my parents, my people. But also about vom Rath. Just like the coat, my Paris topcoat, was about vom Rath but also Genève. The answer to "Why?" is not just one thing, Maître. Nothing is just one thing. Ever.

And yes, to the France court I chose not to mention it, vom Rath and me. Because the trial was my chance to hold up to the world what the Reich was doing. And this nasty business of vom Rath and me would have distracted from that. Especially in the press. Also, it was not something I would have been happy to talk about in public. But now? Well, things feel different. Quite different. The trial here, I mean. Though again the press is invited. By the Reich. The world press. As I understand.

So, it seems to me time to speak about vom Rath. Regardless.

Which I intend to do. All things to the contrary notwithstanding.

Yours,
Herschel F. Grynszpan

Maître,

I am grateful for your visit yesterday. And for the news that the trial will now be in May.

I have been thinking. It was curious, our little talk. You never actually said you do not believe it, about vom Rath and me. Yet you repeated all the details that Herr Weimann and the other men have seized on, that they think are so important. The contradictions, you called them. I am appreciative of your concerns, Maître. That I might not be believed when I speak about these things in court. And so put myself in a bad light. Also that it might distract people from what was most important to me, the bigger reason I went to the embassy. You are most kind, Maître, to point this out to me.

Well, yes I can see the risk. Or rather, half the risk. Because you are right, it may be very distracting, especially to all the newspaper and radio people who will be there. Something they may be very keen to report. Perhaps as much as what the Reich did to the 12,000. So I will have to be very clear, that both things were part of what I did that morning at the embassy. That will be my difficult job. Believe me, Maître, I understand.

And yes, I also understand that the court itself might not believe me. But answer me certain things, Maître—as the court, and the others listening, will have to answer.

First, if I was not setting out that morning for vom Rath in particular, why would I go to the embassy, where I had never been before, instead of to the consulate, in a different part of Paris, where I had been many times and where it was simple to gain entry?

And if I had not in fact asked for the Third Secretary himself at the embassy, how was it that I got to see him? Alone in his office? Instead of just a receptionist? Or some clerk? A 17-year-old boy, unknown to the embassy? Answer me that.

Also, Maître, if I feel at trial that I must, there is vom Rath's brother. Who was thrown out of the Wehrmacht. For outrageous relations with boys. Yes, they can check. I know it to be true. It does not matter how I know. And even if it is not entirely proper that I speak of this, once it is out of my mouth it will be difficult for the court to have me unsay it. You cannot unring a bell, was how de Moro-Giafferi put it.

Most of all, Maître, there is no way to refute me. As Moro taught me, the hardest thing is to prove a negative—to prove that vom Rath did not abuse me, once I have said in court that he did. Do you recall what Herr Weimann told me, when he said I must confine my remarks about the 12,000 at Zbonszyn? That because I was not there, I would not be a proper legal witness to speak about what happened. A rule of court. And he was right—I know it from Moro. But the same legal rule means that the only person who could properly contradict what I will say about the things vom Rath did with me in private—is vom Rath himself. Who will not be making an appearance.

Also, Maître, in the end, how important is it if the court itself does not believe me? Because others who are listening will believe. Or at least consider. And report.

So, again thank you for your concerns. I have taken them to heart.

Oh, and a reminder. To send more writing paper and envelopes. And a new pencil. To continue preparing for trial. Details of vom Rath and me. If you think it necessary.

Yours sincerely,
Herschel F. Grynszpan

16 April 1942
Sachsenhausen

Maître,

I have not seen or heard from you for a fortnight. And for the past month I have not had any visits from Herr Weimann or the men from the court—or Reich ministry, wherever, no one has ever told me—who were questioning me about vom Rath. Not that I miss their company.

Trial is coming in just a few weeks. I think we need to prepare. Especially my connection with vom Rath. And I would have expected those men to question me more. But nothing. From anyone.

I am still here.

Yours,
Herschel

22 April 1942
Sachsenhausen

Maître,

Another postponing. So be it.

I am sorry you could not stay longer so that we could discuss it. Why the delay has been ordered. But anyway, I understand that these things happen. Just like in Paris—there was always someone, on one side or another, who did not think the time was right. Or that something more, something else, had to be decided before the story— whatever story different people wanted to tell—could be laid before the court. And before the public. The world. Perhaps when you are here next we can discuss what all those somethings are.

Also the other news you gave me, that struck me silent. That only the Führer himself will now decide about the trial. About me. And as part of it, the Führer's Personal Protection Order—I think that was what you called it—that everything having to do with me remain the same until he personally commands otherwise. I have been thinking about it, and I have to say, this is how things should be.

Well, I would suppose this means you will continue to visit me, yes? That we will continue to prepare? Or can that now wait?

I hope all this has not caused you any troubles, Maître.

Yours,
Herschel

Honorable Maître Herr Rosenhaus,

It has been so long. For so many things. Since I have seen you. Or even a word. I have been here at Magdeburg since last September. I imagine you know. But then?

I am writing even though I have only a small hope that this will reach you. Because I have tried before to convince the guards here that they are duty obligated to send my letters to you. As part of the Führer's Personal Protection Order. I am in a separate section for special prisoners—"politicals," we are called—and they know that I am kept with instructions for extra care. But getting them to understand about my letters to you has been so difficult. Especially because they are not meant to speak with me. So I can only talk at them, hoping that someday one of them will listen.

I cannot even get them to recognize who I am, Maître. Which would make them realize my importance, and therefore how closely they should follow the orders. Because here at Magdeburg I am once again registered as Otto Schneider. The same as they did to me back on Prinz Albertstrasse, the Gestapo jail there, two years ago now. Do you remember?

But getting them to understand who I am is a double sword, Maître. Not too long ago one of the guards finally answered me when I explained who I was. "If that is who you really are," he said, "then rot in hell."

I was going to explain to him that we do not believe in heaven and hell, but I thought better of it. Did you know that, Maître? That we believe in God—well, our God, I have never quite understood whether it is the same—but not in heaven and hell? Although I must say, in this deep dark hole, I might be starting to change my mind. And getting a push in that direction from one of the guards here, who plays music, very badly, late in the night, in a room close to my cell. To keep himself awake, I suppose. Which of course means I must also hear it. Night after night. On an accordion. Hell.

When I first heard talk of heaven and hell as a child, my mother explained what they were, what the Christians believed in, and how the idea could sometimes help them through difficult times. Well, at least the heaven part. And that for our people, she told me, the miseries of this world may be harder to bear because we believe in God but not in afterlife. Lately, though, after months in this place, without a word from anyone, I have begun to wonder whether there might be something worse—to believe in afterlife, but not in God.

I have little paper left, Maître, and a tiny stub of pencil. Only two of your envelopes. So I must keep this brief. Just to ask that you let me know if there is still to be a trial. Which will also tell me that you are still out there.

If you receive this, at least that means they know who I am.

I wish you a Happy New Year.

Yours faithfully,
Herschel

28 January 1945
Sonnenburg prison camp

My Most Honorable Maître,

Two years since last I wrote. Of course, I have no way of knowing whether that letter ever reached you.

Last year they moved me and many of the other politicals from Magdeburg to the Sonnenburg camp here, near the Poland border, when the bombings around Berlin became so heavy. Just like the French did, moving me out of the Fresnes prison when the Luftwaffe attacks on Paris began. First bombs against France, then bombs against Germany—wherever they fall, I seem to be underneath.

These months here at Sonnenburg I have been hoarding this last scrap of paper and your envelope. I am sorry how battered they are. It seems to me that the time has come to use them—things are happening quickly here. Last night and again tonight prisoners have been dragged from cells here in the special politicals section. And there has been much shooting—not outside, not a battle, but within the camp walls. So I am writing you now, in a hurry, tonight.

There is one guard here in this section who is about my age. And from Hannover, my hometown. He is lonely. And frightened. We talk. Well, actually, that is not true, our ages. He is 17. I am now 23. It is just that I have been in jails and prisons since I was his age, so that is still how I think of myself—and I do not believe I have become any taller. Anyway, this boy has said he will post this letter for me.

What to say? I send you good wishes. And your family. As for me, well, though I am in a special section here at Sonnenburg, I do not seem to be as special as I once was. After Sachsenhausen, when again they began calling me Otto Schneider, things have become steadily worse for me. No, of course, not just for me. I have seen that. And hear it, the shouting, the doors slamming, the shots.

On this single sheet of paper only so many words, Maître. I am near the end. And I want to tell you what I have been thinking about these past days. Which is whether a life should be judged by its highest moments or its lowest? The best a person has done? Or the worst? But here is the other part—How to decide which is which?

Perhaps when this is over, Maître, we can talk again. About such things. And others.

Yours most truly,
Herschel

Author's Note

There are many large gaps—indeed, far more gaps than not—in the historical record about Herschel Grynszpan. But the primary elements are not in dispute: his inability to get sponsorship by Zionist organizations for emigration from Germany to Palestine in 1935–36; his fleeing to Paris alone in 1936, at age 15; the necessarily meager but steadfast support for him there from a struggling uncle and aunt who had migrated some years earlier; the failure of official French Jewish organizations to help him regularize his status in France and survive while waiting to do so, and later their unequivocal public disavowal of him; the refusal of the French state to recognize him as a refugee, and its ultimate order in 1938 that he immediately leave the country; the Nazis' expulsion of his parents and siblings from Hannover to the Polish border in October 1938; Herschel's shooting of the German embassy official vom Rath; the vast pogrom against Jews all across Germany, known as Kristallnacht, in supposedly spontaneous response to Herschel's act; the 20 months he languished in a Paris prison awaiting a French trial that was never held; his removal south by judicial authorities as the Nazis were about to occupy Paris in June 1940; his disappearance in the countryside amid the chaos of the French population's flight from the invading German army; his reappearance weeks later at the prison in Toulouse, soon after which the now-Vichy authorities handed him to the Gestapo; the Nazis' plans for a major show trial to demonstrate that Herschel was part of a conspiracy of Jews, Bolsheviks, and "big capitalists" to provoke France and Germany into a war that Germany had not wanted; and the trial's eventual postponement, *sine die*, due to the Nazi state's worry that Herschel would manage to subvert its premise and purpose.

About Herschel's fate thereafter, nothing is certain. Documents and testimony suggest that he was still alive in German custody near the very end of the war, but Nazi record-keeping had begun to break down by then and no official notation has surfaced of Herschel's last months of imprisonment or of his death. Neither is there evidence of his postwar survival. The most likely scenario is that he was among the many hundreds of prisoners shot, at either Brandenburg or Sonnenburg prison, during the Nazis' final killing frenzy during the last days of the war.

It was not only these basic elements, however, but also the interstices between them that provoked and fascinated me from my first awareness of the story, and that I have sought to give life—albeit fictional—in this novel: What might have been Herschel's experiences trying to get out of Germany? As a *sans-papiers* refugee on the roiling streets of 1930s Paris? Alone on the roads and in the villages of *la France profonde* during the great debacle of June–July 1940? What might have been his encounters with the French state, official Jewish institutions, and immigrant and refugee milieux? With class formations, issues of identity, and other politics of the times? And perhaps most tantalizing, what might have been his voice?

•

My first contact with the Grynszpan story came in 1988, on the 50th anniversary of Kristallnacht. A brief news item mentioned the teenage "assassin" as the spark that set off the infamous night, and it struck me that I had never heard the name. I made a note to myself to learn more. When I finally got around to looking, I was surprised to find almost nothing about Herschel in the library of the University of California, Berkeley, one of the country's largest collections: two books there about Kristallnacht briefly sketched the Grynszpan story, and there was a copy in German of the Nazis' detailed outline for the show trial they had planned. But nothing that looked closely at Herschel.

Years later, when I began more serious inquiry, I came across two obscure monographs about Herschel, as it turned out both highly dubious: a self-serving tract by a Nazi propaganda ministry cohort, under a French pseudonym, published in French during the war; and an erratic, eccentric unpublished manuscript prepared by a French physician in the early 1960s. Several popular histories have since been published in English, but they rely almost exclusively on these extremely unreliable earlier sources (though one book did add new primary material regarding Nazi preparations for and doubts about the planned show trial). And none of them made much of an attempt to reconstruct Herschel's daily life—in Hannover, in Paris, in jail, on the run in the French countryside, or in Nazi prisons. Several professional historians have examined individual aspects of the story, but the saga still awaits a full and proper scholarly treatment.

Soon after my first research foray, through a fortunate coincidence I met Ron Roizen, who for years had been investigating the case. Ron introduced me to Ben Brand, another Herschel devotee. Both wound up sharing with me all the Grynszpan materials they had collected as well as the results of their own independent research. Over the years, the information they provided me, and our extensive conversations and correspondence, greatly enriched not only my grasp of Herschel's story but also my feeling for, my sense of, the boy himself—at least, so I hope. I am deeply grateful to both of them, but of course they bear no responsibility for any of the specifics in the portrait of Herschel, and of others, that I have imagined in this novel.

Herschel Grynszpan in French police car, immediately after the shooting, Paris, November 1938.
Photo credit: Yad Vashem

About the Author

Joseph Matthews was born in Boston and raised there and in California. For a number of years he was a criminal defense lawyer in San Francisco and taught at the law school of the University of California, Berkeley. He spent considerable time in Greece in the 1970s and 1980s, where his novel *Shades of Resistance* is set during the period of the military junta there. His other previous books are the short story collection *The Lawyer Who Blew Up His Desk* and the post–September 11 political analysis *Afflicted Powers: Capital and Spectacle in a New Age of War* (with Iain Boal, T.J. Clark, and Michael Watts).

ABOUT PM PRESS

PM Press was founded at the end of 2007 by a small collection of folks with decades of publishing, media, and organizing experience. PM Press co-conspirators have published and distributed hundreds of books, pamphlets, CDs, and DVDs. Members of PM have founded enduring book fairs, spearheaded victorious tenant organizing campaigns, and worked closely with bookstores, academic conferences, and even rock bands to deliver political and challenging ideas to all walks of life. We're old enough to know what we're doing and young enough to know what's at stake.

We seek to create radical and stimulating fiction and non-fiction books, pamphlets, T-shirts, visual and audio materials to entertain, educate, and inspire you. We aim to distribute these through every available channel with every available technology—whether that means you are seeing anarchist classics at our bookfair stalls; reading our latest vegan cookbook at the café; downloading geeky fiction e-books; or digging new music and timely videos from our website.

PM Press is always on the lookout for talented and skilled volunteers, artists, activists, and writers to work with. If you have a great idea for a project or can contribute in some way, please get in touch.

PM Press
PO Box 23912
Oakland, CA 94623
www.pmpress.org